"I can't say that I'm happy with the notion that the only way I might have kept my fiancée was if I'd ruined her."

Eugenia laughed. "There is ruination, Mr. Reeve. And then there is . . ." She stopped, as a small voice in the back of her head was insisting that she had abandoned all principles. She decided to ignore it. "And then there is chocolate."

His eyes blazed and he reached across the table and laced his fingers into hers. She had noticed his body. But it had never seemed as brawny as when he sat across a small, elegant table designed for whispering secrets.

"We're back where we began," he said huskily. His thumb rubbed a circle in her palm that made her want to squirm, but she didn't pull it away. "I should have plied my fiancée with chocolate."

"Only," she dared, "if you were certain that the chocolate was of the very best quality."

Ward brought her hand up to his mouth and kissed the back swiftly, just a touch of his lips. He turned it over and pressed a kiss on her palm that sent sweet heat up her arm. "Please tell me how one determines the very best chocolate."

By Eloisa James

ELOISA JAMES

Seven Minutes IN HEAVEN

AVONBOOKS

An Imprint of HarperCollinsPublishers

Excerpt from *Wilde in Love* copyright © 2017 by Eloisa James, Inc.

SEVEN MINUTES IN HEAVEN. Copyright © 2017 by Eloisa James, Inc.

First Avon Books mass market printing: February 2017
First Avon Books hardcover printing: January 2017

ISBN 978-0-06-238945-9

Avon Trademark Reg. U.S. Pat. Off. and in Other Countries, Marca Registrada, Hecho en U.S.A.
Avon, Avon Books, and the Avon logo are trademarks of Harper-Collins Publishers.
HarperCollins® is a registered trademark of HarperCollins Publishers.

17 18 19 20 21 QGM   10 9 8 7 6 5 4 3 2 1

This book is dedicated
to my eldest niece, Nora,
who has not only gobbled up my books,
but given me inestimable help
with plot points.
Her taste is flawless:
if she begins running in circles,
clutching manuscript pages,
and threatening to murder me,
I know a book will succeed.
Thank you, Sweetheart!

Acknowledgments

My books are like small children; they take a whole village to get them to a literate state. I want to offer my deep gratitude to my village: my editor, Carrie Feron; my agent, Kim Witherspoon; my Web site designers, Wax Creative; and my personal team: Kim Castillo, Anne Connell, Franzeca Drouin, and Sharlene Moore.

People in many departments of Harper Collins, from Art to Marketing to PR, have done a wonderful job of getting this book into readers' hands: my heartfelt thanks goes to each of you.

Finally, a group of dear friends (and one teenage daughter) have read parts of this book, improving it immeasurably: my fervent thanks to Rachel Crafts, Lisa Kleypas, Linda Francis Lee, Cecile Rousseau, Jill Shalvis, and Anna Vettori.

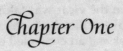

Chapter One

Wednesday, April 15, 1801
Snowe's Registry Office for Select Governesses
14 Cavendish Square
London

Nothing ruins a dinner party like expertise. A lady who has attended fourteen lectures about Chinese porcelain will *Ming* this and *Tsing* that all evening; a baron who has published an essay about vultures in a zoological magazine will undoubtedly hold forth on the unpleasant habits of carrion-eaters.

Eugenia Snowe's area of expertise, on the other hand, would have made dinner guests howl with laughter, if only it were appropriate to share. For example, she knew precisely how the Countess of

Ardmore's second-best wig had made its way onto the head of a terrified piglet, which dashed across the terrace when the vicar was taking tea. She knew which of the Duke of Fletcher's offspring had stolen a golden toothpick *and* an enameled chamber pot and, even better, what he had done with them.

Not only did she have to keep those delicious details to herself, she couldn't even burst into laughter until she was in private. As the owner of the most elite agency for governesses in the whole of the British Isles, she had to maintain decorum at all times.

No laughing! Not even when her housemaid ushered in a boy wearing a brocade curtain pinned like a Roman toga—although the gleaming blue that coated his arms and face clashed with the senatorial drape of the curtain.

The boy's mother, Lady Pibble, trailed in after him. Eugenia didn't see many blue boys in the course of a day, but she often saw mothers with the hysterical air of a woman ill-prepared to domesticate the species of wild animal known as an eight-year-old boy.

"Lady Pibble and Marmaduke, Lord Pibble," her housemaid announced.

"Good afternoon, Winnie," Eugenia said, rising from her desk and coming around to greet her ladyship with genuine pleasure. Her old school friend Winifred was lovely, as sweet and soft as a soufflé.

Alas, those were not helpful characteristics when it came to raising children. Fate or Nature had perversely matched Winnie with her opposite: Marmaduke was a devilishly troublesome boy by any measure, and Eugenia considered herself an expert on the subject.

"I can't do it!" Winifred wailed by way of greet-

ing, staggering across the room and collapsing on the sofa. "I'm at my wit's end, Eugenia. My *wit's end*! If you don't give me a governess, I shall leave him here with you. I mean it!" The way her voice rose to a shriek made her threat very persuasive.

Marmaduke didn't seem in the least dismayed at the idea of being abandoned in a registry office. "Good afternoon, Mrs. Snowe," he said cheerfully, making a reasonable bow considering that he was holding a fistful of arrows and an extremely fat frog. "I'm an ancient Pict and a smuggler," he announced.

"Good afternoon, Marmaduke. I was not aware that smugglers came in different hues," Eugenia said.

"Smugglers may not be blue, but Picts always are," he explained. "They were Celtic warriors who painted themselves for battle. My father told me about them." He held up his frog. "I started to paint Fred too, but he didn't like it."

"Fred is looking considerably plumper than last time I met him," Eugenia observed.

"You were right about cabbage worms," he said, grinning. "He loves them."

"I can smell beeswax—which I gather turned you blue—but is that odor of river mud thanks to Fred?"

Marmaduke sniffed loudly, and nodded. "Fred stinks."

"Don't say 'stinks,' darling," his mother said from the depths of the sofa, where she had draped a handkerchief over her eyes. "You may describe something as smelly, but only if you absolutely must."

"He smells like a rotten egg," Marmaduke elaborated. "Though not nearly as rank as Lady Hubert when she came out of the river."

Winnie gave a stifled moan, the kind one might hear from a woman in the grips of labor. "I almost forgot about the river. Eugenia, I am *not* going home until you give me a governess."

"I cannot," Eugenia said patiently. "I've explained to you, Winnie, that—"

Winnie sat up, handkerchief clutched in her hand, and pointed to her son. "Tell her!" she said in throbbing accents. "Tell her what you said to Lady Hubert! I wouldn't drag him here if it was simply a matter of turning blue. I am inured to dirt."

For the first time, Marmaduke looked a bit fidgety, shifting his weight to one leg and tucking the other up so that he looked like a blue heron. "Lady Hubert said that I should always tell the truth, so I did."

"That sounds ominous," Eugenia said, biting back yet another smile. "Where were you when Lady Hubert gave you this advice?"

"We were having a picnic by the Thames, at the bottom of our lawn," Winnie said, answering for her son. "Did I mention that Lady Hubert is Marmaduke's godmother and has no children of her own? We had hoped . . . but no. After today, *no.*"

"She gave me a sermon just like those in church except that she's a lady," Marmaduke said, apparently deciding to get it over with. "She said as how deceit and hippocrasty are barriers to a holy life."

"Hypocrisy," Eugenia said. "Do go on."

"So I did that."

"What?"

"Well, first I entertained her by doing the dance of the Picts. They were wild savages. They howled. Would you like to see?" He gave Eugenia a hopeful look.

She shook her head. "I shall use my imagination. Did Lady Hubert enjoy your performance?"

"She didn't like it much," Marmaduke conceded, "but she wasn't too crusty. She asked me what I thought about the book of church history she had brought me for my birthday last month, and had I read the whole thing."

"Oh dear," Eugenia said.

"I was being honest, like she said to. I told her that I didn't like it because it was boring and three hundred pages long. Mother was ruffled by that, but she settled down and after a while, Lady Hubert asked me what I thought of her new gown. I said that it would look better if she hadn't eaten an entire side of beef. Father always said that about her."

"It was not kind to repeat your father's comment," Eugenia said. She had discovered over the years that children learned best from simple statements of fact.

He scowled. "I was being honest and besides, after I did the warrior dance she said that my father likely passed on because he needed a rest cure."

"That was *deeply* unkind," Eugenia said with her own scowl, "and very untrue, Marmaduke. Your father was a war hero who would have done anything to stay with you and your mother."

She glanced over at Winnie, who was flat on her back with an arm thrown over her eyes. Her husband had been a naval captain who lost his life at the Siege of Malta while serving under Rear Admiral Lord Nelson.

Marmaduke hunched up one shoulder by way of reply.

"Did you throw, push, or otherwise inveigle Lady

Hubert into the Thames?" Eugenia said, feeling a wave of dislike for the lady in question.

"No! She fell in all by herself."

"After a horned beetle that my son had about his person found its way onto her arm and ran inside her sleeve," Winnie clarified.

"I wouldn't have thought she could leap like that," Marmaduke said, with an air of scientific discovery. "Being as she was large and all, but she did, and into the water she went."

"Head first," Winnie added hollowly.

"I wish I'd seen it," Eugenia said, pulling the cord to summon her housemaid.

"It was funny," Marmaduke confided, "because her clothes were all frilly pink underneath. I had to run for the footmen and two grooms as well, because the bank was slippery with mud. The butler said that it was like hauling a Hereford steer out of a mud-hole."

"That's an extremely vulgar description," his mother said in the weary voice of a vicar sermonizing in Latin to an audience of squabbling children.

The door opened. "Ruby," Eugenia said, "I should like you to take Lord Pibble into the garden and throw a few buckets of water over him."

"Mrs. Snowe!" Marmaduke said, dropping back a step, his eyes widening.

"It's not only Fred who smells. What did you mix in the beeswax to get that color?"

"Indigo powder from my paint box."

"It seems to be pungent, which means smelly. A good washing should get off the indigo," Eugenia said, turning to Ruby. "I'm not sure about the beeswax."

"I don't want to," Marmaduke wailed. "Mummy said that I could keep it on until bedtime."

"Fred is looking very dry," Eugenia said firmly. "He needs a rinsing as well."

After four years in her position, Ruby was adept at handling unruly children. She took Marmaduke's arm, and marched him straight out of the room.

Winnie sat up to watch him go. "He wouldn't have gone with me, nor with Nanny either. May I borrow your housemaid?"

Eugenia sat down beside her friend. "Marmaduke needs to go to school, dear."

"He's my baby," Winnie said, her eyes filling with tears again. "He merely needs a governess, Eugenia. Why won't you give me a governess?"

"Because Marmaduke needs to be around other boys. Didn't his father put his name down for Eton?"

"I can't let him go."

"You must."

"You don't understand," Winnie wailed. "Darling Marmaduke is all I have left of John. You just don't know how hard it is to be widowed and all alone!"

There was a moment's silence.

"I didn't mean that," Winnie said hastily. "Of course, you know; you're a widow too."

"But it's different for you," Eugenia said. "For me, it's been seven years."

"That's what I meant," Winnie said, blowing her nose. "I just want my son home with me, where he belongs."

"He belongs with other boys. This is the third time you've been to see me in as many weeks, isn't it?"

Winnie nodded. "That thing that happened to the cat—its fur is growing back in, thank goodness—and

after that, the title pages of the hymnals. Yesterday the vicar greeted me in a wretchedly stiff manner. And my Uncle Theodore still believes that we have a monkey as a pet; I daren't tell him what really happened to his corset."

Eugenia wrapped her arm around Winnie. "Eton," she said firmly. "Write a letter to them saying that Marmaduke will attend Michaelmas term. I'll send you a tutor, a young man who can take your son fishing when they're done with studies."

"His father meant to teach him to fish, just as soon as he returned from Malta," Winnie said, hiccuping and dissolving back into tears.

"I'm so sorry," Eugenia whispered, easing Winnie's head onto her shoulder. When she had opened the registry office six years before, she'd had no idea that she'd find herself at the center of many domestic crises. She could write a book about the hidden dramas of polite society.

Though when it came to widowhood, one's birth or place in society was irrelevant.

Her desk was piled with letters, and there were undoubtedly mothers waiting to see her. Eugenia rocked Winnie back and forth as she watched Marmaduke scampering around the back garden.

"I suppose I'll take him home now," Winnie said damply, straightening up. "Nanny will not be pleased by what's happened to the nursery curtain."

"I think tea and cakes are in order," Eugenia said. "Eight-year-old boys are always hungry."

"I couldn't! You don't want him to sit on your lovely chairs."

That was true.

"Take him to a tea garden," Eugenia suggested.

"You can sit outside, which means Fred won't cause a commotion either."

"Only if you come with us."

"I'm afraid I can't. I have appointments this afternoon."

Winnie's eyes widened. "Oh no, I'm sorry!" She scrambled to her feet and snatched up her reticule. "My dear, you are such a comfort to me! Send me a tutor!" she called as she trotted out the door.

Eugenia ought to have returned to her desk, but instead she stood at the window and watched as Winnie chased her son, still faintly blue, around and around the fountain where Fred was enjoying a bath.

Even through the beveled glass, she could hear Marmaduke's screams and Winnie's laughter.

It seemed to her that widowhood would be bearable if your husband had left behind a child, a part of himself.

The door opened behind her. "Ma'am, may I send in Mrs. Seaton-Rollsby?"

"Yes," Eugenia said, turning about. "Certainly."

Chapter Two

Later that afternoon

Theodore Edward Braxton Reeve—Ward, to his intimate friends—climbed the steps to Snowe's Registry Office thinking about how many governesses he'd chased away as a boy.

He had vivid memories of the sour-faced women who had come through the door of his house—and what their backs looked like as they marched out again.

If his father and stepmother hadn't been in Sweden, he would have dropped by their house to apologize, if only because his young wards seemed capable of topping his score, and it was a pain in the arse to be on the other side.

Frankly, his half-siblings, Lizzie and Otis—whom he hadn't even known existed until a few weeks ago—were hellions. Devils. Small devils with trouble stamped on their foreheads.

Their governess, a Snowe's governess, had been in the household for only forty-eight hours, which had to be a record.

The registry wasn't at all what Ward had expected, from the burly guard posing as a footman to the unoccupied waiting room. He had envisioned a cluster of women sitting about, waiting to be dispatched to nurseries—and he had planned to choose whichever one most resembled a colonel in the Royal Marines.

This chamber looked more like a lady's parlor than a waiting room. It was elegantly appointed, from the tassels adorning striped silk curtains to the gilt chairs. In fact, it was about as fancy as any room he'd seen in a lifetime of living in his father's various houses.

And his father, Lord Gryffyn, was an earl.

That said, Snowe probably had to put on airs in order to convince people to pay his outrageous fees.

Since Ward needed to impress the House of Lords with his nonexistent parental abilities in order to secure guardianship of his siblings—not to mention getting Otis up to snuff before his brother entered Eton in September—he was prepared to pay whatever it took to get a first-rate governess.

A young housemaid appeared from a side door. "I'm here to see Mr. Snowe," Ward told her.

A few minutes were needed to sort out the salient facts that *Mr.* Snowe was deceased, that *Mrs.* Snowe had opened the agency some years before, and that no one saw Mrs. Snowe without an appointment.

"They are arranged weeks in advance," she told him earnestly. "You might request an appointment now, and we would inform you if she had an earlier opening."

"That won't do," Ward said, smiling because her voice took on a reverential tone whenever she mentioned her mistress. "I sacked the governess you sent. I require a new one, but I have a few stipulations."

Her mouth fell open and she squeaked, "You *sacked* one of our governesses? A *Snowe's* governess?"

He rocked back on his heels and waited until she stopped spluttering and ran off to inform someone of his crime as regards Miss Lumley.

To be fair, even withstanding Miss Lumley's regrettable habit of weeping like a rusty spigot, she had been better than many of the governesses he'd had as a child.

All the same, she hadn't been right for this particular position. His recently orphaned half-siblings were opinionated and idiosyncratic, to say the least.

He needed a really fine specimen of a governess, someone special.

Eugenia hadn't moved from her chair in three hours, and yet, to all appearances, the pile of correspondence on her desk had hardly diminished.

She stifled a moan when her assistant, Susan, entered with another fistful of letters. "These arrived this afternoon, and Mr. Reeve is asking to see you."

A drop of ink rolled from Eugenia's quill and splashed in the middle of her response to a frantic lady blessed with twins. "Bloody hell, that's the third letter I've ruined today! Would you please repeat that?"

"Mr. Reeve is here," Susan said. "You will remember that we sent Penelope Lumley to him a week ago, on an emergency basis."

"Of course. He's the Oxford don with two orphaned half-siblings to raise," Eugenia said.

"Likely born on the wrong side of the blanket, just as he was." Susan leaned against Eugenia's desk and settled in for a proper gossip. "Not only that, but Reeve was jilted at the altar last fall. I suspect the lady realized what that marriage would do for her reputation."

"His father is the Earl of Gryffyn," Eugenia pointed out. She didn't add that Reeve was outrageously wealthy, but it was a factor. Registry offices didn't pay for themselves.

"He's as arrogant as if he were an earl himself. I peeked at him, and he's got that look, as if the whole world should bow to him."

Eugenia gave a mental shrug. It was unfortunate that the conjunction of a penis and privilege had such an unfortunate effect on boys, but so it was.

Without just the right governess, they never learned how to be normal. Having grown up in a household that prided itself on eccentricity, Eugenia was a fierce proponent of the virtues of conventional living.

Better for oneself, and infinitely better for the world at large.

"He's wickedly handsome, which probably plays a part in it," Susan continued. "I could tell that he always gets his way. Though not," she added with satisfaction, "with the lady who jilted him."

Rich, privileged, and handsome, for all he was a bastard: a formula for disaster, from Eugenia's side of

the desk. She crumpled the ruined letter and threw it away. "I find it hard to believe that he has a complaint about Penelope."

Some of Eugenia's governesses were formidable, even terrifying women who could be counted on to train a child as spoiled as a week-old codfish.

Others were loving and warm, just right for orphans. Penelope Lumley was sweet as a sugarplum, and, admittedly, about as interesting. But to Eugenia's mind, grieving children needed love, not excitement, and Penelope's eyes had grown misty at the very idea of two waifs thrown into an unknown brother's care.

"He told Ruby that he had sacked her," Susan said. "I have a tear-stained note from Penelope to prove it."

"Did she say what happened?"

"Lines were struck through and she'd wept over it. I couldn't make out much beyond a reference to a locust, though perhaps she meant a swarm of them, à la the Book of Exodus."

Miss Lumley's Biblical reference was unsurprising; Snowe's specialized in hiring daughters of vicars, as that circumstance often resulted in ladylike accomplishments with a total lack of dowry.

"I can't think of a reference in the Bible to a single locust," Eugenia said.

"I wouldn't know," Susan said with an impish grin. "My father's Bible lessons never took hold."

Eugenia leaned forward and gave Susan a poke. "There's a reason I never sent you out as a governess. You'd unleash a plague of locusts on the man who tried to sack you. I suppose I'll have to see him, but I shan't give him another governess."

"I would guess Penelope's nerves got the best of

her," Susan said, standing up and shaking out her skirts. "She has masses of them and they make her twitchy."

"That is no reason for dismissal," Eugenia said firmly. "She is an excellent governess, and just what those children need."

Mr. Reeve should have thanked his lucky stars that she had sent him anyone—twitchy or not—but the fact that he'd appeared in the office suggested that he didn't appreciate the value of a Snowe's governess.

The mother to whom she'd been writing—not to mention poor Winnie—was one of many begging her for help. Mr. Reeve had been sent Penelope only because of his orphans.

Snowe's Registry office was the most elite establishment of its kind, renowned for its promise to take children "to majority or marriage, whichever came first." As Eugenia saw it, that vow was a pledge to "her" children. She had been known to keep a governess in place, the wages paid by the agency, even if a family lost its funds.

But if a family simply didn't *like* the governess? That was something different altogether. She couldn't spend her time shuttling women around England because one interfering man thought his charges deserved someone better than Penelope Lumley.

"Please ask him to join me," Eugenia said, coming out from behind her desk and walking over to the window looking onto Cavendish Square.

Every year she swore that she would take more fresh air and exercise, and somehow the days spun by in the whirligig that was Snowe's. Her house was only a few steps from the office, which meant she often worked until she went home and fell into bed.

"Shall I order tea?" Susan asked.

"No," Eugenia replied. "I mean to dispense with him quickly and go for a walk in the square."

"I doubt you have time," Susan said apologetically. "You have the Duchess of Villiers, and I squeezed in Lady Cogley after that."

"Is there a problem in Her Grace's nursery? I thought Sally Bennifer was very happy there."

"Sally has accepted a proposal from the vicar. He must have behaved in a most unvicarish fashion, because she needs to marry spit-spot. Ergo, the duchess needs a replacement."

"Is 'unvicarish' a word?"

"I suppose not," Susan said. "But the man took his post only a few months ago, so he must have jumped on Sally like a cat on raw liver. My father would not approve."

"How about sending her Penelope Lumley, since she's now free?"

"Penelope might be put off by the irregular nature of the Villiers household," Susan said doubtfully. Most of Villiers's children were now grown, but he had raised six illegitimate children under the same roof as the three born to his duchess.

"Mary Tuttle," Eugenia suggested.

Susan nodded. "I'll ask her. And I'll be listening during Reeve's visit, in case his claim to being a gentleman isn't as accurate as it might be. I don't think I've ever seen him in a ballroom."

After a few unfortunate incidents during which degenerates had acted on their conviction that any woman engaged in commerce had no morals and would welcome their advances, Eugenia had had a discreet peephole drilled in the wall between her

office and Susan's; Susan could dispatch their footman to the rescue, if need be.

"Don't worry," Eugenia said now. "I'll brain him with the poker." Their fireplace implements were topped with solid brass knobs for just that reason.

"Actually, Mr. Reeve is so handsome that women likely just drop at his feet," Susan said, with a smirk. "If I hear a thump as you fall to the floor, I'll be sure to leave the two of you alone."

Eugenia rolled her eyes. "I might prostrate myself before a freshly baked crumpet, but never a man."

Susan took herself away, and a moment later the door opened again. "Mr. Reeve," Ruby announced.

The man who strode into the room was tall, with thick brandy-brown hair and darker eyebrows, the color of tarnished brass.

He had a lean rangy look, but something about the way his coat fit across his upper arms made Eugenia suspect he was muscled. What's more, his nose had been broken in the past.

This was not the sort of person who typically appeared in Snowe's refined drawing room. He breathed a different kind of air than did the mothers she dealt with daily.

Abruptly, Eugenia realized that she was staring, her thoughts straying in directions they hadn't gone for years.

Since Andrew's death.

She didn't give a damn what Mr. Reeve's thighs looked like!

And she would do well to keep it in mind. He was a client, for goodness' sake. Did she see . . .

No she didn't.

And she didn't want to, either.

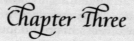

Chapter Three

Ward entered Mrs. Snowe's office and checked in his stride.

No governess he'd ever seen had hair that was a curly, swirly mess of red caught up on her head, a delectably curved figure, and lips several shades darker than her hair. Her lips were lush, even erotic, despite being pressed together into a hyphen.

Ward paid little attention to women's clothing, but he remembered his governesses in gray and black, like dingy crows.

Mrs. Snowe was wearing a pale yellow gown that celebrated her breasts. Her absurdly wonderful breasts.

A delicate jaw, a straight nose . . . Their eyes met.

There was the look he remembered from governesses of old.

She was cross as the dickens, likely because he'd dismissed Miss Lumley. Under her controlled façade, she was practically vibrating with exasperation.

Mrs. Snowe was a former governess, all right, and she'd already summed him up and found him lacking.

He bit back a grin. The governesses he'd chased from the house as a boy hadn't cared for him either. It was strangely comforting to realize that at least one type of woman was absolutely honest in her assessment of a man.

Eugenia took a deep breath and pasted a smile on her face. No matter how foolish Mr. Reeve had been to sack one of her governesses, it wasn't his fault that she was irritated by her unexpectedly desirous reaction to his appearance.

She began to walk toward Mr. Reeve, but before she could take more than a step, his long legs had carried him across the room.

"Good afternoon, Mrs. Snowe." He extended his hand with an unhurried confidence that Eugenia recognized.

She ought to: she had grown up with it. It meant that Mr. Reeve, like her father, generally found himself the most intelligent man in the room.

She touched his fingers, thinking to withdraw her hand immediately and drop a curtsy. A good part of the allure of Snowe's was that she was a member of the peerage. No one ever forgot that.

His large hand closed around hers and he shook it briskly.

Unless they had no idea.

Now he was nodding to her with all the detached civility with which one greets an upper servant. A housekeeper. Or, more to the point, a governess.

It had never occurred to her that he wouldn't know who she was. They'd never met, but their fathers were friends. Though she had a vague memory that he'd spent years abroad . . . perhaps at university?

"How do you do?" she asked, withdrawing her hand. Her accent usually informed even the most bumptious father that in the current social hierarchy, she belonged at the top.

No such recognition seemed to occur to Mr. Reeve. He glanced about the room with lazy curiosity.

"Very well, thank you," he said, bending over to look more closely at a small Cellini bronze that stood on a side table. "I wonder if we could come straight to the point, Mrs. Snowe."

Eugenia's registry was situated in a small but beautifully proportioned house in the most fashionable area of London. The chairs were Hepplewhite and the rug Aubusson. The wallpaper had been hand-painted in Paris in an exquisite lattice pattern of violet and cerulean blue.

The chamber was so elegant that its atmosphere served as a correction to clients deluded enough to think that they were bestowing a favor on Snowe's by seeking a governess. Moreover, it had a dampening effect on reprobates in pursuit of her person or her fortune.

Mr. Reeve was obviously as unaffected by his surroundings as by her person.

"May I offer you a cup of tea?" Eugenia asked, forgetting that she had intended to push him out the door without ceremony.

He straightened and turned, and the pure masculine force of him went through her like a lightning bolt.

"I would be grateful if we could dispense with formalities."

There was no question about it; she was facing the rare client who had no idea who she was.

At all.

It was rather . . . fascinating.

The appeal of her agency lay in her rank—by right of being born to one nobleman and married to another. Her enormous inheritance didn't hurt, but it was her birth that allowed her to be accounted "eccentric" for running a business, instead of being banished from polite society.

Although to be fair, there were a few who considered her to be a disgrace to her name. Still, even those recognized that her father was a marquis and her late husband the son of a viscount.

Mr. Reeve appeared to believe that *she* was a governess.

Eugenia was appalled to find that he was rattling her nerves. This was absurd. He was just another client, to be soothed or squashed as his complaint merited. Considering his termination of Penelope's employment, he needed to be squashed.

She would be polite but firm, as was her practice. He was far from the first parent to whom she'd refused a governess, let alone a second one.

She sat down and nodded. "Won't you please be seated?"

He dropped into the chair opposite her. "I imagine that you've learned that I had to dismiss Miss Lumley. I need someone else."

"May I know the nature of your dissatisfaction?"

"I see no reason to get into particulars," Mr. Reeve

replied, drumming his fingers on his chair. "She's a pleasant woman, but she won't do."

"Miss Lumley is not a glass of milk that you can send back for being curdled," Eugenia stated.

"'Curdled' is a good word for her. Let me be clear that I'm not blaming you. Or her, for that matter. The blame for Miss Lumley's curdled nature must be put at the feet of her parents."

Since when did Oxford dons have husky voices that made a woman think—not that Eugenia was thinking of *that*, because she wasn't. Still, her tutors had spoken in polished syllables, whereas Mr. Reeve had a gravelly timbre. "Could you be more specific about Miss Lumley's perceived shortcomings?"

"She hasn't the strength of will or the wits needed to deal with my siblings." A hint of impatience passed over his face. "I could make allowances if Lizzie and Otis were fond of her, but they aren't. Surely you can spare a governess? I'm told all the best ones work for you."

"Yes, they do," Eugenia said. "But as a general rule, I do not reassign my employees. Inasmuch as you were not happy with Miss Lumley, you are welcome to look for a governess elsewhere. I can direct you to several respectable registry offices."

Any ordinary client would have panicked at this pronouncement, but Eugenia was forming the impression that panic wasn't in Mr. Reeve's arsenal.

"I'd rather *you* gave me a new one." His mouth curved upward in a smile that—that—

Eugenia spent a second wrestling with the fact that his smile set her heart racing. "Mr. Reeve, forgive me, but you don't appear to understand the nature of Snowe's Registry Office." She sounded like a pomp-

ous fool, but what could she do? He seemed to know nothing at all about her or her company.

"I suspect you are correct." The faint humor in his eyes was extraordinarily irritating, but it was certainly not unusual to meet gentlemen who underestimated her.

"My governesses are highly trained and much in demand," Eugenia stated. "They are considered essential in the best nurseries. Parents have been known to hide their children in the country and pretend they didn't exist if I can't find them a governess." She paused in order to emphasize the statement. "I cannot offer you another of my governesses."

Mr. Reeve didn't even blink. "Surely you could spare just one? We didn't have the chance to meet before you sent Lumpy—I mean, Miss Lumley, but—"

Eugenia cut him off. "'*Lumpy*?'"

"The children didn't take to Miss Lumley," he said apologetically.

"'Lumpy' is a highly disrespectful epithet," Eugenia snapped.

"I'm fairly certain they never used it to her face." He seemed to think that was sufficient. "But as I was saying," he continued, "given that you and I did not have a chance to meet before Miss Lumley was dispatched to my household, I came to London in order to ensure that the next governess will be more suited to the position. To be frank, I need a cross between a lion tamer and a magician."

"Never mind the impossibility of that; your request implies that I would trust you with another of my governesses," Eugenia countered. "You will have to seek your lion tamer elsewhere."

By way of reply, he gave her another wicked

smile. The sort that made a woman likely to give in to whatever he asked. "May I first tell you about the children?"

Eugenia spared an incredulous thought for the woman who had jilted him. She must have been as chaste as an icicle to reach the altar without succumbing to that smile. Yet there was no question but that his fiancée had held him off.

This man would never let a woman go after he had made love to her. Eugenia was certain of it.

She drew in a soundless breath. What on earth was getting into her today? She must be having a reaction to being cooped up in the office for the last few weeks. She needed fresh air.

"Lizzie is nine," Mr. Reeve was saying. "I would describe her as excessively dramatic and unnaturally morbid."

"What form does her morbidity take?" Eugenia asked.

"She wears a black veil, for one thing," Mr. Reeve said.

Even after years of hearing about children's eccentricities, that was new.

"I have the idea that only widows wear mourning veils," Mr. Reeve continued, "but most nine-year-olds don't make their governess faint by dissecting a rabbit on the nursery table, either."

"Dissecting, as in, cutting to pieces?"

"Exactly. Though I think Miss Lumley found Lizzie's attempted conjuration of the rabbit's ghost more disturbing," Mr. Reeve added, as if it were nothing out of the ordinary.

"I see," Eugenia said. "I gather the conjuration was unsuccessful?"

Mr. Reeve's sudden grin kindled a hot cinder in her stomach. "No phantom rabbit appeared, if that's what you mean. Lizzie's brother Otis is eight, and far more conventional. He'll go to Eton in the fall, but since neither of them has had any schooling, he has to catch up first."

Eugenia was thinking about ghostly rabbits, but her attention snapped back to him. "*No* schooling?"

What? Had they been raised by wolves? Mr. Reeve's initial letter had only said that he needed a governess, not that he needed a miracle worker.

"No formal schooling," he amended. "They both know how to read. Otis seems to be quite good at mathematics. A few days ago he opened a betting book in the stables, offering proper odds."

"What bets are involved?"

"The question of which horse would produce the most dung collected ha'pennies from every stable boy."

A gentleman *never* mentioned excrement before a lady but, of course, Mr. Reeve didn't think she was a lady.

"Until it was discovered that Otis had gifted his chosen steed with fistfuls of carrots in the middle of the night. The bets were returned," Mr. Reeve added.

"My uncle is a member of the Thames River Police," Eugenia said. "I could arrange to have him give Otis a stern talking-to. Has your brother been informed that gentlemen do not take money from stable boys, no matter how interesting the wager?"

"That's a very good point," Mr. Reeve agreed. "Perhaps I should explain that our mother spent the last decade of her life in a traveling theater troupe."

Oh, for goodness' sake.

She had known—all polite society knew—that Mr. Reeve was the illegitimate son of an earl. But the information that his mother was an actress had been concealed.

Once people learned about his mother, Mr. Reeve would never receive another invitation. He clearly didn't care—which explained why she had never met him, and why he had apparently never heard gossip about the widowed lady who opened a registry office.

In fact, she'd guess that Reeve was so arrogant that he didn't give a damn what society thought of him.

No, "arrogant" implied that he had an inflated sense of his own abilities. Eugenia had a shrewd feeling that he judged himself in relation to other men without exaggeration.

"Do Snowe's governesses tutor only the children of the rich and titled?" he asked. A note in his voice made Eugenia's nerves flare in a primitive response, like a rabbit cornered by a fox.

She was no rabbit.

She gave him her frostiest look. "Certainly not. My governesses can be found in more than one irregular household; the Duke of Clarence's five children share three Snowe's governesses at Bushy Park."

Amusement lit his eyes and the air of danger about him evaporated. "I am far more proper than Clarence. There is no counterpart to the lovely Dorothea in my household."

Her heart skipped a beat at his lazily flirtatious reference to the royal duke's mistress.

"Do you expect commiseration for your household deficiencies?" It was a feeble answer, but all she could come up with.

Ward shouldn't be teasing a respectable former

governess, but Mrs. Snowe was irresistible. That peony pink in her cheeks was the prettiest thing he'd seen in weeks.

And she *was* widowed, after all. He never flirted with married women, or members of his household, but she wasn't his servant, no matter how much he had paid her for Lumpy's lachrymose services.

"I suppose I shouldn't have mentioned my lack of companionship," he offered. Her scent was sweet and elusive . . . like dewberries. Tiny berries that smelled sweet but were tart on the tongue.

"Gentlemen do not bemoan their lack of companionship. Nor, I might add, do they speak of excrement in the presence of ladies."

He let out a bark of laughter. She was tart, indeed. "I can tell what you're thinking, Mrs. Snowe. You think that *I* need a governess."

"It's too late for you," she said roundly. "More to the point, I'm afraid that it's also late for your siblings. How can your brother possibly go to Eton if he's had no schooling whatsoever?"

"Otis will learn anything required in no time," Ward said. "Both children are remarkably intelligent." After a pause, he qualified reluctantly, "Not that I know any other children their age."

She smiled at him—for the first time?

When she smiled, her whole face changed.

Every damn bone in Ward's body—including his most private one—flared with heat. Mrs. Snowe had eyes, a nose, a chin . . . all the ordinary features every woman had. But that smile turned her face into the most beautiful he'd ever seen.

Maybe they weren't ordinary features.

Red lips. Porcelain skin. Hair the color of autumn

leaves on fire. She was speaking and he should be listening, but instead he was—

What the hell was he doing?

Simmering with desire for a governess, albeit a former governess? He'd lost his mind. At least she was a widow; he'd truly disgust himself if he found himself lusting after a married woman.

He'd never felt this madness when he was with Mia—

He seized on that idea with relief.

This all had to do with his former fiancée. He'd been rejected. This extreme wave of desire was the result of that unpleasant surprise.

It explained the insistent beat of his heart, which echoed right down his body to—

It made sense.

More or less.

He'd always enjoyed bedding women, and clearly the months of abstention during his betrothal to Mia had taken a toll. He needed to take a mistress.

Or perhaps make an appointment with a cheerful, welcoming tart. A woman who expected nothing but guineas, and would be surprised by pleasure.

With an effort, he wrenched his mind back to the present.

"Miss Lumley is capable of teaching both of them everything they needed to know," Mrs. Snowe was saying. "She is an excellent teacher of Latin, history, *and* etiquette—as well as crucial skills such as how to run a household, play tennis, and bake a cake."

"Bake a cake!" Ward said. "Why on earth would they be taught that particular skill?"

Eugenia watched as Mr. Reeve's face cooled into that of an offended peer. Susan was right: he had a distinct resemblance to an earl.

"I can assure you," he stated, "that my siblings have no need for culinary skills. I had a succession of governesses as a child, but not one ventured into the kitchen."

"Snowe's children all learn to bake a sponge cake," Eugenia explained. "Baking requires concentration and precision, and it has the potential for serious injury. Children enjoy it."

He gave her a wry smile. "Knives. Fire. I suspect I would have loved it."

"I suppose that you were a very naughty child," Eugenia observed, despite herself.

"'Wicked' was the word most often employed," he offered. That smolder in his eyes should be outlawed. It sent a frisson, a little shock, right down to her toes.

Occasionally she would catch a glimpse of a gentleman turning the corner in front of her, and something about the set of his shoulders or the gleam of his hair would make her remember the excitement she felt on seeing her husband for the first time.

No gleaming hair here. Mr. Reeve had tumbling brown curls that he clearly hadn't done more than glance at. Probably no valet.

Definitely no valet, she amended, glancing at his neckcloth, which was tied with a knot. Not a gentlemen's knot, but the knot children learned how to tie.

"Snowe's cakes have become something of a secret code," she said hastily. "An excellent way by which Lizzie and Otis can fit in with their schoolmates."

Mr. Reeve shrugged. "They show no signs of anxiety about their manners and are, in fact, astonished when dealt a rebuff. I doubt the ability to bake a sponge cake will prove a magic talisman."

"Social bonds come from shared experiences,"

Eugenia said. "In the normal course of events, most children will never touch a kitchen implement again, though they are hopefully more respectful to kitchen workers than they might have been. What I have been trying to say, Mr. Reeve, is that I think you should take Miss Lumley back, if she will agree to return."

He frowned at her.

"I have some twenty families waiting for a governess," she added, "and I think we'd both agree that you have a pressing need."

"Miss Lumley will not do."

"I exchange governesses only in extremity," Eugenia said. And, in answer to his raised eyebrow, "For example, one governess attended an extraordinarily compelling sermon on her day out, and thereafter swore off dancing and French lessons. I moved her to a Quaker household."

"I wouldn't mind that one," Mr. Reeve said. "Lizzie and Otis could do with a reminder of the Ten Commandments, especially the one about honoring your older half-brother."

"Which doesn't exist," Eugenia pointed out. "My point is that no one rejects a Snowe's governess merely because he doesn't like her. 'Liking' is not the point."

"Tears roll off her like fleas from a wet dog," Mr. Reeve said flatly.

Eugenia narrowed her eyes. "None of my governesses should be compared to a canine under any circumstances. Nor a flea."

"My siblings have recently lost their mother." He gave Eugenia a plaintive glance that didn't fool her for a second. Susan was right; he was used to getting his way and he had no scruples about how he got

it. "A sobbing governess—who faints at the slightest distress—is a drawback, to say the least."

Eugenia felt a prickle of misgiving. "I know that Miss Lumley is plagued by nerves, but I wouldn't have thought her anxiety would take the form of constant weeping."

"You can take my word for it. It's not a good example for Lizzie. My sister is already preoccupied by death."

"It's unfair to condemn Miss Lumley for fainting at the evisceration of a rabbit. It's likely a messy business."

He shrugged. "Everyone else managed to stay on their feet."

Mr. Reeve had an air of defiance about him now, as if he expected Eugenia to censure his little sister, but she couldn't hold back her smile. "Lizzie sounds like a most unusual and interesting child, something of a natural philosopher."

She almost confessed to her own childhood interest in mathematics, but thought better of it.

"My sister has arrived at an intriguing theory about bone formation and blood circulation. I am virtually certain that she is wrong, but it hardly matters."

"I wish that I were able—" Eugenia began, but she was interrupted.

Mr. Reeve clearly realized she was about to refuse his request for the last time. His face changed, all its humor gone, his mouth thinned to a tough line. He leaned forward and met her eyes.

"The children have no family on their father's side, but their maternal grandmother is pressing to become the guardian of Lizzie and Otis. Given my irregular birth, she has a strong case."

"Oh dear," Eugenia said.

"She attempted to wrench Lizzie's veil away from her, and I only found my sister hours later, hidden in the attics. Otis has a pet, Jarvis, to which he is deeply attached and his grandmother has demanded that Jarvis be disposed of."

Eugenia frowned. "A dog or cat can be a wonderful companion for a grieving child. If you'd like, I could—"

Again, she was cut short. "Jarvis is a rat."

"A rat," Eugenia echoed faintly. She had a horror of rodents, having nearly died of rat-bite fever as a young girl.

"If Jarvis is banished to the stables, Otis will follow," Mr. Reeve said. "I have no parental experience, but I believe that taking Lizzie's veil by force was not a good idea."

Eugenia nodded.

"Their grandmother is a harridan, Mrs. Snowe, who has already expressed her belief that the children should be whipped into shape. Whether or not she means it is hardly the point: she is not a suitable guardian for children who have lost both their father and mother in a matter of a few years."

"You make a very good argument," Eugenia said, adding, "None of my governesses employ corporal punishment under any circumstances."

"I need a governess," he stated, eyes still focused on hers with unnerving force. "When you signed a contract giving me Miss Lumley, you promised me just that. A woman in constant floods of tears cannot persuade the House of Lords that my household is a suitable place to raise Lizzie and Otis. I need a governess with backbone, who can stand up to their grandmother during her visits."

He was right.

"I believed Penelope Lumley would do well because she is loving and an excellent model for conventional behavior," Eugenia explained. "I do see that she was not ideal under the circumstances. I shall find you a replacement." She hesitated. "Is there anything else I should know about the children? They are eight and nine years old, am I right?"

"Yes."

"Perhaps you could tell me more about the veil?"

"It is black lace, falling to Lizzie's shoulders. She removes it only for meals and dissection."

Eugenia felt a sudden twinge, remembering how she herself had longed for a mother as a young girl. "She must desperately miss her mother," she said softly.

"So it seems," Mr. Reeve replied.

That was an odd answer, but Eugenia didn't have time to investigate; she had a prickling awareness that the Duchess of Villiers had certainly arrived for her appointment by now. One did not keep a duchess waiting.

"I shall do my best to find you a new governess," she assured him, holding out her hand. "In three days at the most."

He shook it, briskly. "I appreciate that, Mrs. Snowe. I shall return on Monday."

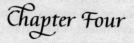

Chapter Four

Early evening, two days later

𝔈ugenia stared down at the proposed advertisement for the registry office that Susan had plunked down on the desk. SNOWE'S . . . BY ROYAL WARRANT OF APPOINTMENT was inked at the top, with a flourish.

Below that an artist had drawn her profile—with a halo of flourishes.

It wasn't a terrible likeness, though her maid wouldn't recognize that tight chignon. Eugenia touched her hair lightly, just to make sure that her loose curls hadn't transformed into a head of snails, à la Medusa-turned-governess.

"*Lady's Magazine* is requesting approval," Susan said. "And the afternoon post has arrived."

She put it on top of that morning's post, still untouched.

At the bottom of the advertisement, under Eugenia's portrait, an ecstatic mother was raising her hands heavenward. OH, RHAPSODY! MY DARLING DAUGHTER IS BETROTHED TO A LORD!

"Is that woman supposed to resemble Mrs. Giffton-Giles?" Eugenia asked. "Because I doubt she'll enjoy discovering her likeness in print."

"Certainly not! That lady represents all of our happy mothers."

"At least those whose daughters married lords," Eugenia corrected. "Won't it foster unrealistic expectations?"

"Last season alone, girls in our charge became the new Lady Bartholomew, Lady Festers, and Lady Mothrose. Everyone knows that our governesses launch a girl better than anyone else can."

Eugenia pushed the advertisement across the desk. "I suppose it will do." She hated the use of her image, but the truth was that her standing as the widowed wife of a lord was the backbone of the registry office's success.

Without warning, her heart gave a little jerk. How could *she* be a widow? Even after seven years, it still seemed impossible. Surely Andrew would stride through that door any moment—

"Genevieve Bell has agreed to go to the Duchess of Villiers, though they'll have to wait a month since she's in Bath with an elderly aunt," Susan said, interrupting her train of thought. "Alithia Midge will join Mr. Reeve in Oxford, but only if he agrees to pay her a resettlement bonus every month until Michaelmas term begins and his brother leaves for Eton."

"Excellent," Eugenia said, pulling her thoughts back to the present.

"I'll send a note by post asking that Mr. Reeve pay us a visit at his earliest opportunity," Susan said. "Or would you prefer I send a messenger directly?"

"The latter," Eugenia said. "Charge it to his account."

Her remarkable attraction to Mr. Reeve was surely the result of exhaustion. That man merely walked in the room, a twinkle in his eye, and she had felt slightly dizzy.

It was only natural that she felt a bit unsteady at the thought of seeing him again. She would be calm, cool, and professional.

"Right," Susan said. "It's time for a sherry." She headed to the other side of the room. In the last few years, the two of them had fallen into the habit of sharing a glass of wine at the end of the day.

It wasn't always easy to determine which governess to send to which household, as well as contending with imploring letters sent by those governesses a week later, asking for advice. Any of them could handle a routinely wet bed, but a boy who takes to pissing on the walls, for example?

Snowe's—in other words, Susan and Eugenia— had to weigh in with advice. (In that case, it took two glasses of sherry to decide that one nursery wall should be temporarily sacrificed until bribery lured the boy to a chamber pot.)

"I've been thinking," Susan said, once they were both settled in front of the open French doors facing the back garden, "how odd it is that the two of us are such good friends."

"I don't find it odd in the least," Eugenia replied.

"My father was a gentleman, but you—you're nobility."

Eugenia shrugged. "You forget that my father is Lord Strange, or he was before being made the Marquis of Broadham. He certainly lived up to his original title."

"Well, you and I *are* friends, and that gives us the right to tell each other home truths, because that's what friends do."

"I'm not interested in hearing any," Eugenia said instantly. Nor did she need to hear any. Everyone told her one truth over and over. Likely Susan had moved into the enemy camp.

They all wanted her to forget her husband, to forget Andrew.

"Let him go," her stepmother, Harriet, had said when she'd last visited London, as if Andrew were waiting around the corner, and it was up to Eugenia to send him off to a warmer climate on holiday.

"You needn't waste your breath," Eugenia added. "I know what you're going to say. My father and stepmother have done nothing but throw men at me for the last six years. Sometimes I think Harriet opens their house in London for one reason only: to introduce me to a new flock of prospective husbands."

"She means well. Surely you don't want to live alone for the rest of your life?" Susan sipped her sherry. "Is this the bottle that Mrs. Selfridge sent us? The touch of apple is lovely."

"Quite likely," Eugenia said, uninterested. Happy clients were always sending them tokens of their appreciation. "I enjoy living alone."

"It's lonely."

"As a matter of fact, it's not."

Susan gave her a squinty look. "Don't try to tell me that you have a lover of whom I'm unaware, because I happen to know that you are in this office every moment that you're not in bed."

"Perhaps I have a companion in my bed," Eugenia said daringly. The wine had gone to her head and she felt pleasantly giddy.

Susan snorted. "I won't even dignify that with a reply. You've attended only two or three events this season."

"Everyone I dance with grumbles about their children," Eugenia admitted. "The only man I could fancy is the Duke of Villiers, and he's my father's age. Not to mention happily married."

"His Grace is enormously fanciable," Susan agreed. "Every time I dance with him, I almost dissolve into a puddle on the ballroom floor."

"Now I think on it," Eugenia said, "Villiers must be glad that Sally fell in love with the vicar. He complained that his daughters were so spoiled that they'd need a ride on a flying pig to get to the stables to exercise their ponies."

"Nonsense," Susan said. "His Grace affects that sardonic look and can't bring himself to say that he's wildly grateful to Sally. I wish I could meet a man like Villiers, but one who was twenty years younger."

"Find someone more cheerful," Eugenia suggested. "Andrew used to make me laugh, but I cannot imagine Villiers telling his wife a bawdy joke, can you?"

"Absolutely not. But who would care, if he looked

at her the way Villiers looks at his duchess, as if he'd lay down his life for her?"

Eugenia sighed. "Andrew used to look at me that way." And he laid down his life for mine, she added silently.

"I am sorry he died, Eugenia, but do you really mean to be alone for the rest of your life in memory of your husband's soulful glances and his facility with rude puns?"

"It is taking me a long time to get over Andrew's death." Every other widow mourned for a year, perhaps two. But here she was, seven years on, still dreaming about her dead husband.

Except for last night, when she'd had a most improper dream about Mr. Reeve, which had nothing to do with anything, and which she meant to forget immediately.

"You are a loyal person," Susan said. "Mr. Snowe was lucky to have married you. But would he have wanted you to mourn him your entire life?"

"Who knows that?" Eugenia asked helplessly. "You make it sound easy, Susan. You and Harriet, and even Papa. I thought—when Andrew first died, I thought terrible thoughts."

Susan wiggled her toes. "It would have been extremely foolish to end your life for love. I always thought that Juliet was absurd."

"I disagree. She was very young, and that sort of grief"—Eugenia kept her voice matter-of-fact—"is like being in a storm that's ripping everything away from you: all your wishes and dreams, your clothes, your hopes, your future. Gone."

"I am sorry that happened to you," Susan said.

"But it didn't rip *you* away. *You* weren't swept away, *you* didn't fall off the cliff. You were older than Juliet's thirteen, as well. You have a good fifty years, if not more, left to live.

"*Fifty,*" she repeated, giving Eugenia a pointed glance. "*Alone.*"

"You're as old as I am, and you've never given your heart even once, let alone twice!"

Susan turned her head and met Eugenia's eyes. "How do you know that?"

Just because a woman has never married doesn't mean she hasn't been in love. Eugenia knew that.

For goodness' sake, she'd grown up in a house notorious for parties welcoming actresses of the most dubious reputation, as well as opera dancers and courtesans. The ladies—to use the term loosely— were always in love with someone, and marriage was rarely a consideration.

"It's time you thought about finding a second husband," Susan stated.

"Do you know what would happen if I married again?" Eugenia asked, taking another healthy swallow of sherry. It burnt its way down her throat.

"You'd come to work with a smile and circles under your eyes?"

"Susan!"

Susan shrugged, unrepentant.

"The moment I turned from the altar, my husband would own Snowe's. He would own my inheritance from my mother, the dowry my father gave me, and Andrew's settlement. He would own the house that Andrew bought for our marriage."

"Well, but—"

"There are no 'buts.' A woman has no legal rights

to her own property. I'll be damned if I've built this company up to be the very best of its kind in all England, only to hand it over to a man as his plaything, to sell if he wishes." Eugenia discovered that her voice had risen to a fierce pitch.

Susan finished her glass and set it down. "Right."

"'Right,' what?"

"You don't want to marry again."

"For good reason, you must admit."

"I certainly don't like the idea of a man in charge of Snowe's. But does that mean you're going to live alone forever? *Be* alone forever?"

"I gather you're not talking about our friendship," Eugenia said dryly.

"I am not."

"What about you?" Eugenia demanded. "You haven't had even one husband. Any number of men would love to marry you, and don't tell me that you haven't a dowry. I pay your wages, and you've worked with me for years. Your dowry must be larger than many men's estates."

Susan shook her head. "I've never met anyone remotely like the Duke of Villiers and even if I did, I'm too fat for the current styles."

"You are not; you're delicious and the right man will adore every curve."

Her assistant just waved her hand dismissively at that idea. "So, you don't want to get married. But you do know what that means, don't you?"

"No," Eugenia said cautiously.

"You must take a lover," Susan announced. "Discreetly, as not to tarnish the reputation of Snowe's. You cannot go on like this, Eugenia, working day and night. It's no way to live."

"Why am *I* being singled out?" Eugenia protested. "You work as hard as I, and don't tell me there's a man in your bed, because I'd never believe it!"

"I can't," Susan said with a sigh. "Vicar's daughter and virginity . . . those two impediments hang like millstones around my neck, even if I did want to fall into bed with a handsome man. But *you* are free, Eugenia."

"Free?" She'd never thought of it that way.

"No husband and no children, and an impeccable reputation. You can please yourself."

"I suppose . . ." Eugenia began.

"It's that, or wither into a dull woman who never takes pleasure for herself," Susan said.

"I will consider it," Eugenia said, surprising herself. But inside, she knew that something had to change. The challenge of making Snowe's a success had been remarkably diverting.

But now that her agency was the best in all London. She needed a new challenge.

All the same, she had the distinct sense that she could walk into a ballroom and have her pick of unattached men.

What kind of challenge was that?

Chapter Five

Later the same night
Fawkes House
Wheatley, near Oxford

Ward put down his quill and yawned. He'd been working all day and half the night on incorporating a steam engine into the continuous paper-roller that had made his first fortune.

He heard a creak from deep in the house as it shrugged off the heat of an unusually warm spring day.

A different creak sent him to the door of the library. "Are you on your way to the kitchens?" he asked the thin white ghost coming down the stairs.

"No," his sister Lizzie said, with the patient air of a

person explaining the obvious. "I'm not on the back-stairs, am I?"

Ward pushed the door further open and stood aside.

As a child, he'd spent a good many sleepless nights wandering his father's mansion; it seemed his siblings possessed the same tendency. They went to bed at the appropriate time and fell sound asleep—for a while. He hadn't seen Otis, but the night before his brother had spent several hours in the library working on a mousetrap he was building.

"I came to speak to you," Lizzie said serenely, walking past him into the library.

"May I say how pleased I am to see you without your veil?"

Sans veil, Lizzie promised to grow up to be as beautiful as their mother, Lady Lisette. Of course, that did not necessarily indicate that his sister would end up mad as a hatter. As their mother had.

"Mother always said that it's inappropriate to mention a lady's sartorial choices, particularly if they are somewhat original."

"You wouldn't wear it if you didn't want attention," Ward said, following her to the sofa.

"I wear it because I see no reason to show my face to the world. Nuns feel the same way."

"I think their veil has to do with being a bride of Christ."

"A veil is useful," Lizzie persisted. "What if I wish to keep bees, for instance? At any rate, I need to talk to you about something important."

"Yes?"

"I have decided that you ought to marry," Lizzie announced.

"I'd prefer not," Ward told her. He had decided to be honest in dealing with the children, or at least not to lie to them outright. To his memory, Lady Lisette had an extraordinary ability to bend the truth. He had the idea that Otis and Lizzie would benefit from a different model.

"Otis needs a mother."

Otis wasn't the only person who would benefit from a woman's presence; Lizzie was only a year older than her brother. He thought of mentioning his stepmother, but what if his sister thought he meant to drop them on his father's doorstep?

Dump them like unwanted puppies.

It wouldn't be like that.

"I don't believe people should marry for practical reasons," he said, instead.

"What's an impractical reason?"

"Love."

"I can understand," Lizzie said after a moment. "It is easy to make a mistake. One of the stable boys told Otis that your fiancée gave you a kick in the goolies. That wasn't very pleasant."

"It isn't precisely true," Ward said, adding, "Ladies don't mention goolies."

Lizzie shrugged. "It is tasteless to have recourse to violence. It's a good thing you didn't marry her."

"I agree," Ward said, wondering if it would set a bad example if he got up and swigged brandy straight from the decanter.

"I hope she gets crump foot," Lizzie said. "I could help you."

"With crump foot?"

"No, with finding a wife."

"I appreciate that," Ward said gravely. "However,

I'm hoping that we can get along by ourselves—with a governess's help, of course."

"A wife would convince Otis that you won't die alone. You're the only one left, you see. No family."

They were back to death. Somehow they always arrived at the subject of death; last night they'd had a long discussion about whether tigers had a separate heaven where gazelles were provided for breakfast, or whether a tiger would have to fast in heaven.

Lizzie had expressed the view that if tigers weren't allowed to eat, the place wouldn't be heavenly. It was a tricky subject about which Ward had no particular insight. More troublingly, it was clear to him that she was not thinking exclusively about a heaven for tigers.

But now she had a clearer point.

"I am not alone," he promised. "Remember that I told you about my stepmother and father, and my other half-siblings? I'll introduce you as soon as they return from Sweden. Of course, we have a grand-mother as well."

"I don't like our grandmother," she said flatly.

"My family will return to London in three months." Not that he was counting. "Didn't we make a rule last night that you wouldn't discuss death for at least a week?"

"I don't consider it a rule," Lizzie said. "More of a suggestion."

That was the problem, right there. Something ran through his family bloodline that converted rules into mere suggestions.

"I hope to return tomorrow with a new governess."

"Lumpy was good-hearted," Lizzie said, as if she were discussing a newly deceased acquaintance.

"It's just that she had a tendency to overlook the big things for the small ones."

Ward had the unnerving conviction that the world had gone awry; before Lizzie came along, he'd always understood grammatical English sentences. "What big things?" he asked.

"She was very upset by Otis's betting scheme, whereas she might have seen it as an example of ingenuity, or even resourcefulness."

"Miss Lumley considered it an ethical lapse."

"That's the small thing. She could have looked at the bigger part of it, and seen that Otis is afraid and that's why he is hoarding money under his mattress."

Ward was silent.

Because he didn't often have instincts, he tried to obey the rare ones he had. He reached out and pulled his sister across the sofa and wrapped an arm around her. She was stiff for a moment, and then her thin, knobby body leaned against him.

"Do you suppose that you could tell your brother that as big parts go, my fortune is a very big one indeed? And that I already changed my will and the two of you will inherit the whole thing?"

The room went very, very quiet while Lizzie thought about it.

After a while, Ward looked down and found that she had fallen asleep. Dark eyelashes lay on pale skin. He took a moment to look, because he rarely saw her without that blighted veil.

She had the promise of great beauty. Right now, she was too thin, and her face was too strained, even in sleep.

Anger is a reasonable response to having a mother like theirs, a terrible mother in anyone's judgment.

It's just that there's nowhere for that anger to go when the lady is dead.

Ward picked up Lizzie and carried her upstairs to bed.

Otis had crawled into Lizzie's bed. Ward carefully laid her next to him and watched as they adjusted themselves on the narrow bed as if they'd been sleeping together their whole lives.

There couldn't have been much room in a traveling theater caravan.

He pulled up the blanket to their chins. A mother—a real mother—would give them each a kiss. He knew that to be true because the moment his father married his stepmother, Roberta started popping into his room at bedtime to kiss him.

He had disliked it, as he recalled. Or at least, he had complained at the time.

He bent down and gave Otis and Lizzie kisses.

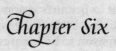

Chapter Six

Monday, April 20
Snowe's Registry

*W*ard arrived at Cavendish Square a good half-hour early, only to have the housemaid at the registry inform him that he'd have to wait, as Mrs. Snowe was busy.

Within ten minutes, he felt like a wild animal trapped in a china shop. He'd just spent five hours cooped up in a coach; the last thing he wanted to do was sit. He prowled restlessly around the room, spindly gold-and-pink furniture seeming to edge closer, like yapping dogs aiming to take a leak on his boots.

He set his jaw. He'd be damned if he'd quit the

place simply because the room was stifling and close. The sensation was merely an odious consequence of the time he spent in Britain's worst prison.

He'd go mad living in the midst of all this ladylike clutter. A good reason to be happy his betrothal had died on the vine. It was a hell of a lot easier to find a new governess than to find a wife.

All he'd had to do was persuade Mrs. Snowe to give him a replacement. Whereas a replacement for his fiancée? Who was, by the way, blissfully married to a duke?

Not so easy.

More to the point, the debacle of his engagement had clarified how little he understood women. He had truly believed he and Mia were in love.

In retrospect, it was more accurate to say that he'd deluded himself into believing it. His jaw still clenched involuntarily when he thought about the months he'd wooed Mia, gently coaxing her to kiss him, never touching her improperly, curbing his impatience to make her his.

Only to be thrown into prison by one of Mia's relatives the night before his wedding. He'd escaped two weeks later, but his fiancée had already married the Duke of Pindar.

Whom—as it turned out—Mia had loved since she was a girl.

Hurrah for His Grace.

Ward had talked himself into believing sugary twaddle about their feelings for each other, when in reality Mia had been hankering after another man.

By the time the housemaid reappeared, Ward had reached the same conclusion he had had the night before: he would use every weapon he had against

the children's grandmother—*his* grandmother—before he'd marry.

No, that wasn't true. If he wished, he could threaten the dowager with a public description of the one visit he had paid to her daughter, Lady Lisette, as a boy. The House of Lords would relish hearing the details of Lisette's lunacy.

But he refused to do that. Mad or not, Lisette had been his mother, and he owed her respect.

Ward strode into Mrs. Snowe's office feeling as irritable as a hungry tiger pacing through high grass. If he'd had a tail, he'd be lashing it from side to side.

She was waiting for him by the same grouping of chairs in which they had sat before, her elegant figure outlined by sunshine coming through the windows. All that red-gold hair of hers was piled on top of her head in a smooth style that dared a man to begin pulling out pins and throwing them to the ground.

All of a sudden, he felt better. The tension in his back eased. No wonder her agency was the best; one instinctively felt that this woman, with all her contained energy and bright intelligence, could solve any problem.

She walked toward him, holding out her hand to shake his. "Good afternoon, Mr. Reeve. How are you? And Lizzie and Otis?"

"We have survived the last few days, Mrs. Snowe. Dare I hope that you have found a governess for us?"

Mrs. Snowe nodded. "I believe so. Her name is Alithia Midge. It's very difficult to imagine Miss Midge weeping for any reason and, equally important, she is fully capable of preparing Otis for the fall term."

She took a sheaf of papers from her desk and led

him to a chair. "Please take your time in reading the contract; I'm happy to answer any questions you might have."

He sat, but didn't read the document. "Does it differ from that pertaining to Miss Lumley?"

"Yes. Miss Midge's salary is considerably higher than Miss Lumley's, as Miss Midge is not only highly experienced, but will need all her resources to bring your brother up to an appropriate standard to enter Eton by September."

"Fair enough," Ward said, glancing through the first few pages.

"The agreement also allows her more time to herself than a governess normally receives."

"The registry isn't charging a larger fee?" he asked, looking at the last page.

Mrs. Snowe shook her head. "My fee is always the same, no matter the situation. We don't merely place governesses; we support them throughout their tenure with a family. Some will require more help and others none at all. It evens out."

"I suppose that makes sense."

"Governesses bear the burden of the household and its children, so I adjust their salaries according to my opinion of a position's complexities. Miss Lumley was charged with the care of two fragile and darling orphans in need of a soothing environment. She was well-suited to that particular task."

Mrs. Snowe had a way of saying things in a direct manner although her eyes shone with secret humor. Ward suspected that had she been present at the conjuration of the rabbity spirit, she would have burst out laughing rather than swoon.

"Lizzie and Otis are neither darling nor fragile,"

he agreed. "I cannot argue with your assessment that Miss Midge deserves special terms."

She smiled at him. "The children are fortunate to have you as their guardian."

"I would not describe them as fortunate," Ward said, hardness entering his voice. "Three months passed between our mother's death and the theater troupe's arrival at my house, whereupon the children were literally dumped on my doorstep. I had no idea they existed."

He didn't add that he doubted his mother had loved her children, or had treated them kindly.

Eugenia had thought Mr. Reeve's eyes were brown, but now they had darkened to the color of burnt amber.

Which was completely irrelevant.

"May I ask how your mother died?"

"According to the children, she developed a lung complaint and was gone in two days. She scrawled a note to me, instructing me to care for them, and sent along her husband's will, which said the same. And she directed the manager of the theater troupe to leave them off whenever the troupe next visited Oxford."

A curl of anger lit in Eugenia's belly, but his mother's shortcomings were scarcely Mr. Reeve's fault. "The children's father . . ." She paused and added delicately, "I gather he passed away as well. Was he known to you?"

"Yes." His face was stony.

"It will be difficult for Lizzie and Otis to enter society, owing to their irregular parentage." That was an understatement. Mr. Reeve was illegitimate and it seemed that his siblings were similarly disadvan-

taged. Thanks to being surpassingly wealthy and the son of an earl, he was welcome anywhere—if he had cared to go.

His young brother and sister, however, would not be so lucky. Otis would have a difficult time at Eton, and Lizzie's hopes of making a good marriage were nil.

Mr. Reeve cleared his throat. "As you may be aware, Viscount Darcy died almost two years ago." His voice was grim. "He and my mother were married."

Eugenia's mouth fell open.

Viscount Darcy?

The late Lord Darcy was notorious for having run away from home at age fifteen, accompanied by a much older woman, the daughter of a duke. They disappeared without a trace, and he had remained unaccounted for until news came of his death around a year ago.

There had followed a series of unsavory—if riveting—revelations about the temptress who had lured him from his home. His mother had bitterly blamed the woman for Darcy's death and had made no bones about sharing her opinion with everyone in society.

"Lord Darcy! Your mother—that means the children's mother—"

His jaw tightened. "She was Lady Lisette Elys, daughter of the fourth Duke of Gilner. Unlike myself, Lizzie and Otis are legitimate, though the product of a Gretna Green match that could not in any way be considered ordinary."

Well.

This changed things.

Or did it? Lizzie and Otis were the children of a woman notorious for—to call a spade a spade—

being as cracked as an egg. Eugenia hadn't known about Lady Lisette's decade with an itinerant theater troupe, but the lady's seduction of an underage boy had been feverishly discussed.

After all, she had been more than thirty years of age, and Lord Darcy scarcely half that. Society had gossiped about it for months.

"I'm sorry," she said, a beat too late.

"Obviously, our mother's identity will become public when the children are introduced to society. I suppose it was too much to hope that it would not be discovered."

"I'm shocked that no one recognized Lady Lisette on the stage."

"I asked the children that. Apparently she stained her hair black and always wore a great deal of paint on her face."

Eugenia had an absurd wish to ease his bleak expression, but there was no escaping the truth. Lady Lisette had been fascinating in all the wrong ways; no one would wish to claim her as a relative.

"I resigned my place at Oxford after the children arrived," Mr. Reeve said, his voice without inflection. "The university has a morality cause, and they were already winking at my parents' irregular union. A mother depicted in the popular press as being as foul as a privy would have been the last straw."

"I won't tell anyone," she offered.

"Thank you, Mrs. Snowe. A woman with your connections could spread gossip without even entering Almack's. I've never been there myself."

Eugenia had.

Many times.

"I suppose you already know about the assembly

room; you're as ladylike as any lady I've met. I don't mean to condescend," he continued, digging himself deeper.

"I'm grateful for the compliment," Eugenia said, saving it up to tell her father—the marquis. He'd roar with laughter at the idea that she was as ladylike as a real lady.

She cleared her throat. "You will have considered this, but your mother's clandestine marriage means that Otis is the rightful heir to his father's title and estate." The current—or soon to be deposed—viscount was a portly man with a wispy beard that gave him a resemblance to an amiable goat.

Mr. Reeve nodded. "The Court of Chancery appointed me guardian after proving the late Lord Darcy's will and testament. The former viscount agreed to care for the estate until Otis comes of age."

"You don't wish to live there?"

Mr. Reeve shook his head. "I have a considerable estate of my own, and he seems to be doing a good job. My people will keep an eye on Otis's property, of course, but the man is genuinely fond of the people and has kept the house and lands in good condition. I don't like the idea of taking his title, lands, and occupation in one blow."

Eugenia nodded.

"The real problem is that the children's maternal grandmother, the Duchess of Gilner, has filed a plea for a Private act in the House of Lords, which would transfer guardianship of the children and estate to herself."

"Due to your irregular birth?" Eugenia asked. Her Grace was a stickler when it came to polite society. In fact, she was one of that small group of dowagers

who felt that Eugenia should eschew the ton altogether, now that she was "in trade."

"Precisely. There will be a hearing in a few weeks in response to her plea."

"Her Grace is a powerful woman," Eugenia said carefully.

His mouth quirked in a rueful smile. "I considered marrying a lady—any lady—without delay, to atone for my illegitimacy, but I can't bring myself to do it."

"It would be difficult to woo under these circumstances," Eugenia agreed, not allowing herself to smile back.

This wasn't funny.

Well, it was a little funny.

"But I doubt that the circumstances of your birth are sufficient to overturn Lord Darcy's will," she said. "I think Court of Chancery follows paternal wishes whenever possible."

"Yes, but I was thrown in prison last year. It was an illegal imprisonment by my fiancée's uncle, but the duchess plans to ask that I be barred from guardianship on that basis."

"That is terrible," Eugenia said, losing all wish to laugh.

"The Duke of Pindar, my former fiancée's husband, will testify on my behalf."

Eugenia narrowed her eyes. "Don't you think it's odd that the Duchess of Gilner is acting as an arbiter of polite society even though her only daughter ran away with Lord Darcy when he was merely fifteen?"

Ward shrugged. "I'd rather not use that against her. After all, the late Lord Darcy's will has been proved. If I can demonstrate the ability to raise the children

according to their station, it would be reasonable to follow their father's wishes."

Eugenia had an inkling that it would take more than a good governess to wage war against the contemptuous old woman, but there was nothing she could do to help. "Have you sent in Otis's name for admission to Eton?"

"Better," Mr. Reeve answered, with that quick smile of his. "I sent a large donation to commemorate Otis's father. Darcy was only two years ahead of me."

Mr. Reeve had been at Eton with his future stepfather? It was a small world, and an odd one.

"I can see Otis racketing around Eton without difficulty," he added. "It's Lizzie who poses a problem. I could send her away to school, I suppose, but she wouldn't fit in with the other girls."

Eugenia had to agree. "Where did Lizzie acquire her headgear?"

"It was part of Lady Lisette's costume for playing Lady Macbeth."

Mrs. Snowe's eyes melted in sympathy. "That's heartbreaking."

Ward wasn't sure why Lizzie wore the veil, but he didn't think it was because she wanted to feel closer to her mother. For one thing, she always referred to her mother as "Lady Lisette."

Mrs. Snowe cleared her throat. "I gather that your mother was not playing minor parts."

"Lady Lisette took all leading female roles, as I understand. Cleopatra and the like. I suppose I'm fortunate that Lizzie isn't wearing a gilt Egyptian headpiece."

"Miss Midge is versatile and creative," Mrs. Snowe said, sounding as if she were reassuring herself. "I

shall dispatch her to you tomorrow; she should arrive in the late afternoon."

With that, she rose and headed toward the door. Ward followed suit. The way Mrs. Snowe's hips swayed was transfixing.

He'd like . . .

No.

She was a respectable widow. She wasn't a woman who would entertain thoughts of an illicit liaison. Anyone could tell that.

Mrs. Snowe stopped at the door. "I believe that Miss Midge will enjoy coming to know your children."

"Is she likely to faint at the sight of entrails?" Not that Ward thought Lizzie had plans for further dissection.

"I cannot imagine Alithia Midge being unnerved even by the events described in the Book of Revelation." Mrs. Snowe replied. "She would likely offer the Four Horsemen a cup of tea."

With that, she opened the door, making it clear that he was expected to leave.

"Lizzie and Otis will be fine," she said, placing her hand lightly on his for a second. "Children are remarkably good at weathering unusual living arrangements. In fact, placidity produces tiresome adults."

"That bodes well for their future."

"Was there anything else, Mr. Reeve?"

Ward had the impulse to tell her everything: that Lizzie was filled with fury instead of grief, that Otis never mentioned his mother and was obsessed with money.

That Lizzie seemed to believe she had magical

powers and that Otis saw no ethical problem with stealing money in lieu of earning it, even though gentlemen did neither.

He shook his head. "No, thank you."

Mrs. Snowe had been a governess, but she was obviously something of a lady as well. Perhaps she'd been a vicar's daughter.

She was making a deep curtsy, for instance . . .

That bosom.

No man could ignore it.

Surprisingly, Mrs. Snowe extended her hand, not to be clasped but to be kissed, for all the world as if they were taking leave of each other at a ball.

Ward had been instructed by the best—his father's title ensured that—so he swept a bow and kissed her hand.

His lips brushed her skin and he caught that elusive scent again. Sweet berries, warm woman . . .

"What did you just say, Mr. Reeve?" a confused voice asked.

Had he spoken aloud?

Ward straightened with the urgency of a soldier on review. "I'm most grateful for your forbearance and generosity," he said, probably laying it on too thick.

But she smiled at him again, so it seemed not.

It was demoralizing to realize just how much flummery a man might babble in order to see that smile again.

Chapter Seven

Ward's butler, Cyrus Gumwater, was not the imperious, stately butler whom one might expect in a great house. Instead, he was a failed inventor, going on fifty and surly to boot. He was tall and lanky with ferocious black eyebrows that seemed to go upward and sideways, in vague harmony with his hair.

Ward had come across Gumwater's design for a "flying aerial machine adapted for the Arctic Regions," and considered that he had saved the man's life when he persuaded him that butlering was preferable to landing face down in a pile of snow.

These days, Gumwater spent his free moments making things for the house, like an improved pickle fork, and a portable holder for multiple umbrellas, even though Ward had only one umbrella.

If that.

Inventions aside, Gumwater was a fine butler, and managed to keep Fawkes House running as smoothly as a well-tuned clock. It was the house Ward had bought for Mia, because betrothed gentlemen were expected to buy a big heap of stone and set up a nursery. Lucky him: if he ever did get married, he had the house, and the nursery was already full.

"Miss Midge has arrived," Gumwater said now.

"You may show her in," Ward said, looking up from a diagram of a steam engine.

Mrs. Snowe had followed through on her promise and dispatched the new governess directly. He had the feeling that she never broke her promises.

Unlike Mia.

Not that it was relevant in the least.

"Miss Midge is refreshing herself after the journey." This was followed by a meaningful pause, so Ward put down his quill.

"She is one of *those* women," Gumwater stated.

Ward raised an eyebrow.

"A managing woman. She demanded fresh goat's milk for breakfast every day."

"Surely you can obtain some? I suppose we could keep a goat, if need be."

Acres of land had come along with the house. They could have a herd of goats. They could even house them in the picture gallery—what was he supposed to hang up there? A portrait of his late mother cuddled up to her fifteen-year-old lover? Or

the grandmother who was suing him on the basis of immorality?

When Gumwater scowled, his brows turned into one line, like the hedge around the kitchen garden. "Goat's milk is not the issue. She asked for the where-abouts of the tennis court, and when I told her that it was in some disrepair, she announced that it would have to be up to snuff by tomorrow or the day after, latest."

"I think Mrs. Snowe mentioned tennis," Ward said.

He was surprised by how often he'd found him-self thinking about Mrs. Snowe. Yes, she was lovely. Beautiful, even. And luscious. Even thinking about the way her gown clung to her rounded hips made him—

Really, it was preposterous. He should go to London and do what every other unmarried gentle-man did: pick out an opera dancer and set her up in a house in Knightsbridge.

He wouldn't pick an opera dancer with a mop of red curls because that would be . . .

No.

Gumwater was nattering on about the tennis court, and Ward was starting to get the general idea of his complaint. Unlike Miss Lumley, who had been tear-fully submissive to the household structure, Miss Midge meant to challenge it.

She and Gumwater had already skirmished, and Gumwater had lost.

An odd name, Alithia Midge.

It made him wonder what Mrs. Snowe's given name was. Likely it was something flamboyant; in his experience people who grew up on the outskirts of society had grandiose names.

Georgette, perhaps. Marguerite. Wilhelmina.

Rosamund. That would be appropriate, in keeping with the color of her hair. An extravagant name would suit her. Something more exotic than the names given to high-born ladies.

"Mia," for example, was short and ladylike, just like his former fiancée. Another reason he was lucky to have escaped that marriage. He would have developed neck cramps kissing his wife.

Georgette Marguerite Wilhelmina Snowe—or whatever she was called—was tall for a woman. She made him think of a wildflower with slightly ragged, velvety petals and a deep perfume.

"Gumwater," he said, interrupting a diatribe that could be summed up as "women don't know their place these days."

"Yes, sir."

"What do you know about Mrs. Snowe and her registry office?"

"Nothing, sir," the butler said promptly. "An office run by a woman. I shall say no more on the subject."

"You look as if you've taken a bite of a green persimmon," Ward observed.

The door opened and a tall, thin woman entered, wearing a navy blue gown with a discreet silver cross at the neck. She looked dispassionate and utterly competent.

One look and he knew Mrs. Snowe was right: there would be no tears from Miss Midge.

In fact, if he were asked to place a wager on this particular governess's response to events in the Book of Revelation, he'd come down on the side of Miss Midge's responding with unruffled civility to any

number of horsemen raining from the sky to herald the end of days.

Ward rose and found his hand being shaken with brisk efficiency.

"I have been thoroughly briefed," Miss Midge announced, as if she were reporting for duty aboard a naval vessel.

"Indeed," Ward said, taken aback.

"The betting ring will have to be shut down. Gentlemen do not profit by taking ha'pennies from their inferiors. It is common." Clearly, vulgar inclinations would be rooted out, just like dandelions from a rolled lawn.

Ward managed not to wince. Although he had not known Lizzie and Otis long, he was certain that the children's instincts were lacking in refinement, as were his own.

He himself had had at least eight governesses as a boy, and none of them had succeeded in weeding out the tasteless interest in making money that his brother also seemed to have inherited.

Ward had never encountered a boy more focused on profit and loss. In fact, most grown men didn't have Otis's fierce ambition.

"My mother wore a veil on the occasion of my father's death," Miss Midge was saying. "I sympathize with the wish to cover one's face during the exigencies of grief. I shall allow the veil, though not during vigorous exercise."

Ward tried without success to imagine his sister bouncing around a tennis court. "I am quite certain that neither Lizzie nor Otis know how to play tennis."

"I shall do my best," Miss Midge said, unexpect-

edly taking his hand again and giving it another shake. "I believe myself capable of miracles, although never having been called upon to perform one, I cannot be sure. The Lord tests us in order to make us stronger."

Ward had no opinion on that doctrinal point, but luckily Miss Midge didn't pause for agreement.

"You must choose a healthy activity with which to engage in with the children," she said. "Fresh air is a great facilitator of family harmony."

Did they need facilitating? Ward felt as if Lizzie and Otis had lived with him forever, even though it had been scarcely a fortnight.

His father and stepmother had picked a bloody inconvenient time to accept a diplomatic mission to Sweden. King Gustav was a hare-brained fool, and he couldn't imagine his father's diplomatic skills would do much to change that.

"No tennis," he said. "I cannot see myself chasing around after a small ball. I suppose I could teach them to fish."

He gave the butler a look that had Gumwater moving forward instantly.

"I should be glad to meet my charges now," Miss Midge said. She seemed to be very given to pronouncements. "Gumwater, I'll thank you to introduce me, if you would."

The butler bowed in Ward's direction, his rigid frame implying silent reproach.

"You know, Gumwater, I could recommend a hair tonic," Miss Midge said, in a clear, carrying voice as they left the room. "It would tame your resemblance to Samson, before his encounter with Delilah, of course."

As the door closed behind them, Ward gave a little kick to the massive wooden desk that dominated the room. "Come out from under there, Otis, and tell me what you think."

Otis crawled out of his hiding place and straightened up. "Look what I made, sir."

It was some sort of grimy wooden box. "What is it?"

"It's a mousetrap," Otis said. "The mouse walks up this ramp, you see, and he falls through this hole. He doesn't realize it's there, because he doesn't know that cheesecloth won't hold his weight."

"Why does he walk up that ramp?"

"Because there's a piece of cheese in the box!" Otis lifted up the cheesecloth. "See?"

"That doesn't look like cheese."

"Monsieur Marcel is frightfully stingy, so I'm using a corner of my bath sponge. Rubbing it with a smelly cheese is better than wasting money on food for a mouse."

"That was your new governess."

"Yes, I heard," Otis said, completely unconcerned. "I'm going to charge six pence for this trap, sir, what do you think? I expect I could make quite a lot of money in the market."

"Would you pay that amount?"

"No, but I don't mind living with mice."

"I doubt that a mouse will be fooled by the cheesecloth, because it would feel unsteady," Ward pointed out. "What does Jarvis think?"

One of the reasons Miss Lumley had to be dismissed was that she had been adamant that Jarvis, a plump rat with long whiskers and bright black eyes, live in the stables.

"Jarvis is asleep," Otis said, peering into the small canvas bag he had slung over one shoulder. "But I see what you mean." He walked a dirty finger along the ramp and paused on the cheesecloth. "It wiggles."

"You'd better go upstairs and meet Miss Midge," Ward said. "She's expecting to find you in the nursery."

"I'll go up there in a bit. If I put a ramp inside, balanced on a rock, the mouse would step on it and the ramp would plummet down. He'd be stuck in the box."

"Possibly," Ward said, choosing not to commit himself. A blind mouse might be fooled, although he'd have to be terribly hungry to mistake a piece of bath sponge for cheese.

"It will take more wood for the ramp, so I'll charge seven pence for it," Otis said, starting for the door.

"Would you like to learn to fish?" Ward asked.

Otis stopped and cocked his head. "Not particularly. I imagine that Lizzie would be interested in dissecting a fish. She wouldn't like to see it die, though."

"We could keep it in a bucket of water," Ward said.

"They gasp for air as they die. I don't think it feels very good for the fish. Lizzie wouldn't like it." He slipped out the door.

Otis had never said a word about their mother's death. Not a single word. Was that normal? Ward had no idea.

Surely his brother hadn't been present when their mother died. Or had they been living in a one-room caravan at the time? He didn't even know. And he didn't know whether he should ask.

Was it better to look into a tragedy of this nature, or simply let the memories fade?

That was surely a question for an expert.

Chapter Eight

Fawkes House
Wheatley
Wednesday, April 22, 1801

Dear Mrs. Snowe,

You will be glad to know that Miss Midge has arrived. She clearly has great ambitions for my brother and sister. They had a preliminary skirmish when it came to light that my siblings were not in the habit of saying bedtime prayers, but Miss Midge prevailed and the household is the more holy for it.

Otis showed me a mousetrap he has designed, so if he is unable to attain the heady heights to which Miss Midge aspires, he can make a living as a rat-catcher which, I believe, is a thriving business in London.

Do you think it is normal that neither Lizzie nor Otis have mentioned their mother since the day they arrived? As you know, Lady Lisette was not conventional in her opinions nor her behavior. She was as fizzy as champagne, and not in a good way. A hedgehog might have made a better mother.

> *Your most obedient servant,*
> *Edward Reeve*

P.S. I have made up my mind that your given name is either Georgette or Rosamond.

Eugenia's clients occasionally sent notes to her, when a son won the house tennis cup, for instance, or a daughter trounced her suitors at archery. This letter was altogether different.

She was trying to decide how to respond when the door opened and Susan's head appeared. "I'm making up a list of our waiting families, and we're short twenty-three governesses. Shall we schedule another training course for next month?"

When Eugenia had first opened the registry office, she had thrown herself into the enterprise. She had loved conducting training courses and watching *her* newly minted governesses go out into the world and put her ideas into practice.

It was only now that she'd reached the top of her profession that she found the business growing wearisome. She pushed away the stack of letters and stood up.

"I suppose we must. Come have a glass of sherry. It's already late."

Eugenia went to a cut-glass decanter that had belonged to Andrew's mother. She poured two glasses of sherry and handed one to Susan, along with Mr. Reeve's letter. "Have a look at this."

"That's a lot of cheek!" Susan exclaimed a moment later.

"How so?" Eugenia sank into a nearby chair and took a healthy sip of golden wine.

"You're a respectable widow."

"He's merely asking for advice."

Susan snorted and handed back the letter. "I must say, Eugenia, sometimes I think you're as old as the hills, and the next moment, you're as naïve as a cloistered nun."

Eugenia skimmed the letter again. "There's nothing salacious here, other than that improper postscript about my given name." If her stepmother were in London, she could show it to her. But Harriet was in the country and although Eugenia often intended to visit, she hadn't managed it in . . . a year? More than a year.

Luckily, her darling papa and Harriet often came to London to see her, dragging children and dogs with them.

Somehow, in the last few years, Eugenia's world had both expanded and contracted. Expanded, because most of the female side of the ton trooped through her registry, and contracted because she rarely had time to attend balls or parties.

She spent every day in her office with Susan, meeting parents in an often fruitless attempt to determine whether they were sane before she committed one of her employees to their household.

"Do you suppose that Mr. Reeve can possibly believe that I might engage in an *affaire* with him?"

Susan crowed with laughter. "Don't you think it's more likely that he's wooing you? After all, *he* doesn't know that the woman with the most irreproachable reputation in all London has been contemplating a turn toward sin."

"*Sin?*"

"Deliciously wicked propinquity with a gentleman of your choice," Susan amended.

"He knows nothing about my reputation," Eugenia said. "As a matter of fact, he hasn't the faintest idea who I am. He's never been to Almack's. He thinks I'm a former governess, one who runs a registry office for the benefit of my fellow workers."

Susan began giggling madly. "You? A governess? That's absurd!"

"I could have been a governess under different circumstances," Eugenia protested.

It was shocking to imagine that big, beautiful man writing her a letter. Not that she wanted any man to write her a letter. She had Andrew—the memory of dear Andrew—that was enough.

She looked over the sheet again. "I honestly don't see anything indecent, other than that odd remark about my name."

"You can take my word for it: if Mr. Reeve is not thinking of you in a marital light, then his letter is a prelude to an attempted seduction."

Eugenia couldn't stop herself from smiling, so she raised her glass and swallowed the last drops of sherry. It rolled over her tongue, tasting first of apples and then salty, as if splashed with seawater. "Do you think I should consider it?"

"Why not?" Susan got up and fetched the decanter. She refilled Eugenia's glass and her own. "I would, if I liked that sort of man."

"What sort is that?"

"Broad chest . . . too broad, really," Susan mused. "One of those brawny types. He could probably pick even me up and carry me to bed. And there's his hair. I prefer a more well-groomed man."

"Really? Because I—" Eugenia stopped. Took another sip of wine.

"All that disheveled hair," Susan said, wiggling her toes again. "And his eyes . . . like hot chocolate. Alas, Mr. Reeve is a bastard, and thus ineligible to be my husband. Can you imagine my father's response?"

"My father always says that a man should be judged by his accomplishments, not the circumstances of his birth."

"That's not a vicar-ish idea," Susan said briskly. "The more pertinent fact is that you aren't looking for a husband, and Mr. Reeve wrote to you, not to me." She put her glass down with a click. "He asked for professional advice as regards his two forlorn, grief-stricken charges, and we cannot ignore his plea."

"*We?*" and, "I don't think that was a plea. I'm not sure what it was."

Susan ignored her. "I'll reply, after which we'll think about who should sign it." She jumped up. Sitting at Eugenia's desk, she started writing, the scratching sound of the quill providing an accompaniment to her voice as she read aloud.

"*Snowe's Registry, Cavendish Square, London, April 23, 1801. Dear Mr. Reeve, Thank you for your letter. Miss Midge is an excellent tennis instructor, among her other*

abilities. You will enjoy the game; it was one of King Henry VIII's favorite pastimes."

"Is that true?"

"I have no idea," Susan said. "But that's what I always tell parents who fuss about building a court. Now, what should we say about his wards?" She put the quill down and picked up her sherry instead.

"He ought not to push the children to talk about their mother."

"You know, if you'd talked more about Andrew since his death, it would be easier to forgive yourself for surviving."

Eugenia almost spit out something about how that was absurd . . . but was it?

"I'll write that if you wish," Susan said, tapping ink from her quill. "It's your letter." She started writing, reading aloud once more. *"I advise that you not press the children for particulars regarding their mother. I still dislike talking about my husband, who died some years ago."*

"You didn't write that!" Eugenia gasped.

"Yes, I did," Susan replied, and went on, *"I realize, of course, that Lady Lisette was your mother as well, and perhaps, like the children, you feel her loss but are reluctant to speak of it."*

"This is an appallingly inappropriate letter," Eugenia noted.

"It's not inappropriate; I'd prefer to call it candid. Don't you ever tire of bland conversation?"

Eugenia looked at her over her glass. "I grew up in a house in which polite subjects were far too tedious to be discussed. So no, I don't get bored."

"Considering your father's disreputable house parties, it's amazing that he has settled down to such happy domesticity with your stepmother."

"I spent my early years in a chaotic mix of the most intellectual, albeit debauched, company in all England, until Harriet taught me the joy of an ordered life."

Eugenia shook her head at Susan's frown. "My father never allowed debauched behavior in front of *me*. He was ferociously protective, but children aren't stupid. They instinctively understand the tenor of a household."

"All that debauchery led you to appreciate polite conversation," Susan said, summing it up.

"I'm dreadfully boring, aren't I?"

"No. On the contrary. You are a lady who observed enough unconventional behavior to give her the courage to start her own business and turn it into a wild success."

Eugenia gave a startled little laugh. "I opened Snowe's because Andrew died."

"I find myself wondering if Lizzie wears her veil to bed," Susan said aloud, turning back to the letter.

"How did you know about Lizzie's veil? I didn't tell you that!"

Susan raised her head. "The peephole, you ninny. After I realized that a gorgeous man, who appeared undaunted by your pedigree and accomplishments, was paying you a second visit? I was glued to the wall."

"I didn't . . ." Eugenia fell silent.

"How is Otis?" Susan said, scribbling away. *"I expect that Miss Midge put a stop to his gambling activities, yet a boy that creative will find ways around her rulings."*

"We will not post this letter," Eugenia stated.

"Certainly not," Susan said soothingly. "We're merely fooling about." She dipped her quill back into the ink.

"You know, Lady Lisette was completely mad," Eugenia said. "The newspaper accounts were right about that."

"Did you ever meet her?" Susan tapped the nib carefully against the lip of the bottle.

Eugenia nodded. "Once. When I was around ten, she came to one of my father's house parties. She was beautiful, in a threatening sort of way. She had lovely blue eyes, but there was something vindictive about them. She glittered."

"'Glittered'?"

Eugenia waved her hand, and nearly spilled her sherry. "Like Rundell & Bridge's window when coal smoke turns everything dark, and the street lamps light up the diamonds."

"Very poetic," Susan said approvingly. "I do believe that Mr. Reeve brings out your romantic side."

"It's the wine," Eugenia said, and set her glass down. "After a day or so, my father summoned a carriage to take Lady Lisette away. He said she was the type who would keep drinking tea while faint screams came from the dungeon."

"I can see where you inherited that poetic bent," Susan said. She was still scrawling on the letter.

"It's no wonder the children don't mention their mother," Eugenia said. She stood up and stretched. "I must go home. I have appointments from eight in the morning straight through the day."

"I cannot remember the last time you left London."

"There's always something to do," Eugenia pointed out as she placed the empty glasses on a silver tray in the corner.

She turned. "No, you cannot!"

Susan was carefully sanding the letter. "Certainly

I can. Mr. Reeve is a client like any other. He wrote a letter asking you about a delicate situation with his orphaned wards. The poor man deserves the courtesy of a reply. Unless you want me to rip up his letter?"

That seemed impolite. But Susan's letter was impolite as well.

"All right," Eugenia said reluctantly. "I suppose it's best to respond."

Susan gave the letter a final shake and closed the sand box. "I am curious to see his reply."

"What else did you put in that letter?" Eugenia asked suspiciously. "You stopped reading aloud toward the end."

"I merely said that Snowe's is always here to provide support for our governesses."

"Lord knows what he'll think of me."

"You are scarcely a good judge, since you're generally bosky as a goose after a second glass of sherry, and we have had three. It's a good thing I wrote the letter—since I'm not the one wildly intrigued by a certain Oxford don. Who knows what you might have written!"

Before Eugenia could swat her, Susan escaped, laughing.

Chapter Nine

Fawkes House
Wheatley
April 29, 1801

Dear Mrs. Snowe,

You asked about Otis, and I regret to report that he has disgraced himself. I believe it is normal for eight-year-olds to shed teeth, and indeed, Otis takes great pleasure in pulling down his lip to display bloody gaps in his lower jaw.

When the children first arrived at my house, Lizzie informed me that Otis should be paid for every tooth he shed, after which those teeth should be burnt or Otis would risk hardship in the afterlife. Pretty much every aspect of this scenario struck me as unlikely, but I have decided it is best not to challenge Lizzie's authority in questions of death and its repercussions.

Otis began to collect payments from my butler, Gumwater, who paid for 14 teeth over the course of a fortnight. Gumwater's excuse is that he has never looked into the mouth of a small boy and has no wish to begin.

What I have dubbed the Great Tooth Swindle came to an end when Gumwater at last queried an enormous molar whose former owner turned out to be a bull. Miss Midge is justly worried about this lapse in ethics, but I assured her that Otis would eventually learn respectable ways to make money. She didn't like this answer either, as she has a strong conviction that Otis should concentrate on lordly skills such as using a handkerchief and making a gentlemanly bow. He is exhibiting a marked lack of skill in both areas.

I have no reluctance to speak of my mother, although I know little about her. By the time I reached my majority and might have pursued a relationship, she had disappeared with Lord Darcy.

I expect that your late husband was a model of comportment and sanity in contrast with the speckled, rotten apples on my family tree. What was Mr. Snowe's profession? His demise must have followed hard on your wedding, so I picture him as an elderly man.

Surely you meant to ask about my first name, which is Theodore. I was called Teddy in my childhood, but at Eton I realized that the diminutive did not convey the kind of bravado that a bastard must exhibit to thrive. My friends call me Ward, by the way.

> Your most obedient servant,
> Edward Braxton Reeve

P.S. I take your silence to indicate that your given name is neither Georgette nor Rosamund. Wilhelmina? Josephine?

There was no question but that Eugenia should not reply to this appallingly intimate letter. She'd never done anything in her life as scandalous as taking part in this exchange. She managed to stop herself for a whole day before she sat down at her desk.

May 4, 1801

Dear Mr. Reeve,

Snowe's gives an annual party just before the opening of Parliament every year. In the crowning glory of the evening, each of my employees climbs on a table and presents an argument that her charges deserve the title "Most Misbehaved." We also award "Most Improved," but the competition is never as formidable. I am considering calling the whole thing off next year, on the grounds that Miss Midge should win by fiat.

Your letter made me laugh, not only at Otis's resourcefulness (although I do agree with Miss Midge that gentlemen ought not to engage in chicanery), but at the idea that Mr. Snowe was elderly. My husband was only one year older than I. He drowned in a boating accident, which was a tremendous shock to all who knew him.

I have been thinking that my advice that you not discuss your mother's loss with Lizzie and Otis may be mistaken. After reading your letter, I realized that no one ever asks me about Andrew. It was such a tragedy that from the day after his funeral, people have tried to avoid uttering his name in my presence.

> *Please give Miss Midge my best wishes,*
> *Mrs. Snowe*

May 13, 1801

Dear Mrs. Snowe,

Once again you have forgotten to reveal your given name. Petunia? Claudette?

We have had an exciting few days, Mrs. Snowe, and if only for the reputation of your agency, I believe that you must pay us a visit. I spent two years in the Americas, and can assure you that ever since what is known as The Incident, Miss Midge has taken on a distinct resemblance to a rabid raccoon I encountered in that country.

I still agree with you as regards the Four Horsemen of the Apocalypse, but only because that eventuality is foretold in the Bible and therefore Miss Midge has been warned. For all her experience as a governess, Miss Midge is constantly shocked by my siblings' lack of moral fiber.

In an effort to please our estimable governess, I took Lizzie and Otis fishing in the lake that lies at the bottom of my gardens. It was not a successful excursion. It turns out that Lizzie's fascination with dissecting animals does not extend to being in at their death.

One of my footmen is delivering this note in a well-appointed coach. Please accept my invitation to accompany him to Fawkes House—as my esteemed guest, it hardly needs saying—and lend us the benefit of your experience.

On another subject, I am sorry to hear of Mr. Snowe's tragic accident. Why have you never married again? That question may seem invidiously personal, so I offer you an unpleasant truth of my own: I have lost the appetite for marriage after my fiancée married a duke.

*I would be happy to share the details over a glass
of brandy, which is what I poured down Miss Midge's
throat last night. Does that not whet your curiosity?*

I never beg, but I am begging. And so is Miss Midge.

All best wishes,
Ward Reeve

"I shall not travel to Oxford," Eugenia told Susan,
"because it would be akin to agreeing to an indiscre-
tion." She had lived her entire life in opposition to
her father's easy ways, and somewhere deep inside
herself she was shocked that she was contemplating
what she was contemplating.

Sin, to call a spade a spade.

"I cannot judge the urgency of Mr. Reeve's request
insofar as you haven't allowed me to read his letter,"
Susan said in a wheedling sort of way.

And, when Eugenia frowned at her, "Have you
looked out of the window? A splendid aubergine-
colored traveling coach awaits your answer. I'm sure
it was made by Brundel & Fibbs. Mr. Reeve must be
fantastically rich."

"I don't care how splendid it is," Eugenia said. "It
would cause a scandal if I were to visit him."

"Much though I dislike reminding you of your
age and marital status," Susan replied, "it would do
nothing of the sort. You're a widow and well over
twenty years old."

"Hush," Eugenia said crossly. "I can't imagine why
Miss Midge is having so much trouble."

"Why shouldn't you pay a visit to one of our
clients? In my case, it might damage my reputation as

a virginal old maid, although it's unlikely anyone would believe that Mr. Reeve would bother to seduce me."

"That is not true. I'm sure Mr. Reeve would be happy to seduce you, if you expressed a willingness to accept his suit."

"I'd have to see him without his suit before I decided," Susan said with a naughty chuckle.

Eugenia rolled her eyes. "I shall not travel to Oxford," she repeated. "I'm certain that Miss Midge has it well in hand."

"I can clear your calendar for two days. Or better yet, a fortnight. You have scarcely left the office in a month. As for Alithia . . ." She fished a note from her pocket and waved it in the air. "She would be grateful for any assistance we can offer, and she implores me to send her a new prayer book. What could have happened to the one she had?"

"Perhaps she dropped it in the bath," Eugenia said. "I am not at the beck and call of Mr. Reeve, no matter what he thinks."

Susan was expert at radiating silent disapproval.

"I shall write a note informing Mr. Reeve that I do not pay nursery visits," Eugenia said. "Send it back in the carriage, if you please."

Susan went away and Eugenia sat down to write a stern, brisk reply but ended up staring into space.

To tell the truth, Mr. Reeve's very maleness was tantalizing. These days, she lived in a world of women. Barring the occasional father, she saw men only at balls and danced at most once or twice, because young mothers continually begged for her advice.

But she had grown up in a world of men. For years, it had been just herself and her father and his wide circle of witty, argumentative, male friends.

Secretly, she loved the way men smelled. She liked their cigar smoke, their bawdy jokes, and their deep laughter. She even enjoyed their foolish habits of mind.

Andrew possessed the same extravagant masculine confidence that Mr. Reeve exhibited. Her husband, too, would have sent a traveling coach on a five-hour drive to London, certain that a woman he scarcely knew would leap into the vehicle at his command.

Not that Mr. Reeve resembled Andrew in other ways, because he didn't. Andrew, for example, had been lean and languid, a marvelously graceful dancer, whereas Mr. Reeve entered a room with explosive force. Andrew had been quietly proud of being one of the best-dressed gentlemen outside of Paris; Mr. Reeve clearly didn't give a damn.

She had no need to ask how Reeve escaped from prison—an adventure that sounded as if it belonged in a novel, to be frank. He had fought his way out. He had a warrior look about him. She found it irresistible.

Like a Pict, but without all the blue paint.

His letter sounded as if it had been written by a medieval lord ruling over his territory. Fawkes House was Ward Reeve's fiefdom, and if she were to go there . . .

She might never leave.

Ridiculous though it was, the idea made her shiver with an instinctive sense of danger and something deeper as well. More pleasurable.

May 14, 1801

Dear Mr. Reeve,

No, I will not pay you a visit. To do so would be monstrously improper.

No matter what you seem to think, I am a lady and was brought up to eschew illicit correspondence with members of the male sex. I am not the merry sort of widow.

I will go so far as to tell you, however, that I have never remarried because my marriage was a happy one and I have never met a man who would suit me as well as did my late husband.

It will not surprise you that I am aware your fiancée's identity. I have heard tales of the Duchess of Pindar's adoration of her husband, which began at age fifteen, as I recall.

If I may be candid, I believe you to have had a lucky escape. I cannot imagine a lonelier existence than being married to a woman in love with another man. Or, in my case, a man in love with another woman.

She paused and stared into space because a memory of Andrew, laughing across a room in the midst of a soirée, had jumped to her mind.

That particular soirée had been at Buckingham Castle, only a few months after their marriage. They had intended to stay only the requisite forty minutes.

But Andrew had looked at her from the other side of the room, and he'd headed toward her, a little smile at the corner of his mouth. She had hardly been

able to breathe, a state her corset made all the worse.

He'd taken her hand and drawn her into the corridor . . .

Eugenia discovered that she was smiling. It was a lovely surprise to find that her heart felt no more than a pinch at the memory, not unbearable sadness.

Perhaps she was ready to let Andrew go? A frightful phrase. But she saw what Harriet meant by it. Let go of the wrenching, vital pain of his loss. Keep the bright, teasing memory of the young man who had adored her.

They had been introduced at her debut ball, after which he blithely ignored her seventeen suitors—among them two viscounts and a duke—and made her fall in love with him using little more than his wicked sense of humor.

And his thighs, to be honest.

Ward Reeve also had legs that a woman could appreciate.

She had to remember that—Snowe's and the new century notwithstanding—she was a conventional woman. That quality was essential to her sense of self. It was her father who was, or at least, used to be, unconventional.

For her part, she liked conformity. Morality.

My secretary will see to it that Miss Midge receives a new prayer book. May I suggest that if Miss Midge's personal belongings, or person, were involved in The Incident, that you give her a holiday and transportation to Oxford? Contractually, she is due every other Sunday, but an exception can do much for household cheer.

There was something disquieting about this exchange of letters. Eugenia read over what she had written, acknowledging the uncomfortable truth that

her mind was completely engaged by a man whom she scarcely knew. By Ward Reeve's strength and control, the legs she couldn't dismiss, his strong jaw and beautiful teeth.

As if he were a horse she were contemplating buying!

But how thrilling it had been to have Andrew's body at her command. To have him walk toward her with that intent look on his face, as if nothing in the world could satisfy him but her.

Damn it.

Ladies didn't curse, she reminded herself.

Damn, damn, damn, damn . . .

The quill was back in her hand, unbidden.

> *My given name is not Henrietta, nor Julietta, although you are correct as regards its extravagance. It is Eugenia, but no one other than my close family ever addresses me as such, and I will thank you to adhere to my wishes in this respect.*
>
> > *All best wishes,*
> > *Mrs. Snowe*

Fawkes House
Wheatley

May 21, 1801

Dear Mrs. Snowe,

> *I don't know whether it was Miss Midge or I who was more disappointed when my coach returned empty. I wish I could tell you that the household has taken a turn for the better, and that Miss Midge has succeeded in her campaign to reshape my siblings into respectable members of polite society.*

But I cannot.

This week, Lizzie posed an even greater problem than Otis. Yesterday she staged some sort of hocus-pocus that persuaded one of the more gullible stable boys that he was invisible. The young man intruded on the washhouse when a maid was engaged in private ablutions.

Alas, he proved all too solid when the girl whacked him in the face with a washboard. The doctor says that when the swelling goes down, he'll likely be able to see out of the afflicted eye again.

Miss Midge was quite disturbed by Lizzie's spell casting. Our governess's father is a vicar, as you doubtless know. He would not approve of my unruly siblings. For my part, I was quite impressed by the Latin incantation Lizzie used to achieve 'invisibility,' the pluperfect subjunctive conjugation for 'I love,' 'I tell,' and 'I listen.' Who would have thought the pluperfect could be so powerful?

It seems that Lord Darcy taught his children Latin from the age of 6 until his untimely death. Miss Midge confirms that both children can practically babble in that tongue, one I never learned, for all my schooling. Otis and Lizzie both readily speak of their father, but remain mum on the subject of their mother.

In the hope you had a better day than mine,

Your most obedient servant,
Ward

Chapter Ten

Fawkes House
Saturday, May 23, 1801

The butcher's eyes were bulging like a Pekinese in a too-tight collar, although he was the one gripping Otis by the collar, not the other way around.

"What seems to be the problem?" Ward asked, his eyes moving from his brother's defiant face to the irate butcher to Miss Midge. In the distance he could hear Lizzie protesting all the way up the stairs after being banished by the governess.

"This boy here," Mr. Biddle roared. He gave a shake that went all the way down to Otis's boots.

"Surely you didn't mean to handle my brother so violently, Mr. Biddle," Ward stated. One of the con-

sequences of his unexpected sojourn in prison was an extreme disinclination to see anyone mistreated, physically or otherwise.

"I did, and I didn't," the butcher said, chin jutting forward, although he released Otis's collar.

Ward pulled the boy into the crook of his arm and stepped back. "What happened?"

"I caught him stealing," Mr. Biddle thundered. His mustache puffed out like the tail of an indignant squirrel.

Otis, now looking more put-out than scared, peeked up at Ward. "I didn't steal anything."

"He took me chain of office! That's the symbol of me office as mayor and I caught him with red hands!"

Bloody hell.

It was one thing to pilfer scraps of wood from the stables and entirely another to steal valuables from the villagers. Miss Midge apparently agreed; she was frowning at Otis with all the boot-faced disapproval of a Puritan encountering an unrepentant adulterer.

"Were you a witness to this alleged crime, Miss Midge?" he asked.

"I regret to say I was in the haberdashery with Miss Lizzie." She gave her charge a direct look. "Otis, explain yourself."

"What's to explain?" the butcher said, his voice hard. "The boy tried for me gold chain. I caught him. He's as crooked as—" He caught Ward's eye and cut off the insult.

Otis jerked against Ward's arm. "I'm not crooked!" he shouted. "He said I was a by-blow, and I'm not! My parents were married. What's more, I have a title, because my father was a lord!" He burrowed his face into Ward's ribs.

Mr. Biddle snorted contemptuously.

"You may scoff, but Otis is correct," Ward stated. "He is Lord Darcy, the fifth in his line and the owner of a considerable estate in Devon."

"I don't care if he's the king of England! I know about him and his sort. We hear things in the village. Lord knows what he was planning to do with me chain."

"I was only hanging it on his rosebush," Otis cried.

What the hell?

"Why on earth would you do that?"

"Lizzie said she would give me a shilling if I did it and brought her back four roses," Otis said miserably. "I was going to put it right back on the hook in his shop. The rosebush is in his yard."

Lizzie was apparently up to some sort of magical foolery. Miss Midge's eyes narrowed. Ward sighed and turned back to the butcher.

"It seems, Mr. Biddle, that your chain of office never left your premises. My butler will give you a guinea for your trouble, and I will make certain that my siblings stay far away from your rosebush and your chain."

"I demand that you do something about that thief," the butcher shouted.

Otis snuggled closer to Ward's side.

"We villagers need to be able to sleep without fear. Why was he hanging my chain on a bush? I have to reassure me wife there's no hocus-pocus going on."

"You are speaking about an eight-year-old boy," Ward said with quiet ferocity. "I suggest you return to your shop, Mr. Biddle, and contemplate your orders. You have no need to think of my household now or in the future."

Biddle's mouth fell open, so wide that Ward could see his fat tongue. Apparently it just dawned on the butcher that he was berating the man who owned the largest house this side of Oxford, and who employed twice as many servants as other estates in the vicinity.

"Good day, Mr. Biddle," Ward said. Gumwater took Biddle by the shoulder and turned him smartly toward the front door.

Ward scooped up his brother and carried him to the library, followed by Miss Midge. He sat down before the empty fireplace, the boy in his lap. "Bloody hell, you're a nuisance, Otis."

"I hate Mr. Biddle," Otis cried.

Miss Midge sat down opposite them, her hands folded and her heels neatly together.

"Tell us what happened," Ward said.

"I wasn't stealing his chain," his brother said with an angry sniffle. "I was just nimming it for a little while."

"Nimming it?"

"Thieves' cant," Miss Midge put in.

"I was hanging it between heaven and earth." Otis dragged his sleeve across his eyes.

"I do not understand," Ward said, with Herculean patience.

"I was hanging it in Mr. Biddle's rosebush. His own rosebush, between heaven and earth."

"It sounds as if Miss Lizzie made another attempt at a magic spell," Miss Midge said. Her voice was tight.

Ward's heart sank. Since her arrival, the new governess had shown herself to possess no discernible sense of humor, which meant she took Lizzie's foolery too seriously.

"We must speak to Lizzie," he said.

Miss Midge nodded and rose.

Otis collapsed against Ward's shoulder and said something unintelligible.

"What did you say?"

And, after catching the import of it, Ward said, "You're my brother, Otis. You're stuck with me, no matter what. Forever."

He didn't reply, but Ward added, "Lizzie too. You're wretched nuisances, but you're *my* nuisances."

He surprised himself.

It seemed he wasn't going to hand his brother and sister over to his father and stepmother after all.

Chapter Eleven

Fawkes House
May 23, 1801

Dear Mrs. Snowe,

    Miss Midge is adding her own note to this missive. I will keep my part brief. Otis was caught borrowing our village mayor's chain of office, a crime which his sister instigated. His motive was not personal gain; Lizzie intended to use the power of the chain to transform a few roses into tools for finding true love.

    If you find this confusing—never mind improbable—so do I. My sister has shown herself to have a prodigious imagination; unfortunately, her creativity is in direct proportion to Miss Midge's dislike of magic, no matter how ineffectual (it promotes paganism and undermines

Christian values). Miss Midge will no doubt expound
on her feelings when she sees you.

The wherefores of the conjuration are vague, but
apparently Otis was to hang the chain in a rosebush in
order that the sun could shine "full" upon it, and there-
after bring four roses back to his sister.

> *We need your help,*
> *Ward*

"What on earth does he think I could do?" Eugenia
asked, looking down at the letter. "Go back in time
and stop the boy from stealing a livery collar?"

"I suppose Lord Darcy could have started his career
as a burglar by taking something less valuable," Susan
remarked.

"Have any of our children stolen valuables before?"
It was the sort of detail she should have at her fingertips, but she couldn't bring anything to mind.

Susan snorted. "Surely you haven't forgotten last
year's Most Misbehaved contest? One of the Duke
of Fletcher's children, I can't recall which one, stole
heaps of things. Don't you remember the golden
toothpick?"

"Well, of course, but that was different. It wasn't
for material gain."

"Neither is this," Susan pointed out. "The Fletcher
governess didn't even win Most Misbehaved for the
toothpick, although after she mimicked the duke's
reaction, she earned a few nominations for Most
Pitied."

"I can't remember anything like this before," Eugenia said.

"I try not to burden you with unpleasant details,

so that you can maintain a pleasant relationship with the parents." Typically, Susan worked with the governesses, while Eugenia dealt with their employers. "Some of our children are proper little rotters."

"We oughtn't to insult our own," Eugenia said, frowning.

Susan blithely ignored her. "If I were to embark on a life of crime, I'd take a gold chain instead of, say, a gold toothpick. It suggests that Otis possesses more intelligence than the Fletcher offspring, although I don't imagine His Grace would agree."

"I have no idea how to respond," Eugenia said.

"He is begging you to come, Eugenia. Obviously, you must go to Oxford," Susan said. "I will take your appointments for three days. And I'll add my own plea: travel from there to your father's estate and enjoy a proper rest."

"I cannot go to Oxford," Eugenia said, the words wrenched from her throat. "I just can't, Susan. Mr. Reeve is too . . . *No.* I'm not ready."

The thought of entering Ward's house— shamefully, Eugenia couldn't help thinking of him with the name he used to sign his letter—made her feel weak. Cracked. Overheated.

Susan scowled, but Eugenia shook her head. "No."

"All right, we'll have to rely on Miss Midge," Susan said with obvious reluctance. "I'll write to Mr. Reeve and explain that we have no expertise as regards larcenous behavior. I won't mention that Otis has bested the Duke of Fletcher's offspring," she added, with a chuckle.

"Thank you," Eugenia said, heaving a sigh. "If your father only knew what you are urging me to do, Susan—"

"He'd disown me," Susan said cheerfully. She leaned over and dropped a kiss on Eugenia's cheek. "It's only because I love you. You have no appointments tomorrow. Stay home."

That evening, Eugenia walked through the house where she and Andrew had begun their married life, servants moving in a swirl of activity around her. A footman brought her a light meal that she ate in her bedchamber. She bathed, put on her nightgown, cleaned her teeth . . .

Went to bed and dreamed.

Of course, she dreamed of Andrew. There was nothing unusual about that; she dreamed of him at least once a week. He had been her rock, the stable fulcrum of her world.

In her dream, they were in the dining room, and Andrew was lounging at the table, rolling something between his hands. She couldn't see what it was. He was talking on and on about a horse he'd bought that had the eyes of a unicorn.

Starting awake, Eugenia lay in the dark, remembering how much Andrew talked. She'd loved to listen to him in those days. He had such definite opinions. And he always, always, knew what was right.

If he claimed a horse had the eyes of a unicorn, it had. No matter that neither of them had ever seen such a creature. Andrew's certitude had been a refuge after the ebullient chaos in which she grew up.

Her father's house had been comfortable, untidy, stacked with books, crammed with curiosities from all over the world. He had a penchant for fencing in the long picture gallery, lunging and parrying with competitive fervor while Eugenia watched from behind the shelter of a glass cabinet.

Andrew would never have fenced in the house, any more than he would have left a stack of books on the piano. He furnished their house in perfect taste. No detail was too small—from the way a horse's mane complemented the carriage he pulled, to the color of a bride's trousseau. His instinct for perfection dictated every detail of their life.

One night he had even discarded a silk nightgown that her stepmother had given her, because Prussian-blue was unbecoming to Eugenia's hair. "You look like a firework, all red and blue and ready to explode," he had said, laughing as he'd bundled it up and thrown it into the hallway. "The only place you're allowed to explode is in bed with me."

Then he had gathered her up in his arms and taken her to bed, and she'd forgotten about the nightgown.

Until now. Oddly enough, she felt a prickle of sadness for the girl she'd been, who had loved that nightgown and had felt beautiful in it.

She'd been so impossibly young.

And her life had been so simple.

Chapter Twelve

Tuesday, May 26, 1801
18 Cavendish Square
Mrs. Eugenia Snowe's residence

*T*he next morning, her maid laid out a muted green gown that complemented Eugenia's red hair without making it blaze like a wildfire.

Not that Andrew disliked her hair. He had adored winding her curls around his fingers and arranging her hair over her breasts as if she were a naiad in an old painting.

But he didn't want her to look flashy in public. Ladies sparkled in private; they gleamed discreetly in public.

It would have been easier to recover from his death

if she had unpleasant memories of their marriage. Instead, all she had were wistful fragments, like a few pearls strung on a thread. But pearls that are never worn lose their luster and shine. Perhaps that was the problem.

"I don't wish to wear that dress today," she told Clothilde. "Don't I have a gown somewhere that is the color of the sky?"

"Yes." Clothilde ducked into the dressing room and returned with an armful of cerulean silk. "With slippers?"

"No, something more sturdy. I intend to go for a walk in the park."

Clothilde groaned. "Madame, there is mud from yesterday's rain."

"You needn't come with me," Eugenia said. "Ladies my age have no need of a chaperone."

"That is true," Clothilde said, brightening. She hated mud, rain, dirt, and anything else that posed a threat to her immaculate appearance.

"You are larger in the bosom than you were when this dress was ordered," she observed a minute later, wrestling Eugenia's bosom into place.

"My breasts look like two cream buns on a tray," Eugenia said, regarding herself in the glass. "If they keep growing, they'll end up the size of ostrich eggs."

"Ostrich? What thing is that? Your *décolletage* is most attractive. Unfortunately, there are no gentlemen to be seen at this hour." Clothilde sniffed disapprovingly.

"I should like a new wardrobe," Eugenia said, making up her mind. "From the modiste who dresses the Duchess of Villiers."

"Oh là là," Clothilde cried, helping her slip into

her merino pelisse. "An excellent choice! Now, *now*, madame, you will meet the man."

"*The* man?"

"A man." Clothilde gave a Parisian giggle. "Or many men!"

Eugenia crossed the road and walked into the park, ambling off on a brick path. While she'd been hidden in her office, spring had come to London. Everywhere she looked there were masses of spring green and clumps of pale purple violets.

With one surreptitious glance to make certain she was not observed, Eugenia stepped from the path and crouched down in order to gather a fat handful of violets.

She had the vague sense that they were edible, though she doubted her cook knew—

Wait.

She froze. She wasn't alone.

In front of her, a pair of stout boots came into view. The owner of those boots presumably had an excellent view of her bosom, not to mention her purloined posy.

A dark, gravelly voice washed over her like the smell of brandy in a small room. "Mrs. Snowe, may I help you to stand?" His hand was large and powerful: the quintessence of all the things she enjoyed about men.

No glove.

Of course, Ward Reeve probably never wore gloves.

She put her gloved hand in his bare one and allowed him to draw her to her feet. "Mr. Reeve, this is a surprise." She had liked his smile when they first met. But now, after their exchange of letters, it was different: deeper, warmer . . . intimate.

A gallant would raise her fingers to his lips, fall back and bow, perhaps with a flourish. Ward did none of these, but simply held her hand tightly as he said, "You would not come to me, so I had to come to you."

Eugenia could feel herself turning pink. She pulled her hand away. "I have no advice to offer you, Mr. Reeve."

"Shall I collect your violets?" Without waiting for an answer, he bent down and gathered most of them in one sweep. His thighs strained against his tight-fitting breeches. Sunshine made his hair gleam with hints of gold.

He rose and presented the violets to her. "I consider myself extremely fortunate that Snowe's doesn't merely dole out governesses to various households, but offers them support throughout their employment."

"Yes, well—"

Ward slipped his hand under her arm and guided her back onto the footpath. "Your assistant, Miss Lloyd-Fantil, was kind enough to point out your house, and your butler directed me here. May I escort you to tea at Gunter's, Mrs. Snowe?"

For goodness' sake, why had Ward's fiancée run off to marry another man? Eugenia was having trouble not simply nodding in agreement to everything he said.

It was his voice and his eyes.

She had the feeling that, had he disappeared on *their* wedding day, she would have waited for him.

For years.

Just as she was doing for Andrew, she thought uneasily. Waiting for a man who would never come back.

Ugh. She pushed away the thought and focused on Ward's face again.

"Even though you claim to have no advice, you could choose the right concoctions to dazzle my siblings into obedience."

"I—"

"Miss Lloyd-Fantil assured me that you had no appointments today." His coaxing, deep voice brushed over Eugenia's skin like silk. He drew a little closer, and she smelled a mixture of leather and soap.

And man. Man sweat, to be utterly frank.

It was demoralizing to realize that she wasn't a good woman after all.

Apparently all her conventional behavior was simply a façade, because in his presence her limbs felt heavy and her skin prickled.

"Very well," she said, "I suppose we could go for tea."

If he kissed her, she would quiver like a rabbit caught in a vegetable patch. Not that he appeared to have any intention of kissing her.

The man was asking for help and she was staring at his mouth. Shameful!

"I shall ask them to prepare a hamper that I can bring back home with me," he said, taking her arm.

"You mustn't accept ices," she told him. "They'll never last. Gunter's always promises that properly packed, their ices won't melt, but they do."

His eyes crinkled at the corners in a devastatingly attractive way.

"You see? You are a veritable fount of good advice. I'll bring Otis and Lizzie to London one day, and we can take them for ices," he said.

We?

He turned her around the way she'd come before

she could think of a response. "My carriage is just there."

Sure enough, a carriage awaited in the street, so luxurious that one might expect a royal duke to clamber out of it, full of gallantry and brandy. "Miss Lloyd-Fantil mentioned that your vehicle is remarkable," she said, trying to fill the air so that the silence between them didn't seem quite so potent.

"It was made to order for the Duke of Clarence," he said, confirming her impression that it was meant for a prince. "It's a bit grandiose for me, to tell the truth. But when Otis and Lizzie turned up, I needed something larger than a high-perch phaeton, and this was the only suitable carriage I could buy in a hurry."

"Merely a practical decision?"

"I am convinced that Otis would have tried to drive my phaeton the moment he found time. Taking bets on his prowess, no doubt."

"You've had to turn your whole life upside down, haven't you? You gave up your profession and your carriage. It's admirable," Eugenia said, meaning it.

He shrugged as if it had been no hardship. He probably always put the people in his life above everything else; he was that sort of man.

A groom in smart livery stepped forward as they approached. A small mounting box was already positioned at the door. In truth, Eugenia was tall enough to climb into even a high-perch phaeton without assistance.

Nevertheless, Ward held out his hand. She looked down at the box just as her boot was about to descend on the painted image of . . . She gave a startled gurgle of laughter, dropped his hand, and put her foot back on the ground. "Is that a *chamber pot*?"

"Unfortunately," Ward said solemnly, "there's no mistaking it, is there? Given the . . ."

"Stream of piss," Eugenia supplied, having just worked out what she was looking at. "What admirable realism."

He grinned at her. "We mustn't speak of manure, but piss is acceptable?"

Eugenia could feel color flooding her cheeks.

"I won't tell anyone," he said with a twinkle in his eyes. "It is my firm conviction that those of us who needn't mind those rules shouldn't. And as for realism, I beg to differ. I gather that is a representation of the Duke of Clarence's private part," Ward said, pointing to one corner of the box. "Surely you agree that it is an optimistic—if not grossly inaccurate—rendering of the royal privates."

Eugenia smiled. This whole conversation—with its brash, irreverent attitude toward polite convention—reminded her of her girlhood.

Her father would love the absurdity of this mounting block.

"The organ in question does appear to be approximately the same size as the chamber pot," she said, stepping directly on the painting on her way into the carriage.

"More than optimistic," Ward said dryly. "Catastrophic."

Eugenia waited until he was seated opposite and the groom had closed the door before she asked the obvious question. "What on earth is the justification for the rampant vulgarity of that mounting box, Mr. Reeve?"

"*Rampant?*" he repeated, with a bark of laughter.

Her cheeks heated. "I didn't mean it that way."

"And am I truly still Mr. Reeve?"

She raised her chin. "Of course."

"I think of you as Eugenia—which, by the way, suits you."

"The chamber pot?" she insisted, trying to ignore the heat flaring in her cheeks.

"Caricatures have poked fun at the royal duke's inamorata, the lovely Dorothea Jordan, owing to her surname."

Eugenia's brows drew together.

"'Jordan' is an inelegant name for a chamber pot," he explained.

"Of course." She thought about that for a moment. "Why would the duke wish to remind Mrs. Jordan of such unpleasant remarks every time she climbed into her coach?"

"His Royal Highness apparently agrees with me that ignoring unpleasantness doesn't make it go away." His eyes took on a wicked sparkle, and he drawled, "After all, no matter how much polite society would like to pretend otherwise, such pots are in daily use in the most respectable of households."

"Stop that!" Eugenia said, though she couldn't hold back a smile. "You forget that I come across naughty boys all the time in my line of work, Mr. Reeve. At your age, one should aim for behavior suited to a grown man."

He laughed. "I haven't been labeled 'naughty' in years. I actually think that Clarence's idea is rather gifted in its simplicity. This way Dorothea stomps on her detractors every time she enters the carriage. Or she would have, if Clarence had accepted delivery of the vehicle."

"Why did you not have the scene painted over?"

Ward shrugged. "It made Otis laugh so hard that he almost coughed up his breakfast. Laughter is all too rare in the house at the moment, so if we have to tread on a few royal chamber pots, I'm happy to oblige. I'm more worried that the boy will grow up feeling inferior, considering the dimensions of the royal appendage."

His laughter went to Eugenia's head like a third glass of sherry. She almost—almost!—retorted something about how disappointment is a woman's lot in life.

Susan would make a jest like that, but it was untrue in Eugenia's case; Andrew had been more than appropriately accoutred, according to what she'd learned from marble statues of Greek athletes.

"Why did His Royal Highness decide against the carriage after having it designed to his specifications?" she asked instead. The seats were Spanish leather, and every detail was exquisite, if flamboyant.

Andrew wouldn't have liked it. She wasn't sure whether he would have loathed the chamber pot or the royal tool more, but she knew that the mounting box would have been repainted a sober black before the carriage ever drew up to their house.

The shiny trim would have been ripped from the exterior. The velvet tassels embellishing the curtains would have been exchanged for something more somber.

"Clarence couldn't afford it," Mr. Reeve said. "Must have outrun his allowance again."

Eugenia glanced at him from under her lashes. Her stepmother had suggested that she double her fees since Mr. Reeve was outrageously wealthy. She hadn't. Snowe's would never profit from the misfortune of two orphans.

"Luckily, I can afford it," Mr. Reeve said, guessing her train of thought.

"How pleasant for you," Eugenia said coolly. She was one of the richest woman in London, but she kept it to herself.

Mr. Reeve leaned forward and touched her knee. "I just wanted you to know that I am financially solvent."

"In—in my—that is entirely irrelevant," she spluttered.

He sat back and grinned at her. "I'm happy to hear it."

"Finances have no part in our discussion of your siblings' misbehavior," she managed.

"No, but I wanted to make a point."

"Quite," she said. Perhaps he was offering . . . surely he wasn't offering her money? A clammy feeling broke out all over her. Men had made improper proposals in the past, but no one had actually offered her *carte blanche*.

"Happily, Snowe's fees will not bankrupt me." But his eyes caught her face and his expression changed. "What have I said?"

She swallowed. "Nothing at all," she croaked. Of course, he hadn't intended anything of the kind. She was being a fool.

A fiendish grin spread over Ward's face and he leaned forward again. "I do believe that you thought I had made a respectable widow an offer, as if she were a lady of the night."

She cleared her throat. "Certainly not."

"Mind you," Ward went on, paying no attention to her feeble denial, "that gown does rather put your assets on display, like apples for purchase in front of a theater."

Eugenia narrowed her eyes at him. "Even given your disdain for polite discourse, Mr. Reeve, you should avoid such an invidious comparison."

"You are far too marvelously endowed to be likened to apples," he said, nodding agreeably.

She must be going a bit mad, because she heard herself say, "Earlier today, I was thinking that they'll be the size of a pair of ostrich eggs in a few years."

His eyes glittered with a dark emotion that she had no trouble interpreting, though she hadn't seen it for years. Lust.

Desire.

"All mankind lives in hope," he said. A husky note in his voice made her want to both leap toward him—and out of the carriage.

Andrew had been not much older than a boy when they married. He had looked at her with sunny pleasure in his eyes. Ward was a man, with a more abandoned, burning, and sinful emotion in his gaze.

A voice deep inside was shrieking about duty and morality, ethics and Snowe's, *her reputation.* But it was a small voice, and far away.

For seven years, she had been extraordinarily careful of her reputation. This was madness, but an oh-so-potent madness.

She was in the grip of a strange calm, like being in the eye of a storm: just the two of them, and the walls of this preposterously luxurious coach. No sounds but their voices, the rumble of wheels on stone streets, the slight creak as Ward's perfectly matched horses drew up in front of Gunter's.

It was an unfashionable time of day for tea, and the tearoom was all but empty. As they entered, the

ladies in the room turned toward Ward like sunflowers in the morning.

Lady Hyacinth Buckwald's gaze, for example, drifted over Ward as if he were one of those Greek statues: head to foot and back up with a pause in the middle.

"Mrs. Snowe!" the lady raised her hand and curled it closed two or three times in the sort of greeting with which a duchess might greet a chimneysweep. "I am surprised to see you here. One thinks of you as immured in that little house of yours. I would introduce you to my eldest daughter Petunia but she has retired to the ladies' waiting room."

Eugenia paused by her table. "Good morning, Lady Hyacinth. How are your younger children?"

"I can assure you that we found a *most* respectable governess," the lady said, her face darkening.

Ward had been exchanging a few words with Mr. Sweeney, the headwaiter of Gunter's, but now he came up behind Eugenia.

"If it isn't Mr. Reeve," Lady Hyacinth cried. "I haven't seen you in years."

"It was lovely to meet you again, Lady Hyacinth," Eugenia said with a nod, after which she allowed Mr. Sweeney to escort her to a table in the back, more or less protected from prying eyes by a well-positioned fern.

Behind her there was a brief murmur, and Ward followed. It was extraordinary, the way she could feel his presence behind her. She eased into a voluptuous walk, the faintest swing of her hip.

She didn't feel like a governess, nor like the successful proprietor of Snowe's Agency.

She felt like a woman.

Ward watched as waiters loaded their table with

delicacies, and then told them to prepare a hamper for his siblings. "But no ices," he added.

"I assure you that Mr. Gunter has devised a way of storing ices that can keep them stiff for hours," Mr. Sweeney said earnestly.

"Mrs. Snowe told me in the park that promises of that nature are never kept," Ward replied. The look he gave her should probably make a bolt of lightning come right down and consume the two of them.

The headwaiter blinked madly for a moment and closed his mouth. He bowed and promised to return with a hamper in due time.

"I'd like a small hamper for my return to Oxford as well," Ward said.

"Certainly, sir. What would you like in it?"

"Roast beef and a bottle of red wine."

Eugenia laughed. "You're such a man."

"Yes, I am," Ward said.

Color crept up her face. "I meant that ladies generally prefer white wine and chicken."

"We men have to keep up our stamina. But today I shall order like a lady. White wine and chicken it is. And some of those ices, because I'm certain they can stay stiff enough to eat for luncheon."

Eugenia choked back a giggle as Mr. Sweeney left.

"I must say that it's tragic to think you've been disappointed in this particular area," Ward said. "Stiffness." His gaze was purely wicked.

"I haven't been," Eugenia retorted. With a reckless grin, she added, "After all, I married when my husband was eighteen."

Ward's eyebrow shot up. "In case you're wondering, many of us retain the abilities we had at eighteen well into our later years."

Eugenia looked at Ward's body under her lashes. Eighteen-year-old men were . . . well, slender. Ward was muscled. A shadow on his jaw would be considerably darker by the end of the day.

"Are you already planning for your old age?" she asked.

The intensity in his gaze was a little unnerving. "When it comes to that part of my life, absolutely."

Eugenia was amazed to hear the husky giggle that came out of her mouth. She was not the sort of woman who giggled. Ever.

Except, it seemed, when a man whose eyes were full of lust boasted about his prowess in the bedroom some sixty years on.

Chapter Thirteen

Ward could not have been less interested in Eugenia's story of some dreadful child who had painted himself blue. But he recognized at the same time that he would happily listen to anything she wanted to tell him.

Damn it. She was irresistible.

"Who was that woman when we came in?" he asked her, after the story of the blue boy was over. "The harridan who implied that you shouldn't be allowed out of the registry office and claimed she'd met me, although we have definitely never met."

"That's Lady Hyacinth Buckwald," Eugenia replied. And, at his blank look, "You haven't heard of her?"

He shrugged. "I don't go into society, and my family knows I loathe gossip. So, no."

"She knows of *you*," Eugenia said mischievously. "Or at least, she knows of your fortune. The poor woman has four daughters to marry off. I think Petunia is second eldest." She pursed her lips. "Theirs is an unblemished family line. Petunia might be the solution to your prayers."

"No," Ward stated without hesitation.

"Lady Hyacinth doesn't care for me because I removed her governess after Boris—her husband—chased the poor woman around the ballroom at eight in the morning."

"Is it the time of day relevant?"

"His behavior was inexcusable at any hour; the time of day simply magnifies his transgression. One feels that a gentleman ought to be doing . . . doing whatever gentlemen do in the morning."

"The poor sod is likely desperate," Ward said. "Putting Boris to the side, I assure you that gentlemen are prone to chasing women around at eight in the morning."

"Be that as it may, they should never chase their governesses!"

One moment her eyes were flashing at him with amused, sophisticated desire, and the next she was as prim as a patroness of Almack's. Or at least what he imagined those ladies to be.

It was almost as if there were two Eugenias. One real, and one . . . not precisely unreal. The perfect lady and the real Eugenia.

That ladylike Eugenia was surely the result of pure will, inasmuch as she hadn't been born to the position. Her performance was quite impressive; he actually felt like applauding.

He genuinely liked and admired her. She'd not only made a life for herself following the death of her husband, but presumably a prodigious fortune with Snowe's Registry.

She was fascinating.

Damn it, if he didn't have to marry a gentlewoman for the sake of his siblings, he would give serious thought to courting her.

No matter what, he meant to pursue her. The truth of that was throbbing through every limb. Eugenia would be *his*. He would make love to her until this flame between them burnt out. Hopefully it would take only a night or two.

There was nothing to stop them but the eggshell-thin layer of respectability to which she clung.

Thinking of that, he gave her a slow smile, so suggestive that she froze, fork halfway to her mouth.

She blinked at him and carefully put down her bite of cake, uneaten.

"I don't think you're listening to my diatribe about gentlemen who consider a governess to be fair game simply because she lives under the same roof."

"No," Ward admitted.

Eugenia knew that smile. Was there any woman who hadn't seen that particular smile on a man's face, if not on many men's faces?

Ward had apparently come to the conclusion that she was his for the taking.

The problem with that—well, the problem with that, obviously, was that she was a respectable widow.

"What are you thinking?" she asked warily.

His eyes stayed on hers, happy and alert. A cheerful, anticipatory look that most married women knew.

Perhaps not *every* married woman. Perhaps not Lady Hyacinth.

"I've just realized how much I like you," he said.

"If you are thinking of chasing me around a ballroom at eight in the morning, or any other time, dismiss the thought," Eugenia said, trying in vain to ignore the melting sensation in her stomach.

"I am a respectable widow," she clarified. "It's essential to Snowe's Registry that my reputation remain as such. Nothing unbefitting, no matter the hour."

He threw back his head and laughed. "*As such*? Sometimes I feel as if I'm talking to a dictionary when I'm with you."

"There's nothing wrong with my sentence construction," she said, a bit stiffly.

Ward nodded. "Not at all." His eyes were dancing.

"The more important thing is that whatever conclusion you've drawn, Mr. Reeve, you'll have to discard it. I mean that."

Ward leaned forward, his eyes intent on hers. "You must stop calling me Mr. Reeve, or I shall do something drastic."

Eugenia couldn't stop herself; the corners of her mouth twitched into a smile.

"There it is," Ward said, settling back. "That smile of yours means that you will call me Ward. And I shall call you Eugenia, so that's settled. I notice that you haven't tried the strawberry trifle."

"I've already eaten more confections than I've had in months," Eugenia protested. On her side of the table were three untouched sweets. On his, five empty plates.

He snorted. "A bite or two of this or that? Mr. Gunter's *pâtissier* will weep if all this is sent back to

the kitchen." He reached across the table and helped himself to a forkful of her trifle. It was light and airy, cream whipped with bits of sweet fruit.

"I mustn't taste any more, because I won't be able to stop," Eugenia protested. "I have a terrible sweet tooth, and no self-control whatsoever."

But the fork was coming toward her mouth. "Just a taste," he coaxed.

The taste was so sublime that she closed her eyes for a moment from pure pleasure.

"You adore sweets, don't you?"

She opened her eyes and put a hand to her heart. "This may be the best trifle I have ever eaten." She plucked the fork from his hand and took another bite.

"*That's* why you have all the children learning to bake," he said, watching her. "You love sweets. You are an epicure."

"More of a glutton," she said honestly. "Everyone should be able to make something that gives people so much joy."

Ward's face wore an odd expression as he watched her eat. "Describe the taste for me."

She took another bite and closed her eyes again. "The cream is velvety smooth with just a touch of liqueur. The strawberries are tangy and not too sweet."

Ward made a sound precariously close to a groan. She opened her eyes and said, "My cook is forbidden to make confections like this. I can't indulge myself, or my hips wouldn't let me through the door. No cakes, unless I have company to dine with me."

Except she never had company, now she thought about it.

"If this were my cook," she added, surprising her-

self, "I would ask her to macerate the strawberries in liqueur first, making them even more tart."

"Your late husband must have plied you with sweets every chance he got," Ward said.

She shook her head. "Andrew was an ascetic man. It was one of the things that I loved about him."

Ward nodded.

"My own father, by contrast, has spent most of his life pleasing himself," Eugenia said, feeling a twinge of disloyalty.

"He must be a happy man."

"Yes. He is most happy when inventing things. Rather like you, I believe," she added, wondering if she should have a bite of the chocolate cake.

So she could compare it to the trifle.

"Yes, you ought to eat it," Ward said, meeting her eyes. "It's one of the best cakes I've ever had."

"Don't you dare try to feed me again," Eugenia said. "It's lucky we are screened by that fern so no one saw you."

"Not lucky," Ward said. "I slipped Mr. Sweeney a pound note."

Eugenia winced. "Privacy is dreadfully expensive." But she was glad. She'd hate to know that Lady Hyacinth was watching her, and probably eavesdropping as well.

"Your reputation is important," Ward said. "I would never do anything that might hurt you in any way."

Ward wasn't talking about taking tea together. His eyes were so heated that she lost all desire for the chocolate cake.

"You haven't told me why you came to London," Eugenia said, taking a hasty sip of tea. It had gone cold and had that bitterness of tea that has steeped too long.

Ward raised a hand; a second later a waiter was bowing at their side, then hurrying away with the rejected teapot in hand. Ward was the sort of man to whom waiters and their like always paid attention. It was a bit irritating.

"I need advice," Ward said.

"How are Lizzie and Otis faring with Miss Midge since you last wrote?"

"Therein lies the problem."

Before he could elaborate, a high-pitched voice interrupted them. "Mrs. Snowe, Mr. Reeve, I trust you will forgive me; I wish to present my darling Petunia."

Ward looked up warily. On the rare occasions he found himself in the company of ladies—usually at his father's house—he had a devil of a time with marriage-minded mothers. They seemed to hunt him with all the determined enthusiasm of a foxhunter who's glimpsed a bushy tail. His fortune clearly outweighed his irregular birth.

What he needed was a portable foxhole.

Next to Lady Hyacinth stood a younger version of herself: the same brown hair, lanky figure, long chin. It couldn't be easy to be Lady Hyacinth's daughter.

Especially once you realized you'd inherited the family chin.

"I'm sure you won't mind if we join you," Lady Hyacinth said, breaking about ten rules of polite behavior all at once.

By the time fresh tea arrived, Ward had been pushed around the table so that he was shoulder-to-shoulder with the marriageable daughter.

"One must assume you have been discussing governesses," Lady Hyacinth said, "though I cannot imagine why. Mrs. Snowe is an expert." She patted Eu-

genia's hand. "There are those who reprove a woman for engaging in commerce, but I always defend you, Mrs. Snowe. Your endeavors clearly spring from the anguish of having no children of your own."

To Ward's admiration, Eugenia's smile didn't slip a bit.

"I have asked Mrs. Snowe for a governess," Ward said, "as I have recently become the guardian to two children."

"Not your own, surely?" Lady Hyacinth said. "That would make you entirely ineligible, Mr. Reeve, earl in the family or not. Even a paper-rolling machine can't make up for *everything*, you know."

At this grotesquely tactless statement, Eugenia's smile disappeared.

"They are not mine; their parents are deceased," Ward stated. He saw no reason whatsoever to reveal any further details, even though all London would know as soon as the Duchess of Gilner's private act was heard in the House of Lords.

"Mrs. Snowe has been kind enough"—he interpreted a twitch from across the table and smoothly changed direction—"to endeavor to find me a governess. They seem to be in short supply."

"I knew there could be no unsavory reason for this tête-à-tête," Lady Hyacinth said. "That's why I thought it was the perfect moment to introduce my darling Petunia. Mr. Reeve, how is your dear father, Lord Gryffyn?"

"I believe he is well," Ward said. "He and my stepmother will be traveling in Sweden on a diplomatic mission for a few more months."

"So brave of them," Lady Hyacinth said. "I was told that they brought the family with them. Surely

it would have been more prudent to leave their precious children at home."

"My parents would never expose my siblings to danger," Ward said, showing his teeth in a faint approximation of a smile.

"At the very least, they should have left the heir at home," she pronounced. "I am proud to say that Petunia has never had even a sip of water from nonnative soil. I don't believe in it."

Ward glanced at Eugenia, but she was gazing into her teacup as if she were reading the leaves.

"So few people understand the intricacies of polite society," Lady Hyacinth continued. "It is best not to spend too much time with young children, for example. It excites them and makes them feel that they are important. Time enough when a debut nears. Don't you agree, Mrs. Snowe?"

"In my experience, it depends on the parents," Eugenia said, less than diplomatically.

Lady Hyacinth took no notice. "At one's debut, delicate questions arise that can be answered only by a mother. Take, for example, the problem of elbows. I imagine that you have paid a great deal of attention to that question, Mrs. Snowe."

Ward enjoyed seeing Eugenia nonplussed. He had the feeling it didn't happen often.

"I cannot say that I have," she said, finally.

"Unclothed skin," Lady Hyacinth pronounced, "is of vital concern. Does one wish naked elbows at the dinner table, or will the gentlemen find it too stirring?" She turned to Ward with a ferocity he'd once seen in a hawk's eye. "What is your opinion of naked elbows, Mr. Reeve?"

"I have no opinion at all," he said. This was not

strictly true. He had noticed, for example, that Eugenia's slender arms were quite bare. A man could ignore the conversation and contemplate kissing his way up from her fingertips.

"Fashion is for people of low account," Lady Hyacinth pronounced. "Those of us born to a high station ignore such trivialities."

"Mother!" Petunia interjected. "I quite forgot something significant. Mr. Simon Briggs asked me to accompany him for a drive." She looked mortified, but Ward didn't think her memory was the cause. In fact, he'd bet Mr. Briggs wouldn't appear.

The lady surged upright. "My dear Petunia, you mustn't make a habit of this negligence."

They all stood and Mr. Sweeney appeared. Lady Hyacinth turned to him. "I shall require my French silvered fox-fur stole with the intact head, if you please. I entrusted it to one of your lackeys when we arrived, and I shall want it returned without a single hair disturbed."

"Immediately, my lady," he murmured, sending a waiter scurrying.

"What a charming time we have had," Lady Hyacinth said, bestowing a wide smile on Ward, who bowed and kissed her hand.

Mr. Sweeney dropped the fox stole around her neck with such zeal that the fox head flew up, appearing to leap for freedom.

Lady Hyacinth arranged her stole so that it hung over her right breast. "Mrs. Snowe, I am gratified to discover that even though you were taking tea alone with a gentleman, it was for unimpeachable, albeit mercantile, reasons. I promise you that I shall con-

tinue to defend your reputation when the question arises. As it inevitably does, unfortunately."

Eugenia didn't let on by a quiver of a hair how she felt about that, but Ward had the idea that anger was vibrating in the air. Instead she smiled sweetly and said, "You are just as so many have described you as well, Lady Hyacinth."

"It is a cross to bear," the lady answered. "When one has generations of fine breeding behind one, society ogles. But as I tell Petunia and my other girls, it is responsibility that makes us what we are. And our responsibility is to display the best of breeding."

Eugenia had drawn Miss Petunia aside and was murmuring something to the poor girl. Ward said, "Your daughter is a lovely young woman, Lady Hyacinth. She seems very tactful."

"Oh, the very essence of tact," the lady agreed. "We do not have a governess from Snowe's—they found themselves unaccountably without a woman who could serve a household of our caliber—but true manners must be learned at home. Why, look at you, Mr. Reeve."

Ward was beginning to enjoy himself. "What about me?"

"With your, ahem, *background*, one would never dream of meeting you in Gunter's or elsewhere, but given that you were brought up in the earl's household, you are . . . more. *More*," she repeated firmly. "Breeding tells. Why, you go everywhere, don't you? I believe I saw you with the Duke of Villiers the other day."

"His Grace is a good friend of my father's," Ward said.

"I believe you went to Eton, and you didn't learn to bake a cake *there*, did you? The aristocracy ought not to labor in the kitchen, no matter what Mrs. Snowe's governesses require!"

Eugenia turned from her conversation and said, "This has been a pleasure, Lady Hyacinth." She dropped a curtsy.

Lady Hyacinth inclined her chin, and turned back to Ward. "Mr. Reeve, I feel that we have reached a new level of amicability. A friendship, as it were. I shall call on your dear father as soon as his lordship returns from Sweden—hopefully with all the younger family members still in tow. But even if they find themselves in blacks, I shall call upon him."

Ward couldn't bring himself to comment on his father's happiness at that prospect, but an answer was irrelevant.

"I can see that my darling Petunia has formed a true appreciation for you, Mr. Reeve. I hope to see you at an event soon—she dances like a blossom on the wind."

"Mother!" Petunia said in an anguished voice.

"I must escort my daughter to her next engagement," Lady Hyacinth said. "The mother of a diamond of the first water like Petunia has no time to dilly-dally over tea."

Her curtsy was so brisk that her bosom rose in the air and bounced as it settled back into place.

As did the fox, its bright glass eyes fixed on Ward.

"If I heard rightly, you recently acquired Fawkes House, did you not?" Lady Hyacinth said, dilly-dallying. "Perhaps you should rename it, Mr. Reeve. That name was all very well back when Lord Fawkes lived in the manor."

"I hadn't considered," Ward said, taken aback.

"You could hardly call it Reeve House, could you? It sounds like a weevil. Or a German vegetable. Such a complicated language for such simple people. I never did meet one who wasn't thinking about turnips."

And with that she sailed away, the fox head flapping and her daughter—red-faced from pure mortification—following.

Chapter Fourteen

Eugenia dropped into her chair, looked at Ward, and burst out laughing. He was apparently a man who would happily fight a legion with one hand tied at his back, but when faced with a bumptious mother, was desperate for rescue.

"If you allow another woman of that sort to join us," Ward told the headwaiter, "I will never darken the door of this establishment again."

"I am extremely sorry, sir," Mr. Sweeney said earnestly. "If another woman like that brings her custom to this establishment, I shall follow you out of the building."

"Excellent. I think we'd better have more tea and a few pastries. How are the hampers coming along?"

"We are ready whenever you wish, Mr. Reeve," Sweeney said before slipping away.

"Lady Hyacinth is infamous," Eugenia told Ward when they were alone again. "She truly is one of a kind."

A waiter arrived and placed an assortment of new cakes on the table, murmuring that they were a gift of the house.

"Pure guilt," Ward said. "Sweeney permitted that disaster to happen, just as if he'd waved good-bye as our boat capsized."

Eugenia took in a sharp breath. She wasn't going to think about Andrew.

Not about boats capsizing.

Not today.

"What have I said?" Ward asked. "Bloody hell, you wrote me that your husband died in a boating accident, didn't you?"

His eyes were an intense blue. "I'm truly sorry. Here, have a bite of cake." He forked up a large bite and extended it toward Eugenia's lips. She oughtn't to. She'd eaten too much. "And describe how it tastes," he added.

"Chocolate is everything a woman wants," Eugenia said. She took the bite. "This is sweet, bitter, decadent, unbearably delicious . . . pure pleasure."

She smiled at his stunned expression and ran the tip of her tongue over her lips.

"Go on." His voice was hoarse as he extended the fork again.

Eugenia closed her eyes and allowed herself to savor the taste. "Chocolate tastes like all the good things in life swirled together." She opened her eyes. "It's like happiness."

"You are the most sensual woman I've ever met," he growled.

Eugenia blinked and jolted back to herself. "Me?" Her voice came out in a surprised squeak. "Not at all! I'm a very sedate person. I simply like chocolate. Everyone does."

"Not the way you do."

"Did you give Miss Carrington chocolates when you were betrothed?"

He shook his head. "Do you suppose she would have refused the opportunity to become a duchess if I had?"

"It's possible," she said, grinning at him.

"I didn't bed her," he said abruptly.

"I suspected as much." Eugenia silently congratulated herself on not betraying shock at this rapid shift into a topic that she had never discussed with a man.

"I'm amazed that you have given my cursed betrothal any thought."

His heavy-lidded eyes sent a bolt of pure sensation down Eugenia's body. It was terrifying—exciting. It raced straight to her head.

"You wouldn't have allowed Miss Carrington to leave you if she had truly been yours," she said. "I spend a good deal of my time analyzing young boys, you know. Grown boys aren't so different."

"Indeed."

"Men in general are remarkably primitive," she said, pouring him a cup of tea and taking one herself.

"Would you have expected me to beat my chest in a display of possessiveness upon my return from that regrettable incarceration? Remember, I came back to discover my fiancée happily married."

"Had the two of you been intimate, Miss Carrington would have been waiting for you."

A rueful look crossed his face. "I can't say that I'm

happy with the notion that the only way I might have kept my fiancée was if I'd ruined her."

Eugenia laughed. "There is ruination, Mr. Reeve. And then there is . . ." She stopped, as a small voice in the back of her head was insisting that she had abandoned all principles. She decided to ignore it. "And then there is chocolate."

His eyes blazed and he reached across the table and laced his fingers into hers. She had noticed his body. But it had never seemed as brawny as when he sat across a small, elegant table designed for whispering secrets.

"We're back where we began," he said huskily. His thumb rubbed a circle in her palm that made her want to squirm, but she didn't pull it away. "I should have plied my fiancée with chocolate."

"Only," she dared, "if you were certain that the chocolate was of the very best quality."

Ward brought her hand up to his mouth and kissed the back, swiftly, just a touch of his lips. He turned it over and pressed a kiss on her palm that sent sweet heat up her arm. "Please tell me how one determines the very best chocolate."

"It has the qualities of the very best ices," she said, drawing her hand away. The tearoom had gradually filled since they had first entered, and probably clients of hers were seated on the other side of the fern.

"You know so much more about delicacies than I do," he said, his voice dark and unbearably sensual.

"The very best ices are sweet, so cold that they feel hot in the mouth. So sweet they taste bitter. So smooth that they slide down your throat."

"And stiff," he said. "Don't forget stiff."

"Mmmm, yes," she said. "So stiff as to be . . . ravishing."

Ward leaned forward. "How would you change that chocolate cake you just tasted, Eugenia?"

"What do you mean?"

"Just what I asked. If that cake had been made by your cook, would you be perfectly satisfied?"

"It's not a question of satisfied," she said. "It was wonderful. But . . ."

"What would you ask her to do?"

"It would benefit from a touch of cardamom," she said readily. "Just a crackle of spice. And the texture could be improved. Perhaps by beating for another half-hour, or another egg yolk. Or one might try putting steaming water in the oven during the baking process."

Ward sat back and grinned at her. "You are a master baker. I predict that at some point you will throw off this façade of respectability—"

"Mr. Reeve!" Eugenia squeaked. "There is nothing hypocritical about my behavior!"

"The pretense of prudence," he said without a pause, "that stops you from eating the food you most desire. Perhaps you'll open a pastry shop someday. Like this one."

Eugenia scoffed. "Nonsense! I can scarcely make a sponge cake, I assure you."

"I am confident that you could make a success of any endeavor, Eugenia."

He sounded sincere.

She smiled, trying to ignore the way her heart was galloping, and rose. "I think we've had enough sweets, don't you, Mr. Reeve?"

"I hope I do not shock the ladies in the room,"

he said, also rising. "It would be best if we sat back down and talked about something more mundane, like my siblings."

It took tremendous self-control not to glance at his breeches. Instead, they simply looked at each other, desire hanging in the air like smoke.

But his reference to his siblings struck a chord, and her hands flew to her mouth. "Oh dear," she breathed, "we forgot to discuss the problem of Lizzie and Otis."

"We can talk about it in the carriage," Ward said, and nodded to Mr. Sweeney, who had brought Eugenia's pelisse.

Ward took it from him and held it as she slipped it back on. His strong hands touched her shoulders, paused for a moment in a caress that made her knees go weak.

She felt different. Freer, as if chains had fallen away. It was ridiculous, but true.

As they moved toward the door, threading their way between now-crowded tables, she heard a growled word behind her. She glanced over her shoulder at Ward.

"The Dowager Duchess of Gilner just entered," he said. "My grandmother."

Oh.

Sure enough, Eugenia's way out of the tearoom was blocked by a hard-eyed old woman with the bearing of one who had once been considered a great beauty.

"Good afternoon, Mrs. Snowe," the duchess said.

Eugenia curtsied. "Good afternoon, Your Grace."

The lady's violet turban was adorned with a plume so long that it swept her shoulder when she turned to Ward. "Mr. Reeve."

"A very good afternoon to you," Ward said, bowing.

The lady rested her hands on the ornate brass ball which topped her cane. "I am too old to prevaricate, Mr. Reeve. A Snowe's governess is hardly enough to qualify your household to raise children of the nobility, insofar as that you are not only unmarried, but illegitimate. I would prefer that you did not contest my petition to the House of Lords. An institution in which you do not belong, I might add."

"My father brought me up under circumstances similar to those under which I intend to bring up Lizzie and Otis," Ward replied. "I assume you approved of his guardianship, Grandmother, since you yourself dropped me on his doorstep."

Eugenia had the feeling this was the first time Ward had used the word "grandmother" in direct address.

Her Grace's gloved fingers tightened on her cane, the only outward sign of irritation. "I regret that you force me to put the truth in such blunt terms, Mr. Reeve, but you are my daughter's by-blow, and I fully expected your father to place you in the country."

The implication was clear. To her, Ward was little more than rubbish, but legitimate children were another story.

"If their other grandmother were alive, she would beg me to raise them," the duchess added.

Eugenia thought that the late Lady Darcy must be turning in her grave at the idea her grandchildren had any contact whatsoever with the family of the woman who seduced her fifteen-year-old son.

"You are unfit, Mr. Reeve," the lady concluded. She shifted her eyes to Eugenia. "It is highly irregular of you to take tea with one of your clients, Mrs. Snowe.

In your situation, reputation is paramount. Yours is already compromised by your choices."

The Duchess of Gilner was one of a cabal of society despots who considered Eugenia to have irredeemably lowered herself to the level of a merchant. Most of them hid their opinions because they—or their daughters-in-law—were well aware of the crucial importance of not alienating the proprietress of Snowe's.

The dowager was apparently incapable of such diplomacy.

Eugenia didn't care what the lady thought of her. "I gather that you do not wish your grandchildren raised by one of my governesses," she said, with a syrupy smile. "Should you succeed in your petition against Mr. Reeve's guardianship, I shall be happy to direct you toward another registry. One hesitates to call other agencies *lesser*, but I'm confident that they will be able to find you a good enough governess in due time."

The dowager's eyelids twitched.

Eugenia turned to Ward and dropped a magnificent curtsy. "I am very sorry to disappoint you in this matter, Mr. Reeve, but it's clear that Her Grace does not feel the need for her grandchildren to have one of my governesses. What a pity, since they seem to have been disadvantaged in their early life."

The tearoom was now bustling with patrons and virtually every table was listening avidly to their conversation.

Ward picked up Eugenia's lead. "Mrs. Snowe," he said, voice dripping with pathos, "I implore you not to withdraw your promise to send me a governess, as a consequence of the duchess's rash statement."

He turned to the dowager. "As I understand it, a Snowe's governess is essential to my orphaned wards' future." His voice turned cold, implacable, and decisive. "I am certain that their late father—who explicitly left them to my guardianship—would wish them to be raised with the best possible care."

The duchess's nose twitched as if a rotten egg had cracked nearby. "I comprehend that you are angling for better terms, Mrs. Snowe. Although it offends propriety to engage in such a distasteful negotiation in public, I shall compensate you double Mr. Reeve's fee."

"I was not negotiating," Eugenia corrected her. "All London knows that I send my governesses only to the very best houses, Your Grace. I shall carefully consider your petition, should you win your lawsuit."

And with that, she left, with Ward close behind.

Chapter Fifteen

*B*ack in the carriage, Eugenia settled in her seat, feeling as if she'd run the gauntlet. "I see exactly why you want to keep the children under your care," she told Ward.

"It's a wonder my mother wasn't even more cracked than she was," Ward replied.

Eugenia gave him a sympathetic smile. There wasn't much to say on that subject. She pulled aside the velvet curtains pinned to the bottom and top of the windows. Clearly, His Royal Highness hadn't wanted passersby catching a glimpse of himself and Mrs. Jordan inside the carriage.

"Your coachman is headed in the wrong direction," she exclaimed. "Did you instruct him to return to my house?"

Ward was lounging on the opposite seat, eyes eating her up with burning intensity. "No."

She was nearly waylaid by the husky growl of his voice, the unspoken promise, but then his response sank in. "I cannot spend the day with you." Even though the idea sent a pulse of warmth through her stomach.

She plucked the curtain aside again. "That's Chiswick House!"

"We must be making excellent time."

All trace of desire fled Eugenia's body. She sat upright, feeling a jolt of alarm. "What do you mean?"

He smiled at her. "We're heading for the post road to Oxford."

The words whirled in her mind until they settled into place. "*What*? I don't . . . What are you doing, Mr. Reeve?"

"Kidnapping you."

She stared at him, trying to read his expression. "Are you joking?"

"Not at all."

"Did I somehow convey the mistaken impression that I planned to visit your house?" she demanded, her voice rising as anger flooded her.

"You did not. I—"

She cut him off. "You have made an enormous mistake, Mr. Reeve." She was so outraged she could scarcely form the words. "Turn this carriage around on the instant or I shall have you imprisoned again!"

He leaned forward. "Eugenia, please hear me out. I need your help. I'm damn well desperate. I spoke at length to Miss Lloyd-Fantil this morning, and we

agreed that you are my best hope—perhaps my only hope—to keep the children."

All morning and afternoon his voice had been light—even when it was husky with desire or laughter—but now his words were somber.

She stared at him. "If you need my help so badly, why did we dally in a teashop? Why did you not explain yourself directly?"

"Miss Lloyd-Fantil suggested I take you to Gunter's while your trunk was being packed."

"By Clothilde?" Eugenia asked, turning her head as if her maid had magically appeared in the carriage.

"Your maid is following in a separate conveyance, accompanied by the young woman Ruby, Snowe's housemaid."

Eugenia gaped at him. "Ruby as well?"

"Miss Lloyd-Fantil told me that Ruby is adaptable and used to naughty children. She's optimistic that Ruby will be helpful. You see, Miss Midge left her post day before yesterday."

Eugenia's eyes rounded. "Voluntarily," he added. "She declared my house a godless wilderness and my siblings, particularly my sister, to be heathens in word and deed."

Eugenia felt as if the breath had been knocked out of her. Her outrage was dissolving into shock. "I'm—I'm sorry to—no, I'm *appalled* to hear this. My governesses do *not* desert their posts without extraordinary justification and ample warning, I assure you!"

"She informed me that Lizzie's dabbling in what she referred to as the 'black arts' was impious, if not blasphemous, especially after she learned of the attempted conjuration of a rabbit," Ward said. "She

also has strong feelings about Otis's insistence that his pet rat has a soul. Her instruction in evening prayers, for example, foundered after Otis refused to stop praying that Jarvis would enter heaven with him."

In all the years she'd managed her registry, Eugenia had never had to contend with a circumstance like this. "I instruct all my governesses not to intercede in matters of doctrine. Whether or not rats have souls clearly poses a theological question that we are not qualified to answer."

She was in shock. She couldn't believe that Alithia Midge had deserted her post. "She left without a word of warning? Without offering six weeks' notice?"

"In her defense, given her strong views on religion, she found my siblings dangerous to her spiritual well-being. Yesterday Lizzie refused to pray for her mother's eternal soul, and informed Miss Midge that if Lady Lisette was in heaven, she'd prefer to go to the other place."

"Oh dear," Eugenia gasped.

"After that, Lizzie confessed to deliberately throwing her governess's prayer book in the lake in an attempt to stop Miss Midge from reading aloud prayers for the dead."

"I'm dreadfully sorry," Eugenia said helplessly. "I've placed Miss Midge in two households, and while she isn't the sweetest woman in my employ, she could be relied upon not to weep or faint."

"Our next governess must not weep, faint, or pray," Ward said dryly.

"All the same, this does not justify an impromptu trip to Oxford. I should be at Snowe's, helping Susan find a third governess for you."

Ward folded his arms across his chest. "Unfortunately, when Miss Midge decided that her soul was in mortal danger, she unburdened herself on our local vicar, Mr. Howson."

"I don't suppose you've been attending matins and ingratiating yourself with the local clergy?" Eugenia asked, hopefully.

He threw her a sardonic look. "I'm a bastard, Eugenia. The Church of England refuses to even baptize bastards, so I doubt I'd be welcome at a church service."

"That's terrible," Eugenia exclaimed. "I'm sorry you are excluded."

"I don't give a damn. But it is essential that gossip not reach the Duchess of Gilner's ears, so I need to placate Howson, before his outrage—Miss Midge found a kindred spirit in him—spreads beyond the village. Lizzie and I have an appointment with him tomorrow morning."

Eugenia turned the predicament over in her mind. Ward was right: rumors of paganism at Fawkes House would destroy his defense against the duchess's plea for guardianship. "Can you impress upon Lizzie that she can't talk about your mother's posthumous locale?"

"She and I have discussed the advisability of allowing people to believe that our mother is sitting on a fluffy cloud singing hymns, even if Lizzie doesn't agree. I was fairly certain a short morning call to the church would be effective, especially if a large donation was forthcoming. But last night I learned that a bishop is paying a visit to the vicarage."

"That is most unfortunate," Eugenia observed.

"I daren't wait until his visit has concluded. Pastor

Howson has strong views about magic—that is to say, he believes in it."

"For goodness' sake," Eugenia said. The shock she'd been feeling was quickly being replaced by exasperation. "I can't believe that Miss Midge took those silly spells seriously."

"I don't believe she did, but she was horrified by my siblings' indifference to the Anglican faith. Your assistant, Miss Lloyd-Fantil, agreed with me that the formidable directress of Snowe's Agency would be a valuable support before the bishop."

"I see," Eugenia said, nodding. "Nevertheless, that doesn't explain why you did not simply ask me. You cannot have imagined that I would refuse your request, under the circumstances." Despite herself, a trace of hurt feelings leaked into her voice.

Ward curled his fingers around her clasped hands. "There was no doubt in my mind that you would come with me." He gave her a wicked grin. "But I have always wanted to kidnap a woman."

A startled laugh broke from Eugenia's lips. "Really?"

He nodded solemnly. "Truly. Dash off into the night—"

"Afternoon," she corrected.

"Into the afternoon—with a beautiful, witty woman, a bottle of white wine, and a cold roast chicken."

Eugenia shook her head; this day was growing odder and odder. "Kidnapping as a fashionable pastime?"

"I've never done it before. But if you wish, I'd be happy to make it a regular pastime."

"Just conceive if you had succumbed to this way-

ward impulse and kidnapped Miss Petunia instead."
Eugenia laughed as her exasperation melted away.
"Any woman you kidnap has the right to demand
marriage. You have put your future in my hands."

"I don't mind being in your hands," Ward said. A
flash of raw, sensual hunger crossed his eyes.

Eugenia felt giddy, as if champagne was fizzing in
her veins. She slipped her hands from his and settled
back, because it was that or lean forward and kiss
him. "You are a lucky kidnapper, Mr. Ward. I am not
inclined to marry again at the moment."

"Nor am I."

For a moment, a sense of perfect harmony filled
the carriage. With a thump of her heart, Eugenia realized that they had just agreed to . . . to something.

When she was about to panic—was she truly certain that she wanted to have an *affaire*?—she looked at
Ward again. He would readily accept it if she changed
her mind.

"Miss Lloyd-Fantil assured me that as a widow,
you could travel without a chaperone. But if you have
even the slightest qualm, we can stop and your maid
will join us in this carriage."

"There's no need," Eugenia said.

Ward felt a surge of exultation.

Eugenia was his, and whether she wanted to acknowledge it or not, she would soon be his in all ways.

He felt as lustful as an untried boy, his tool rigid,
fueled by desire smoldering low in his belly, his balls
sending warning throbs. His response had little to
do with how beautiful she was; what he found enchanting was her confidence, her wit. She was ferociously alive—at least, after she dropped the ladylike
visage that she wore like a mask.

"I sense you've come to a decision," he said, taking the bull by the horns.

"About what?" She cocked her head and a glowing cascade of red hair fell over her pelisse.

"About us."

"'Us'? There is no us."

But in reality they were communicating without words. The true conversation was unspoken.

I'll make you blissfully happy, he promised her. Silently.

She raised an eyebrow. *But is it worth the possible loss of my reputation?*

"There will be an us," he stated aloud. "You are mine, Eugenia Snowe."

"I am no man's," she said with a shake of her head.

"You were your husband's," he said, absolutely certain of that. He knew without a shadow of a doubt that Eugenia had given herself heart and soul.

Blasted Snowe.

He was starting to dislike the fellow, no matter how dead he was.

"I was his, and he was mine," she said with a lopsided smile.

"Just like a fairy tale," he answered, not even trying to disguise the growl in his voice.

"Didn't you mean to offer me a glass of wine from that excellent hamper?" Eugenia asked.

He bent over and pulled open the hamper. "Tell me about him." He drew out a bottle of wine. "Was he as pretty as you are?"

"Far more so," Eugenia said, her eyes going a bit dreamy. "He was like Adonis. Every debutante longed to catch his eye."

"But he chose you?"

"We danced all night."

"That *is* like a fairy tale." He handed her a glass of wine.

She took a sip. "In the fairy stories, the prince doesn't die saving the princess."

Ward choked on his wine. "The boating accident?"

"I was drowning and he saved me," she said, lifting her glass in a clear salute to her husband.

The wine's flowery fragrance floated into the carriage. Ward watched her throat working as she swallowed. "Can you tell me what happened?"

She twisted up one shoulder. "The sailboat capsized; I didn't know how to swim. It was so foolish! We were within sight of the shore, but as it turned out, it is possible to drown very close to land."

The only response Ward could think of was a curse, so he kept silent.

"All these years later, I've forgiven myself for surviving, but at the time it was unbearable. I watched him go under and never come up again."

"He would never have chosen differently," Ward said, keeping it matter-of-fact. He finished his wine, took her glass, and placed them both in the basket.

Her smile was rueful. "I do remind myself of that."

The carriage rocked under them, and she shook her head with a sudden impatient gesture. "Why are we discussing such a dismal subject?"

"We are tracing the steps of a particular dance," Ward said, standing for a moment in the swaying carriage before he sat down beside her. So closely that his leg touched hers.

"A dance?" she asked.

"A dance." His lips brushed the curl of her ear. She smelled of berries again, not sweet or insipid, but something wilder than flowers, with a bite.

She drew away, and the coolness in her eyes insisted that she didn't welcome his kiss or the press of his thigh.

But he was learning to read her. To understand her.

When Mrs. Eugenia Snowe felt threatened, she drew her ladylike guise around herself like chain mail.

"In this particular movement of the dance, I am offering myself," he said. "A gift, though I will admit to thinking that diamonds would look lovely here."

When Ward's callused finger touched the hollow at the base of Eugenia's neck, she felt warm all over, as if he radiated heat. The neck . . . such an innocuous place. But when Ward's fingers slid slowly, slowly under her ear, his eyes intent on her face, she could feel his touch in all her most sensitive places.

His hand curled around the back of her neck as he watched her for permission. She couldn't remember desire like this, as if liquid fire ran over her skin. No, that was wrong, she must have felt this with Andrew. It was a physical reaction, a mating response . . .

"I loved my husband," she heard herself say.

The caressing fingers paused and Ward nodded, eyes respectful. "I'm certain he was a good man, Eugenia."

"He was a *great* man," she said fiercely. "He was going to change things in the House of Lords. He was—he would have done so much."

Sweet hunger thrummed through her so strongly she could scarcely believe she had waited seven years to feel this again.

"May I kiss you?" Ward asked.

"Yes." Her head turned to the perfect angle for his kiss, making it clear to him, but also to herself. She was going to do this thing, this . . .

This step away from Andrew. This step away from death and into life. It was only a small step, but she knew that it would change everything.

She would stop hiding in her office. She would attend balls and the theater—she used to love plays—and someday a man would come along who had Andrew's elegant charm and *joie de vivre*.

Not quite yet, though. She would enjoy herself first, learning to live in the world and not in the cloister that was Snowe's Registry.

As Ward's lips touched hers, her body shuddered, as if she were waking from a seven-year sleep. She raised her arms and slid them around his neck.

She was no longer married. Or a virgin. Or young. Perhaps she should be clear about the future, though. She didn't want to hurt him, because Edward Reeve may be one of the strongest, toughest men she'd ever met, but she had the idea he was capable of being hurt.

She drew back just as he was about to deepen the kiss and cradled the strong planes of his face with her hands. "Ward," she whispered.

Intelligent eyes, ferocious and desirous. "Eugenia," he replied. Her voice throbbed with desire, but his was calm.

She took a deep breath. She had learned while running Snowe's that clarity was important. "I may always be in love with Andrew. I am not ready to marry again and I wouldn't want you to think of me in that light."

"I understand," Ward said. He put a hand over hers, braced on the seat between them. "We are considering courtesies that can be exchanged between friends, Eugenia."

Her gaze darted down to their ungloved hands. His hand dwarfed her slim fingers.

"Friends," she said, amused by that evasion.

"Between good friends, any number of intimacies might take place, never to be mentioned in public or in company."

Her hand moved under his like a rescued baby robin fallen from a nest. Even so, he bent toward her slowly, allowing her to turn away if she wished.

She did not wish. In fact, Eugenia held her breath until Ward's lips brushed hers, and her mouth slipped open on a sigh. For a moment, they merely breathed each other's air, and then his hand curled around her fingers and the other pulled her toward him, and his tongue slid into her mouth.

Chapter Sixteen

Eugenia Snowe was not a reckless woman. She had always lived within clearly defined boundaries, relishing rather than rebelling against the rules of society her father chose to ignore.

But now, in a dark carriage with a man who had abducted her, a rash sense of abandonment welled up in her, spilling to the ends of her fingers.

She wanted Ward Reeve with every fiber of her being. She wanted his burly body, and the burning hunger in his eyes, and the lock of untidy hair that had fallen over his eyes.

He was kissing her with a primal hunger that brought her body to life. And yet she felt like laughing.

That was new; she didn't remember laughing when Andrew kissed her. Even as she leaned closer, melt-

ing against Ward, curling an arm around his neck, she realized why.

This was not making love.

This was making *fun*.

The delight, exhilaration, whatever it was, went straight to her head. She opened her mouth wider and forgot everything except for the sensual touch of Ward's tongue, the firm clasp of his hand at the back of her head.

Desire was rougher than she remembered, and yet that unfamiliar joy kept bubbling up along with it.

At length, she couldn't suppress it any longer, and a gasp of laughter broke from her. He murmured something that she didn't understand.

She tilted her head so that she could lick the pulsing vein of his neck as her hands moved to his powerful shoulders. "Did you just lick me?" His voice was a surprised growl.

"Mmmm," she said, licking him again. "I should think that licking is a greeting in some part of the world . . . China, perhaps?"

A warm tongue ran over the curve of her ear. "In a distant part of the world, two people meet each other by . . . *this*?" His touch sent a wave of heat straight between her legs.

"Perhaps it isn't all that common," she murmured.

The carriage swayed and the impetus drove his body against hers. He ran his fingers through her curls and gently tugged her head back. "I reckon kisses are greetings in some part of the world . . . Russia, perhaps."

She brushed his lips with hers. "This sort of kiss?"

He shook his head. "Deeper, wench."

"I'm not a wen—" But he crushed her lips between

his, raw desire stealing away her words and giving her something else in return.

They kissed until her head was spinning, a warning that her common sense was losing a battle with longing.

"Ward." It was a gasp, a song, a prayer.

He hummed deep in his throat, and his lips slid across her cheekbone. Under his caress, the planes and angles of her face felt new, as if they were being remade by his touch. By the very way he was exploring her, memorizing her.

Eugenia pulled back; it was that or slide down on the seat and offer her breasts to Ward's mouth. His face was defined by a strong jaw and eyebrows that peaked in just the right spot to emphasize his cheekbones.

In short, he was devastatingly beautiful. Masculine, but beautiful.

"What may be decent in China or in Russia is *not* decent in a carriage traveling to Oxfordshire," she managed. Had she just promised to be indecent with him at a later time . . . out of the carriage?

His wanton grin confirmed that she had.

"Just a minute," she said hastily.

"I would wait a lifetime for you, Eugenia."

She rolled her eyes. "Whatever happens between us, I would rather be spared a flood of empty gallantry."

"Disturbingly, I didn't mean it as an empty compliment."

She put a hand to his chest and gently pushed him away. Her hair had fallen over her shoulders and her lips felt bee-stung. She began bundling up her hair and sticking hairpins in at random.

She didn't dare look at his face because if that vivid hunger was still in his eyes, she would succumb. Again.

When her hair was more or less secured and her heart had settled back to its normal rhythm, she said, still not meeting his eyes, "Before we reach Fawkes House, I would like to hear how the children are. Were they affected by Miss Midge's departure?"

Ward's voice was deep and rough, but he answered. "Otis showed no sign of noticing. He has spent most of the week working on his mousetrap."

"Is your house infested by mice?"

"I expect so. It's an old house, after all."

"You would know. Mice are not silent companions," Eugenia said. "They chatter and run in the walls; they endlessly plague the kitchen staff; they will eat the candles if they're left out."

"A mouse will eat a candle?"

She nodded. "As will a rat."

"The only rat in our house is Jarvis, Otis's pet."

Eugenia gave a shudder. "I hate rats."

"It's hard to believe, but I have grown inordinately fond of Jarvis."

"You haven't!"

"I have," Ward said, the corner of his mouth kicking up.

Eugenia shuddered again, involuntarily.

"I understand a lady's hesitation to be around small beasties, but you seem particularly vehement."

"I grew up in a house infested by rats."

Ward absorbed that statement with shock. He had pictured Eugenia as a little girl with rosy curls and porcelain skin and a few freckles on the end of her nose. That child . . . grew up in a house with *rats*?

He kept forgetting that she wasn't born into the gentry. Still, he'd assumed she'd grown up on the outskirts of society. The daughter of a vicar, perhaps.

A rat infestation implied a household fallen far below the gentry.

He suddenly realized he was scowling ferociously. "I don't like to think of you in such conditions." Had she ever been hungry? The thought bit into his gut like acid.

"I prefer not to remember the details myself." Her voice had the perfect cadence of a lady's, but that was part of her mask, the role she had assumed. "I was bitten at the age of eight."

The acid spread through his veins. "Did you contact rat-bite fever?"

She nodded.

"It's often fatal." He was starting to understand her. As a child, all her energy, fierce intelligence, pure joy for life must have focused on escaping her circumstances. No wonder she hungered for the life of a lady.

"I came very close to dying," Eugenia said. "My stepmother—whom I adore—later told me that she learned how to pray during my illness."

Ward raked his fingers through his hair. Many houses in England were infested with rats. It was a fact of life.

The little whiskered face of Otis's best friend leapt into Ward's mind. Whether she wanted to or not, Eugenia was about to meet a rat.

"How far is it to your house?" she asked.

"Approximately four hours. We'll be pulling into an inn to change horses in half that time."

"Would you mind if I took a nap? This wine has made me terribly sleepy."

She was clearly avoiding further intimacies, but he rejected the impulse to persuade her otherwise. He didn't want to make love to Eugenia Snowe for the first time in a carriage.

"A good idea," he said with a nod. "I shall sleep as well." After all, he didn't mean to sleep at night.

Though it wouldn't be appropriate to leap on his guest the moment he had her over the threshold. He ought to ply her with . . . with flowers or something. He'd be damned if he treated her like a courtesan or a merry widow.

Her virtue was as spotless as any lady's; he'd bet his honor on it. Still, she wanted him.

That was enough to stake his happiness on.

Chapter Seventeen

Some two hours later, the carriage drew into the courtyard of the Holy Cheese. He touched Eugenia's shoulder to wake her. When she sat up, rosy and blinking from her nap, he had to swallow a groan.

Her hair had fallen from its pins again and her dress was on the verge of displaying her breasts to the open air. She would look like this after making love.

"Oh," she said in a sleepy purr. "Have we arrived at the inn?" She pulled her thick hair over one shoulder and started twisting it, the way he imagined women did flax at a spinning wheel.

"Yes, we need to change the horses," Ward explained. "I thought you might like to refresh yourself inside. We'll still be in good time for dinner. And it will give the second carriage a chance to catch up with us."

"Where are we?"

"The Holy Cheese."

"The Holy Cheese? 'Holy' as in sacred, or 'holey' as in full of holes?" Her hands flew around her head until her hair was pinned in place as firmly as shingles to a roof. After her nap, she looked more relaxed, which he liked. Very much.

"Both," Ward answered. "They take cheese very seriously in these parts."

He pushed open the door and helped her down before the groom could take out that ridiculous mounting block. It was coming on twilight, and the air was fresh and clean as it never was in London.

"Do you enjoy living in the city year-round?" he asked, taking Eugenia's arm.

"I grew up in the country, and I do miss it," she said. "But Snowe's is in London, and I find it hard to escape."

As soon as they were seated in a snug private parlor, the innkeeper entered, accompanied by a serving man carrying a bowl of fruit and a platter of cheese. "Good evening, madam, sir."

Before his eyes, Eugenia, who had been smiling in a fashion that made Ward want to snatch her into his lap, straightened her back and transformed into a perfect impersonation of a lady.

The innkeeper responded to her airs and graces as if she were an actual duchess, bowing and scraping and generally making an obsequious ass of himself as Ward looked on.

Eugenia's uncle was with the Thames River Police; she could not have come from the gentry, let alone the aristocracy. And yet she would effortlessly fit into one of his father's dinner parties.

"Governesses teach their charges far more than letters and sums, don't they?" Ward asked, following his train of thought after the innkeeper left. "After all, children come into the world as little savages. I know I did."

"Left to their own devices, yes," Eugenia agreed. "Lizzie and Otis seem to be in a class of their own." She twinkled at him. "Perhaps naughtiness runs in the family."

"Among other crimes, I refused to sleep the night in my own bed—as do my siblings, by the way. Apparently, I told endless stories and bored everyone around me. I also sucked my thumb, or so my step-mother tells me; I don't remember that."

She laughed. "There's nothing unusual about that."

Their eyes caught and his head swam. She was so damn beautiful, and so intoxicating. He wanted to kiss her again.

He cast around for another subject. "Do you see your family often?"

Despite himself, his voice was hard. If he ever met her father, he would have words with him about those rats. What kind of man raises a daughter in those conditions?

"Not often enough," Eugenia said with a warm smile. "But in fact this unplanned journey has caused me to make up my mind to travel from your house to my father's and to take at least a week away from Snowe's. Perhaps longer." She fiddled with her knife. "Do you know, I had the oddest idea this morning."

"What was that?"

"I might hand over the registry to my assistant, Miss Lloyd-Fantil."

Ward looked up from the apple he was peeling. "You would give up control of Snowe's?"

"I would like a new challenge," she said, looking as unruffled as a lady talking of learning a new dance step.

"I can be challenging," Ward said.

The smile that blossomed on Eugenia's face made lust rise in his body like a tidal wave. He wanted her with an absurd ferocity. The thought of bedding her was like a prickling spur that made his balls ache.

Hell, he didn't need a bed. The wall would do. The table.

No.

"In fact, you appear to be offering no challenge at all," she said, eyes glinting mischievously.

That was true.

"I'm at your service," he agreed. He leaned over and dropped a kiss on her mouth and the touch of her lip sang through his bones like fire.

"Tell me more about your childhood," Ward said. He twisted his wrist and the last bit of peel fell from his apple.

"My mother died when I was very young, before I knew her."

"I'm sorry to hear that," Ward said, giving her the fruit. "I never knew my mother, either. My grandmother, the Duchess of Gilner, handed me over to my father when I was a mere infant."

She accepted the apple. "Why do I feel as if the Holy Cheese is actually the Garden of Eden, and you're playing the role of serpent?"

"Nonsense," he said. Anything they did together wouldn't be sinful.

"The duchess gave you up because her daughter

gave birth to you out of wedlock? I have known courtesans who would never do that, unless driven to it
by the extremes of poverty."

"You are acquainted with courtesans? As in, ladies
of the night?"

"In my youth," Eugenia said placidly. "My father
is generously disposed toward those rejected by conventional society."

Not only rats, but strumpets as well? It was no
wonder that Eugenia was determined to play the
lady. "One might argue that the Duchess of Gilner
saved my life. My mother was markedly unstable."
He cleared his throat. "Were the courtesans part of
your father's household, along with the rats?"

"I would hate to think that you are implying any
similarity," Eugenia said, her voice clear and strong.
"I was brought up not to disparage others, whether
for their profession or their parents' marital status."

Ward grinned. "A fair hit."

"In fact, my aunt runs Magdalene House, a home
for women who wish to escape that life."

"That is charitable of her."

"Well, she—" Eugenia stopped. "Yes, she is a good
woman. She taught me a great deal about what truly
matters in life." She rose from the table. "Surely your
coach will be ready by now."

Eugenia couldn't be implying that her aunt taught
her the tricks of that particular trade. Ward couldn't
control the swirl of heat that went through him at the
idea that the ladylike Eugenia might be adventure-
some in the bedchamber.

He pushed his chair back and came around the
table to escort her. "What did your aunt teach you?"

She turned and looked back at him over her shoul-

der. His breath caught at the pure sensual beauty of her sculpted cheekbones and peony-pink mouth. "The differences between the sexes, for one thing."

"What differences are those?"

"Differences to do with bedding."

With one stride, Ward moved close enough to pin Eugenia against the wall, though their bodies didn't touch. He braced a hand above her head.

"Didn't Mr. Snowe teach you about bedding?"

Eugenia's eyelashes lowered, dark against her cheek, and then she looked directly at him. Her eyes were as green as new leaves in springtime. "Of course he did."

Jealousy felt sour in his gut. "You've been faithful to his memory for how many years?"

"I have been a widow for seven years," she stated, chin up. Back straight.

"He was a fortunate man," Ward said. To kiss or not to kiss? He felt as if he might expire from pure lust. "Still, your husband couldn't have taught you everything there is to know about intimacy. In fact, how do you know he was any good, if you've slept with only one man?"

She broke into a peal of laughter. "If you don't know the answer to that, my friend, nothing I can say will enlighten you. Perhaps I shall give your future wife a hint or two."

"My wife won't need any hints," Ward said, easing closer. He could smell her now, that sweet berry fragrance that was all her own.

"Perhaps it's *you* who needs advice," she said merrily.

"Your husband did not, I gather."

"He took me to heaven and back," she said, her voice softening with the unmistakable ring of truth.

Well, damn.

Some shamefully envious part of Ward's soul had hoped that the man had been less than accomplished.

"It's a tragedy you haven't been with a man for years."

"That's a woman's lot," she pointed out. "Either we marry, or we fend off unwelcome advances."

"Seven years without a moment's pleasure," he said musingly.

Her eyes dropped, and pink rose in her cheeks again. Ward's balls tightened and sent a throb through his lower body. Damn, but she was delicious.

She'd pleasured herself.

"Without a man's touch," he clarified.

"This conversation has gone from improper to obscene," she observed.

He shook his head. "Haven't you noticed, Eugenia, that almost all of our conversations start at improper?"

"That speaks ill of both of us," she retorted. "Would you please allow me to pass so that we can continue our journey?"

"I'd rather discuss your experience of heaven."

She pushed at his shoulder. "Absolutely not!"

Ward brushed the pretty curve of her ear with his lips. "Why not let me teach you *my* version of heaven? Your husband wouldn't have wanted you to be alone for the rest of your life."

"No," Eugenia agreed, giving Ward a clear-eyed look. "Andrew also wouldn't want me to engage in any sort of unsavory relationship. I bear his name now, and that was very important to him."

"I wasn't thinking about an unsavory relationship," he clarified. "There's nothing unsavory if a

man were to give a woman pleasure, to make up for years of widowhood. No 'relationship,' so to speak, is required."

"The vicar would not approve."

"What about something so small that the vicar would never need know?"

"Small?" She gave a naughty giggle.

He leaned closer and breathed in that elusive scent of hers again. "She-devil." If there was anything he needn't worry about, it was the size of his rod. "What if I offered you one minute for every year since your husband's death?"

She burst out laughing, and brushed past him. "Only seven minutes? That is very like a man."

Ward watched her leave the room, an unwilling grin on his face.

Ladies—that is to say, *true* ladies, with birth and titles and the rest of it—were tiresome; all the humor and life was bred out of them by the time they reached the age of twenty. Eugenia, on the other hand, was funny and wry, indisputably brave and intelligent—and wickedly sensual as well.

He prowled behind her, riveted from head to toe.

If she granted him only seven minutes, he wanted every one of them. If he could lure her to his bedchamber, seven minutes would turn into seven days.

Just as Eugenia was about to leave the front door of the inn, he caught her waist and spun her to face him.

She let out a sound between a squeak and a gasp, tipped back her head and gazed at him from under those lovely, curling lashes of hers. "Mr. Reeve," she said. "Was there something I could help you with?"

"Yes," he said tightly, pulling her against him.

Her eyes closed as their bodies came together, fitting like two spoons.

"Give me seven minutes," he breathed. Her mouth opened, her tongue met his, and lust shot up his spine. She tasted like fresh apples and spice and Eugenia.

"Seven minutes," he repeated hoarsely, when he could speak again. "Please."

Her wide, gleaming smile made his pulse race even faster. "Seven minutes? I deserve more than that, Ward." She leaned forward and put a finger on his lips, stopping his offer to turn seven into seventy. "No."

Denial was as heady as a kiss. His blood was pounding a litany that went something like, *Mine, mine, mine.*

She turned her head with a flip that made her hair glow in the waning daylight like strands of fire, and walked outside with a swing in her hips that was enough to bring a man to his knees.

Chapter Eighteen

The private drive leading to Fawkes House was almost a mile long, and if Ward's sumptuous traveling coach hadn't already convinced Eugenia, his estate would have: he was as rich as Croesus.

As rich as she, quite possibly.

It was an interesting thought. She was used to suitors who had an eye to her fortune. But, of course, Ward was no suitor; he was a client.

Client or no, as they entered the marbled entry hall, she half expected Ward to sweep her off her feet and carry her straight upstairs.

But Ruby and Clothilde were just behind them; the second carriage had caught up and followed them closely the last few miles. So decorum was maintained.

Ward introduced his butler, Gumwater, a man with extraordinary eyebrows that jerked up and

down like furry caterpillars. He immediately sent a footman to escort Clothilde to Eugenia's bedchamber, with her trunk to follow.

"I would like to introduce you to the children," Ward said to Eugenia. "Shall we accompany Ruby to the nursery?"

The nursery was a large, pleasant chamber with tall windows. It had rained sometime earlier; the ivy that framed the windows held glistening drops caught in the warm glow of lamps set round the room.

Eugenia's attention went directly to the little girl across the room. She wore a dingy-looking black veil and stood on an overturned chamber pot, one arm flung out in fine declamatory style. Her audience was a cross-legged boy, his back to them.

As they entered, Lizzie stopped in mid-sentence, and Otis twisted around to look before politely standing.

"Down from the chamber pot, Lizzie," Ward said. "I hope to God it was empty when you converted it to a stage?"

"Of course it was!" she said, hopping down.

"I'd like to introduce both of you to Mrs. Snowe," Ward said. "She has kindly agreed to stay for a few days until we can arrange for a new governess."

Eugenia smiled at them. "How nice to meet you. Miss Darcy. Lord Darcy."

Otis jerked a bow and mumbled something. Lizzie didn't curtsy, but proclaimed from behind her veil that she was positively enchanted. Clearly, there was a great deal to be done before the children could be introduced to society.

"This is Ruby, who will be your nursery maid until a governess joins us," Ward added.

Ruby crossed the room, smiling with the brisk kindness that made her such an excellent housemaid for Snowe's. "Do you ever remove that veil, Miss Lizzie?"

"Not often," Lizzie said.

"As long as you wash your face and behind your ears, I suppose it'll be all right," Ruby said. "But if you don't mind, I would like to give it a good wash tonight after you're in bed."

Lizzie didn't seem to mind.

"And you, Lord Darcy, what have you got there?" Ruby asked.

"My rat, Jarvis," Otis reported, sitting back down on the floor. At this, Eugenia fell back a step, instinctively grabbing Ward's arm.

He leaned over and said in her ear, "Jarvis is a very well-mannered fellow."

"Jarvis, is it?" Ruby was saying. "What's that he's wearing?"

"His opera cloak," Otis explained. "We're having a night at the theater."

Reminding herself that she was no coward, Eugenia forced herself to move a bit closer in order to see what an opera cloak made for a rat looked like. The tiny garment had been fashioned from a scrap of fine crimson velvet. It was fastened around the neck of a sleek little rat with golden fur and shiny black eyes.

Jarvis was sitting on Otis's knee, showing no inclination to leap at Eugenia and run up her skirts, so she eased closer still.

"Does Jarvis mind wearing clothing?" she asked.

Otis had the knobby knees and ruffled hair of all boys his age. He also had a disconcertingly direct gaze that she'd seen on another male, his brother.

"Jarvis is agreeable," he informed her. "He has four or five costumes for different occasions."

"But the red velvet is his favorite," Lizzie said. "He didn't take to breeches."

That seemed reasonable. "What play were you performing?" Eugenia asked, turning to Otis's sister.

Lizzie was extremely slender, too thin for a girl of nine. But her voice emerged from behind the veil with all the strength of a woman twice her age. "A scene from Congreve's *The Way of the World*. It was one of our father's favorites."

"I memorized that play when I was about your age!" Eugenia exclaimed.

Lizzie gave a little squeal and threw back her veil, revealing a pale face with huge brown eyes. She pointed her finger directly at Eugenia. "'Sirrah, *Petulant*, thou art an Epitomizer of Words!'"

"'*Witwoud*,'" Eugenia retorted, "'you are an Annihilator of Sense.'"

"I can't imagine why you have both memorized that particular play," Ward said with a touch of reproof in his voice. "If I remember it correctly, it is quite improper."

"My favorite is Etherege's *She Would If She Could*," Lizzie said, ignoring him. "Do you know it?"

"Old Sir Oliver Cockwood?" Eugenia exclaimed. "Of course!"

"'Oliver *Cockwood*'?" Ward repeated, his brows knitting.

Lizzie jumped back onto the chamber pot and threw out her arm again. "'Jealousy in a husband—Heaven defend me from it! It begets a thousand plagues to a poor woman, the loss of her honor, her quiet, and her—'"

She paused dramatically. Eugenia sensed that Ward was not enjoying the performance—he was glowering—but she filled in the word obediently. "Pleasure."

"'And what's as bad almost, the loss of this town,'" Lizzie finished. "She's sent to the country, which is what has happened to Otis and me, as a matter of fact."

"You have a fine declamatory style," Eugenia said to Lizzie. "Didn't those lines come from *The Country Wife*, not *She Would if She Could*?"

"They get mixed up in my mind," Lizzie said, stepping down from the chamber pot again. "It's one of the reasons that Papa said I was an awful actress. Did you know my father, Mrs. Snowe?"

"I regret to say that I did not," Eugenia replied.

"He was rotten on the stage too, so he managed the curtain."

"I shall have to ask the two of you to help me get you ready for bed," Ruby intervened. "Does Jarvis sleep in the house?"

Otis clutched the rat to his chest. "Yes!"

Ruby didn't bat an eyelash. "Does he sleep in a box? I don't hold with animals in the same bed as people."

"He sleeps with me," Otis said, his voice rising.

"I have a little box I use for ribbons that would be just the right size," Eugenia said. "It's lined in soft green velvet, and I think a refined rat like Jarvis would find it most agreeable."

"That would be safer for him," Ruby said. "What if you rolled over on him one night?"

"I never would," Otis stated.

"I can't say for certain that my maid will have packed my box, but we could quickly ask her, if Mr. Reeve would show me to my chamber," Eugenia said.

"I suppose," Otis said reluctantly. "Jarvis and I will come along and see if he likes it."

"Jarvis travels outside the nursery in a canvas sack," Ward said.

"That's for every day," Otis said, popping Jarvis into a velvet bag with tasseled ribbons.

They left Ruby behind to supervise Lizzie's bath. "Jarvis has a refined wardrobe," Eugenia said.

"Mother made his cloaks before she died," Otis said.

Surprised, Eugenia glanced at Ward, but she couldn't grasp his expression. It was hard to imagine Lady Lisette sewing. It suggested a motherly side that Eugenia, for one, wouldn't have predicted.

"You are giving the boy your ribbon box, madame?" Clothilde whispered a few minutes later, disapproving. "It was a gift from your father, no?"

"It's just an old cigar box," Eugenia said, tumbling out the ribbons and handing it to Otis. He inspected the green velvet lining carefully and declared that Jarvis would probably like to sleep there.

Once Otis and Jarvis had been entrusted to Ruby's capable hands, Ward ushered Eugenia out of the nursery. Her mind was whirling as they walked down the corridor back to the guest wing. "Lizzie is remarkable," she told him.

"For her capacity to memorize, albeit inaccurately, salacious dialogue?" he answered dryly.

Eugenia squinted at him. "Surely you aren't cross because she has learned a play, or at least parts of several plays, by heart?"

"I was surprised that you encouraged her."

"Oh pooh," Eugenia said lightly. "I was fascinated by plays at her age."

Ward looked down at her and shook his head. "Forgive me if I don't find that reassuring. She has to become a lady, Eugenia. A *proper* lady."

"I promise you that the next governess we send will help."

"Just imagine if Lizzie were to quote a character named Oliver Cockwood in a ballroom. Perhaps it would be better to allow my grandmother to raise the children." A note in his voice suggested he was truly considering it.

Eugenia shook her head. "The duchess would crush her spirit, whereas you will nurture it."

They reached the door of her bedchamber and Ward leaned against the wall, looking down at her. "Now that Lizzie knows you too have a passion for the theater, she'll be pestering you every time she sees you."

"Would you feel reassured if I were to steer her toward more acceptable plays?"

"I would greatly appreciate it."

"Shakespeare is an obvious choice," she said. But she couldn't stop herself. "I could teach her *Much Ado about Nothing.*"

"Excellent," Ward said, with the heartiness of a man who has no interest in or knowledge about England's greatest playwright.

"Benedick is one of my favorite characters. 'I will live in thy heart,'" Eugenia quoted, grinning at him, "'*die* in thy lap, and be buried in thy eyes.'"

"'Live in thy . . . die in thy lap'? Wait. What did he mean by 'die'?"

"What do you think?" She was still laughing as she closed the door behind her, laughing so hard that she had to lean against the wall.

Chapter Nineteen

The night had turned chilly, and after Eugenia's bath Clothilde laid out an evening gown of rose-colored velvet.

The fabric clung to her curves and turned her skin the color of milk, so she drifted downstairs feeling luscious and ready to be seduced, and was disappointed to find the drawing room empty.

"Mr. Reeve has been temporarily delayed," Gumwater announced. "May I offer you a glass of sherry?"

"Yes, thank you," Eugenia said. When he was gone, she positioned herself on a sofa before a great mirror and tried out various postures. If she sat with her ankles crossed, her waist looked appealingly small. If she bent forward, her bosom appeared more ample than it already was.

Gumwater reappeared with a tray on which a

crystal decanter and two glasses were balanced. He wordlessly filled her glass and disappeared again. With a rush of nervous energy, Eugenia surged to her feet, picked up her glass, and began surveying the sparse furniture.

At length the door opened, and she turned to see Ward enter. Despite her wait, she couldn't stop smiling. He was devilishly handsome, with hair tumbling over his brow.

"Please accept my apologies," he said. "We had something of a crisis upstairs."

"What happened? Can I help?"

"Thank you, but Ruby and I seem to have brought things under control." He went to the tray and took up the remaining glass with the enthusiasm of one greeting a long-lost friend. "Jarvis was not happy to discover that Ruby believes even rats need nightly baths, so he retired under the grate and would not come out until lured forth with cheese. Once he'd emerged, I helped Otis negotiate a weekly bath for Jarvis."

If Eugenia were not a lady, she would walk over to Ward and run her hands down his shoulders. And perhaps even farther. His silk breeches left nothing to her imagination. She tipped up her glass so he didn't guess where she had been looking.

"I have been thinking about our meeting with the vicar tomorrow," she said untruthfully. "What can you tell me of him?"

"Very little. His name is Howson. According to Gumwater, the bishop's visit is the result of complaints arising after the man accused an elderly woman of running a brothel when, in fact, she was raising orphans at the expense of the county."

"Rash at the best and dangerously irrational at the worst." Eugenia set her glass down. "Does tomorrow worry you?"

Ward shrugged. "He sounds as cracked as a walnut, but I'm confident that between the two of us we will knock some sense into him. Figuratively speaking, of course. I believe that our supper awaits us." He held out his elbow. "May I?"

He ushered her to a small room, paneled and appointed, though it had the same empty feeling as the drawing room. It held a table, a sideboard, and a few chairs, but nothing embellished the walls or the floor.

When they entered, Gumwater was fussing with dishes on the sideboard. "Everything is as you requested, sir," he said. "I'll return to—"

"Thank you," Ward said. "I'll ring if we wish for anything else."

The butler withdrew, glancing at Eugenia from the corner of his eye in a way that suggested he knew her to be a woman of easy virtue.

She wasn't.

But she couldn't blame him, since she fully intended to become one.

Mrs. Snowe of Snowe's Registry was a woman of impeccable moral rectitude. But Eugenia was discovering more clearly every second, that Eugenia Snowe, née Strange, was not.

As evidence of which, she was having a meal alone with a man with whom she had determined to have illicit relations. Susan would be proud.

"What are you thinking about, Eugenia?"

"I was wondering if I am the sort of woman who will take to debauchery," she admitted. "Perhaps I will surprise myself and become adept at depravity."

She couldn't help but laugh at the appalled expression on Ward's face.

"What depravity?" he demanded. "We have done nothing more than kiss. You and Lizzie traded ribald speeches, but I hardly think that qualifies."

"According to all the ballads I've heard on the subject," Eugenia said, "a widow is halfway to moral decline once the chimes ring after midnight for the first time."

A laugh rumbled from his side of the table. "What on earth do chimes have to do with it?"

Eugenia threw him a naughty glance. "Once a man has kept a widow awake after midnight, she sees no reason to go to bed alone again."

"I wouldn't want you to be alone."

The need in Ward's eyes was so potent that she looked down at her soup bowl. The soup was pale green, with an aroma of new peas and delicate herbs. Eugenia gave an involuntary moan upon tasting it. "This is superb."

He slid his bowl across the table. "Have mine. I haven't touched it."

"I couldn't," she protested.

"Please do. Frankly, I would happily give up my meal to watch you eat."

She took another spoonful, and since he was observing her, she let the spoon slip extremely slowly from her lips. "You have a wicked side," he muttered. "I may not survive the next course."

"Pooh," she said. Then, changing the subject: "How long do you wish Otis and Lizzie to remain in mourning, if you don't mind my asking?"

"I had thought to take them out of blacks after six

months, but if you think they ought to be in mourning a full year, I'm happy to follow your lead."

"Given Lizzie's veil, I think your instincts are correct. It would be good to ease the children away from outward expressions of grief as soon as possible."

She took another spoonful of soup, glancing at Ward from under her eyelashes. He was wearing an exquisitely cut tailcoat, cut from a dark blue kerseymere. "You decided not to wear black?" she asked.

He shook his head. "I scarcely knew Lady Lisette; it felt hypocritical to claim grief at her death. How long did you remain in mourning?"

"Oh, I was very conventional," she said, taking another spoonful of soup. "Full mourning for a year. After that, half-mourning."

"Half-mourning is gray, am I right? And violet."

"Gray," she agreed. "Who knew there were so many shades of gray?"

"Five? Ten?"

She smiled at him over her wine glass. "There are forty at least. No, likely fifty. Fifty shades of gray."

"I have a gray cravat," Ward said. "My valet went through a brief infatuation with French fashion, during which canary-yellow, gray, and aubergine cravats entered my closet. Alas, I refuse to be the dandy that he wished me to be."

"I can picture you in a gray cravat," Eugenia said. "But not for mourning," she added. "Merely because gray is *au courant*."

"You wore gray for how long? Two years? Longer?"

Her eyes fell under his gaze. "I found it difficult to counterfeit joy. Color is a language, after all. A statement." She took her last spoonful of soup.

"What time are we expected at the vicarage tomorrow morning?"

"Nine o'clock."

"Ought we to have a plan?"

Ward removed the cover from a serving dish holding fragrant lamb stew. "I have a plan. If Howson makes any sort of fuss about my sister's foolery, I'll have him removed from his position."

"How will you do that?"

"Only two things matter in this country: money and rank. I have both, even as a bastard, and if that's not good enough, Lizzie and Otis do as well."

"Are you referring to Lord Darcy's estate?" Eugenia asked.

He glanced at her, and back at the stew. "That, and I settled thirty thousand pounds on Lizzie. I want to ensure that her dowry will overcome any hesitancy owing to her parentage or to my guardianship."

Eugenia felt a pinch at her heart. He was such a good man. He'd given up his independence, his freedom, his place at Oxford, and now a significant fortune, for the sake of a brother and sister he'd never known.

Her father always insisted that titles and blood didn't matter, that the only important thing was what a man did with his life. Watching Ward from under her eyelashes, Eugenia had no doubt but that her father would approve.

Later, at her bedchamber door, he took her hand and brought it to his lips. For a dismaying moment, she thought he would walk away without even kissing her. But at the last second, he bent his head and kissed her greedily, every stroke of his tongue making it clear that he planned to make her his.

There was sensual possession there . . . and restraint too. "Eugenia," he said, voice low and rough. "It's time for bed."

"Very well," she gasped. She turned to open the door, to guide him inside, but he stopped her, a kiss gliding over her throat.

"Alone." He drew back. "I don't want to seduce you before you've had a chance to recover from the journey. It seems less than gentlemanly."

She opened her mouth to protest.

"Tomorrow," he continued, "I mean to abduct you once again—straight to my bedchamber."

It was a vow, a promise.

Chapter Twenty

Wednesday, May 27, 1801

The following morning, the library served as the gathering place for the trip to the parish church, St. Mary the Virgin. Ward was already there when Gumwater ushered in his sister, whose black dress was relieved only by a snowy white collar.

"You look beautiful, Lizzie," Ward said. "Given the circumstances, I'm very grateful that you chose not to wear your veil."

"I wanted to wear it," Lizzie said, sitting down on the sofa. "But Ruby stayed up most of the night making me this new dress, so I thought it would be ungrateful to wear the veil. It covered the collar."

Ward made a mental note to increase Ruby's salary

before he remembered that Ruby came with Eugenia, so she was paid by Snowe's Registry. Perhaps he could lure her away; Otis hadn't even complained at the idea that he should stay home with Ruby while they all set off for the church.

Just then Eugenia walked through the door. She was wearing a dark plum gown that made her skin glow like a pearl. Hell, *she* glowed. The sight of her plump, rosy mouth made him want to kiss her, not bow.

But bow he did. Kissed her hand and asked all the right questions about how she'd slept, all the time thinking that he wanted to pick her up, throw her over his shoulder, and take her straight to bed.

Lizzie hopped off her sofa and bobbed a curtsy, smiling up at Eugenia. It abruptly occurred to Ward that a gentleman wouldn't allow his young sister near the woman he fully intended to seduce.

It was too late now.

Eugenia bent and kissed Lizzie's cheek, and then she set about teaching Lizzie to be just like her. "I want you to pretend that you're greeting a bishop," she said.

"What's a bishop?" Lizzie inquired.

"He's an authority in the church," Eugenia said. "Have you ever been to church on Christmas?"

"I've never been to church at all," Lizzie reported. "That was one of things that bothered Miss Midge."

"Well, just pretend that your brother is a king and curtsy to him. No, don't bob up and down as if you were a jack-in-the-box, Lizzie. Bend your head slightly, take your gown in your fingers, *very* delicately, and slide your right foot forward and shift all your weight onto that foot."

It took four or five tries, but Lizzie was an excellent mimic. Ward leaned against the mantelpiece and watched. Lizzie was ordinarily a somewhat reticent child, but this morning words poured from her.

"I didn't like her because she fainted," she was explaining.

"I expect that Miss Lumley didn't have the fortitude to deal with a dissected rabbit," Eugenia said.

"We have guts too," Lizzie said. "A cow's insides could stretch all the way down the drive."

"Ladies don't say *guts*," Eugenia said.

"Why not?" Lizzie demanded.

Ward had the distinct impression that Gumwater's entrance rescued Eugenia from a question she wasn't prepared to answer. Though how could that be, if she was once a governess?

Somehow, now that he knew her better, he simply couldn't accept that she was ever a governess, or indeed, an underling in any household.

Once in the carriage, Lizzie kept Eugenia entertained by pointing out all the sights—a tumbledown house supposedly haunted by the ghost of a nun, the great oak that housed a family of owls, and then, when they reached the village of Wheatley, the shop belonging to the irascible butcher, Mr. Biddle.

When they arrived at the parish church, Ward stepped down, turning to assist Eugenia. Once on the ground, Eugenia held out a hand and Lizzie jumped to her side as if she were iron and Eugenia a magnet.

"I'm ready!" Lizzie said cheerfully, and they marched toward the church without looking to see if Ward was following.

Was this what it was like to have a family?

He strolled behind, thinking about that.

Chapter Twenty-one

The Parish Church and Vicarage
  of St. Mary the Virgin
Wheatley

"*I* don't believe in magic," Hirshfield Chatterley-Blackman, the Bishop of Oxford, grumbled at his manservant, Rowland. "I never have. All that business about getting naked out on the heath in the rain. The women I know wear at least ten articles of clothing at any given time."

Rowland was kneeling at Hirshfield's feet, buttoning up his gaiters. He coughed an assent.

"In fact, make that twenty. You wouldn't catch my sisters going around *in puris naturalibus*, would you? No one would do it, not even imbeciles like Howson.

Do you know how much trouble that man has caused me?" The grumble escalated to a bellow.

"England is full of nice, quiet parishes, thick with vicars who do no more than shag the occasional parishioner or fall into the ditch, cock-eyed on drink, but *I* am the one who ends up with Howson. The man won't listen to reason. Not a bit of it. This is as mad as that supposed brothel he discovered a few months ago."

Rowland murmured something before he came to his feet with a slight creaking of joints.

"I suppose he thinks that the gal is out at night lopping off toad fingers and hedgehog whiskers and all the rest of that rot that's supposed to go into a cauldron," the bishop—known to his intimates as Chatty—moaned. "At nine years old!"

Rowland said something, the clearest word of which was "earl."

"That's bloody right," Chatty said, twitching his tippet out of his man's hands. "Let go, that's good enough. Reeve may be illegitimate, but he's the by-blow of a peer and that makes all the difference. That's the sort of thing Howson doesn't understand. You don't interfere with nobility."

He tramped gloomily along a passage leading from the vicarage to the church's vestry behind the chancel, trying to remember where he'd hidden his flask the last time he had to visit, during the orphanage debacle. It was in the vestry room somewhere.

Hurried footsteps sounded in the passage, and Rowland interrupted his search. "My Lord," he panted. "You forgot your cross."

"Right," Chatty said testily. "I'll put it on." Whenever he had to face a mad churchman, he always

wore a great Palatine cross that some long-ago ancestor had brought back from the Crusades. It had a ruby at the top that winked in the light.

He fancied that it gave him an air of authority.

There was no getting around the fact that Howson had a way of commanding the stage. Taking up all the air in the room.

It was all that bloody zeal of his. Zeal was a dangerous thing. Howson's brain sizzled like a pan of sausages. That energy gave him authority, not to mince words.

"I'd like to mince him," Chatty muttered to himself.

He headed toward the side door that led into the central nave. The curate stood at door, looking nervous. "Is everyone present?" Chatty asked testily.

"Yes, My Lord Bishop," the curate said, nodding madly. He pushed open the door and announced, "The Right Reverend Hirshfield Chatterley-Blackman, the Lord Bishop of Oxford."

Chatty marched to his velvet-cushioned seat looking neither left nor right. He'd just realized that he'd never found his flask after the distraction of putting on the cross, and brandy was the only thing that might make these proceedings bearable.

Before he got his bottom settled on the cushion, Howson leapt in front, blocking his view of the pews.

The vicar looked lean and greasy and full of zeal. Chatty would be the first to admit that he himself had a chin or two too many, but he disliked men who were as thin as pencils on principle. It was indicative of an inadequate diet, and that sort of thing was bad for the brain.

"What did you have for breakfast, Howson?" he asked.

"Cabbage," Howson replied, and started babbling on about witchcraft.

Cabbage. That explained a lot. Probably gave the man wind, which made it particularly objectionable that he was standing so close.

Unless Chatty was mistaken, Howson was starting to hint at satanic possession. Pretentious ass. As if the devil didn't have better things to do than run around dressed like a nine-year-old.

If he were the devil, he'd possess a nubile young woman with buxom thighs.

"Stand aside, Vicar," Chatty said, cutting him off. "I suppose I'd better speak to the girl's brother, but I'll tell you freely that I don't believe there is such a thing as magic in Oxford. Or in England."

Howson's eyes bulged with fermented zeal. He was the sort of man who never changed his ideas about anything, no matter the evidence.

"I am servant to a higher truth," he gasped.

"So am I, and a higher servant than you," Chatty retorted, silently cursing his brandy-less state.

"In this head," Mr. Howson said, raising his voice, "is a compendium of knowledge related to terrible matters such as these. There is no cure for this situation!"

Decapitation would cure Howson all right, Chatty reflected. It would solve a lot of problems.

"Move aside," he said irritably. "I expect you've made a double ass of yourself this time."

"I am a hammer of the Lord," Howson said, demonstrating an adroit avoidance of the topic.

"I wish you were a bloody glass hammer," Chatty said. "I'd open the sessions with a bang, I would."

At last Howson moved so that Chatty could see. His heart sank. The vicar had outdone himself.

That man with his arms crossed over his chest, managing to resemble both a hungry wolf and a duke? That was surely the Earl of Gryffyn's son. The little spell-caster looked like an angel. And . . .

"Holy Bejabbers!" he burst out, "Eugenia Strange, is that you?"

Chapter Twenty-two

The moment she saw the resplendent bishop deposit his generous bottom onto a red velvet cushion, Eugenia started smiling so widely that Ward gave her a puzzled look over Lizzie's head.

She shook her head at him and waited impatiently while the vicar ranted about being a servant to a higher truth and a hammer of the Lord.

Mr. Howson was a withered man who looked as if he considered personal cleanliness—its proximity to godliness notwithstanding—to be a waste of time. When he started holding forth on the devil, she squeezed Lizzie's hand to reassure her, but the girl's blue eyes were entirely unafraid.

Though there was an odd expression in them. A distinct hint of drama.

Eugenia bent down. "Lizzie, I'm very good friends

with the bishop, and we shall be out of here in the shake of a lamb's tail."

"Without speaking to the vicar at all?"

"There will be no need," Eugenia assured her.

"That's not fair," Lizzie whispered. "Everyone has the right to face their accuser."

"Well, if you would like to," Eugenia said, taken aback.

"Yes, I would! I memorized my speech last night." And with that, a look of tragic innocence settled back onto Lizzie's face.

"This isn't theatricals, you little donkey."

Lizzie gave Eugenia an uncannily mature look. "That vicar would love to send me off to a nunnery, you know the way Hamlet said. I have the exact expression my mother had when she played Ophelia."

Just then, the vicar moved to the side, allowing the bishop—or Chatty as he'd always been known to Eugenia's family—to recognize her. A moment later, Eugenia was close in the incense-perfumed embrace of one of her father's oldest friends.

"What the deuce are you doing here?" Chatty demanded. "I know you're not married again, because I'd be very hurt if I hadn't officiated. Very hurt, indeed. But poor Andrew has been gone nearly a decade, hasn't he? Time to think of marriage."

He swiveled about, cassock flying, Eugenia still tucked under his arm, and surveyed Ward and Lizzie.

"No, no," Eugenia said hastily. "Mr. Reeve is a client of Snowe's, that's all. May I introduce Mr. Edward Reeve and his half-sibling, Miss Lizzie Darcy?"

"Of the Northampshire Darcy's?" the bishop asked.

"No, my lord," Ward said, bowing. "In fact, my half-sister's father was Lord Darcy of Darcy Manor."

Chatty's mouth fell open. "*What*?"

"Lizzie's younger brother Otis inherited the title," Ward added.

"If I understand you correctly," the vicar erupted, with an expression that suggested he'd just swallowed turpentine, "this child is the offspring of a notorious—"

"Mr. Howson," Eugenia interrupted, "I'm certain you have no intention of saying anything disparaging before a child who is mourning the recent death of her mother."

"Dead, is she?" Chatty said with interest. "Lady Lisette was barking mad, of course, but a lovely woman." With a little start, he looked over his large stomach at Lizzie. "Forgive me, child."

Lizzie heightened her air of innocent pathos. "My father once told me that madness is a pirouette away from genius."

"My lord, I thought it best if I brought Lizzie to speak to you," Ward said, intervening. "I would be dismayed if the absurd rumors circulating in the village are countenanced here."

Chatty turned to the vicar. "Howson, the truth is that I've allowed your nonsense to go on too long. I'm feeling ashamed of myself. This young girl has no need of spiritual guidance."

He looked down at Lizzie's conspicuously innocent gaze. "She is clearly as guiltless as a lamb," he said, with more vigor.

"We must discuss these events," the vicar spluttered.

Chatty's eyes narrowed. "You just spit on me, Howson! Spit! Do you know what spit does to silk?

The only thing worse is blood. It was bad enough when you accused that old woman of running a house of ill repute, when in fact she was nurturing indigent orphans."

Howson had a desperate look around his eyes. "I know the smell of evil!"

"No, you don't," Chatty snorted. "I've had enough. You're lucky that Mr. Reeve is an understanding man."

Ward was standing with his arms folded over his chest and Eugenia didn't think he looked very understanding. Nor did the vicar, considering the way he edged away from him.

"I'm sending you to Africa," Chatty said. "Or perhaps somewhere farther away; geography was never my subject."

"The Antipodes," Ward suggested.

"Right, that'll do," Chatty said obligingly. "Howson, get your affairs in order because you'll be off on the first boat. I think you'd better apologize to this young lady. If you make it back to England, don't get yourself tangled up in the pastimes of the nobility. This young girl is the daughter of the late Lord Darcy. Her brother is a lord."

"That is irrelevant!"

The curate walked forward and took the vicar by the arm. "If you'll be so kind, vicar, I believe that you might want to begin packing your books," he said, pulling the protesting man straight out the room.

"Eugenia, Eugenia, Eugenia," Chatty said, enveloping Eugenia in his arms again. He smelled of roast beef, incense, and port.

"I didn't get to say my speech," an indignant voice said from behind Eugenia.

Lizzie was tapping her foot for all the world like a frosty dowager who'd been kept waiting.

"You can perform it at home," Ward said, glancing down at her and then back at Eugenia.

She could feel herself getting pink around the ears. Hopefully no one else could interpret that intent look of his. She glanced sideways and realized that Chatty's eyes had narrowed.

"Miss Darcy," Eugenia said hastily, "it is not appropriate to complain when you're in the company of a bishop."

"Why not?" Lizzie demanded. "He sent the vicar away before I could make my speech. I had the right to say it, because the vicar was accusing me of nefilius things. All sorts of nefilius things."

"Nefilius?" Ward repeated.

"I presume you are referring to 'nefarious' things," Eugenia said. "While I applaud your vocabulary, there is a time and place for everything."

Lizzie glared. "This was the place *and* the time," she said, not unreasonably.

"She has a point," Chatty said, interrupting. "I'll be tickled if she doesn't remind me of you, Eugenia. Remember that time when you secreted yourself in a basket and had it brought into the parlor? You were around seven years old."

Eugenia opened her mouth to stop him, but Lizzie got there first. "Why was Mrs. Snowe in a basket?"

"She had memorized a soliloquy from *Othello*, and wanted to give it to the company," the bishop said. "As I recall, her father had made her promise not to recite any more Shakespeare, but she got around him by being delivered as a birthday present."

"I have memorized the whole of *Othello*," Lizzie

said, nodding. "I was the prompter when my mother played Desdemona."

"Lady Lisette playing the innocent Desdemona," Chatty muttered. "Flabbergasting."

Eugenia threw him a quick frown. No matter her reputation, Lady Lisette had been Lizzie's mother, not to mention Ward's.

"Well, go ahead and give your speech," Chatty said. "If you're anything like young Eugenia, you won't relent until you have your way."

"What did Mrs. Snowe do when she didn't have her way?" Lizzie asked, eyes wide.

"I am not a good model," Eugenia said hastily.

"Oh, she was a terror, a right terror," Chatty said. "Burst out screaming, she would. Her papa had spoiled her rotten."

Eugenia swatted her old friend on the arm. "Hush, you beast."

"I am not spoiled," Lizzie said. "I don't mind if no one hears my speech."

"Good girl," Chatty said, bending down. "I hate *Othello* myself. That being the case, would you be so kind as to escort an old man back to the vicarage?"

"I can do that," Lizzie said, as regal as any queen. She and the bishop left the room, her high voice fading as the door swung shut behind them.

"Spoiled, were you?" Ward said, with distinct amusement.

Just a few minutes before, he had resembled an ancient berserker, wanting only an axe resting on his shoulder to complete the picture. Now he looked like an English gentleman again, if handsomer than most.

"Well," Eugenia said briskly, gathering up her reticule and shawl, "we'd better follow them."

Ward took the shawl and wrapped it around her shoulders. "How spoiled were you?"

"Monstrously," she admitted as he drew her down the aisle. "I was the light of my father's eyes, and I spent a good deal of time with him or alone. Thus the plays."

"Is that why you became a governess?" He held open the door.

"I was never a governess. I operate a registry office for governesses, which is not the same thing."

They entered the dim passageway leading to the vicarage. Its only illumination was weak sunlight filtering through narrow windows badly in need of a wash.

Ward took a quick look ahead to make certain they were alone, drew Eugenia to a halt, and slid his arms around her waist. "I thought you were too naughty to be a governess."

"I think we established that *you* were a naughty child, Mr. Reeve. I was quite biddable."

"Only if you weren't crossed, according to your friend the bishop." Ward drew her closer and bent his head. "I can't go on without a taste of you."

Her eyes were luminous in the dark corridor, her skin translucent. "You'd best be careful, Mr. Reeve. You've made Chatty curious, and if he were to drop a word to my father, you might find yourself dumped at the base of an altar. And I don't mean as a pagan sacrifice, either."

"You're a widowed woman," he said, his lips hovering over hers. "Your father needn't defend your honor the way he would a maiden's."

Eugenia shook her head. "You have a great deal to learn about fathers and daughters."

"I have time before Lizzie grows up."

Ward's ready acceptance of Lizzie and Otis into his life was almost as alluring as the muscled leg holding her against the wall.

Or the warm mouth ravaging hers, kissing her with a ferocity that pricked all over, making heat radiate through her body.

"We can't do this here," she whispered.

"No one can see," he growled back, the catch in his voice making her knees wobble because he so clearly wanted her as much as she wanted him. His hand slid past her shoulder and shaped her breast as he drank from her mouth.

"How spoiled are you these days? Will you scream if I don't give you what you want?" He was rubbing her nipple with the side of his broad thumb, making her eyelids droop and her knees tremble.

"Screaming in the vicarage would not be a good idea," she managed. She could scarcely speak. She was boneless against the wall, her hips arching instinctively against the hard muscular curve of his thigh. With a gasp, she pulled away from his kiss and sank her hands into his hair.

"You sound so damn wanton," Ward growled. "You'd let me do anything to you, wouldn't you, Eugenia? The perfect lady is no longer in control."

"No," she whispered.

He pulled at the edge of her gown so that one breast gleamed in the dim light. "Ask me for what you want."

"Kiss me," she cried, helpless in the grip of a desire so potent that she could feel herself tremble.

He bent his head and his warm tongue found her nipple. Her eyes closed and a broken moan floated from her lips.

"Hush," he commanded. His teeth nipped her at the same moment that a hand covered her mouth, stifling her hoarse cry.

"You want everything I'll give you, don't you?" he growled.

"Yes," she breathed.

"Even here, in this church corridor. If I wrapped your legs around my waist, I could take you right here, couldn't I?"

His smoldering voice made her shudder again. Her breasts felt heavy under his restless caress.

"Couldn't I?" Ward repeated, his voice branding her skin. He was kissing her again, taking her mouth as his hands petted her, but even so, when he drew back she had just enough presence of mind to speak the truth.

"Yes," she gasped.

"You'd take every inch of this into your sweet, tight body," he said, kissing her ear lobe at the same time he rubbed her hand against his cock, now straining to break free of his breeches.

A trickle of sense penetrated Eugenia's consciousness.

He was using those words with her—a lady? Not that she wasn't curious about his privates, but—

She heard the low words he whispered in her ear. "Right here in the corridor."

Eugenia was melting, her skin singing, her breasts throbbing . . .

But.

No.

Ward was starting to sound altogether too much like those men who came to Snowe's Registry, thinking they could make her do whatever they wanted.

She summoned every ounce of self-control she possessed, and pulled away. "The answer to that is no, Mr. Reeve."

That man was going entirely too far, thinking that he had her under his command.

Perhaps he did have her under his command, but she was constitutionally opposed to revealing that truth.

She gave her skirts a shake. "Shall we join the others?" She walked ahead of him in the passageway feeling shaken—and triumphant. She'd be damned if she let Ward know how susceptible she was to his charms, simply because he was promising to make love to her.

Make deep, immoral, illicit, debauched love to her all night long.

She was no man's possession, and she wouldn't be—at least, not until she chose to give herself away again.

Chapter Twenty-three

During the time it took for Ward's blood to cool down, he discovered that he couldn't stop grinning. He was entranced by Eugenia's sensuality, by her candor, by her laughter.

Even the way she drew her ladylike cloak around herself and dismissed him, all the time with a glint in her eye that admitted it was a pretense.

She was like no other woman he'd ever met. Just now she was prancing down the hall ahead of him, and he knew perfectly well that every twitch of those rounded hips was calculated to drive him insane.

When she reached the end of the corridor, Eugenia looked over her shoulder, and damned if she didn't look as composed as if he hadn't tried to make love to her. She had been close to coming in his arms.

He knew she had.

Her breath had caught and she had writhed against him, fingers clenching his shoulders, all because he was kissing her breast.

It was the first time that he'd ever ground out a series of demands like that, perhaps because other women in his experience had made it clear that they were happy to do anything he wanted.

Anything, anywhere.

Not inconsequentially, he had walked away from them without a second thought.

But Eugenia?

She had walked away from *him*.

He strolled into the vicarage's drawing room and waited for a maid to pour him a cup of tea, taking the time to add milk and sugar, both of which he loathed. One sip of that revolting beverage, and his cock deflated.

A cup of tea, a chat with the bishop, and he could summon his carriage and return home. Where he fully intended to pull the owner of Snowe's Registry upstairs and ravish her against the bedpost.

Or against the wall.

He turned around, holding his tea. Tears were trickling down Lizzie's cheeks. "What happened?" he rasped, dumping his tea cup on a side table and crouching down beside his sister.

"Nothing," Eugenia said. "Lizzie is demonstrating the art of weeping. She planned to employ the art this morning, but she was thwarted by Chatty's expeditious handling of your vicar."

"Howson was not 'my' vicar," Ward said testily. Granted, the bishop was a middle-aged man, but did Eugenia have to nestle in his arm like that?

What about when she married again? What if he

was crossing a London street and saw her gazing at her husband with that sweet expression?

He would turn the other way, obviously.

"Lizzie, what is the possible good of being able to cry on command?" he demanded.

"It might do her a rare sight of good when she's married," said the bishop—or Chatty, as Eugenia was calling him. "There's nothing that controls a man as quickly as a woman's tears."

"Don't listen to him," Eugenia said. "Ladies never use tears to get what we want. There are other ways. More honorable ways."

Lizzie stopped crying and looked up at the bishop with the air of a young saint. "Please pardon my silliness." The lisp was overdoing it, in Ward's opinion. "My fault is himinous, and if you forgive it not, heaven will not pardon it in the world to come."

Himinous? What did that mean?

He almost missed Eugenia rolling her eyes.

"*Heinous*, not himinous," Eugenia corrected. "*A Woman Killed with Kindness*, and a most inappropriate speech for you to quote."

"I was the prompter for that play too," Lizzie said, dropping her hands, which had been clasped beseechingly. "My father said that knowledge of good literature could never hurt."

The bishop smiled down at her. "You will be a remarkable young woman someday."

"Time to make our farewells," Eugenia said firmly.

As they walked toward the door, Eugenia and Lizzie in the lead, the Right Reverend Chattersley-Dorfmann looked at Ward over his spectacles. "I gather Eugenia intends to travel on to her father's estate?"

"I believe Mrs. Snowe did indicate as much." Of course, Ward wouldn't allow Eugenia go today.

He needed a week with her. No, a fortnight.

"She is a dangerous woman. So much life," the bishop said, his eyes steady. "Such charm and beauty, paired with intelligence and energy. I've known her since she was a child. Young Lizzie reminds me of Eugenia."

"Mrs. Snowe is remarkable," Ward agreed. "If you'll excuse me, Your Honor—"

"Her entire family is extraordinary," Chattersley-Dorfmann said. "I encounter her aunt frequently; she operates Magdalene House, as you may know. Her husband is with the River Police—a former magistrate for the City of London—but Magdalene House is entirely her own."

"An edifying occupation," Ward said. "Well, I must bid you farewell, with my sincere gratitude for your forbearance with regard to my sister's foolery, my lord."

The bishop ignored him. "I expect you think that I am worried about Mrs. Snowe," he said, folding his hands over his considerable middle. "In truth, I am worried about you, Mr. Reeve. She's above your touch, if you don't mind my saying so."

Ward bowed. "Mrs. Snowe travels on directly to her father's estate, my lord, but I thank you for your concern."

A few minutes later, he escorted Eugenia and Lizzie to the carriage with a mental shake of his head.

The bishop apparently believed that being a bastard put Ward out of the reach of a good woman, in the same way that it barred him from the church.

Ward had clear memories of a maid informing him

at around six years old that the Bible itself said that no one of illegitimate birth could enter the assembly of the Lord. That was true enough, but her warning that a bolt of lightning would strike him down on entering?

Not quite so much.

Unfortunately, he had been young enough that he had taken her advice seriously. A couple of years later, he had refused to enter St. Paul's Cathedral for his own father's wedding, though he never told his father or stepmother why.

In the real world, rather than the ecclesiastical one, his fortune paired with the fact that both his parents came from the nobility meant that his illegitimate birth was practically irrelevant.

When he climbed into the carriage, Eugenia was leaning forward, elbows on her knees, listening intently to Lizzie.

"Leonardo da Vinci made drawings of all the muscles," Lizzie was saying, her peaked face glowing. "Papa bought me a book."

"I should like to see it," Eugenia said.

The little girl's face fell. "We couldn't bring our belongings whilst we made the voyage to see our brother."

"A voyage implies that you came over water," Eugenia noted.

"Trip," Lizzie said, with a wave of her hand. Apparently, she had so many synonyms rattling around in her head that she used them indiscriminately.

"Did you leave other things that you now miss?" Eugenia asked.

"My books," Lizzie said. "I took Mama's veil, and Otis had Jarvis, and that was all that really mattered."

"Is there anything you'd like me to retrieve, Lizzie?" Ward asked.

"There's no point to acquiring possessions." His sister rearranged her features into a mask of tragedy. "All golden girls and boys come to dust."

"*Cymbeline*," Eugenia said unsympathetically, "Misquoted, and irrelevant to this conversation."

Lizzie shrugged. "We didn't have very much. The troupe burnt our wagon after Lady Lisette died, because they were afraid that her illness might have been contagious."

Ward pulled his sister in his lap and wrapped both arms around her. "I wish I'd known you were alive," he said, kissing her hair. "I would have taken you and Otis out of there, Lizzie, I promise you that."

He looked up to find that Eugenia was smiling at him.

Chapter Twenty-four

"Would you two mind if I paid a visit to the butcher before we return to Fawkes House?" Eugenia asked, endeavoring to ignore the way her heart was melting at the sight of Lizzie tucked into her brother's arms like a bird in its nest. "The shop is just across the square."

Ward's brow furrowed.

"Butchers and bakers are the heart of a village," she explained. "After the saga of Mr. Biddle's 'borrowed' gold chain, we need him to relay the message that Lizzie was merely fooling. In return, he will be first to know that the vicar is being dispatched to the Antipodes."

"I don't see the necessity," Ward said. "I have important things to do."

"It's best to nip gossip in the bud," she said, ignor-

ing his comment and the heated gaze that told her what he considered important.

"Mrs. Snowe, do you really have to leave this afternoon?" Lizzie asked.

Ward answered her. "Luckily for us, Mrs. Snowe has kindly agreed to stay with us until we receive a new governess from her registry."

Eugenia raised an eyebrow. "Mr. Reeve, is that an attempt to blackmail me into extending my stay?"

"Absolutely," Ward replied.

"But you told the bishop that Mrs. Snowe was leaving directly," Lizzie said to Ward, crinkling her brow.

"I didn't want him to worry that Mrs. Snowe's visit posed a threat to her reputation," Ward explained.

Lizzie shook her head. "He wouldn't have worried. Widows can do whatever they like. Lady Lisette said so, many times."

Eugenia winced. Lord only knew what Lizzie's mother had been doing during the year or so between her husband's death and her own. She suspected that the children were privy to far more than they ought to have been.

Ward tightened his arm around his sister. "Our mother was no guide to proper behavior."

"That's what Miss Midge said," Lizzie confided. "She said that Otis is a better parent to Jarvis, and I should follow his lead. Which is ridiculous, because no one carries a baby in a sack!"

Eugenia leaned forward and nodded at Ward. "If you and Lizzie will give me just five minutes, I'll take care of the butcher and return directly." She jumped down and closed the door behind her before the two of them could follow.

Biddle's Meat was large and airy, as befitted a butcher who served as mayor and was in possession of a gold chain signifying his office.

It was also empty.

Ward's groom gave the counter a sharp rap and bellowed, "Service!"

The sound of a scuffle was heard from the back and a man who resembled a tightly stuffed sausage appeared, a bloody cleaver in his hand.

Despite herself, Eugenia fell back a step.

"How can I help you, madam?" he said, laying the cleaver on the counter and giving her a toothy smile. "I've some excellent chickens, and I'm just butchering a cow of the finest quality."

"My name is Mrs. Snowe," she said. "I was hoping to talk to you for a moment about the incident in which young Lord Darcy tried to hang your chain of office on a rosebush."

His fat lower lip pushed out. "I don't see as there's anything to talk about. It caused me nothing but trouble." He jerked his head toward an empty hook. "I put it away safe enough."

"A man like you, the mayor of the village, holds great influence over his neighbors," Eugenia said. "I am hoping that everyone in the village will understand that no theft was intended."

A woman hurried from the back. "Robbie, what is—" She saw Eugenia, faltered, and bobbed a curtsy. "Ma'am."

"Mrs. Biddle," Eugenia said. "I am Mrs. Snowe, of Snowe's Registry for Governesses in London. Mr. Reeve engaged me to find a governess for his wards. I was just explaining to your good husband that Miss Lizzie Darcy managed to convince a particularly

naïve dairy maid that she knew a spell for revealing true love. One of your roses was an ingredient."

The butcher gave a bark of laughter. "We all heard about the boy who thought himself invisible."

His wife turned to him. "Mr. Biddle, why don't you finish with that side of beef while I talk to Mrs. Snowe."

"I didn't mean to frighten the boy," the butcher said heavily. "I lost me temper and that's the truth."

"As would anyone in those circumstances," Eugenia said warmly.

He took up the cleaver and disappeared into the back, revealing who was the real mayor of the village.

"Mr. Reeve and I met with the bishop this morning," Eugenia said with her best smile. "His Lordship believes Mr. Howson is better suited to being a missionary. In fact, he is sending him out of the country immediately."

"Gracious heavens, that's very good to hear," Mrs. Biddle said. "I never liked him. He didn't eat a bit of meat, can you imagine? Just cabbage, day and night."

"That is certainly peculiar," Eugenia said. "Miss Lizzie was merely being silly, Mrs. Biddle. She is dazzled by her ability to influence people."

The butcher's wife ventured a smile. "She and her veil are well known in these parts, Mrs. Snowe. I'm sorry Mr. Biddle lost his temper."

"Having met Mr. Howson this morning, I believe I put the blame on the vicar," Eugenia said.

Mrs. Biddle gave her a beseeching look. "Might you ask Mr. Reeve not to take away his custom? Mr. Biddle has always been one to fly off the handle, but he's only a blusterer."

A deep voice came from the door. "I'm happy to restore custom, Mrs. Biddle, as long as you promise to keep your husband in check."

Eugenia whirled about with a gasp. "I didn't realize you were there!"

"Good afternoon, Mr. Reeve," the butcher's wife said, bobbing a curtsy. "The village will be better off without the vicar, and everyone will thank you for it."

"Mrs. Biddle," Ward said, bowing. He took Eugenia's arm, murmuring in her ear, "I thought you might need support, but I underestimated you."

"Once again," Eugenia said, with satisfaction.

They climbed into the carriage to the bellow of Ward's laughter.

Chapter Twenty-five

Later that evening

Ward had had enough.

After they returned from the village, Otis had appeared with a new version of his mousetrap. Ward had thought to lure Eugenia upstairs after the demonstration, but Lizzie had taken the initiative, and with a laughing glance over her shoulder Eugenia disappeared into the nursery, not to be seen again until the children were in bed and Gumwater announced the evening meal.

So far, the meal had been perfectly pleasant, but if Ward had to watch Eugenia moan with delight over a *gâteau au chocolate* for another moment, he'd probably spend in his pants like a boy of fourteen.

He wanted Eugenia and she wanted him. Presumably he should ply her with compliments, lure her upstairs, and kiss her until she wasn't thinking clearly. But that didn't seem right. It didn't fit with the manner in which they talked to each other, with a blunt truthfulness that he'd never before experienced with another woman.

He decided to come to the point. "Eugenia, do you intend to sleep with me tonight?"

She laughed aloud, eyes dancing. He felt about her laughter the way she felt about chocolate. It shimmered through him and made him feel like an unschooled lad, raw and unpracticed.

He set down his wineglass, stood, and moved to her side of the table. She looked up, eyes luminous with amusement and intelligence. "I am considering it."

He crouched down beside her, and the laugh died on her lips. "How can I persuade you? I'm tired of talking about inconsequential things."

"Cake, sir, is never inconsequential," she said merrily.

"Please?"

Their eyes met. "Yes," she said. "Yes, I will, Ward."

His hand slipped behind her head and he pulled her toward him, not roughly, but if he wasn't tasting her, possessing her, inside her, soon, he felt as if he might explode.

Her mouth opened to his with a sense of rightness that flooded through his limbs. He toppled her forward from the chair into his arms, still kissing, and rose to his feet. "May I feed you more cake later, if I promise to satisfy you first?"

"If you are still offering only seven minutes," she said, flicking him a wicked glance from under her lashes, "I'd prefer to finish my dessert now."

Her confidence made her glow, as if she were burning through life at a higher pitch than everyone else.

"Seven hours won't be sufficient," he said in a rough voice, putting her on her feet.

Her smile grew.

Eugenia had sadly few memories of marital pleasure, if the truth were told. After Andrew died, recollection was so painful that she pushed it away. With time, her memories had become fuzzy, overlaid with nostalgia.

But this pleasure, the ferocious bliss that Ward sparked in her?

She didn't intend to forget this, *ever*.

Tonight, she would sleep with a burly, gorgeous man for no better reason than desire. Because he made her laugh, and he made her heart race.

Not for love or duty, but for pleasure.

"I would like a tour of your personal chamber," she said, thinking dizzily that she sounded like a lady of the night. Perhaps a courtesan to a king.

It turned out that Ward's bedchamber was enormous, with a huge bed canopied with curtains fringed in gold marooned in the center of the room like a pleasure boat.

Eugenia stopped short in surprise.

"It came with the house," Ward said.

She turned to tease him, but he had torn off his coat and tossed it on a chair, and was pulling his shirt from his breeches.

Who cared about his ostentatious furniture? Without his coat, Ward's shoulders were even broader than she'd thought, muscles rippling beneath the thin linen of his shirt.

She moved toward him feeling unbalanced, as if

she'd drunk the better part of a bottle of wine. He had turned to the mantelpiece to light a candelabra, so she slid her hands around his shoulders from behind.

Even that slight touch made her thighs clench with longing. She rubbed her cheek against his back, happy to be out of his sight. She felt vulnerable and exposed, as if desire were written on her face for him to read.

"I love your smell," she whispered, kissing his neck. It was powerful like the rest of him, the neck of a man who didn't spend his days in tearooms.

He turned in her arms. "Eugenia Snowe," he said, his voice dark and low, "may I remove your gown?"

"You may—after you remove your shirt." When she first married, Andrew had had to coax her to undress. Even after three months as husband and wife, she still prepared for bed in her own chamber before welcoming him into her bed.

That was the memory of a different woman.

Without a word, his eyes on hers, Ward ripped off his shirt. Eugenia sucked in her breath. His skin was golden, stretched over powerful muscles. His nipples were flat coins flanking the faintest trail of chest hair, leading down a stomach grooved in horizontal ridges.

"Why do you have these?" she asked, reaching out and touching the muscles.

"Riding." Ward stepped closer, crowding her hands so they flattened against his abdomen, reached behind her and began deftly unbuttoning her gown.

Eugenia spread her fingers, marveling at how white her skin looked in contrast to his. Sliding her hands to the sides of his waist didn't reveal an ounce of softness. His body was all coiled power.

At last, her gown loosened, and he pulled it open and forward. Eugenia brought her hands to her bodice and took a step back before she allowed the gown to slide down her front.

Ward whispered something, a curse or a prayer. She allowed her gown to slip again, until it barely covered her nipples.

"Eugenia." His eyes were black with desire.

"Yes?" Her corset was doing its job, holding her breasts where they could be best admired.

She fell back another step, until she could feel the warmth of the fire. A king's courtesan would turn undressing into a performance. She dropped her hands even lower, baring her bosom; the scarlet bows adorning her corset nestled along the lower curve of her breasts.

"No chemise?" Ward's voice was no more than a rasp.

"A chemise would interfere with the line of my gown," Eugenia explained. She turned around and peeked over her shoulder. "Do you see how the smoothly my gown hugs my hips?"

She took his groan as agreement.

"If I let go, this gown will fall straight off," she said, whirling about so her skirts billowed around her ankles.

Ward groaned again.

"You first," she breathed.

Ward tore open the placket on his breeches and his cock sprang forward. It was thick and long, bobbing against the base of his stomach as if it had a will of its own.

"No smalls?" she asked, echoing his question about her chemise.

He shook his head.

"Because they would interfere with the line of your breeches?" she teased.

"When I was in prison, my smalls became infested with fleas. I threw them out and never used that particular garment again."

One of those big hands took hold of his manhood and slowly stroked its whole length. Eugenia's heart quickened at the sight. Her eyes fell lower and his legs were—well, they turned her mouth dry with one glance. They looked carved from warm marble, like those of a Greek athlete poised, javelin in hand.

He stopped just before her, his hands rounding her bottom. As if he somehow knew exactly what would make her dizzy, his right leg slid between her legs and he pulled her forward, grinding her softness against his thigh.

She shocked herself with a panting breath. "That feels. . . ." His thigh was pressing a fold of silk against her most private part.

"Drop your gown, Eugenia," he said in her ear. She heard his order through a blinding flash of sensation from his touch, his smell, his tongue on her ear.

She hadn't even realized that her fingers were still clenched. She looked at him, dazed, and he pried open her fingers and pulled the gown so it slithered to the floor.

She whimpered as he pushed his thigh back between her legs, unprotected by a barrier of silk. "You like that," Ward growled.

Eugenia couldn't find her voice so she nodded, blood thundering through her veins.

He pressed again, harder. "Do you want more?"

In answer, she leaned forward and licked him at the join of his thick neck and shoulder.

"Hell," Ward groaned, his leg abruptly straightening, pitching her against him. His mouth pushed hers open roughly, possessing it without warning or apology.

Eugenia wound her arms around his neck and tilted her head, giving him everything, loving the way Ward plundered her mouth, his tongue thrusting deep, making her legs tremble and her breath turn to frantic pants.

He tore his mouth away and looked down, a curse spilling from his mouth.

Eugenia's corset barely reached her waist. Her only remaining garments were pale silk stockings held up by garters with red bows, and her favorite heeled shoes.

Glancing down, she saw pale skin, curves, and the tuft of red hair that covered her most private place.

"There are no words to describe you," Ward said, his voice strangled and rough. "You're so damn beautiful, Eugenia, like Venus and Diana in one woman. No man could see you without falling to his knees and begging."

"Begging for what?" Eugenia asked achingly.

"This," Ward said, falling to his knees.

Surprised, Eugenia looked down. Was he about to? Andrew had . . . but only months into their marriage, under the covers, and a very few times.

"Oh my God," she breathed as Ward drew her legs apart and his warm tongue ran over the tender flesh on the inside of her thigh.

She held her breath.

When his tongue touched her again, a broken

cry came from Eugenia's lips, and her knees shook so much that she fell against the chair at her back. Ward's hands tightened on her legs, holding her steady as he licked and teased, sending streaks of bliss through her.

Eugenia's mind tumbled from one thing to another, from the acute waves of pure sensation rocking her, to the sight of his bunched thighs crouched before her, to his rumpled chestnut curls, to the way harsh breaths expanded his chest.

Another delicate, twisting caress with his tongue and she sank to her knees. "I want to touch you too," she gasped.

"Not here." Ward leaned forward and scooped her into his arms, coming to his feet in one smooth movement.

Eugenia pressed kisses on his shoulders, loving how they flexed as he carried her across the room to the great bed as if she were light as a meringue.

Her heart was thudding and her body racing with erotic pleasure. All the same, she couldn't suppress a wide smile. Was she meant to be feeling this bubbling laughter, even as a bead of sweat ran down the back of one knee?

Ward laid her on the bed and leaned over her, arms braced on either side. "I see that you are a drunken lover."

"I scarcely had a glass." She arched up, kissing his chin, toeing off her shoes at the same time.

"Drunk on this," he said, taking her hand and wrapping it around his tool, his hand enclosing hers.

Eugenia felt her eyes growing wide. It had been years . . . she'd forgotten what a man felt like, silk and

smooth and hard as rock all at once. Extraordinarily alive, pulsating in her hand.

She tightened her grip.

Ward growled, shifting his weight onto the bed, thrusting into her hand.

"I had forgotten," she breathed.

He pulled back and her hand slid away. "No talk of your husband," he ordered. "Not in this bedchamber, Eugenia."

"I wasn't referring to him in particular."

A flicker of surprise in his eyes as he drew her stockings down her legs, tossing them to the side.

"No, I haven't slept with anyone else." She stretched her arms over her head. Her breasts bobbled, catching Ward's attention, just as she meant them to.

"Just now you kissed my cunny before touching my breasts," she said, thinking about that.

Ward's expression was sending ripples of pleasure through her. Since his legs straddled hers, Eugenia widened her legs just enough to rub against his hair-roughed thighs.

A grin curled the corners of his mouth and he bent over her again. "Your wish is my command. But first . . ."

One of his hands ran down her side, pausing for a second to grip her hip, clenching possessively. "I love this curve."

The hand slid straight down into the sleek warmth between her legs.

Eugenia squeaked and wriggled, arching against the callused, broad finger stroking her. She felt as if little flares of heat were sparking through her, so scorching they should be visible in the air.

"You are going to tell me what you need, aren't you?" Ward's voice came from some deep part of his chest. Commanding her.

"Yes," she gasped, her breath ragged and harsh.

He kept his hand where it was, but bent his head to her right breast. She froze, waiting . . . waiting . . .

"Eugenia."

"Please!" She was shivering all over. "I wish—I'd like to touch you."

A smile ghosted over his mouth. "Anytime."

"Why are you so much larger than other men?" Her hands slid over his shoulders.

"You seem to like it."

"That's not the point. You are not what I imagined an Oxford don to look like."

"When I was thrown in prison, there was nothing to do. I started to plan an escape from the moment the door locked behind me, of course, but it took a few weeks. I passed the time as productively as I could. I discovered that I like physical exertion."

He did something with his fingers, and the flash of heat that streaked through her body made sweat spring out on her brow.

"Enjoy that, do you?" Ward murmured.

Eugenia couldn't even answer because at that moment Ward lowered his body onto hers and finally, finally, put his mouth on her breast.

Andrew—no, she would not think about Andrew!

Men loved her breasts.

Ward loved her breasts.

His hands shaped their heavy weight as his mouth moved from one to the other, as if they were two presents he was determined to enjoy at the

same moment. His tongue trapped her nipple, made her moan and squeak and writhe against him.

"Ward!" she cried. She had managed to raise one knee but the other was trapped under his body. And she wanted . . .

He looked down at her and a giddy smile broke out all over her face. This was more fun than she'd had in years.

"Drunk," he said, with obvious satisfaction, bending over and rubbing her nose with his. Then he slid his tongue in her mouth.

It was strangely erotic to find that he faintly tasted of her.

"More?" he asked, lifting up his head. His eyes were heavy lidded, sensual in a way that made her arch again, impatiently.

"Would you like the same?" she gasped.

"I want everything. I want to taste the two of us intermingled." Ward shifted his hips and the broad head of his cock slid over her sleek opening.

"Tell me," he commanded her, one hand possessively encircling a breast, his words muffled because he was suckling her hard.

"Oh, please," Eugenia cried, feverish and desperate. "Please come inside me."

"One moment," he said, reaching over to the small table at the side of the bed.

"What's that?" she asked, coming up on one elbow.

"A French letter," he said, "a condom for preventing conception."

"We needn't," Eugenia said. "It takes repeated effort and time to conceive a child; I was married for months."

"That is not what my father taught me," Ward said, not bothering to close the drawer. "Apparently I am the result of a single encounter." He held something that looked like a wrinkled sausage casing with an incongruous ribbon stitched at one end.

"You keep it right there . . . in your bedside table?" Eugenia had the queasy realization that she was likely only the latest of several, if not many, women who had visited this bed and listened to Ward's smoky commands.

He was slipping the thing over himself but he looked up and grinned at her. "Are you imagining me as the master of a harem?"

Eugenia's brows drew together. "Not precisely." She peered at what he was doing. "That looks very uncomfortable."

"You might conceive a child if I don't wear it." He slid it back off and held it up. "The function is fairly obvious."

She pulled her legs to the side and came to a sitting position. "I never conceived during my marriage. Although I suppose there is a risk. Perhaps we should reconsider—"

She began sliding toward the edge of the bed, but she broke off with a squeak when Ward grabbed her wrist. A second later she was flat on her back beneath him, one of his big hands locking both of hers over her head.

"You won't force me if I have changed my mind," she said, looking up at him. *She* might be unwilling, but her body wasn't. It was trembling all over, longing for his touch.

It took all her resolve not to arch upwards again, to beg for his body.

"What's wrong?" His voice was dark, implacable and he was looking into her eyes so deeply that she felt as if he could see to the bottom of her soul.

Maybe . . .

No.

She had to keep her self-respect, and allowing that thing inside her would make her feel dirty. Soiled.

"I understand that your life is different from mine," she said, trying to explain in the least objectionable language possible. "I am not suggesting in the least that having that—that object in your possession indicates moral turpitude."

For a moment he just stared at her, and then he threw back his head and roared with laughter. "*Moral turpitude?*"

Eugenia gave him a little frown. "I am trying to be tactful."

"Just be honest," he suggested.

"I don't want that French thing inside me."

His eyes went to the object in question. "You dislike them?"

"Actually, I've never seen one before."

"Well?"

"I prefer not to."

"Why not? I promise to give you pleasure even wearing it."

He shifted. He was rubbing against her and despite herself, her knees fell open and she sucked in a breath. But she reached down and pushed him away. "Don't touch me with that!"

It provoked a flash of frustration that she'd not seen in his eyes before. He came up on his knees, straddling her thighs, and said, "Eugenia, I must ask you to explain yourself."

"I suppose I am more scrupulous than most," she said desperately.

"I don't know you well enough to compare."

"I don't want that thing inside me after it's been inside other women!" she burst out. "I expect you've washed it, but I don't care. I apologize if you think me overly fastidious."

Ward stared at her for a second and then silently reached into the little drawer in the table by the bed, which was still hanging open. He withdrew a handful of French letters, and let them rain down on the bed.

They fell all over her breasts and belly, thin and slippery, sewn at the top with ribbons of different colors.

"I would never reuse one," he said. "But more important, no woman has been in this particular bed, or indeed in any other bed containing me, for almost two years."

"Oh," Eugenia gasped. "I'm so—I'm happy to hear that they are only used once. But why were you so abstinent?" In the back of her mind she began to catalogue the reasons a healthy young man might avoid the opposite sex, none of them good. Her stomach churned.

Ward looked at her and burst out with a bellow of laughter. "No, not illness. Are you always this distrustful?"

She cocked her head, feeling gladness spread through her like warm honey. He didn't have a disease. "It's a consequence of Snowe's. I can assure you that running a registry would cure anyone of optimism."

"Even given my brief acquaintance with Otis and

Lizzie, I see your point," Ward said. He gave her a rueful smile. "I was betrothed to Mia for a year, and I had wooed her for months before that. The betrothal ended when I was thrown in prison, and shortly thereafter, my brother and sister appeared on my doorstep."

Eugenia ran a hand along his cheek. "You have had a trying year."

"That's an understatement," he said, lying down beside her and turning his head, a sinful gleam in his eyes. "Don't you think it's high time someone made me feel better?"

Chapter Twenty-six

*W*ard couldn't get air into his lungs.

Next to him, Eugenia sat up, sending French letters skidding off the bed in all directions, turned onto her hands and knees and crawled on top of him. Her hair fell forward, curtaining his face.

"Hell and damnation," Ward said hoarsely. "You're the most gorgeous woman I've ever seen."

"Good." She lowered her head and licked a path right down to his nipple. Ward propped himself up on his elbows, not bothering to stop the curse word that tumbled from his lips.

Eugenia looked up with a happy grin and wriggled backward.

The moment she put her tongue to his tool, Ward let out a groan that reverberated through his body.

He felt as if he were in a dream. Ruby-red lips, hair

falling like curly silk over his legs, and Eugenia's half-lidded eyes as she plainly enjoyed what she was doing.

"Enough," he said hoarsely. He needed to come inside her, to possess that curvy sensual body.

A moment later he had her flat on her back, a surprised laugh on her lips. He started kissing her ravenously, plunging into her mouth while he grabbed one of the condoms strewn across the bed.

"Wait a minute. Not that one!" she said, laughing.

Was she going to laugh all night? Probably.

"I wanted a *blue* ribbon."

Ward obtained his French letters from the very best purveyor in Bond Street. They were outrageously expensive and guaranteed to please a lady, though he didn't think the establishment had the ribbon color in mind when they promised satisfaction.

He bent down and licked Eugenia's rosy nipple, drawing it into the warm depth of his mouth. She pushed up toward him, her legs moving restlessly. "Ward!"

"I'll give it to you," he breathed. Damn it, he wanted to lick and suck every inch of her luscious skin.

He breached her silky, glistening folds and slowly fed his fat cock into her. She was so tight, much more than he'd experienced before. She felt so good that sweat broke out on his shoulders.

Eugenia was squirming, eyes squeezed shut, trying to help him. He took hold of her leg and pulled it up, allowing him to slide in a fraction of an inch, a grunt breaking from his lips.

"Look at me," he whispered.

Another gasp broke from Eugenia's lips. He had to see her eyes. If she was in pain . . .

Maybe he was too large. Or she was too small.

Or maybe he was a madman because every time he glanced down, the sight of his thick cock entering her made him shake with the need to thrust forward.

Fast and hard.

"Eugenia," he rasped, clearing his throat. "Open your eyes."

Pleasure-drenched eyes opened, staring at him with a trace of indignation. "Excuse me," she said with another gasp and a wriggle. "I'm trying to make room where there isn't any."

No agony in her eyes. Perhaps a tinge of discomfort. Definitely need.

His head fell forward, just enough so he could kiss her. He kept his hips rigid, in place. He pushed her leg higher until she finally understood and wrapped her legs around his waist.

"Ward!" she gasped. But he wanted it to last, slowly, so it was good for her, because damn, once he was seated in her, he wouldn't be able to stop himself.

"Do you need more?" he asked hoarsely. "I'll give you more." He lowered his head again and nipped her lip. "You have to tell me what you need."

Eugenia's eyes opened again. "I'll *take* what I need," she cried, panting. Before he could stop her, she arched up, impaling herself a few more inches.

This was a side of lovemaking that he'd never imagined. Hotter, funnier, sweeter. Better in every way. He held himself immobile, loving the flush high on Eugenia's cheekbones, the way she was biting her bottom lip.

"More?"

"Yes, you miserable fiend. I need you. I need *all* of you. *Now.*"

He saw no discomfort in her eyes, just indignation and desire.

With a deep groan, Ward thrust into the hottest, tightest place he'd ever been. Ever. Without exception.

Eugenia's eyes flew open and a cry broke from her lips.

He froze.

"Do that again," she commanded, her fingers clenching on his shoulders.

He did it again. And again.

He set a hard pace, braced on his forearms, sweat dripping off his body. He was fighting for control, an orgasm always in danger of roaring up his legs.

Beneath him, Eugenia was writhing, broken words rasping from her throat, nails biting into his back.

His balls drew up, ready to give her everything he had.

At just the perfect moment, she whispered, in a tone of greatest surprise, "I can't hold back any longer, Ward."

"For God's sake," he groaned. "Don't."

She gave a ragged moan and clamped around him with her arms, her legs, her cunny. Every part of her tight and warm and holding him.

"Ward!" she cried, her convulsions shaking both their bodies, as if they were one.

Hips pumping, Ward let himself go, heat roaring up his legs, up his spine, blinding him to anything but the pleasure blasting through his body.

Chapter Twenty-seven

Eugenia sprawled on top of Ward in a sweaty heap, trying to catch her breath.

"What were you called as a child?" he asked, his voice rough and satisfied.

"Eugenia. What were you called?"

"Teddy. You had no pet name at all? No one ever thought you were an angel or a duckling?"

"None. I don't like that sort of comparison. I'm the opposite of an angel, I'm afraid, and always was."

"Are you indeed?" He waggled his eyebrows, treating her to a fine display of false surprise. "You, Eugenia Snowe, savior of disobedient children all over England, are not angelic?"

"I'm a savior of their parents. I'm sure there are many children who devoutly wish that Snowe's

would go out of business, leaving them free of a governess."

"It's true that they'd almost certainly prefer to make mud pies than cakes." Ward ran a hand slowly down her back and over the curve of her bottom.

Eugenia was coming to the pleasing realization that Ward's boast had not been a hollow one—it seemed he did possess the stamina of an eighteen-year-old when it came to repeat performances.

He raised his head and pressed a kiss on her mouth. "You are the most formidable, exciting woman I have ever known."

Another kiss, on her nose.

"Definitely the most beautiful."

A kiss on each eye.

"The best lover I've ever had. Ever."

"Thank you," she said softly, kissing him back.

"And the evening isn't over," Ward said, leaning back, his fingers laced under his head. Which put all those muscles in his arms on display, she couldn't help noticing.

"I should return to my room," Eugenia said, not moving. "I'm afraid one of the children will have a bout of sleeplessness and come looking for comfort."

"I locked the door."

"Even so . . . what if they knocked?"

"What if they did?" He rolled over on his side, head propped on one hand.

"Ward! You can't let your brother and sister know that—that we are lovers!"

"I've no intention of telling anyone. If either of them knocks, I'll go to the library and you can stay here. I like the thought of you sleeping in my bed."

She gave him a rueful smile. Rational thought was starting to steal back into her mind. How long did *affaires* last? Surely one day at most when children were in the house.

He read her thought. "No," he said. "Not yet. I still want you, and you want me."

Undeniable. But . . .

His expression changed; he leaned over her, eyes sober. "Eugenia Snowe."

"Yes?" She was obviously a hussy at heart, because the only thing she really wanted to do was pull him into just the right position to start all over again.

"I want you to sleep the night with me."

"It's not proper," she said. Did that mean he merely wished to sleep? His body seemed to be . . .

A smile touched his lips. "I don't care. Do you?"

She tried to think about that. She hadn't realized how long Ward's lashes were. They were warm brown with gold tips that touched his cheeks.

"Yes, I do. I decided as a child that I would be the most proper person in any room."

His eyes softened. "I'm afraid you'll have to give that up, *angel*."

"I'll call you Teddy," she warned.

"If you stay for two weeks, a mere fortnight, I'll let you play 'most proper person' every day. For a while."

Eugenia laughed. "What are you talking about?"

"Propriety," he said, kissing her cheekbone. "It's nothing more than an act, isn't it?"

"What do you mean?"

He finally settled his groin between her legs and Eugenia let out a little moan, her hands curling around his shoulders.

"Think about the royal duke's chamber pot." But before she could bring it to mind, he dived into a kiss so hungry that Eugenia's fingers clenched in his hair. They kissed for long minutes, caught somewhere between lust and satisfaction.

"Were you thinking of the chamber pot?" Ward asked huskily, pulling away.

"What?" Eugenia breathed, running her tongue along the generous curve of his lower lip.

"Everyone uses one."

He was propped on one elbow again, which left a hand free to caress her breast. Eugenia tried to understand what he was talking about. "Are we discussing the mounting block on your carriage?" she asked.

"Propriety is nothing more than an empty game," Ward stated. "All those ladies sitting around in drawing rooms, pretending that they don't sweat, or piss, or break wind, are merely playing."

Eugenia rolled her eyes. "What is your point?" She kept her eyes on his but her hand stole down his front, caressing his taut stomach and then lower.

"Haven't you ever been to dinner when the chamber pot was behind a screen, in the corner?"

"Alas, yes." Eugenia edged closer, feeling a restless surge of energy that had everything to do with the hard length throbbing against her middle.

"I was perhaps fifteen the first time I was bid to join the adults at dinner," Ward said. "I remember hearing a lady—I'll spare you her name—disappearing behind that screen and the most extraordinary sounds soon after."

Eugenia snorted and hid her face against his shoulder.

"It sounded like a waterfall," Ward continued. "Yet

all the guests sat there and made insipid conversation while pretending not to hear anything. It was at that moment I decided that I had no interest in polite society—or any society."

"Is that why you have never attended balls and the like?"

"Exactly," he said, nipping her lower lip. "My point is that you shouldn't worry about propriety, Eugenia. Stay with me." He rolled on top of her. "My body is at your service."

She let out a startled giggle.

"Take me," he said, his voice dropping. "I'm yours. No one will know. As far as the world is concerned, you are generously paying me a visit until a new governess can be found. Miss Lloyd-Fantil assured me that she would send someone as soon as possible."

"Oh, Susan," Eugenia said a bit crossly. "She thinks—"

"I like her," Ward interrupted. "Give me a fortnight." He dropped a kiss on her lips. "The court case is approaching frighteningly quickly. I need you to help with the children's instruction. What if they are summoned before the House of Lords?"

"That is most unlikely," Eugenia said. She considered. "Although it would be well to prepare them for the possibility, however remote."

"My solicitors tell me that they might ask Otis, in particular, about his father's wishes."

Eugenia's mind fell into chaos because Ward had slid down, just enough to kiss her breast.

Why shouldn't she stay? No one knew she was here. No one would care, her mind prompted her. She was a widow.

Squirming under Ward's attentions, she felt *alive*.

"I'll think about it," she said, the words escaping on a pant. "I promise to . . ."

Ward had never expected rational thought to work. He didn't need logic. Eugenia's breast was luscious and perfectly rounded, her nipple a small, ripe cherry. He kissed her until her legs were moving restlessly under him, her hands slipping over his back and shoulder, skating lower.

Then he moved up to take her mouth with a needy moan. She tasted like woman and desire and everything good in life. Slipping one arm around her slender waist, he pulled her tightly against him, loving the way her curves slipped into his body's hollows.

They were made for each other, like Adam and Eve.

He took in a ragged breath and rolled over, bringing her with him so he could run his hands over the silky skin of her back, over her arse, curving inward. "I want you," he said in her ear. His hand slipped between her legs.

His fingers slid through wet folds and air whooshed from Eugenia's lungs in a strangled moan.

Ward reached over and grabbed a French letter—pink ribbon this time. Eugenia slid backward, waiting, her teeth biting into her lush bottom lip so hard that he could see a mark.

"I want to taste you first," he said, tying the ribbon.

"No," she choked. "Now, Ward, now!"

"Or what?"

She shook her head, and the fog of desire cleared from her eyes. "Or I slip this knee toward the middle of your body?"

"Stay a fortnight," he commanded.

"I shouldn't," she mumbled. Ward pulled her over him and rubbed her in all the right places.

"Yes, you should."

Eugenia's eyes flew open. "Are you trying to *blackmail* me?" Her tone was outraged, and pink popped up in her cheeks.

Ward couldn't hold in his laughter. "Would it work?"

"No!"

"I'm begging you. See . . . ? I'm begging." He flipped her over, pulled her legs apart and slid down until his head was close to the pinkest, sweetest part of Eugenia's body.

A cry broke from her lips the moment he licked her. Ward found himself smiling as he loved her until her legs were shaking.

He moved up, positioning himself in just the right place. He let go with the full force of his being, dimly aware that he'd never before made love with this wild, keen concentration, his hips thrusting in tandem with his pounding heart.

He kept just enough presence of mind to note the way Eugenia was whimpering, her hands pulling him closer, crying his name over and over until the word dissolved into a scream.

She was as passionate as he was, wild, clawing his back, her body convulsing in pleasure. He savored every moment, then set her on top of him and watched as she braced herself, found her rhythm, laughed down at him.

And rode him until her body convulsed again, driving him to lose control. A rough shout broke from his chest and he gave her all he had.

"A fortnight," he said, his voice not more than a rasp.

Eugenia turned to look at him, and her lush lips turned up at the corners. She tried to answer, cleared her throat, tried again.

"I'm too tired to depart directly," she whispered.

"You are exquisite," he breathed, running his thumb along her lower lip.

She smiled, eyes drenched with pleasure. "I'm partial to you as well."

They fell asleep wrapped together like puppies.

Or lovers.

Chapter Twenty-eight

Thursday, May 28, 1801

Eugenia woke in her own bedchamber to the sound of Clothilde pulling back the curtains. She sat up, blinking.

She didn't feel like a fallen woman. Though she had certainly played the part, not least when Ward escorted her to her chamber at the crack of dawn.

"Good morning, madame," Clothilde said. "I have brought your breakfast tray. Will we return to London today?"

"I promised Mr. Reeve I would stay until we can provide him a new governess. Probably a fortnight." Eugenia scrambled out of bed. "There will be a hearing in the House of Lords in a few weeks, and the

children have a great deal to learn before they are suited for polite society."

"Ruby is mystified by the two of them," Clothilde said, ringing the bell to order a bath. "Two of *our* governesses they've had, and still they do not wash behind their ears."

"I must teach them the rules of address, how to bow and curtsy, how to comport themselves in adult company. And I must teach Lizzie to be herself, not a character from a play."

"Ruby says the little girl is *trop dramatique*," Clothilde said, nodding.

Eugenia had been longing for a new challenge— and now she had one. Her days would be full, and her nights . . . blissful.

She poured herself a cup of tea and sat on the bed, as the tray occupied the only chair. "Have you noticed that this house is strangely lacking in furniture, Clothilde?"

"It is the same everywhere," her maid reported. "Mr. Reeve bought the house with some furniture, by all reports, and has made no changes. Six bedchambers do not have a stick in them. And, madame, no maids live in."

"None?"

"Not a one. They come from the village every day. Mr. Gumwater considers women in the house to be a nuisance." She wrinkled her nose. "I have met others of his type."

"The kitchen help is all male?"

Clothilde nodded. "Monsieur Marcel, the chef, is from Languedoc, not far from one of my aunts. He has no kitchen maids, not a one. All the same, his bread is *magnifique*. As good as my mother's, madame."

Eugenia felt another surge of happiness. Perhaps she would go to the kitchens and ask if Monsieur Marcel would try a few of her ideas. She had imagined a chocolate cake with a strong ginger flavor. Or a lemon tart with bits of rind to give it extra piquancy.

"I'll take the children downstairs for their first baking lesson today. Is Monsieur Marcel the sort who will dislike children in his kitchen?"

"No, no," her maid said. "He is a true Frenchman, so I am sure that he loves children."

Never mind the fact that Clothilde herself frowned on anyone under the age of ten, owing to their propensity to get dirty.

Eugenia was just out of her bath when a footman delivered a note from Ward.

~Would you like to have Lizzie and Otis at dinner?

She scrawled her reply below his sentence, folded it, and sent it back.

~Absolutely. We must begin instruct them in table manners and polite conversation immediately.

He wrote back.

~I fear that you'll moan while eating chocolate soufflé—which I have requested for this evening.

She began a new sheet of foolscap.

~The presence of your siblings in the dining room should prevent you from lunging across the table.

Her writing was neat and ladylike, his slanted and fast.

~All I can think about is whether you are having a bath.

An image of *his* bath leapt to her mind: water glistening on strong, sleek legs, running down the wide arc of his shoulders. She swallowed hard, hesitated, and ignored his provocation.

~*Will Otis bring Jarvis to the table?*

His answer:

~*Would that pose a problem?*
~*No society, polite or otherwise, allows rodents to share the table.*
~*Jarvis is required to remain in his sack when outside the nursery.*

Apparently Jarvis went where Otis went. Eugenia shuddered at the thought. The sack would have to stay out of sight at all times. Under the table.

~*I might give the children their first baking lesson, if you approve?*
~*Perhaps when the time comes Otis can simply present the assembled Lords with a cake, thereby proving my fitness as a guardian.*

Eugenia considered how best to answer, but in the end, she didn't.

She had the sense that Ward disapproved of the cake baking, for all he kept a jesting tone. He disliked it on principle, as if she were teaching his siblings menial labor.

A short time later, she collected Lizzie and Otis and took them down to the kitchen—because whether their older brother approved or not, thanks to Snowe's Registry, the ability to bake a credible sponge was a calling card in polite society.

Monsieur Marcel had yellow hair and a magnifi-

cent curling mustache. Eugenia nodded her head and introduced herself in his native language, which earned her a beaming smile and a flourishing bow.

To her surprise, Lizzie stepped forward, bobbed an awkward curtsy, and asked in fluent French what he was cooking.

"I am contemplating the evening's meal," the chef responded.

"Contemplating?" Otis echoed, also in perfect French. "Why do you have to think about it?"

Eugenia choked back a laugh. Before her eyes, Lizzie and Otis took over the baking lesson, following directions more or less adroitly at the same time they asked questions.

"How did you come by such excellent French?" Eugenia asked Otis, while his sister watched the chef whisk together eggs and sugar with impressive speed.

"We lived in England only four months of the year," he explained. "We stayed in Paris during the winters, but we also went about France in the wagon."

That went some way toward explaining how Lady Lisette and Lord Darcy had never been recognized in their theatrical career.

When the cake was in the oven, they all sat down at the kitchen table and Monsieur Marcel told Eugenia how difficult it was to manage a kitchen with only one knife boy. "Not even a scullery maid!" he said, shaking his head so vigorously that his mustaches trembled.

"You placed miracles on our table last night, given such difficult circumstances," Eugenia said warmly. "I shall do my best to persuade Mr. Reeve to hire adequate help."

"It's not the master," the chef said. "It is Mr. Gumwater." He glanced at Lizzie and didn't elaborate, but his shrug spoke volumes.

"Did you know that your head looks as if it's covered in snails?" Otis interjected.

"Otis," Eugenia said, "one never makes remarks of a personal nature. Please apologize to Monsieur Marcel at once."

"I apologize," Otis said, looking at the chef expectantly.

"We French adore *les escargots*," Monsieur Marcel told him. "I am happy to resemble my nation's favorite food."

Otis grinned. "I could use wax to make my hair resemble rat tails!"

"You too could be French," Monsieur said, bellowing with laughter. "I assure you that the biggest rats in the world are to be found in my beloved Montpellier!"

This, Eugenia thought, was precisely why she insisted upon baking lessons: young English ladies and gentlemen needed to understand their households were run by real people.

"Monsieur, I wonder if I could beg you to make a variation on a cake?" she asked. "I should warn you that it exists in my imagination only."

"*Intéressant!* I would welcome it, Madame Snowe," the chef replied. "My skills are growing rusty. Monsieur Reeve eats whatever I cook and shows little interest in food." He capped that with a roll of his eyes.

"My visit will last a fortnight," Eugenia said, beaming as she rose from the table. "I shall rejoin you after Mr. Reeve hires kitchen staff. I would not wish to increase your work until you have adequate help."

Monsieur bowed magnificently. "I shall count the

moments, Madame Snowe." He turned to the children. "You shall have your own cake for dessert tonight."

"I should like to use a quince next time," Lizzie said. "I never knew what that play meant when it calls for quinces in the pastry."

"Hush," Eugenia said, taking her hand. "For one thing, quinces are not in season. But more importantly, rather than requesting cakes from *Romeo and Juliet*, you must thank Monsieur Marcel for his kind instruction."

"I am most grateful," Lizzie warbled, and curtsied once more. Otis's bow involved a waggle of the waist that made him look like a crane with a sprained ankle.

Their French notwithstanding, there was work to be done.

Back in the nursery, Ruby supervised as the children washed their hands and faces.

Then Eugenia took over. "I'm going to leave the room and enter it again. I would like you to imagine that I am the Duchess of Gilner."

Lizzie's nose wrinkled. "I don't like her."

"A lady never expresses a negative opinion of another person except in private," Eugenia said. "Greet me as if I was your revered grandmama, come to evaluate the nursery."

"Do you mean, as if I liked her?"

"That's precisely what I mean."

"You want us to lie!" Lizzie cried dramatically.

"I want you to *act*," Eugenia corrected her. "At the right time, in the right way."

Eugenia hadn't seen Ward all day, and by evening desire glowed in her like a banked fire. The mere thought of him made her knees weak.

She chose a gown that promised more than it revealed, since the children were joining them. It was indigo blue, made of a silk so heavy that it fell like a column to the ground.

"Diamonds in your hair?" Clothilde asked. She hadn't said a word, but Eugenia knew perfectly well that her maid knew of her *affaire*. Clothilde plainly approved—she was French, after all—but even after years together, they maintained a certain decorum.

"I believe I would prefer the silver net," Eugenia said. "If you brought it, that is."

"Certainly, madame," Clothilde said, clearly pained by the insinuation that she would make such an error.

"With the silver heels," Eugenia said.

"The blue slippers would be preferable," Clothilde said. "In my opinion, silver might convey the impression that you are expensive."

"I *am* expensive. I fail to see how that is relevant."

"Gentlemen like to pretend that their wives will not be a burden on the household accounts. This gives them license to grumble, and pretend to have been deceived in years after."

"I have no intention of marrying Mr. Reeve," Eugenia stated. "Therefore, I shall wear the silver shoes and look as if I am expensive as the queen herself."

"Certainly, madame," Clothilde said.

"You needn't wait up," Eugenia added, taking up the silk shawl that accompanied the gown.

"I hope it is a pleasant evening, madame." Clothilde's French accent lent volumes to the prosaic statement.

"I have every reason to believe it will be," Eugenia said, her smile widening as their eyes met in the mirror.

Chapter Twenty-nine

On coming down the stairs for the evening meal, Eugenia encountered Gumwater, who informed her that dinner would be served in a small chamber off the ballroom. He offered no escort, so Eugenia walked alone across the ballroom listening to the tap of her heels. The room resonated with an empty, windy sound that suggested no one had danced there since the seventeenth century.

She entered the parlor to find Ward alone, elbow on the mantelpiece, staring at the fireplace, his powerful features lit from below, as if he were a medieval warrior at a bonfire, contemplating the next morning's battle.

It was a good thing that she hadn't met Ward in her debut season. Andrew had been a glowing, golden

boy, but Ward was all man, and not merely because he was burly in comparison to her late husband.

"What are you thinking about?" she asked.

He straightened. "You."

Eugenia grinned. "Complimentary thoughts?"

He glanced at the open door. "Lascivious ones."

They smiled at each other, like two cats sharing a stolen bowl of cream.

"I was also considering whether I would run out of French letters by the end of the fortnight," he added, clarifying things. "May I offer you a glass of wine?"

He moved over to the decanters on the sideboard. "I've banished Gumwater. He's not used to women in the house and it makes him tetchy. A glass of sherry?"

"No, thank you. A glass of red wine would be very pleasant." Ladies were supposed to drink sherry before meals, but Eugenia liked to consider that a suggestion rather than a rule.

"Of course."

"What will you do now that you're no longer at the university?" she asked.

"I am adapting my paper-rolling machine to steam," he answered, handing her a glass of ruby-colored wine.

"What increase in page production do you expect?"

He blinked, surprised.

"Isn't that the obvious question?"

"From one entrepreneur to another, yes, it is."

Eugenia took a sip of wine, eyeing him over the rim of her glass. "I would also be curious to know how large the steam-driven machine will be. Do the printing establishments on Fleet Street have space to accommodate a steam engine?"

Ward's eyes lit up. "The question of the size of the engine itself is only one of the restrictions I'm wrestling with—"

But he broke off as the door opened and Ruby ushered in Lizzie and Otis.

Lizzie swept a deep curtsy. She was, Eugenia realized, wearing her veil, but it was pinned back, giving her the solemn look of a nun.

Eugenia greeted her and turned to Otis, who was wearing a leather bag over one shoulder, trimmed with black satin. He managed a reasonable bow, given that the bag was visibly squirming.

Instead of formally greeting his siblings, Ward gave Lizzie a tug on one of her curls and poked at Jarvis.

"Don't!" Otis squealed, but there was no offense in his voice.

"Jarvis may not leave his carrier until you return to the nursery," Ruby reminded Otis before she left.

Ward put a warm hand on Eugenia's back. "Here is Gumwater with our meal."

Thank goodness the meal was set at a round table, because it would have felt very odd if Ward had been at one end and Eugenia at the other. Once the butler left the room, Eugenia watched closely to ensure that Lizzie and Otis chose the right silverware.

Monsieur Marcel had clearly taken Eugenia's presence as a challenge; Gumwater announced a first course of *la poularde à la Montmorencie*, garnished with a ragout *a l'Allemande* to be followed by a second course with three entrées.

Otis appeared to have easily assimilated the lessons she gave them that afternoon. Lizzie kept forgetting and using the wrong fork, or talking with her mouth

full, mostly because she was so excited to tell Ward about cake baking that she couldn't stop talking.

"Monsieur Marcel is a miraculous marvel," Otis said, trying out a tongue twister.

"He is," Eugenia agreed, "but he won't be your chef much longer, Mr. Reeve, unless you hire a cook, two kitchen maids, and a couple of scullery maids."

Ward looked surprised. "Has he informed Gumwater if he is in need of help?"

"Mr. Gumwater won't have women in the house," Lizzie said, bouncing in her seat. "Ruby says that she—and Mrs. Snowe and her maid, of course—are the only women allowed to sleep under Mr. Gumwater's roof."

Ward raised an eyebrow. "It appears that I lost ownership of my roof."

"In addition to the cook and kitchen maids, you might think about a housekeeper," Eugenia said, "one who might help you furnish the house. Lizzie, you mustn't bounce at the table."

"I feel like it," Lizzie said thickly.

"Please do not speak with food in your mouth," Eugenia said patiently.

The little girl narrowed her eyes. She pulled her veil forward and draped it over her face. "You needn't watch me."

"A lady never wears a veil when dining in company," Ward put in.

Lizzie pulled her veil to the side, just enough so that she could glare at her brother. "Lady Lisette did whatever she wanted to!"

"Our mother was not a lady," Ward stated. "You are, which means you cannot bounce, chew with food in your mouth, or wear a veil while eating."

Eugenia intervened. "I've been wondering what it was like to live in a theater wagon. Did you like it?"

"No," Lizzie said, pushing her veil behind her head once again.

"It wasn't so bad," Otis said.

"It was rubbish," his sister snapped. "It was small, and smelled in the rain. There wasn't anywhere to put books or clothes. And we couldn't go to *school*."

Ward felt his gut tighten. The more he heard about his siblings' life, the more he despised his mother. It was an uncomfortable feeling.

"What do you think that your parents enjoyed about the stage?" Eugenia asked.

"Acting," Lizzie said. "Lady Lisette loved acting parts."

"Mother was very good," Otis put in, apparently undismayed by his sister's earlier snub.

"No, she was not good," Lizzie retorted. "She liked to do soliloquies and take up the whole stage. You're not supposed to do that. The troupe is supposed to work together. That's why—" She broke off and took a bite of creamed spinach.

"Was your father a good actor?" Ward asked.

"He was bollocks at it," Otis said, with a blinding smile that Ward had seen only a few times. "That's why he worked the curtains."

"He also didn't want to be recognized," his sister said, her voice tight. "Lady Lisette would have been very angry."

From the corner of his eye, Ward could see that Otis had illicitly taken Jarvis out of his carrier and was stroking him on his lap. He should probably say something, but he sympathized. The very mention of Lady Lisette made him want to pull Eugenia onto his

lap and kiss her until he forgot about the conversation.

"Do you know what I do when I'm angry?" Eugenia asked, in something of a non sequitur.

"What?" Lizzie asked.

"I shout and scream. I try not to keep it bottled up inside."

Ward frowned. Lizzie needed to learn how to be a lady, not how to shout. She already did that plenty, mostly aimed at her brother.

"Perhaps it is time for the ladies to retire for a cup of tea?" he asked Eugenia pointedly.

Eugenia didn't glance at him. "It can be cathartic to scream. You allow the anger go through your voice and into the air."

"My brother and sister have no need to learn to scream," Ward stated.

"It's not screaming, per se," Eugenia said, looking at him. Her eyes were compassionate, almost as if she thought his siblings were forlorn paupers. As if they'd grown up hungry.

The thought chilled him. "Was there always enough food for you to eat?"

Otis didn't look up, but the curve of his neck stiffened. Bloody hell.

"Until Father died," Lizzie clarified. "Lady Lisette always said that practicalities were tiresome."

"Hell and damnation," Ward snarled.

"That's a gentleman's version of a scream, Lizzie," Eugenia said.

"Did it send your anger into the air?" Otis asked, with the look of a child who has just learned a new phrase and is aware that he isn't supposed to repeat it under any circumstances.

But plans to do so as soon as he's in private.

"Never say that phrase around ladies," Ward warned.

"You just did," Lizzie pointed out.

"It was an aberration. I apologize to you, Lizzie, and to Mrs. Snowe." He managed to arrange his mouth into a line with curves at the ends. A smile, of sorts.

"I like cursing better than screaming," Lizzie said. "I know lots of words already."

"All right," Eugenia said, to Ward's profound dismay. "But never, ever in public. Do you promise, Lizzie?"

"Yes!"

"*I* can do it in public if I want to," Otis crowed.

"Not until you're eighteen," Eugenia declared, "and never in polite company. Now Lizzie—and Otis, if you'd like—I want you to think of something that made you very, very angry. Something you want to forget."

Ward had gone rigid with annoyance. This is what came of introducing the children to a woman who wasn't born and bred a lady. She didn't understand that if Lizzie even whispered "damnation" in a ballroom, she'd be ruined.

"Are you ready?" Eugenia said.

"Will you do it as well?" Lizzie asked. She had a strained look around her eyes, like a horse attacked by a cloud of flies.

"I am not angry," Eugenia said. "This is your turn."

Lizzie closed her eyes and took a breath so deep that her narrow chest expanded visibly.

"What in the *hell* do you think you're doing?" Ward hissed at Eugenia.

She turned her clear eyes to him. "I will be happy to discuss it with you at a later time."

Lizzie's eyes popped open. "I'm ready!"

Eugenia smiled. "Go ahead, Lizzie."

Ward groaned internally. He was new to fathering, but he was certain that encouraging a young lady to curse was not appropriate.

His little sister sat up straight, squared her shoulders, opened her mouth and let out a string of curses in a high, shrill, and very loud voice. After the first three, Ward's ears rang. After seven or eight, Gumwater burst through the door at a breathless trot.

Eugenia leaned forward and nodded, and Lizzie stopped. The silence that followed had the crystal clear precision of early dawn.

"That hurt my ears," Otis cried. He was huddled over, his hands protectively clasped around his pet's head. "You hurt Jarvis, too!"

Gumwater muttered something and walked back out again.

"I feel better," Lizzie said, looking surprised.

"I feel worse," Ward said. "Where did you learn all that filthy language, Lizzie?"

She didn't seem to hear him; her eyes were fixed on Eugenia. "Did I do it right?"

"Absolutely right," Eugenia replied, rising to her feet. "I'm glad it made you feel better. Now it is time for the ladies to retire to the drawing room."

"We needn't honor that rule tonight," Ward said, standing.

Lizzie danced around the table and grabbed Eugenia's hand as if they'd been friends for years. "I thought of something else that makes me angry."

"We will wait for tomorrow," Eugenia said. "You have an imaginative turn of phrase, and I believe Gumwater was shocked."

She glanced at Ward. "As was your older brother."

"They are mostly taken from Middleton plays," Lizzie confided.

"Don't gentlemen stay at the table and smoke a cheroot?" Otis asked Ward. He had dropped Jarvis back into his carrying sack.

"No," Ward said. "You're too young. If anyone tells you differently when you're at Eton, ignore them."

"*Eton*," Otis breathed.

There was a stunned expression on his little brother's face; Ward didn't know if he was horrified or happy. Damn it, it had slipped out; he had meant to tell Otis once the boy was more settled.

There was no keeping the secret now. "I'm sending you at school in a few months, for the beginning of Michaelmas term," Ward said. "I went to Eton and so did your father."

"My father promised that I would go to Eton," Otis squeaked, his voice cracking with excitement.

Thank God: happiness, not horror.

"I know a boy named Marmaduke, Lord Pibble, who will also be new to Eton," Eugenia said. "I believe your brother can arrange to have you share a bedchamber."

"'Marmaduke'?" Otis wrinkled his nose.

"I would bet you a shilling that you and he will be the best of friends by the end of term."

Ladies don't make wagers, Ward thought. But he kept his mouth shut.

"It's not fair that girls can't go to Eton!" Lizzie exclaimed. She was still clutching Eugenia's hand, Ward noticed with a mild sense of panic.

He couldn't have his sister grow fond of his lover. It wasn't done.

It *really* wasn't done.

"Marmaduke has a pet toad named Fred who goes with him everywhere," Eugenia was telling Otis. "I expect you can't bring Fred and Jarvis to the classroom, but your pets could wait in your bed-chamber."

"I must teach you both how to swim," Ward said. "There's a river that runs by the school, and a boy drowned there during my time."

From the corner of his eyes, he saw a shiver run through Eugenia. Damn it, he'd forgotten about her husband again.

"Do you know how to swim, Mrs. Snowe?" Lizzie asked, looking up at her.

"I do not," Eugenia replied, adding faintly, "It's a useful skill. Many people do not realize how danger-ous water sports can be."

"I shan't go in the lake," Lizzie said firmly. "There are dead fish in there, and they might bite me."

"Pooh!" Otis said. "You think about death all the time. If you don't learn to swim, you could be dead yourself someday. Did you think of that?"

"I'll enter the water only if Mrs. Snowe does so with me," Lizzie said.

"I should prefer not to," Eugenia said.

"I needn't either," Lizzie replied cheerfully.

Ward gave Eugenia a look that aimed to remind her that, as her own experience had taught her, swim-ming lessons were very important.

"I changed my mind," she said, with patent reluc-tance. "I'd be happy to learn to swim."

"Excellent," Ward said. "Swimming lessons to-morrow morning. Mrs. Snowe, I think we should

forgo the ladies' teatime. It is the children's bedtime."

Lizzie was still clinging to Eugenia's hand. "I feel angry."

Eugenia bent over and kissed Lizzie on the cheek. "I have a headache, my dear, but I promise you a tea party tomorrow, and you can teach me more of Middleton's creative phrases."

"You know what gave Mrs. Snowe a headache?" Otis demanded. "It was that shouting. I'm lucky not to be deaf."

Lizzie dropped Eugenia's hand and poked her brother hard in the ribs. "You are the most—"

Over the clamor, Ward opened the door. "I apologize for my siblings."

Eugenia smiled at him, and Ward actually found his head bending toward her before he jolted upright again. He wanted that mouth. He wanted to lick inside and see that look she gave him last night, as if she needed him more than her next breath.

"This was one of the more interesting meals of my life," Eugenia observed.

"We must talk about the new skill you taught my sister."

Her smile didn't hitch. "Snowe's Registry makes a point of being readily available to its clients."

He leaned a trifle closer; the children were squabbling and not paying attention. "Are you trying to remind me that you, and not I, are the expert in child-rearing?"

"Yes." Her eyes had a shimmer of desire.

He could have pointed out that he was an expert in the behavior of polite society, but he found he didn't

care. "I want you," he growled, leaning still closer so that his words traveled only as far as their mingled breaths.

"Are you going to kiss Mrs. Snowe?" Otis's interested voice asked.

"No!" Ward said, straightening.

"Of course they're not kissing," Lizzie said scornfully. "When people kiss, they hold their heads like *this*." She flopped her head to the side like a wilting dandelion.

"That's stage kissing," Eugenia said. "It's different in real life, Lizzie. Your brother and I have no interest in kissing."

"I told you," Lizzie said, nudging her brother with her elbow. "They're not married."

"Be careful! You almost poked Jarvis," Otis protested. "Anyway, you don't have to be married to kiss."

"You're not supposed to kiss unless you are husband and wife," Lizzie stated.

"An excellent point," Ward said, feeling that a parental affirmation was required.

"Mother kissed Mr. Burger all the time, and they weren't married," Otis said.

"That's private!" Lizzie snapped. "You were never, ever supposed to tell!" She burst into tears.

Ward managed not to flinch at the revelation that his mother apparently had a lover named Burger. He reached down and picked up his weeping sister. "Time for bed. Come along, Otis."

"Would you like to say goodnight to Jarvis?" Otis asked Eugenia.

"Certainly," Eugenia said, in an obvious lie.

Ward watched as Otis hauled Jarvis, who seemed

eager to be part of the party, from his bag and put him on his shoulder.

Jarvis nudged Otis's cheek with his nose, a rattie kiss, and began combing his hair.

Eugenia tentatively reached out and rubbed Jarvis on his head with one finger.

Ward turned, settled his sobbing sister against his shoulder, and walked on.

Chapter Thirty

At bedtime, Eugenia tried to decide whether she should undo the braid that Clothilde had put in her hair after her bath. She was fairly certain that fallen women greeted their paramours wearing diaphanous nightdresses, hair flowing around their shoulders.

Her nightgown was made from sturdy cotton, just what a respectable widow ought to wear to her solitary bed.

In the end, she undid her braid and slipped between the sheets to await a discreet knock. The next she knew, her hair was tangled around her shoulders. And she was no longer alone in the bed.

Ward was lying on his back beside her, head turned away and one strong arm under her, embracing her. She was snuggled against him, for all the world as if they were man and wife.

Lovers were intimate, of course. But she had thought that lovers didn't sleep together; rather, they engaged in sinfully thrilling debauchery, and then parted to sleep in their own chambers.

Now, though, pearly light was stealing into the room, signaling the dawn. Somehow they had slept through the hours for thrilling debauchery, and it was time for her bedfellow to make his way to his own chamber.

"Ward," she whispered, running her fingers over his naked shoulder and then his neck, and along his jaw. He had finely drawn cheekbones for a man, but they didn't feminize him.

He was the opposite of her godfather, the Duke of Villiers. Villiers was at perfect ease in glittering attire. He insisted on scarlet heels, even as younger men eschewed that fashion for Hessians.

Of course, Villiers's grip over London society was such that red heels still regularly made appearances everywhere from the queen's drawing room to Vauxhall.

Ward's deep bottom lip opened and her finger slid inside a warm, wet mouth.

"Good morning," Eugenia said huskily, pulling her hand away. "Whatever are you doing in my bed, Mr. Reeve?"

He blinked sleepily and ran his free hand through his hair. Chestnut locks tumbled into an arrangement that a valet would need an hour to achieve. "I've never liked to sleep alone. My father says I used to roam the house at night, joining people in their beds."

"What people would those be?"

"Relatives, for the most part. Although on one oc-

casion I made my way into my future stepmother's chamber and wet her bed."

"I'm glad you outgrew that tendency," Eugenia said, heartfelt.

He was wide awake now, his eyes gleaming. He took her hand and placed it on his chest. "Please return to what you were doing."

Eugenia ran her fingers down his taut abdomen.

"Last night it was all I could do not to reach across the dining table and haul you onto my lap," Ward said.

"Not in front of the children."

"I kept my hands to myself," Ward said, his voice breaking in a groan. "Please don't stop."

She obeyed.

Two hours later, Ward pulled himself upright and stretched. Every part of him was content.

Eugenia was prone on the bed, her hair spread over her naked breasts. "Time to get up." He bent over and kissed her cheek.

She moaned something.

"We have a swim lesson this morning," he said. "Surely you haven't forgotten?"

At this, her eyes popped open and she sat up so abruptly that they collided. "I'm doing nothing of the sort."

Ward grinned at the sound of her hoarse voice. Mercifully, the house's walls were thick, so Eugenia had been able to express herself freely.

Scream all she wanted, in other words.

"Lizzie won't enter the water without you. I can't believe I didn't think of the danger when I took them fishing."

She groaned and rolled on her side. He nudged her

over, sat down, brushed the hair from her face, and gave her a coaxing kiss.

"Go away," Eugenia said, pushing at him. "I can't lie about in bed all day. You must leave before my maid appears."

"Your maid won't come upstairs until my man informs her the coast is clear."

"Oh." He watched as Eugenia digested the significance of this; namely that the household was fully aware of their circumstances. "I have no interest in learning to swim."

If he handled this badly, Eugenia might refuse to go near the water for the rest of her life. "Your late husband would not wish you to fear the water," Ward said, as tactfully as possible.

Eugenia sighed. "One thing I've come to understand in the last few weeks is that Andrew's wishes cannot continue to guide my own."

"I didn't know him," Ward said, wrapping an arm around her, "but I suspect he wouldn't want you to mourn him forever."

"No one would say I'm in mourning, considering your presence in my bed!"

Ward pushed her back, pinning her to the bed, their bodies sliding into perfect alignment. "I am jealous of Andrew. Would you give *me* seven years of mourning?" he growled, nipping her ear.

"For you, a month or two," she murmured, laughter running through her voice. "Six at the outmost."

Why were they talking about mourning? Ward felt a shock, like cold water. He couldn't marry Eugenia, and it wasn't right to pretend it was a possibility.

She was undeniably helpful with the children—notwithstanding last night's cursing interlude—but

the woman he married had to vanquish the qualms society had about his birth. His household—his wife—had to be irreproachable.

"Well," he said briskly, rolling off the bed and standing up, "it's time for that swimming lesson."

"I truly don't—"

"Yes, you do." He pulled on his dressing gown. Screw delicacy; it was time to be blunt. "Andrew gave his life to save yours."

Eugenia flinched.

"You can't drown after he sacrificed himself to keep your head above water."

"That's not fair."

"Where does fairness come into it? I'd like Lizzie to be able to save herself, and she won't enter the water without you. The idea that dead fish were floating under the surface almost ruined our fishing excursion before it began."

Eugenia rose and wrapped her arms around his neck, pressing her delicious curves against him. "Couldn't we have our lesson tomorrow morning?"

Ward cleared his throat. "Now *that* is unfair."

She laughed. "I had no idea it was so exhilarating to be improper."

"I promise to give you more chances to be improper," he said, meaning it.

"I don't mean only in the bedchamber. It was very helpful for Lizzie to express her rage, no matter how eccentric my approach."

Ward hesitated, unsure of how to phrase his response. "I am in full approval of *your* embrace of impropriety, but not my sister's."

Eugenia kissed his chin. "I can feel your 'full approval.'" She wiggled against him.

"But please don't teach Lizzie the conduct that you are embracing."

Her brows drew together, and she pulled away from him. "You imagine that I would teach her to—to do *this*?"

"The cursing," he clarified. "If Eugenia utters one of those words in a countess's drawing room, it could ruin her."

"I doubt it," Eugenia said. The hurt in her eyes was changed to unruffled composure. "You'd be surprised by how earthy women can be in conversation." She turned away to retrieve her dressing gown and pulled it on.

"The ladies who rule polite society," Ward insisted, "are fickle, if not cruel. Lizzie could forfeit her chance for a good marriage with a single mistake."

"If your sister does not express her feelings of anger, she will constantly try to express other people's—and her penchant for dramatics will not be viewed sympathetically."

"Lizzie needs to think like a *lady*," Ward said. Damn it, he was having a conversation with his mistress—about his little sister.

That just wasn't done.

"Lizzie needs to put in words her feelings about your mother," Eugenia said.

"She can do it without profanity," he pointed out. "Ladies must act as such, *all the time*, Eugenia. It's—"

He stopped, aware he was about to say something she might take as an insult.

"Lady Lisette is dead," Eugenia said, after pausing to see if he cared to finish the sentence. "Lizzie tried hiding her face—and her anger—behind that veil, but it's not helping."

"She doesn't hide her face for that reason," Ward said. Though in truth he wasn't sure why his sister wore the veil. "The more important point is that ladies do not belch out lists of vulgarities." His gut twisted at the line he had to draw between them, but he had no choice. "The children are my responsibility. I have to conceal the fact that Lizzie knows such vulgar words."

Eugenia dropped down on the side of the bed, and looked at him, clear eyes sober but not indignant. "Would you like me to leave, Ward?"

"No!" The word shot out of him with such force that she couldn't mistake his sincerity. "God, no, Eugenia. You're . . . you're making this ordeal bearable. Please."

"I want to be very clear about what you're asking. You wish to shield your sister from anything that can possibly be construed as ill-befitting the behavior of a lady."

"Yes."

"As such, you are dismayed that I allowed Lizzie to curse. Do you feel the same about our excursion to the kitchens?" Her face was perfectly composed, but her fingers fidgeted with the tie of her dressing gown.

"Eugenia—" he began. "I've bungled this. I didn't mean to make you angry or to hurt your feelings."

"I am not angry," she stated. No one could look more placidly ladylike than Eugenia, when she wanted to be.

Just as no lady could be as ferociously real as she was, when she wanted to be.

Noticeably, she said nothing about hurt feelings. She must often be hurt by the abrasive insouciance

of the aristocracy—witness his grandmother's rudeness and Lady Hyacinth's slights.

"Lizzie's debut will be challenging," he said, trying again. "We have our mother's wretched behavior to overcome, and my irregular birth. I am complicating her marital future by not allowing the duchess to raise her."

Eugenia shook her head. "We both know that the Duchess of Gilner would not be a good choice."

"My point is that Lizzie has to be more ladylike than—than the queen. Her comportment must bamboozle women such as Lady Hyacinth into thinking she is conventional. She has to appear a true lady in every respect."

"I assure you that my reputation as the head of Snowe's will benefit Lizzie. You kidnapped me for that very reason, remember?"

Eugenia was sitting in a pool of sunlight, the tangled hair about her shoulders making her look wild and debauched, nothing like a lady. He couldn't bear the idea that she might think he'd kidnapped her for any motive other than the one now roaring through his limbs: blind, fierce desire.

With a growl, he dived at her and pulled her against his body, taking her mouth in a ravenous kiss. She was unresponsive for a moment, but then her body melted against his and her arms circled his neck.

He pulled back, looked into her smoky eyes. "Unless you want me to flaunt my own command of profanity—which far surpasses my sister's—you won't suggest that I have any motive for having you in my arms except the obvious."

"Which is?"

He pulled her up so her legs curled around his waist. "If I watch you taste one of Marcel's desserts, I damn near come in my breeches."

He loved her cool logic and her dizzy delight . . . but most of all he loved her laughter. He pushed the thick arch of his cock against her. "Forgive me?" he whispered roughly. "I feel guilty about Lizzie. It's not only that I'm a bastard . . . you and I are lovers now. Even though there are children in the house."

A shiver went through her body as he ground against her. "It's dreadfully inappropriate," she said, nodding.

"I can't stop myself." His voice was savage with pure emotion. "Damn it."

If the duchess ever learned that he had dallied with Eugenia—let alone that he had contemplated marriage to her—she would use the knowledge to wrest the children from his care.

"No one will find out," Eugenia said, pressing kisses on his neck.

His heart stuttered at the look in her eyes.

"We will guard the secret," she promised. "No one will guess because, frankly, Mrs. Eugenia Snowe of Snowe's Registry is precisely whom you require by way of a superior governess. They will delight themselves by trying to guess how much money you paid me. What's more, I'll travel to my father's house as soon as a new governess arrives, even if that occurs earlier than a fortnight."

The idea of Eugenia departing caused an iron band to tighten around Ward's chest. He would never have enough of her.

Eugenia pulled free and reached for the cord to summon her maid.

"No," he rasped, too late.

"We have no time to make love." She put her hands on her hips, her dressing gown revealing a sliver of a tender flesh, the rounded under-curve of a perfect breast.

The last shadow had flown from Eugenia's face, replaced by her joyous smile. He lunged at her, but she pushed him back. "Swimming lesson first. If you're lucky, I'll dip a toe in the water." Her eyes were dancing.

The iron band around his chest relaxed. They had made it through.

She'd forgiven him.

She had understood.

Chapter Thirty-one

*I*t took Eugenia a full hour to force herself down to the lake. In the end, she managed it only because of a strongly worded message from Ward, accompanied by a pair of breeches and a shirt borrowed from a stable boy.

Clothilde was scandalized by the breeches, especially viewed from the rear. But given that the shirt fell well below her bottom, Eugenia was far more bothered by the idea of entering the water.

She found Lizzie sitting on a great rock, watching Otis and Ward splash in the water.

The little girl jumped up and bobbed a curtsy. "Good morning, Mrs. Snowe! I was afraid that you wouldn't come."

"I apologize," Eugenia said. "Ladies should never be tardy."

"That side is deep," Lizzie said, pointing to a slice of dark water to her left. "We're not allowed to go there, ever. But it's shallow on this side."

Ward began heading toward them. The folds of his linen shirt clung to every ridge on his chest. Even in the grip of anxiety, she registered how extraordinarily alive and vigorous he looked. A beautiful, wet male.

"Did you see that I'm wearing breeches, just like you?" Lizzie asked, as Eugenia stepped up onto the rock. "They belong to Otis but they fit me. This is one of his shirts."

"Indeed I did," Eugenia said, sitting down. Her breeches tightened on her thighs, making them even more indecent. She tucked her feet to the side and arranged the shirt to cover her legs.

Ward had reached them. "Good morning, Mrs. Snowe," he said gravely, as if he hadn't left her bedchamber a mere hour before. "The water is surprisingly warm for May. May I escort you to the water's edge?"

"I'd prefer to sit and watch for a minute or two," Eugenia said, forcing her voice to remain steady. It was essential that she not communicate her fear to Lizzie. "Otis certainly seems to have taken to the water."

Otis had mastered the trick of floating. He resembled a river otter she'd once seen paddling in circles on his back.

"It's your turn, Lizzie," Ward said. "You wished to wait for Mrs. Snowe, and here she is."

Lizzie's fingers turned into talons clutching Eugenia's hand. "Are you certain there's nothing dead in the lake?"

"Not a thing," Ward said, holding out his arms. "Come on, Lizzie, my girl. No time like the present."

He carried her off without insisting that Eugenia join them, so she sank back on the warm rock instead.

Wavelets glinted in the mid-day sunlight, turning the lake's surface into liquid gold. It was pretty, but a part of her couldn't help remembering the water closing over her head that terrible day. Her screams when Andrew didn't reappear seemed to be echoing in her ears.

Ward had coaxed Lizzie to put a foot in the water. Eugenia let her forehead sink onto her knees.

What was she doing here?

Not at the lake, *here*.

She was quite proud of herself for embarking on an *affaire*. Susan would be pleased; Ward may fancy that he'd devised the idea of kidnapping her, but she recognized the Machiavellian hand of her best friend.

It had taken courage to be intimate with a man who wasn't Andrew. Learning to swim was yet another challenge, another way of living with courage.

The rock beneath her was a gray-and-white color, mottled here and there with lichens. After closing her eyes, she smelled more strongly the wild roses growing on the other side of the rock, past the deep water. Under their strawberry-sweet smell, she caught the soft odor of mud and mown grass.

The water lapping on the shingle had little relation to the thundering wave that had closed over her head and taken Andrew's life. The lake didn't smell briny, the way the ocean had.

She had been brave as a child. She never imagined herself growing into a coward.

Eugenia turned her head, still resting on her

knees, and watched a butterfly alight next to her on the dove-gray rock. Its wings were cream-colored and tattered like cow parsley.

When the butterfly flew away, she told herself, she would walk over to the lake edge and wade in, not too far. Up to her knees was enough for today.

No one floated on their first day in the water. Well, no one except eager little boys.

The butterfly's wings trembled like a lace curtain in the wind, and it was gone. Eugenia lifted her head.

Ward was standing in the water to his thighs, his right hand holding Lizzie's, and his left, Otis's. Both children were floating on their backs, lying on the surface of the water as if they were made of thistle-down. His hair was spangled with sunshine, and the water eddied around the three of them in little waves.

Her eyes met his and Ward broke into the widest, most joyful smile she'd ever seen. His hair was plastered to his head and she could see the contours of his skull.

It was a magnificent skull. That very morning she had run her hands all over it, cupped his face and kissed him with every bit of passion she felt.

The truth struck her like a blow: she was falling in love.

Eugenia had never fainted in her life. Not when Andrew didn't surface, not when they found his body, not when they lowered his coffin into the ground.

No, she saved dizziness, a weightless feeling in her head, the gathering black dots at the corners of her vision, for the moment when her lover smiled at her from the lake.

She came to with cold water dripping onto her face.

"Eugenia," Ward was saying, his voice low and insistent.

"What happened?" she squeaked, brushing water from her face.

"You fainted," he said, not loosening his grip on her shoulders. "One moment you were watching us, and the next you slid over in a heap."

"I thought you were dead," Lizzie said. "I screamed."

"I didn't scream," Otis said loftily. "I knew you weren't dead because you didn't look dead."

Ward glanced at his brother, visibly registering that Otis was familiar with the sight of a dead body.

"I think we've had enough for our first lesson. We shall return to the house for a cup of tea." He drew Eugenia to her feet and helped her down from the rock.

"Jarvis will have missed me!" Otis said and began running toward the house.

"He won't have noticed," Lizzie retorted, but she followed her brother.

Eugenia's knees trembled as she tried to puzzle out what had happened. She had *fainted*? Never. She never . . .

But she knew what had happened. The shock of realizing she was falling in love for the second time in her life had made her faint, just as in a bad melodrama in which the heroine collapses in the hero's arms.

Now her heart was beating as if nothing had happened, yet her whole world had come sharply into focus.

She could smell lake water on Ward, and below

that, Ward himself. The man whom she loved. A man who smelled like mud and man and perhaps just a whiff of dead fish.

Although she would never say *that* aloud, at least when Lizzie was within earshot.

The truth of it had settled into her bones by the time they reached the house.

She was in love.

She loved the bastard son of an earl, an inventor. She loved a man who had adopted his captivating, orphaned siblings along with a pet rat.

She loved a man who had made his own fortune, who had given up a prestigious university post for the sake of two orphans, who made love like a god.

"Are you still dizzy?" the god-like man asked. He had commandeered a coat from a footman and wrapped it around her shoulders, ignoring the lake water dripping all over the marble floor.

Ward looked irritable, which—in her experience— was exactly how men behaved when people they loved were ill.

That idea ran through her mind without warning, but it felt true. Ward was in love with her too, although he would need more time to realize how lucky they were.

They were both alive.

Ward cupped her face in his hands. "I had no idea that the water would frighten you into a faint. Please forgive me, Eugenia."

She was unable to stop the smile that burst from her heart. "I *shall* learn to swim, Ward. I've made up my mind."

"But you fainted before even touching the water!"

"I'll try again tomorrow. It was just nerves. I haven't

been near water since the accident. I should probably rest." Eugenia flashed him a look under her lashes. "An escort to my chamber would most welcome."

The grim lines around his mouth eased. "I see."

"And a bath, because someone dripped lake water on me," she added. The entry was empty because the footman had run off to find rags to dry the floor. "Someone ought to wash my back. Someone who is already wet, perhaps."

Ward held out his arm. "I am, as always, your most obedient servant, Mrs. Snowe."

Chapter Thirty-two

Saturday, May 30, 1801

$\mathfrak{E}$ugenia woke the next morning with conflicting emotions: a lazy, sensual happiness that came from the presence of the man lying asleep beside her, and an icy trepidation arising from the imminent swimming lesson.

She slid quietly out of bed. She was going in that lake, because she was determined never again to put anyone at risk to save her life. Since the accident, she'd chosen to avoid water—but that felt uncomfortably similar to the way she had been avoiding society.

She was no coward.

It was a glorious morning. Standing at the window, she heard a faint clatter and a fragment of distant

song; the new kitchen maids were at their duties. The neat lawn behind the house sloped down to the lake, which looked deceptively benign in the morning light.

If she slipped out the side door, no one would see her. The kitchen and its gardens lay on the other side of the house. She could steal down to the water, wade in as far as her knees, and return to the house with no one the wiser.

Yesterday's breeches were nowhere to be seen, but she could wear her chemise into the lake since she would be alone. Making up her mind, she gathered her robe and slipped quietly from the chamber.

When she reached the pebbly shore, she kicked off her slippers, bent over, and examined the tiny fish swimming among the weedy plants at the water's edge. Her reflection in the water shook with wavelets, but her fingers were trembling in reality.

This was ridiculous! She was twenty-nine years old. She had established a successful registry company. She was no coward.

She had no fear of encountering dead things, fishy or otherwise, below the lake's limpid surface. No, it was the sensation of water closing over her face, the terror of finding herself in a liquid coffin.

Enough!

She folded her dressing gown, placed it on top of her slippers, and inched forward. First her toes met dry sun-warmed stones and then those just under the water. She nearly forgot to breathe as she willed herself not to retreat back to dry land.

Thank goodness she was alone, because she was beginning to think she might vomit.

Ward and Lizzie and Otis were at home in water.

Otis, in particular, had announced that he wanted to be in the lake every day. If she wished . . .

She gulped.

Did she want to be Otis's mother? And Lizzie's?

Knobby knees, earnest face, all chin and eyes. A pet rat named Jarvis, thrust at her like a furry, whiskery version of his boy. Lizzie's fierce spirit and dramatic soul. Her black veil, trailing behind her now rather than sheltering her from the world.

Eugenia knew that answer. She wanted to be the children's mother.

With all her heart.

Emboldened, she took another step so that water trickled over her toes before she froze again. The water was horridly cold and there was a faint smell of dead fish.

She stood as if rooted for what seemed like an age, cursing herself for being a coward, and incapable of going in any deeper.

Just when she was about to admit defeat, she was startled by strong arms wrapping around from behind.

She squealed. "Ward!"

"Good morning, angel," he growled, his voice muffled by her hair.

"Stop teasing," Eugenia said. "I detest that name." He must think her a total ninny for standing in a half inch of water.

Ward moved around in front of her, water lapping over his ankles. He wore breeches and a loose shirt, but his feet were bare.

"What if someone sees us?" she asked.

He leaned forward and kissed her, as hot and needy as if he hadn't woken her up twice during the night.

Eugenia's mind slid away from the lake and into

some special space where she and Ward breathed together, his muscled arms locked around her.

"Bloody hell," he groaned a few moments later. "I feel unhinged around you, mad with lust."

"We could return to my bedchamber," she said. "It's nice and dry there."

"I want to kiss you." He moved backward, farther out. He didn't pull her toward him; he merely squeezed her hands, as if to promise, *you are safe.*

She looked down at their feet. Although he was no more than an arm's length from her, his ankles were completely submerged.

"Are you trying to bribe me?"

"You'll have kisses, either way," Ward assured her.

But he made a little sound of satisfaction in the back of his throat when she stepped toward him.

He crushed her against his body, his hands running over her bottom and pulling her even tighter. Then he took another step back, bringing her with him. Her hands clenched on his shoulders.

"All right?" he murmured.

The water was brushing her calves, but she felt so overheated that its cool caress was welcome.

"Are you certain no one can see us?" she gasped, because his hand was caressing her breast.

"Quite certain," Ward promised in a rusty voice. "Your back is to the house. Close your eyes." Her chemise was no barrier to his mouth. Eugenia's knees weakened, but he supported her.

She didn't notice that he had guided her further out until cold water reached her thighs. Her eyes popped open.

"You're seducing me into the water!" she gasped, pulling away from his arms and standing free.

He threw back his head and bellowed with laughter. For a moment she was struck by the sheer beauty of his face and arched neck. The shadow of lashes on his cheek, the sunlight striking gold from his hair.

He gathered her close again, and picked her up. Her legs curled around his hips just as they had when she lay underneath him in bed. Her chemise billowed around her, floating on the surface.

He took another step backward, bringing her bottom perilously close to the water. Eugenia wrapped her arms around his neck. "You cannot possibly think that we—that we could—"

"Well, we *could*," Ward said, laughter threading through his voice. "But perhaps not during your first swimming attempt?"

"You must be joking!" Eugenia cried, missing the step that brought water all the way to her waist. "This is cold!" she squeaked, huddling against his chest.

"Your body will warm in a minute," Ward said, nuzzling her ear.

Eugenia took a shuddering breath. "Very well, you may go a little deeper."

Ward grinned. "I think you said the same thing last night."

She pinched him in reply, and ordered, "Farther out, please, before I change my mind."

When the water reached her shoulders, Eugenia made two discoveries. The first was that, below the water's surface, her breasts looked enticingly mermaid-like.

The second was when one is plastered against a warm male body, cold water was surprisingly tolerable.

"I do not want the water to go over my head," she

told him. As secure as she felt with Ward, she had reached her limit.

"This is far enough for today," he reassured her. "Uncurl your legs, Eugenia. I'm going to slide an arm under them."

Somehow she forced her legs straight in the water. She trusted Ward with every particle of her being. He wouldn't let her sink.

"You're changing everything," she whispered, squinting up at him as she floated—actually floated!—with the support of his arm at her back.

"I'm making you into a swimmer." He scooped her back up against his chest again. "Enough for the day."

Eugenia couldn't stop smiling. "I floated!" He had opened doors for her, doors inside herself that she never knew existed.

"You did," Ward said, kissing her nose. "Next thing I know, you'll be swimming the Channel."

"Do people *do* that?"

"Not as far as I know," he replied cheerfully. "But you're a woman who goes where others don't, Eugenia."

"Floating is enough," she replied, resting her cheek against his chest.

Ward was plowing steadily through the water and up onto the shingle. "I think we should make this a daily ritual." His voice was dark and needy.

Following his gaze, Eugenia looked down. Her dripping chemise clung to every curve. It was so thin that the tuft of hair between her legs could be seen through the fabric.

Morning ritual, Ward had said. He was planning their life together. They were both experiencing this new, tender emotion carved out of desire.

She felt a bolt of happiness that warmed even her chilled toes. "There's more to us than desire," she said. She could not shout that she loved him and she knew he loved her, even though it was true.

Ladies didn't do that. Not proper, even for those conducting an illicit *affaire*.

Ward said nothing in reply, and they were back at the house and up the stairs before she untangled her thoughts about what ladies could and couldn't do.

Once again in her chamber, he set her down. But there was something she had to clarify before she rang for a bath. "Ward, you are aware that I'm a lady, aren't you?"

Ward stared at Eugenia, not knowing what to say.

What was she asking, exactly? She had freely told him of the prostitutes she'd met as a child, of her aunt's directorship of Magdalene House, of her uncle who was in the Thames River Police . . .

On the other hand, she currently lived in an elegant house in the smartest neighborhood—though she had paid for it herself.

What made a lady? He himself was illegitimate, but he had never considered himself defined by that, any more than he was by being the son of aristocrats.

If he refused to define himself by the circumstances of his birth, he shouldn't define Eugenia by hers. Nor his mother: for all her lineage and privilege, Lady Lisette had been no lady.

There was only one possible answer. "Of course I do. What I see before me," he said, "is a very chilled, shivering *lady*." He pulled the cord to summon her maid. "Who shall have a hot bath and later some champagne."

Her mouth curled into a smile.

"It's not every day that a lady overcomes her worst fear." He brushed a kiss on her lips. "You are a remarkable woman, Eugenia."

Ward needed a few minutes after he'd left Eugenia's chamber to work out why he felt as if walls were closing around him. Then he remembered that just before she'd asked him about her status as a lady, Eugenia had said, "There's more to us than desire." His gut clenched uneasily.

There could be no "us."

She was a delight, a revelation, a pure pleasure. She was a lady and yet not, given the scorn with which the likes of his grandmother and Lady Hyacinth greeted her.

He had to establish distance between them. He couldn't endanger Eugenia's heart; she had already lost one lover.

Actually, it was probably all in his imagination. Likely she didn't give a ha'penny for him. Eugenia Snowe was a woman of common sense. They were enjoying each other with the kind of unbridled enthusiasm that came naturally to people who have been deprived of bed play.

They would always have a special tenderness between them.

That worked, he decided, yanking down his breeches.

Freed from the wet cloth, his erect cock bobbed against his stomach. His body didn't give a damn about the plans he was making for sharing nostalgic glances with Eugenia at some time in the future.

It wanted her, to own her, take her.

Keep her.

Oh, bloody hell.

Chapter Thirty-three

Friday, June 5, 1801
A week later

£ugenia passed the morning in the kitchen—she
and Monsieur Marcel were perfecting a lemon tea
cake—after which she and Ward spent the afternoon
teaching Lizzie and Otis the finer points of croquet.
Neither child had the faintest understanding of good
sportsmanship and both thought cheating was a sen-
sible route to victory.

"They won't be roaming the house tonight," Ward
told Eugenia with obvious satisfaction in the evening. "Lizzie drifted off in my library, and I carried
her to bed."

Eugenia had a sudden image of Ward with a sleep-

ing child draped over his shoulder. But the imaginary girl had a mop of dark curls, the color hers had been before they lightened to red.

For goodness' sake! She took a hasty gulp of wine. Gumwater padded around the table, serving the meal with hearty, if silent, dislike.

"Your butler abhors me," she observed, when the man had left. "And frankly he has done nothing to endear himself to me."

"My stepmother is not fond of Gumwater either," Ward acknowledged. "He's capable in the position, though."

"I can tolerate him for one more week," Eugenia said, silently willing Ward to invite her to extend her stay beyond the fortnight they had agreed on.

One more week.

Or forever.

"I appreciate that," he said easily.

Eugenia was trying her utmost to not blurt out a declaration of love that he might not reciprocate. She felt as if her skin were about to burst, as if she were a plump grape, succulent and sweet. Love and lust were jumbled in her mind.

She shifted in her chair. Ward's eyes narrowed, but Gumwater pushed open the door again, bringing another covered platter. For the remainder of the meal the butler managed to find reasons to keep coming and going, dropping fussy remarks about the provenance of the wine, the paucity of green beans, the exorbitant price of pineapples.

Ward didn't appear to be irritated. Or to want to be alone with her. He kept up a sidelong conversation with Gumwater. Meanwhile, Eugenia practiced being a lady. Ladies didn't squirm in their seats.

But Eugenia was so hungry for Ward that she couldn't think.

Or form sentences.

It felt as if he were torturing her, insisting on every course, peeling an orange so methodically that the peels fell into slow coils on the table. She watched his hands, thinking about those fingers touching her.

Her breath felt hot in her chest, but Ward was genially discussing a dessert wine with Gumwater.

"What do you think, Mrs. Snowe?"

It took her a moment to realize Ward had addressed her. She had grown used to "Eugenia" rolling off his tongue, though he was careful never to use her first name in front of the children or the servants. She ran his words backward in her head and managed to put together a response.

"The hint of walnut is delicious."

Somehow that word "delicious" came out an octave lower than the rest of her sentence.

Ward froze.

"Monsieur Marcel has made a trifle with apricot crème anglaise to your recipe, Mrs. Snowe," Gumwater said, his eyebrows jumping as if he'd seen a rat.

Not Jarvis, *vermin*.

"Would you like me to bring it now?"

"Yes, please," Ward said, glancing at him—and away from Eugenia.

"You look weary, Gumwater," Eugenia said, taking matters into her own hands. "Mr. Reeve, surely your butler may retire for the night after bringing the last course? One of the footmen can clear the table later."

Gumwater cleared his throat with a sound like a dying bullfrog, so Eugenia silently warned him not

to speak with a smile that showed all her teeth. He left, closing the door behind him a bit too sharply.

"I'd hate to make an enemy of you," Ward said appreciatively. "Poor old Gumwater has retreated in great dudgeon."

Some minutes later, the butler shouldered his way sullenly through the door, balancing a crystal bowl that he plunked down on table between them.

"Your trifle, Mrs. Snowe," he said, not making the slightest attempt to conceal his irritation.

"Why do you tolerate being treated so disrespectfully?" Eugenia asked, once the man had taken himself away.

Ward shrugged. "An illegitimate child in a noble household quickly learns not to be bothered by servants silently expressing their opinions."

"You tolerate Gumwater's insubordination, because servants were impolite to you as a child?" Eugenia was incredulous. "Your father should have sacked anyone who behaved in that way!"

"By the time I was old enough to understand, I was also mature enough to understand that nonsense of that sort doesn't matter. I had a few skirmishes at Eton, but once the boys saw that I literally didn't give a damn what anyone thought of my parentage, most of them stopped bothering about it."

Ward was lounging in his chair the way no gentleman was supposed to do. His hair wasn't arranged in waves, or powdered, or even hidden by an old-fashioned wig. It was thick and wavy and so soft that Eugenia's fingers curled into her palm at the memory of clenching them in his hair.

"Eugenia," he said in a low voice. "You oughtn't to look at me like that. Not here."

"But you look delicious," she said reasonably. He leaned forward and her eyes skated hungrily over his broad shoulders, over his strong neck and the cravat that framed his jaw.

Desire felt like a clawing animal inside her, making her breath catch and heat come into her lips. She clenched her legs against the feeling.

"Please allow me to serve you some trifle," Ward said.

He stood up and her mouth went dry. Those silk breeches hid nothing, and there was much to hide. Ward plunged a spoon into the layers of cream, sponge, and apricot, and prepared a plate for each of them.

Ladies never licked their spoon. They didn't close their eyes and nearly swoon, either.

Eugenia did both.

"This is so good," she moaned, her eyes opening to find Ward staring at her. His eyes were dark, and his hands clenched the edge of the table.

"Jesus," he said hoarsely. "Have another bite, Eugenia."

She brought the spoon to her mouth and again closed her eyes. She felt transported by silky cool cream flavored with Armagnac, and the touch of anise that had been her idea.

Ward's chair shoved back and she heard footsteps. But she didn't open her eyes, not even when cool silver nudged her lips, prompting her to open for another bite.

"Good girl," Ward said, his voice rough.

Hands ran over her shoulders, fingers gliding down her arms. She swallowed and took in a stuttering breath.

"A man could lay you down on this table and cover you in trifle, even the pale pink parts of you— or those parts especially—and lick off all that lovely cream," Ward murmured.

Eugenia was hardly able to breathe.

"That's not what you want, is it?" he asked.

"No," she murmured. "Well, perhaps."

"I know what you want," he said. "I know what you need."

A sobbing breath escaped, but she still said nothing, because Ward was drawing her to her feet and pulling her gown up, right there in the dining room. If she kept her eyes shut, this could be happening to someone else.

Some other lady was trembling and helpless in the grip of big male hands that were stroking fire into her legs—no, the fire was already there.

Ward turned her about. "Bend over, Eugenia." It was a command, but she would have obeyed a suggestion, a hint, anything. She bent over the table, quivering.

His hands ran up her legs, sliding over her arse.

"Do you want me?" A warm, large body covered her from behind. Part of it was hot and silky, and throbbed against her bottom.

"Yes," she panted.

There was no French letter in the dining room, of course, so nothing came between them. Every inch pulsed as he pushed inside. They cried out in unison, shock radiating to the ends of Eugenia's fingers and toes.

Her hands curled on the tablecloth and she dimly heard a glass topple. Ward pulled back and thrust forward again.

"I've never felt anything like you." She thought the words were forced through his teeth, because "you" was lost in a groan as he thrust home.

"More," she said fiercely. She felt shameless in her hunger. For years, she had paid little heed to her body other than to dimly note if she was hungry or tired. Now her priorities had reversed.

His hands slipped to her hips and gripped so hard that she might have bruises. "You want me to take you, Eugenia?"

She couldn't answer, the words wouldn't shape in her mouth, but he understood and began thrusting harder and harder. As a child, she'd visited the belfry of St. Paul's Cathedral when the bells were ringing. Their deep clang had pounded through her, leaving her deafened afterwards.

Now white heat rang through every part of her, roaring all the way to her fingers and toes.

After she stopped convulsing, she discovered she was limp on the table, Ward's sweaty body curved protectively on top of hers, both of them gulping deep breaths of air. The tremors of that huge pleasure, that great voice, still throbbed in her legs.

"I've never felt anything like this," Ward said, his voice hoarse.

Eugenia had never experienced anything so earthy, so animal-like, so primitive. It turned her into a different woman.

The kind of woman who stands and lets her skirts fall down, takes her lover's hand without words, and draws him to the door.

Takes him upstairs.

Chapter Thirty-four

The four of them swam every morning. Eugenia learned to float on her back unaided—though she still didn't put her face under water. They played enough croquet so that Otis and Lizzie grasped that cheating made the opposing players walk directly off the lawn.

At night, every night, Ward made love to Eugenia with the skill, passion, and endurance of a primitive, profane kind of god, not the one worshipped in the parish church. Certainly not the one that Vicar Howson believed in.

After Howson was dispatched abroad, the vicarage stood empty for a week or so before a young

man with yellow hair and cornflower blue eyes moved in, and after that, the butcher's gold chain was forgotten and all anyone talked of in the village was his eyes.

A letter came and went from Susan. A new governess was to arrive on the following Wednesday. With Eugenia's blessing, Ruby, who was enchanted by Lizzie and Otis, had decided to stay on as nursery maid.

"They're not like other children," she told Eugenia.

"I know," Eugenia said. "I know."

The fortnight fell behind her like a fever dream.

One night Gumwater set the dining table as if for a royal banquet, and Eugenia took the children through the entire meal. She invented problematic situations and quizzed them about proper behavior.

"If your hostess spills water on the table, how would you behave? What about if the person to your right becomes inebriated and bursts into song?"

It was only because Ward was a silent witness that she realized how many societal rules dictated that dinner guests ignore the truth or look the other way if a man urinated against the wall, if someone cast up their accounts, or if an irascible guest berated his wife.

Letters flew between Ward and his solicitors as they prepared for a spirited battle over Otis's guardianship. He mentioned them occasionally, but never shared them. Of course, there was no reason to allow her to read them.

Eugenia wasn't certain why, or how, but her blissful certainty that Ward had fallen in love with her was fast slipping away.

She was in love. Ward? It no longer seemed so.

One night at supper he mentioned in passing her return to London, as if it meant nothing to him. The day before, she had overheard Ward tell Otis that he and Lizzie would escort him to Eton in the fall.

No mention of her. No glance at her, either. No silent acknowledgment that by the fall their *affaire* might be regularized.

Every time she felt a burning pain in her heart, Eugenia sought refuge in the kitchen. She and Monsieur Marcel had perfected her tea cake. Not only was that enormously satisfying, but more importantly, she had discovered what her next challenge would be: she meant to open a tearoom.

It would be a tearoom that welcomed children, the only one of its kind. Delicacies would be offered in small portions. A child with Otis's appetite could eat five or six. Or twelve.

After Ward described how hungry he had always been at Eton, she decided to offer special hampers that could be sent directly to boarding schools. They would include sweets and pastries, naturally, but also hearty meat pies.

She spent hours in the kitchen, trying one recipe after another with Monsieur Marcel's help. Lizzie often spent the afternoon there as well, stealing raisins and ranking delicacies. In the evening, Eugenia scribbled notes and imagined new combinations of flavors.

"Perhaps you should abstain from the kitchens tomorrow," Ward said one evening, after Gumwater had brought in a tray holding five different confections.

"I know," Eugenia said ruefully. "It's just that one cake leads to another . . . I have an idea or Monsieur

Marcel does, and we adjust the amount of butter or other ingredient, and before I know it, we have four versions on our hands."

"What on earth is enjoyable in that?" Ward asked. "It sounds hot and tiresome."

"Baking is like mathematics," Eugenia explained. "I'm fond of numerical problems, and baking demands precision. I promise that nothing will go to waste; we could have a picnic tomorrow afternoon, for example, and Otis would eat every crumb."

They had their picnic on a linen cloth spread under a willow near the water. After eating luncheon, they lay on the grass reading books until Lizzie fell asleep, using her bundled veil for a pillow. Otis was building a hut of twigs for Jarvis.

Eugenia was drowsily watching drifting clouds from under the shade of her bonnet when a long blade of grass tickled her nose.

"Good afternoon, Mrs. Snowe," Ward whispered. They were scrupulously formal with each other in front of the children, even while swimming.

"Mr. Reeve," she murmured.

"You are wildly beautiful." The grass blade was sweeping back and forth over her lower lip.

"Thank you," Eugenia said, suddenly shy. They rarely spent time together during the day; Ward was usually in the library working on his steam engine, while she instructed Lizzie and Otis, or rattled around the kitchens.

"I wish we had more time together," Ward said softly.

Eugenia didn't dare answer; she was afraid that her aching love couldn't be disguised.

"I received a letter from the dowager duchess yesterday."

Dread clenched her gut.

"She informs me that she plans to visit," Ward said, his eyes dark with obvious regret. "I suspect that she will look for ammunition to bolster her case."

Eugenia reflexively glanced over to make certain that neither child was listening. "When is she expected?"

"This Tuesday."

"In three days," Eugenia, shocked to hear how calm her voice was.

"The children will miss you," he said. "*I* will miss you. Damn it, I . . ."

He fell silent as her heart pounded in her ears, certain he was about to say something, ask her to stay, promise to woo her in a year, a few years, if need be. Lying awake by his side at night, she'd come up with a thousand possibilities.

"There's a fair in the village tomorrow," he said abruptly.

That wasn't a declaration.

"We could take the children."

"Certainly," Eugenia said. Her heart was thudding a dirge because Ward wasn't going to say anything. He would not ask her to stay, or even promise to court her after he gained legal guardianship of the children.

He meant to say good-bye.

Years of self-control led her to say, with perfect equanimity, "I love country fairs."

Something flickered in his eyes, and a horrible truth dawned on her: he'd brought up the fair because he expected her to depart directly afterwards.

Just when the silence became unbearable, a shriek echoed over the lawn: "How *dare* you!"

Ward's face disappeared from her view as Eugenia sat up. Lizzie was chasing after Otis with a book in her hand.

"What is going on?" Ward called.

"He let Jarvis chew my book!"

"I didn't," Otis protested.

Lizzie stopped, hands on her hips, looking unnervingly like a miniature version of the Dowager Duchess of Gilner. The family resemblance was undeniable. "I doubt another rat wandered over and gnawed it!"

"Let's have some cake," Ward said. "We'll have your book re-bound, Lizzie, perhaps with a special binding with your name inscribed on it."

Eugenia brushed away an unwelcome tear and busied herself by pulling from the basket the assortment of delicacies that Marcel had packed for them. Otis threw himself down and dived for a piece of spice cake, but Lizzie just sighed.

"I no longer care for sweets," she said, in a voice of doom.

"And why is that?" Ward asked, accepting a plate with a slice of chocolate cake, another of the orange tea cake (not entirely successful), and a sweet bun.

"I watched that spice cake being made. It took hours," Lizzie said. "Now it's just here to eat."

"It can't have been as much work as a sponge cake," Otis said. "I thought Monsieur Marcel's arms would fall off as he beat the eggs."

Like Lizzie, Ward didn't want cake. In fact, he'd be just as happy never to taste another dessert, though he would never say such a thing to Eugenia.

Soon she wouldn't be here to tell.

The thought provoked a surge of emotion so strong he nearly leapt to his feet. He wanted to take Eugenia to his room and make love to her so many times that she'd never—

No. He sensed that if he gave her the slightest hope, Eugenia might wait for him, even through the many years until Otis came of age. That was impossible and unfair.

She deserved to have children of her own, not be the mistress of a man who could not marry her until his young siblings grew up.

"I thought Snowe's governesses taught children how to bake a sponge, not a spice cake," he said, controlling his untidy emotions.

"Not just a sponge," Lizzie said importantly. She counted on her fingers. "I can make sponge, orange cake, jelly roll, sweet buns, and lemon tart."

Ward turned to Eugenia, frowning. "You led me to understand that children are required to learn how to make one cake."

"I can do one," Otis said, with his mouth full.

Eugenia glanced at him, and he swallowed and said thickly, "Sorry."

"I've been in the kitchen almost every day," Lizzie said. "I asked Mrs. Snowe to name her tearoom 'Lizzie's Teas,' but she says no. When I grow up, I shall open a shop and name it 'Lizzie's Emporium.'"

"What tearoom?" Ward demanded.

"I am thinking of opening a tearoom," Eugenia said. "Did I not tell you, Mr. Reeve?"

No, she bloody well did not tell him. Was she planning to serve people tea herself? Show Lady Hyacinth to a table?

He was careful to keep his voice even. "Mrs. Snowe, I wonder if you would care to walk toward the lake?"

"Jarvis ought to go home to his box and take a nap," Otis said. He had finished three pieces of cake and he looked sleepy.

"I expect he was exhausted by ingesting the history of the Punic wars," Lizzie said acidly.

"Children, why don't you return to the nursery?" Eugenia asked, rising. "Inform Mr. Gumwater that our picnic is finished, if you please."

She had a governess's trick of asking questions that were actually indirect orders, so Otis immediately turned to go.

"Otis," Eugenia said.

He paused. "Oh." He came back and made a fairly credible bow. "Thank you for a most enjoyable picnic, Mrs. Snowe."

She nodded. "It has been my pleasure, Lord Darcy."

Lizzie dropped a grand curtsy. "It is such sweet, sweet sorrow to part after this enchanting interlude."

"Overdone," Eugenia said, but she smiled and touched Lizzie's hair before the child ran away.

As Ward looked on, she knelt and began collecting the luncheon debris and placing it in the basket. No lady would do such a menial thing.

"Please refrain," Ward said, more sharply than he intended. "That is the servants' responsibility, to be carried out by a footman, not by you."

She rose again and met his eyes. "May I assume you are angry because you believe that Lizzie has spent too much time in the kitchen?"

"You told me that Snowe's children never again touch a kitchen implement. And yet you have appar-

ently given Lizzie ambitions to open an emporium, as if she were a baker's child who might well spend her life in a kitchen."

He didn't raise his voice, but he also didn't try to disguise his exasperation. "I've explained how important it is that Lizzie, in particular, be brought up a lady. I trusted you, and instead you have taught her a trade."

A stark moment of silence passed between them. "I apologize," Eugenia said at length. "I had no intention of undermining your efforts. I assure you that Lizzie is, and will be, a lady."

"Not if she says 'bloody hell' in a ballroom and follows that by announcing her plans to open a shop. Damn it, Eugenia, I think it's wonderful that you established a registry office. I'm sure your tearoom will surpass Gunter's and be the most fashionable in London. But Lizzie won't have your life, don't you see?"

Eugenia did see.

Ward had never made explicit precisely how he felt about her profession—but he wouldn't have, would he? He needed her. Two governesses had failed him; he needed someone to instruct Lizzie and Otis.

No, that wasn't right. That bitter comment didn't represent reality.

Ward did respect her. She simply hadn't comprehended the extent to which he believed that her ownership of the registry was of more consequence than her birth. In essence, he agreed with the Duchess of Gilner that Eugenia was no longer a lady.

"What if Lizzie tells our grandmother of her ambitions?" Ward demanded, as if he'd read her thoughts. "The House of Lords will not be sympathetic to the

fact that I allowed my mistress to keep my sister in the kitchen, training to be a *pâtissier*!"

Eugenia felt a sharp pain in the region of her heart. "I am not your mistress," she managed.

"Lover, if you'd prefer," Ward said.

Apparently, to him, it was a distinction without meaning. But not to Eugenia. Lovers were on a par with each other and money never changed hands. A mistress, on the other hand, was a dependent.

She would never be a kept woman of any man.

"We can impress discretion upon Lizzie," she said, rallying a calm tone. "I would add that your sister seems to believe that merely being *in* the kitchen while something is baking is the same as knowing how to make it. I can assure you that she has not had an apprenticeship in baking."

"The distinction is immaterial," Ward growled. He ran a hand through his hair.

God, she'd been such a fool. She thought that giving Ward her body proved that she belonged to no man, but he obviously saw it otherwise.

She drew herself upright and met his eyes. No one could shame her unless she allowed it. She had learned that harsh lesson when some of the dowagers—such as the Duchess of Gilner—had sneered at her for opening Snowe's.

"There is nothing less ladylike than being anxious about one's status. You would do well to remember that when you are tutoring Lizzie in what she may and may not say to the duchess."

His jaw flexed.

"A *lady* may bake a cake simply because she wishes to, which is one of the reasons Snowe's governesses teach it. A *lady* can straighten the picnic basket if

she knows that the butler is slothful and won't come down until the plates are swarming with ants. A true lady can do virtually anything she wishes without it having any effect on her status—except, perhaps, have an *affaire* with a blooming idiot!"

Another moment of silence, punctuated only by the irregular chirps of a sparrow.

"I take your point," Ward said. "In the main, you are right, but the rules are more strict for those on the margins, Eugenia, as surely you know."

She narrowed her eyes. "I gather my ownership of Snowe's puts me on the margins."

"No," he said, his face implacable. "I'm saying that if the news emerges that Miss Lizzie Darcy spent her early life in a traveling caravan with Lady Lisette, people will watch her like a hawk for evidence that she does not fit her station."

Eugenia was wrestling with her temper. Ward was a deeply protective man, fighting for those he loved. His ideas were wrong—owing to the fact that he had been scorned by servants, and by boys at Eton.

Their scorn didn't matter to him, because he had never given a damn.

The same was key for Lizzie was well. If Lizzie comported herself with perfect confidence and poise at her debut, she would set the rules, not follow them. But if she radiated anxiety, the vultures would circle, waiting for mistakes.

She, Eugenia, would simply have to manage that debut. Even if her relationship with Ward was long over.

He took a step toward her. Taking her hand, he pressed a kiss into her palm. "I don't want you to go."

She drew her hand away. "Yes, you do, because you

are right: if the duchess were to discover our intimacy, she would use it to disqualify your guardianship."

"Gumwater is loyal to the bone. He would never tell anyone, and he controls the household."

Hopefully, that was true. "I shall depart tomorrow morning," Eugenia said.

He visibly flinched. "I don't want tonight to be our last together."

"You received the duchess's letter yesterday, so you were already aware of that," Eugenia pointed out, head high. "I think I would feel more comfortable if I left as soon as possible."

His jaw tightened. "We just agreed to take the children to the fair."

Eugenia bit her lip, willing tears not to come. Part of her wanted to flee, but another, larger part, couldn't bear the idea of leaving. Not just Ward, but Lizzie and Otis. "In that case, I shall leave the following morning," she said, somehow managing to keep pain out of her voice.

That evening Eugenia fell asleep waiting for the soft click of the door opening, the rustle of sheets being pulled back, the touch of callused fingers on her cheek. She woke in the night to find that she was panting, trembling with desire.

"May I?" Ward's voice was soft in the darkness, so tender that she could fool herself into thinking she heard love.

She pressed a kiss on his mouth by way of answer. Her nails dug into his rock-hard arse as he held her steady, hands clamped on her hips as he pumped into her, driving her to euphoria, letting her rest for a moment, before silently driving her higher again. And again.

He came one last time with a desperate groan, his eyes raking her face in the faint light of early dawn.

He left without words. Perhaps there were none to be said? Her feeling for him was irrelevant.

The four of them swam that morning as if nothing had changed, and after luncheon, set out for the fair in Wheatley. Within moments of arriving, to Eugenia's dismay, they split into pairs. Lizzie wanted to visit the animal pens and Otis was interested in—if offended by—a game called bat-a-rat.

Eugenia would have liked them to stay together. She was shot through with anguish at the idea of her coming departure. But Ward merely bowed and left with his brother.

She and Lizzie examined all the hens for sale, while Lizzie pointed out the fact that blood went right down into their feet. Apparently in some breeds, you could see the veins.

"Some people eat chickens' feet," Eugenia told her. "Or consider them a good-luck token. My father has a large collection of curiosities, among them a necklace of chickens' feet worn by a tribal chief in the American wilderness."

"I would love to see that," Lizzie told her, tugging her on to the next tent.

Eugenia nearly said, "You shall, some day," but she stopped herself.

"Let's go to that lecture," Lizzie cried, pointing.

A placard outside a tent read, A DISCUSSION OF CHEMISTRY IN PROOF OF THE SCIENTIFIC SUBLIME, BEING GIVEN BY A FAMOUS SCIENTIST AND DIFFUSER OF USEFUL KNOWLEDGE.

"*Diffuser*?" Eugenia said dubiously.

"Come on," Lizzie said, tugging at her hand. "It's already begun!"

Eugenia looked around for Ward, but he was nowhere to be seen.

The tent was small and crowded with men who frowned at them, but when met with Eugenia's most peremptory stare, quickly vacated two seats in the last row.

Ten or so lines of chairs were arranged in a tight semicircle facing a man with a shock of ferocious black eyebrows.

"It's Mr. Gumwater!" Lizzie squealed.

Ward's unpleasant butler, it seemed, had a secret life in which he diffused useful knowledge for the royal sum of tuppence a head. Famous scientist, indeed!

"I can learn whatever he has to say at home for free," Lizzie hissed. "Let's go."

Eugenia whispered back, "It would be rude to leave now, as it would make a commotion. If possible, a lady should never hurt people's feelings at the expense of a small inconvenience to herself."

Lizzie subsided with a sigh. "Being a lady is tiresome. And I can't see."

Eugenia pulled her onto her lap. "How's this?"

"Better," Lizzie said, leaning against Eugenia's shoulder. Ruby had pinned Lizzie's veil against her shoulders as if it were a cape and rolled it up under her pelisse, so her little frame felt particularly bony.

These days the veil, like Jarvis, was ever-present but mostly invisible.

Gumwater was holding forth about the composition of water, something about the affinity of oxygen for elements other than hydrogen.

Eugenia let her mind wander. She was trying to decide whether she and Ward should speak again, more frankly, before her departure.

But what could she say? "Why don't you want me to stay?" sounded plaintive and humiliating. It wasn't the right question.

Ward *wanted* her. His lovemaking had only become more passionate, if that was possible. They hardly slept; last night she had awoken to find him stroking her, her sleepy body already flying toward release.

The question was whether he loved her.

Suddenly Lizzie began shaking with laughter. Indeed, the whole audience was laughing. Eugenia frowned and tried to concentrate, but her mind refused to hold on to facts about decomposition in the state of water.

Let alone understand what was funny about it. She missed that joke, and Gumwater turned to the mysteries of chemical affinities.

Obviously, her feelings were stronger than Ward's. Her skin prickled with embarrassment at the idea.

If that was the case, she didn't want to hear it said aloud. The humiliation would be devastating.

Lizzie was laughing again; Eugenia's arms tightened around her. She felt a near unbearable sadness at the thought of leaving in the morning. She would have been a good mother to Lizzie and Otis. They liked her and trusted her.

Eugenia, better than anyone, would have been able to navigate the choppy waters of Lizzie's debut, shaping Miss Darcy's season in such a way that her parentage was viewed as an immaterial fact, far outweighed by her beauty, her composure, and her fortune.

She rested her chin on Lizzie's hair, wondering if Snowe's was the main reason Ward was sending her away. If he didn't raise the subject, she had to say

something. If only to assure him that she would discard the idea of a tearoom if he sincerely believed it would imperil Lizzie's future.

If she said nothing, she would regret it for the rest of her life.

Chapter Thirty-five

Eugenia was dressing for the evening meal when the footman delivered a note.

The children and I await you in the drawing room.

It wasn't the note of a lover.

She chose a raspberry-striped evening gown with a revealing bodice; no matter how unmoved Ward pretended to be, she knew he still wanted her, even if she wasn't sure he loved her. With that dismaying thought, she added ruby earrings and lip rouge as well.

In the drawing room, Lizzie was dancing up and down, chattering to Ward, and Otis was sitting on the floor with Jarvis.

Ward was wearing a coat the color of smoke that accentuated his shoulders and made him look so

handsome Eugenia felt a painful throb of need. A somewhat humiliating throb, inasmuch as she was about to be summarily evicted from the house.

She nodded to Ward, and crouched to greet Otis, using one finger to stroke his rat between the ears. "Master Jarvis is wearing a very fine cloak tonight." It was dark green, with gold trim.

"It's his favorite," Otis told her.

As whiskery, intelligent-looking animals went, she was forced to admit that Jarvis had charm. Of a sort.

"He must go into his bag during the meal," she said to Otis. She could hardly ignore Ward, so she straightened and turned. Lizzie was talking a mile a minute, words bubbling out of her as if she were a river.

As she watched, Ward's brows drew together and he said something sharp. Lizzie scowled right back.

Eugenia smiled reluctantly. Lizzie would drive Ward mad when she came of age. She was too independent and original to blindly obey the intricate codes that governed polite society.

Ward met her eyes, and with a shock she saw that he wasn't displeased at his sister; he was angry at *her*. "I gather that you took my sister to a tent-talk, Mrs. Snowe," he said. "I would that you had sought my permission first."

Eugenia went over to them, and bent to kiss Lizzie's cheek before responding. "Permission? To attend a lecture about the composition of water? One doesn't usually ask for permission to be bored into a stupor."

"I wasn't bored!" Lizzie cried. "The talk was funny, even if it was by Mr. Gumwater! I learned—"

"There's no need to repeat what you learned," Ward said, cutting her off.

"You are being protective to a fault," Eugenia observed. "The subject of the lecture was chemistry. Some people may not believe young ladies capable of comprehending scientific concepts, but I hope you are not among them."

"In fact, Lizzie is showing all too much comprehension," Ward said grimly. He turned away, as if he couldn't look at her any longer. "Otis, I think it would be best if you and Lizzie made your farewells to Mrs. Snowe now, and returned to the nursery. You can take your supper there."

"I don't want to!" Lizzie protested.

Ward's jaw tightened.

"It is Mrs. Snowe's last meal with us," Lizzie added, jutting out her stubborn little chin.

Apparently, the "tent-talk"—whatever that was— had been the last straw. Eugenia felt a burst of pure rage at the idea that her sins were so egregious that she was no longer invited to dine with the children, but she choked it back.

"You and I have not seen the last of each other," she promised Lizzie. "I shall ask Mr. Reeve to allow you to pay me a visit in London. Would you like that?"

"Yes, I would!" Lizzie exclaimed. "Do you truly have to leave, Mrs. Snowe?" Her mouth wobbled.

"Indeed I must," Eugenia smiled, although her cheeks felt stiff. "My father is waiting for me."

She saw the pain that streaked through Lizzie's eyes, and pulled her into an embrace. "I'm sorry," she whispered. "I'm truly sorry about your father, Lizzie."

"Miss Midge said that all things have their season. She said my father is in heaven."

Hopefully Miss Midge, for all her failures when it

came to evening prayers, had provided some comfort. Eugenia gave Lizzie another squeeze, then went to Otis, hugged him, and gave Jarvis a little pat.

"I thought we were to take supper with you," Otis complained.

"Ruby will bring you supper in the nursery," Ward said. His eyes were flinty.

The butler held the door open for the children and was turning to go when Ward stopped him.

"Gumwater," he said, "would you be so kind as to summarize the content of your tent-talk? Mrs. Snowe somehow did not catch the essence."

"I regret I was unaware that any women were present," Gumwater said, his tone plummy with ill-disguised disdain. "Until afterwards, of course. There were those who felt only women of a certain class would attend a tent-talk, but I gave them your name, Mrs. Snowe, and assured them you were a widow of good standing."

"You cannot imagine how distressed the unfavorable judgment of your acquaintances makes me feel," Eugenia remarked.

"The talk wasn't intended for ladies," Gumwater said, flashing her a look of potent dislike. "No tent-talk is."

Eugenia skewered him with a gaze that she had learned at her father's knee, a stare that spoke to generations of aristocrats as ancestors. It made it clear that she was capable of summoning a servant to have a commoner's head cut off.

Or at least, she would have been three hundred years before.

"What, exactly, is a 'tent-talk'? I understood from the placard outside that you were offering a lecture

on 'chemistry in proof of the scientific sublime.' Furthermore, no one barred me and Miss Darcy from entering."

Gumwater cleared his throat. "I was expounding on the benefits of chemistry. Teaching the local men about the composition of water."

"You were billed as 'diffuser of useful knowledge'; what, pray tell, has that to do with the composition of water?"

"I have a gift for humor," the butler said, his bushy eyebrows twitching madly. "It was my free afternoon."

"Give us a précis of the content," Ward said.

"It's the way I teach it. So that it sticks in men's brains, as most are simple-minded."

"I fully understand that most men have simple minds," Eugenia agreed.

"I put it in terms of relationships. Hydrogen is like nitrogen, a dependent friend of oxygen, continually forsaken for new favorites."

Eugenia had the strange feeling that she was performing in a Punch and Judy show, but without lines. What on earth could be offensive about hydrogen?

"Come to the point, Gumwater," Ward said, folding his arms over his chest.

Suddenly Eugenia remembered a phrase from the tent that was followed by a roar of male laughter and Lizzie's body shaking with giggles. At the time, it had seemed innocuous, but . . .

"I suppose that you explained chemical relations by drawing an analogy to intimate matters," she stated.

Gumwater nodded. "The connection between oxygen and hydrogen is much more friendly in the state of water." He coughed. "It takes two hydrogen atoms to satisfy an oxygen atom."

Her father would say Gumwater was a prick, Eugenia thought. A woman-hating prick, who probably thought she shouldn't know that word, and never mind it went back to the time of Shakespeare. "In other words, you turned the chemical composition of water into a jest about the difficulty of satisfying a woman?"

"The men always laugh when I explain what it would take to see water split up," Gumwater elaborated. "It wasn't meant for a young lady. I've never had a woman enter the tent before and certainly no governess would bring her charge to something meant only for men, as is a tent-talk."

Ward had stood silently through this entire exchange. Now he indicated the door with a jerk of his head.

He said nothing until Gumwater left, at which point he turned to her. "Why in God's name did you enter that tent? Even if you didn't understand the aim of a 'tent-talk,' surely you noticed that the audience was entirely male?"

"If scientific information were not viewed as the sole province of men," Eugenia snapped, "you might well find more women inadvertently wandering into what was actually a ribald harangue."

"Educational principles aside, I would like to know why you exposed my little sister to a vulgar, if not lewd, performance."

"I had no such intention," Eugenia said, drawing composure around her like a suit of armor. "I am truly sorry that I didn't recognize the true nature of your butler's so-called lecture. Lizzie has a thirst for knowledge that should be nurtured, but obviously I chose the wrong venue."

"As I have repeatedly told you, Lizzie is a young *lady*," Ward stated, his arms locked over his chest.

Anger swept through her with the same burning ferocity with which she had experienced desire the night before. "I am fully aware of Lizzie's place in society," she said, fighting to keep her voice from rising. "I see no reason why her status should preclude scientific knowledge. When I was a girl, I especially enjoyed learning mathematics."

"If you'll excuse my bluntness, Eugenia, that is irrelevant. Lizzie will be raised in a house without strumpets, or the other lamentable aspects of your upbringing, which is precisely why I came to Snowe's Registry in the first place."

Eugenia flinched. She hadn't expected to have her confidences thrown back at her; she'd never told anyone but Andrew about the courtesans in her father's house. "We are in agreement on that point," she said, striving for composure.

"Then why did you bring my sister into a tent full of men enjoying a string of lewd jests? You, who train governesses, *you* took my sister to see a debauched tent-talk." Ward was furious—and rightly so.

She had made a mistake, and she'd learned long ago to acknowledge her mistakes. She would apologize again.

"There are instinctual rules that govern polite society." He raked a hand through his hair, frustrated. "I don't know how to explain it."

How could he possibly think she was ignorant of the rules of polite society? Her power to grant a family a governess was linked to the children's success in marriage. It was as if he still thought she was

a former governess—but she'd clarified her rank, she was sure of it.

"A lady would never have dreamed of entering that tent, and if under some misapprehension she were to enter and see the audience, she would remove herself immediately," he went on. "Yet you sat unmoved while my little sister absorbed jests alluding to three people in one bed. Not to mention an illuminating disquisition on *watery froth*, Mrs. Snowe. In short, my sister is now curious about the composition of semen, as well as unusual erotic combinations!"

Eugenia forgot her resolution to apologize. "Your sister, Mr. Reeve, was already in possession of far more knowledge of adult life than are most children her age," she pointed out. "Need I remind you of your mother's friendship with the charmingly named Mr. Burger—which friendship her children had been instructed never to mention?"

"My intent is to help them forget their unfortunate childhood, not deepen their knowledge of dissolute behavior."

"I had no intention of teaching your sister immorality!"

"Let me repeat: what were you doing in the goddamned tent while she was learning it?"

"I have apologized for that, and I will apologize again," Eugenia said, pulling herself together. "I was very wrong to enter that tent. I was not paying attention to your butler's sordid lecture, and I freely acknowledge that I should have been."

"What in the bloody hell *were* you doing?" This was a shout.

Eugenia shouted right back. "Thinking about you, about *us*!"

His face went utterly expressionless, stony. "*Us?*"

"Yes, *us!*" she cried. "I was wondering why you had taken yourself off with Otis, why you were acting so strangely, why you had said—" She stopped.

"Had said what?"

Her breath was rasping in her chest. "*Nothing,*" she said, her voice quieting. "Why you had said nothing. About us."

Chapter Thirty-six

In the silence that followed, Eugenia discovered that she was clinging to the back of a chair for support. Ward's arms unfolded and his lips tightened into a line before he walked over to stand beside her.

"I apologize," he said, looking into her eyes. "This is my fault for not being more clear at the beginning of our intimacies. Our *affaire*."

Affaire. So that was what it was.

All it was.

She couldn't delude herself that she hadn't known. She had always known.

"You were perfectly clear," Eugenia said, chin up. She refused to betray any sign of the devastation she felt. The trembling, however, she couldn't hide: she was shaking slightly from head to foot. "You begged me to stay with you a fortnight."

"A man does, in the throes of passion."

That was unforgivable.

But at the same time, she caught a glimpse of something in his eyes. This wasn't the man who had coaxed her into the water, who had celebrated making love by eating trifle at midnight. This was someone different.

The thought steadied her.

They had *made love*.

"Our intimacies were not merely the throes of passion," she said, making up her mind. She had blazed trails by starting her own business; she might as well confound another preconception, to wit, that a woman must not speak of love before a man proposed marriage. She would speak the truth.

Ward said nothing.

"I am in love with you," Eugenia said, meeting his eyes. "I believe you are in love with me as well."

Just as the silence grew unbearable, he said, "I am terribly sorry to disappoint you, Eugenia."

It was as if he taken out a pistol and shot her in the leg. Not a fatal blow, but pain tore through her all the same. The worst of it was that his voice was genuinely regretful.

"I see," she managed.

He turned away, clearly giving her time to collect herself. Eugenia clenched her hand on the back of the chair with such force that her knuckles turned white with strain.

Standing with his back to her, gazing out the window, Ward cleared his throat. "Even if I felt more for you, I could not keep a mistress in the house with my siblings. I was very wrong to countenance these two weeks."

Taking a breath felt like inhaling fire.

Felt *more* for her? He could go to hell.

"I am *not* your mistress," she said, fierce and low. "That would imply a financial exchange between us. I have been your guest, and helped with the children with no thought of recompense."

He turned back and put his hand over hers again. "Forgive me, a lover."

It was patently obvious to her that he had never considered marriage. He was using the term "lover" as a sop to her feelings. Back in the carriage when he first abducted her, he had offered "courtesies" between friends, never to be mentioned again. Why hadn't she listened to him?

"Do you mean that you did not think of me as someone to marry," she asked, shaping the words carefully, "or that you did not think of me as a doxy owing to my giving myself to you with such . . ." Her voice trailed off.

"Such joy," Ward said, that disconcerting flash of emotion in his eyes again. "We took pleasure in each other, and there's nothing wrong with that, Eugenia. But the world has intervened, and now we must go our separate ways."

"I see."

He hesitated. "Even if I had—if I wished to offer you marriage, I cannot."

She couldn't bring herself to answer.

"I must marry someone who will make up for my irregular birth and launch Lizzie into the ton. My wife must be a model of conventional behavior. If I marry, my wife has to be a paragon."

She swallowed hard. It wasn't as if his words were surprising.

"In the ancient phrase, she must be a lady *to the manner born*," he continued, his hand tightening over hers. "You are all that is ladylike, Eugenia, but there is an incalculable part of being a lady—an instinctual part—that cannot be learned. My stepmother would never have entered that tent, let alone taken a seat among a crowd of guffawing men."

"To the manner born?" She not only understood society's manners better than most, but she was born in a manor!

Apparently he had lied when he said that he knew her status. She nearly snapped back a précis of her family tree, but she stopped.

It was irrelevant.

What Ward was really saying was that she wasn't ladylike enough. That meant he didn't respect or love *her*, the Eugenia who started Snowe's Registry.

If she informed him of her pedigree—that she was not merely gentry, but a peeress, one of the highest in the land—she might be able to convince him that her family's position in society meant she could successfully launch Lizzie on the marriage market.

But there was no persuading a man to love you, the real you.

Right. She had to push back her hurt and fury, and find the strength to be polite.

"Your sister is eager to learn about the natural world," she said, withdrawing her hand from under his. "You would do well to encourage her, Ward, no matter how unconventional her studies might seem."

His face was expressionless, closed off to all feeling. "Thank you for the advice, but I mean to avoid pushing her toward further eccentricities. She's already

talking of opening an emporium and has learned to bellow strings of curses. Ladies don't curse."

Funny. A string of curses was the only thing going through her head.

Ward took a breath, and she steeled herself.

Surely there wasn't more?

There was more.

"I blame myself," he said, looking at her with compassion and regret—a combination that made her nearly choke with rage. "I never should have brought a lover into a household with children. I had to send the children to the nursery tonight because I realized that Lizzie has grown overly fond of you."

"I was fond of some of the courtesans I knew as a child," Eugenia said. He'd already decided she was irredeemable; she might as well shock him further. "I learned much from them. One young woman named Augusta, for example, locked her lover inside a closet until he agreed to have her carriage relined in canary-yellow satin."

Instead of looking appalled, he looked even more sympathetic. As if he pitied her.

It was time to retire. Thank God for her training—because no matter what Ward thought of her, she was a lady who had been presented to the queen. Several times, in fact.

As if from afar, she watched herself curtsy, step forward and kiss Ward's cheek, saying all the right things about taking a small meal in her chamber. She apologized yet again, and mentioned her hope of remaining in the children's lives.

With a touch of self-deprecation, she promised that if he would entrust his sister to her on a visit to

London, she would never again to expose Lizzie to science.

She played her part, but Ward didn't play his. He stood silently and said nothing in response to her charming remarks about the children.

She curtsied again, the sharp, organized part of her brain assuring herself that Ward could not keep her from Lizzie when the time came for her debut.

Thinking of that, she paused in the doorway and turned. "When you marry, please do introduce me to your wife. *This*"—she waved her hand in the air— "shall never be mentioned again between us, as you specified two weeks ago. I trust you to make certain your household doesn't breathe a word."

She waited. Still he said nothing. "I would ask you to have a word with Gumwater in particular." She didn't bother to keep her disdain out of her voice. "But what I really mean to say is that I would be happy to help your wife in any capacity with Lizzie's debut."

He still didn't answer, so she slipped out the door and closed it behind her.

Chapter Thirty-seven

Monday, June 15, 1801

Eugenia had been awake all night. She spent hours reeling between fits of burning tears and equally intense bouts of rage, imagining scenes in which she threw heavy objects at Ward's head.

Just as she talked herself into celebrating the natural end of their friendship, she found herself curled in a ball again, tears soaking into the sheet.

The truth was that she loved him just as much as she'd loved Andrew. And wasn't that damnable? She had lost them both. By dawn, her throat ached and her eyes were swollen.

Sleep was impossible and there wasn't any point

to lying wretchedly in bed. She got up and went over to the window.

The lawn stretched down to the lake, where little tendrils of steam rose from the surface. It looked irresistible.

Clothilde entered with a gentle knock just as Eugenia was pulling on her borrowed breeches.

"I've decided to have a last dip in the lake before we leave," Eugenia said, not even trying to conceal her swollen eyes. Gumwater had undoubtedly been at the drawing room door last night, eavesdropping on every word she and Ward exchanged and reporting them to the household with relish.

"I shall finish packing your trunk," Clothilde said, adding, "Reeve is a *connard*, madame, and we are well rid of this house."

Eugenia pulled on her slippers and made her way down the hill to the water, trying not to slip on the dewy grass. When she reached the shore of the lake, she took a deep breath and looked around with mixed emotions. The woods across the small lake were dreamy, soft green in this light. Birds were waking, calling to each other.

No matter the grief with which their love affair had ended, in teaching her to enjoy water, Ward had given her a gift beyond value. She toed off her slippers and placed them neatly on the shingle along with a length of toweling.

She was determined to go into the lake alone—and furthermore, to put her head under water.

In the end, it wasn't even difficult. She steeled herself and waded into the water, flinching at the chill against her legs, gasping when it covered her breasts.

She took a deep breath and bent forward, and water flowed like a benediction over her burning eyes . . . and she was floating.

Face down, the way the children did.

She thrashed a bit, got water in her mouth, and turned over, floating on her back. The sky was pale, pale blue and far away. She remembered the faint reassuring pressure of Ward's hands as he held her up, but she didn't need him.

She could float by herself.

She could find a husband as well. She sent thanks into the air, thanks and a farewell to Andrew.

Another farewell.

She made little waving motions with her hands, the way that Ward had taught her. Her hair worked itself free of its loose braid and spread around her in the water, making her feel like a mermaid.

The cool soothed her eyes and she tried turning over again and floating on her face, but only for a minute. She had done it. That was enough for now.

Her feet found the bottom and she ducked down to slick back her hair and return to the shore, but stopped in surprise.

"Mrs. Snowe," Otis called, "I hope you don't mind that I came down to the water. Jarvis wanted to say goodbye."

He was sitting on the big rock, arms wrapped around his knees. Jarvis was next to him, belly up, enjoying the sunshine.

Eugenia walked toward the shore until the water was lapping just above her breasts. "I am happy to see you, Otis. I do hope you'll visit me in London."

He looked down and gave Jarvis's stomach a scratch. "I thought perhaps you would visit me at Eton."

"I shall," she promised. "I shall send hampers full of lovely things for you and Marmaduke."

"*If* I share rooms with him," Otis said. "I might be put with some other boy." His hand closed on Jarvis and the sleepy rat squeaked in protest and woke up, struggling free.

"I shall make certain you are placed with Marmaduke," Eugenia promised. "One of the school's governors is a close friend of my father's."

"Lizzie said that the bishop was one of your father's friends as well."

"Yes, he is. Are you worried that Jarvis will fall off?" The rat was exploring the side of the rock that led to deep water, the side where she and the children were forbidden to swim.

"Oh no," Otis said. "Jarvis knows better. He never jumps if he might hurt himself. Is your father acquainted with everyone important?"

"He's a marquis, and the peerage is small. As you will learn yourself, Otis, once you grow up."

"A marquis is better than a lord, isn't he?"

"It's not a question of better than," Eugenia said. "It's—"

She heard a splash, and Otis's shriek cut off her reply. "Jarvis! Jarvis fell in!"

"Don't worry," Eugenia said, pushing through the water toward the rock.

"I'm coming, Jarvis!" Otis shrieked, throwing himself from the rock into the dark water on the far side.

Eugenia uttered a low curse, put her face in the water, and kicked. She moved her arms and legs the way she'd seen Ward do. Within a minute, to her surprise, she was on the other side of the rock.

Otis was thrashing in the water; he hadn't gone

under, thank goodness. When she saw him, she stopped kicking and promptly sank. Water filled her mouth and she plummeted into colder water.

Terror seized her and reverberated to her fingers and toes like a lightning bolt.

No! Otis needed her. She fought her way back to the surface.

She emerged sputtering and choking. Otis was still crying and thrashing in a circle, sending plumes of water in every direction. There was no sign of Jarvis.

Eugenia's heart fell. She shouted, "Otis, please be calm!"

He looked very small with his hair plastered to his skull. His mouth was open, screaming "Jarvis! Jarvis!" over and over.

At least he wasn't sinking.

"You must go to shore," Eugenia shouted. She tipped forward to try to move toward him, which caused another panic-inducing plunge toward the bottom of the lake. But she kept her head and broke the surface again.

Taking a gulp of air, she shouted in a voice learned from many governesses, "Otis, get out of the water this instant so I can save Jarvis!"

His scream broke off in mid-air. He stared at her in surprise, stopped thrashing, and promptly disappeared.

Heart pounding with fear, Eugenia swam to where he'd gone under, filled her lungs, and let herself sink. The water was murky, darker and colder here where the lake was deepest and the sun never quite warmed it. *There!* Otis was just to her right, struggling about, his hair flying around his face.

Her lungs were aching, but she reached him,

grabbed his shirt, and kicked upward with all her might.

They broke the surface coughing. Now they had to swim around the rock somehow. Otis was clinging to her shoulder, and he was surprisingly heavy.

Just as she took a breath to start kicking, she heard a bellow and saw Ward charging down the lawn. "Your brother's coming," she gasped.

"Jarvis!" Otis wailed.

A moment later, Ward grabbed the boy first by one arm and then by his waist. As Otis was hoisted into the air, Ward's eye caught Eugenia's. He shouted something at her but she sank below the water before she could catch it, feeling pure relief at having Otis's weight lifted from her.

Her legs were exhausted, but she set out for the other side of the rock. Four kicks and she was there. When her feet at last touched the bottom she was nearly overwhelmed by a flood of relief, followed by exhilaration.

She'd done it!

She had not only swum for the first time, she'd saved Otis from drowning, as Andrew had once saved her. At the thought of what could have happened if she had failed, her knees weakened and she felt dizzy.

She pushed wet hair from her eyes and stepped up onto the rock. Otis was crouched down on the far side, staring into the water. Beside him, looking sleek and unconcerned, was Jarvis, grooming himself.

"I'm fine," Eugenia called, and broke into a fit of coughing. Otis started to his feet, gave a shriek, and hurled himself into her arms. "We thought you sank!"

All that could be seen on the other side of the rock was a spreading pool of bubbles. Just as Eugenia was wondering whether she ought to jump in the better to reassure Ward of her safety, his head broke the surface.

When he saw her, his face filled with an emotion she couldn't interpret. Her heart thumped; perhaps the near tragedy would make him realize that he loved her.

"I had no need for a rescue," she called, "but I thank you for your effort."

"Don't move," he shouted. "I'd like to speak with you, Mrs. Snowe."

His bellow was manifestly not that of an anguished man arriving late to the realization of true love.

"We can speak later," she called, retrieving her slippers and turning to go. Otis prattled all the way back up to the house, mostly to Jarvis but also to her.

As if she had eyes in the back of her head, Eugenia was aware that Ward cut through the water to the shore in a couple of irritated strokes. He picked up her forgotten length of toweling, rubbed his head, and started up the lawn after them.

"I saved myself," Eugenia whispered to no one in particular, as she crossed the threshold into the entry.

Gumwater was there, his eyebrows twitching as she and Otis dripped lake water over the marble floor.

"Your maid awaits you, Mrs. Snowe," he announced. "Your trunk is already stowed on the carriage, but she held back a dry garment for you."

"Thank you, Gumwater," she said. She bent down and kissed Otis and, when a plump, wet rat was thrust toward her, she kissed the general area

around Jarvis's whiskers. "I will visit you at Eton," she promised the boy.

The door slammed open and Ward strode in. "I thought I made it clear there would be no swimming on that side of the rock," he barked at the two of them.

Apparently he thought she had willfully put a child at risk. Lovely.

Eugenia managed a smile. "I think that Otis and I both learned our lesson as regards deep water, Mr. Reeve." She bent down and gave Otis a tight hug, causing the two of them to drip even more water on the floor. "You were very brave," she whispered, loving the feeling of his spindly arms wrapping tightly around her waist.

Then she straightened, turned to her host, and held out her hand. "Mr. Reeve, I shall take my leave as soon as I have changed into a gown, so I will bid you goodbye now."

He merely looked at her proffered hand.

"I can scarcely curtsy in soaking-wet breeches," she said, exasperated. Apparently he insisted upon ladylike behavior to the end.

She bobbed a curtsy and turned to climb the stairs. Sadness weighed as heavy as her drenched clothing. It was truly over. The next time she saw Edward Reeve, it would be as mere acquaintances.

At the same time, she was proud of herself in a way she hadn't been in years. She had broken—no, shattered—the glass coffin that had encased her since Andrew's death.

She had conquered her fear of water, taught herself to swim, and had an *affaire* with a beautiful man.

Fallen in love with him.

Ward didn't return her feelings, which was pain-

ful, but even that was good. Pain was . . . Pain was proof she was alive.

Andrew had loved her with everything he was, and he had respected her too. She deserved that kind of love. True, she was no longer the same docile young lady whom Andrew had known.

But someday she would meet a man who valued her for the strong person she had become.

Chapter Thirty-eight

Eugenia was gone.

At the end of the day, Ward sat in his library, collapsed onto a chair like a puppet with no strings. She was gone.

Lizzie had burst into tears at luncheon. Gumwater said something snide, so Ward sacked him. He didn't want his sister growing up around that kind of overt dislike.

Yes, he had grown up with servants' disrespect, but what the hell was he thinking, allowing his sister to be subjected to the same contempt, albeit for her sex, not her birth?

Otis had cried at bedtime, and Ruby was treating Ward with cool disdain whenever he entered the nursery. Monsieur Marcel? He hadn't gone anywhere

near the kitchen, but tonight was the first time he'd been served burnt chicken.

Followed by dry cake. There was no mistaking the message.

All the same, he had made the right decision.

He tossed back his brandy with a jerky movement. For all intents and purposes, Lizzie and Otis were his children, and their futures were at stake. Every time he thought about Lady Hyacinth's syrupy condescension toward Eugenia, or his grandmother's patent scorn, he realized once again that the choice he'd made wasn't really a choice at all.

He could not allow Lizzie and Otis to be raised by the duchess, a woman who had abandoned him as a baby. His father had been scarcely eighteen years old, but he hadn't banished his infant son to the country to be raised by a cowherd. The earl had visited the nursery every day, frequently more than once a day.

As a small boy, Ward had roamed the house at night, and more often than not had ended up in his father's bed. Looking back, he had to suppose that the earl took lovers, but he had never met them.

Lady Lisette, on the other hand, made no sacrifices for the sake of her children. That sad fact became clearer with every story that Otis or Lizzie blurted out. She had never put her children's interests before her own: neither their safety, nor their comfort, nor their futures.

And the Duchess of Gilner had shaped their mother into the monster she had become.

The next morning he woke with a groan as his man snapped back the curtains and announced, "Her Grace, the Duchess of Gilner, has arrived, sir. She awaits you in the south parlor."

Ward rolled over, throwing his hand over his eyes. "Coffee."

"I regret to inform you, sir, that Monsieur Marcel reports that he used the last of the coffee refining Mrs. Snowe's Arabian mocha soufflé. Would you care for tea instead?"

He loathed tea, and Marcel knew it. Ward got himself to his feet, silently cursing the brandy he'd downed the night before, and headed for the bathing chamber.

"The bath is slightly chilly," his man said, after he stepped in. "I'll add some hot water." He emptied the smallest kettle Ward had ever seen into the freezing bath, then sailed out of the room. Another convert to Eugenia's charm.

Once Ward stopped shivering and got himself into clothing—his valet had unaccountably left the chamber—he went to the nursery. Otis jumped to his feet, Jarvis clutched in one hand, and ran toward him. Ward bent just as Otis reached him.

He caught his brother up into his arms, thin legs dangling. He smelled like raisin scone and little boy. "I had a bad dream about Jarvis drowning," Otis said, settling the rat on Ward's shoulder.

"Jarvis is a remarkably healthy animal and a good swimmer," Ward said, putting Otis down. "Just look at him."

Sure enough, Jarvis's black eyes were gleaming with good health as he launched himself from Ward's shoulder to Otis's.

"If that rat ever jumps on me, I shall let him plummet to the floor," Lizzie said with relish, joining them.

"Our grandmother has arrived," Ward told them.

"Ruby, would you please bring Lizzie and Otis downstairs in half an hour? Without Jarvis," he added.

"Oh horrors," Lizzie moaned. "I loathe the duchess. She's a gut-griping maggot-pie."

Eugenia would know which play that fragrant turn of phrase came from. Ward pushed the thought away. "Please do not refer to Her Grace as a maggot-pie," he said. "The Duchess of Gilner deserves our respect."

"Why?" Otis asked.

"She is an elder member of our family," Ward said.

"Mother said she was—"

"Our mother is dead, and I think we would all agree that she was not a good model for proper behavior."

Lizzie sniffed. "Mrs. Snowe said—"

Ward cut her off again. "Ruby, please dress the children in their best attire to greet the duchess."

"I will put my veil back on," Lizzie threatened.

Ward cupped one hand under her defiant, pointed chin. "I will not allow Grandmother to take your veil from you."

His sister came a step closer and leaned against him. Ward looked up and discovered that Ruby had deigned to give him a smile.

Out in the corridor, Ward realized that he would give almost anything not to have to walk down the stairs to the drawing room. He had never met the duchess before he'd written a letter informing her of the children's existence.

Her response to the news that she had two more grandchildren had been joyless, and their further encounters downright horrible. For example, when they'd met outside Gunter's, the expression she'd had on meeting Eugenia—

He stumbled and nearly fell against the wall of the corridor. It felt as if he'd been shoring up a seawall with sand, and the tide rushed in.

Now the truth slammed into his head like that tide. All those ideas he had, about the kind of woman he should marry, a woman who was a proper lady? They were all rubbish. Worthless.

He had been focused on whether Lizzie would be able to marry well—why? In order that his sister could turn into someone like the duchess—or Lady Hyacinth, for that matter? A person who talked about others in such a withering fashion? So that Otis could marry a lifeless young woman like Lady Hyacinth's daughter?

God forbid.

The best person to help him raise Lizzie and Otis was the woman whom they loved, and who loved them in return: Eugenia.

Equally importantly, *he* loved her. He loved her more than life itself.

It was true that people like the duchess were rude to Eugenia—but only because she was too intelligent to be confined by their narrow strictures. They were rude to her and scorned her . . .

The way he had.

Regret punched through him, searing his heart. His body. This is what anguish feels like, his brain helpfully told him.

He felt as if he'd walked naked into a snowstorm and the consequence was frostbite, a cruel pain in his limbs, and a huge, tearing loneliness in his heart.

A strangled rasp burst from his chest. Damn it, this was unacceptable.

He had hurt Eugenia. Cut her to the bone. He ran

an unsteady hand through his hair and forced himself to continue walking toward the staircase.

None of the things he'd thought to be important truly mattered. He had thought he wanted a demure wife, but he didn't. Eugenia broke all the rules.

He had wooed Mia, asked for her hand in marriage, and now he understood that she had been right to leave him: he hadn't felt enough for her.

The honest truth was that he had been mildly irritated when he discovered that Mia had married a duke in his absence. He had congratulated himself on comporting himself like a gentleman, and relinquishing his fiancée without violence.

Yet the mere thought of Eugenia with another man made rage course through him. He would never be able to marshal civility if he saw *her* with a new husband.

He reached the top of the flight of stairs and started down. Beauty, laughter, intelligence like a flame, the berry scent that was hers alone, the way Eugenia screamed when he gave her pleasure . . .

Anguish, he discovered, was not unlike a case of pneumonia he'd had as a child. His limbs throbbed in tandem with the pain in his chest.

With an effort of will, he forced himself to nod to the footman standing by the door to the drawing room. He would see the duchess and then he would repair this. Somehow.

There had to be a way by which he could be with the woman he loved and still win guardianship.

His grandmother was perched on the edge of a chair, her eyes fixed on the mantelpiece clock. He bowed. "Please forgive me for not attending you immediately, Your Grace."

"I have been waiting for an hour and forty-three minutes," the lady said in a voice that could have kept frozen one of Gunter's ices.

"I apologize," Ward said, seating himself without being asked, because he had the feeling that the duchess would prefer he stand in front of her like a schoolboy being reprimanded.

"Where are the children?" she demanded, clamping her hands around the knob handle of her cane.

"Their nursery maid will bring them down shortly."

She pounced on that. "Nursery maid! Hadn't you engaged a Snowe's governess?"

"Miss Midge left, but we are expecting a new governess tomorrow."

"When did the governess leave?"

Her eyes had a distinct resemblance to Jarvis's, though Otis would not like the comparison. "A fortnight ago," Ward said.

"So you—"

"Miss Midge left her position without giving notice, and Mrs. Snowe very generously agreed to take her place until a substitute could be arranged. She only left us yesterday. I believe you'll see a remarkable difference in the children's behavior."

"If Mrs. Snowe managed to teach Otis to bow, I shall be astonished," the duchess said acidly. "She acts as a governess on occasion, does she? The Countess of Sefton will be interested to hear it." Her tone turned from disdain to satisfaction, which struck Ward as ominous. "I suppose you have no idea what I'm talking about."

"I confess I do not," Ward answered. The duchess smiled toothily, like a shark wearing a pearl necklace.

"Lady Sefton, one of the patronesses of Almack's, did not revoke Mrs. Snowe's voucher after the woman opened her registry, although obviously she ought to have done so. It hardly need be said that those who engage in trade are not welcome at Almack's."

She opened her reticule, took out a handkerchief, and dabbed her nose with it.

Lizzie and Otis entered the room before Ward could fashion an answer that didn't include a threat of violence. Well, not violence, since she was an elderly woman and his own grandmother—but he would defend Eugenia and her choice to open Snowe's Registry with his last breath.

He went to greet the children, which gave him time to rein in his temper. Lizzie was not wearing her veil, and Otis was not carrying Jarvis's bag.

They were both dressed in black, of course, but Lizzie's pale blond hair gleamed and her face appeared healthier than he remembered. To Ward's eyes, the children looked shiny, well-mannered, and a trifle boring. Perfectly conventional, in other words.

"Miss Darcy and Lord Darcy," their grandmother said, nodding. "It appears that Mrs. Snowe is a satisfactory governess; your bow was nearly graceful, Lord Darcy."

"Mrs. Snowe is not a governess," Lizzie said.

The duchess's thin lips grew thinner.

"She is a *lady*," Lizzie clarified.

"A lady acts as such," their grandmother replied, with a sniff. "A governess teaches girls to curtsy, and a lady does not. Equally important, children do not speak until they are spoken to."

"Mrs. Snowe was our guest," Otis said, ignoring that rule.

"Indeed? How do you define *guest*? Would a guest teach you how to bow?"

Otis's brows knit together. "It doesn't matter what a lady does. She is still a lady."

Ward grinned at that. Otis was right.

"I beg to differ," Her Grace stated.

"Mrs. Snowe's father is a marquis, and that means she's a lady," Otis said defiantly.

Wait.

The word rattled around in Ward's head.

"*Marquis*?" he echoed.

"What's more, she gave me a box for Jarvis to sleep in," Otis said, "and governesses don't give gifts."

The dowager duchess looked at Ward. "I don't blame you for your incredulity. One rarely finds peers plummeting down the social ladder in such a definitive fashion. Mrs. Snowe's late husband would be aghast. And *his* father, the viscount? Turning in his grave, without a doubt."

"I'll show you the box!" Otis exclaimed. He turned toward the door, stopped, spun around, and bowed, before he dashed out.

"No governess can perform miracles in two weeks, but Mrs. Snowe must be competent," Her Grace pronounced. "Perhaps if I offer her three times her customary salary, she would agree to join my household."

Ward barely registered that Otis had left the room, because he was still trying to make sense of the conversation. Eugenia was the daughter of a marquis, and had been married to a viscount. Or the son of a viscount? Wouldn't that make her Lady Snowe? Maybe not. Maybe she was just the Honorable Eugenia Snowe.

Damned if he knew. He'd never paid much attention to the governesses who tried to drill such things into his memory.

Besides, her title was irrelevant; clearly she chose not to use it, if she had one. More importantly, why in hell hadn't she told him? It would have been a good opportunity when he'd told her that she wasn't ladylike enough, for example.

He suddenly remembered Eugenia asking him if he knew she was a lady.

He'd said yes; what else could he possibly have said?

Bloody hell, why hadn't he gone to a few soirees over the last seven years? He might have met Eugenia in the proper setting. He would have known her status, instead of making a fool of himself by assuming she had been a governess.

"I do not agree," Lizzie said, in reply to something he'd completely missed.

He wrenched his attention back to the venomous old woman, who still had not invited his sister to take a seat. The woman was trying to intimidate Lizzie, but he had a shrewd idea that she would fail. Nothing frightened his sister.

Other than dead fish.

The duchess's own characteristics had bred true, and Lizzie was more than a match for her grandmother.

"It is not your place to agree or disagree," Her Grace stated. "You are a child, and as such, you ought to be quiet and obedient." She raised her clasped hands and thumped her cane onto the ground.

Lizzie's eyes narrowed. "I recognize you!"

"I should hope so," her grandmother said acidly.

The little girl dropped into the chair opposite the duchess. Her slim figure went rigid and a glare settled on her face. Her hands extended before her, clasping the invisible brass knob on top of an invisible cane.

Before anyone could say a word, she rasped, in a fair approximation of the duchess's aristocratic drawl, *"Look like the innocent flower, my lord, but be the serpent under it."*

Lizzie was a far better actress than Ward had recognized, not that it was relevant. Shock, and perhaps pain, creased the old woman's face.

"I know how tender 'tis to love my babe," Lizzie went on. *"I would, while it was smiling in my face, have plucked—"*

Ward suddenly knew which play—and which character—Lizzie was performing. Those were Lady Macbeth's lines when she was about to say that she'd murder her own child in order to become queen. "That will do," he said hastily. "Lizzie, you have been extremely rude. Apologize to Her Grace at once."

Lizzie hopped to her feet and curtsied. "I apologize, Grandmama."

"Are you saying that Lisette portrayed me on the stage?" the duchess said, her voice strained. "Her own mother?"

Happily, Otis trotted back into the room before Lizzie could confirm the uncomfortable truth.

"My mother was a troubled woman," Ward found himself saying. "I know from my own experience that Lady Lisette was prone to unkindnesses she later regretted."

The duchess met his eyes and then looked away, turning from a desolate mother to a haughty, disdainful aristocrat.

"Here's the box!" Otis said, taking advantage of the momentary silence to thrust Jarvis's bed toward his grandmother.

She recoiled, her gloved hands flying into the air. "Do you think to give *me* an object touched by a rat?"

"You can see how nice it is," Otis said, opening the lid. "This box was given to Mrs. Snowe by her father, the marquis, and she gave it to me. No governess would do that."

Had everyone in the house known of Eugenia's pedigree? Yet Ward had no one to be angry with except himself. He had jumped to a conclusion about Eugenia's upbringing rather than trust the evidence of his ears and eyes.

Then, like a kick to the belly, he grasped the significance of Eugenia's status.

They could marry. She was an aristocrat, for God's sake. That marquis, her father, was probably sitting in the House of Lords: how could they possibly object to her as the children's mother in front of *him*?

His heart leapt, and he only just managed to keep a sober expression on his face.

"That box is revolting," the duchess was telling Otis. "The lining is tattered, and the wood appears to have been chewed. A stable boy might have given you a gift of this value."

"It's only because Jarvis likes to sharpen his teeth," Otis said, looking uncertain.

"What is *that*?" Her Grace demanded, her tone deepening as she pointed a thin finger at the inside of the lid. "Is that a painting?" She plucked the box from Otis's hands and tugged at the tattered green velvet lining.

"You're tearing off the velvet," Otis cried. "That's what makes Jarvis feel safe and warm!"

The duchess dropped a shred of cloth to the floor and hissed. "Mrs. Snowe *gave* this box to you? This is an obscenity!"

Ward only just managed to pull Otis back before he could assault his grandmother in order to retrieve Jarvis's bed.

"Not even a rat should sleep within sight of this depravity. I'll say this much for you, Mr. Reeve," his grandmother said, handing the box to Ward. "You had no idea just whom you were entertaining under your roof. It seems that Mrs. Snowe is *considerably* more sophisticated than most think her to be." There was a grim satisfaction about her that made Ward's eyes narrow.

He glanced under the lid of the box, quickly closed it again, and turned to the children. "Lizzie and Otis, say farewell to your grandmother, if you please. Otis, I shall find a new bed for Jarvis."

"Good afternoon, *Grandmother*," Lizzie said with a curtsy. Otis bowed, his entire body rigid with reproach.

They had turned to go when the duchess stopped them, her voice chilly. "Children must say farewell to every adult in a room, which in this case includes Mr. Reeve."

Otis turned around, grabbed Ward's hand, and gave it a kiss before he ran for the door. Lizzie curtsied. "Good afternoon, dearest brother." Her lisp made an appearance again, accompanied by a roll of her eyes.

"Go on, you little donkey," Ward said.

When Lizzie was safely out the door, he opened the lid of the box again. Inside was an exquisite depiction of a wildly erotic scene—and he'd seen his

fair share. A nude man was kissing a naked lady's nether parts, while she pleasured herself. The lady's luxuriant curves were as painstakingly detailed as her lover's enormous and rampant phallus.

Eugenia would be horrified at the idea she'd unwittingly given it to Otis. In fact, it was lucky that Jarvis hadn't shredded the velvet already, giving his little brother an early education in erotic art.

"Utterly revolting," the duchess snapped, rising to her feet with the help of her cane. "I feel quite faint."

He couldn't let her leave, not before ensuring that she would not ruin Eugenia's reputation by talk of the box.

"Clearly Mrs. Snowe had no idea that the painting existed," Ward said. "I would ask that you keep its existence a secret, Your Grace."

"You dare defend—"

"I will always defend my brother and sister to the best of my ability. Knowledge of this image would attract the worst sort of attention. I would not be surprised if gossip about the box attached to your daughter, rather than Mrs. Snowe."

"Nonsense! The proof is in your hands!"

"A painting depicting an erotic act found in the possession of a very young man," Ward said, looking hard at his grandmother. "Do you follow what I'm saying, Your Grace? Neither of us wishes to remind the world of Lady Lisette's amorous proclivities. My own father was her junior, as you may know—although not nearly as young as the late Lord Darcy."

The dowager duchess abruptly sat again. In the silence that followed, the sharp lines around her mouth tightened. "No one would dare accuse my daughter of the debauchery you imply. Otis is her *son*."

"One would hope you are correct." He let the silence grow because, frankly? The world wouldn't hesitate to accuse Lady Lisette of any manner of depravity.

"There is absolutely no need to discuss this appalling incident again," the duchess announced. "The fact that Mrs. Snowe has been acting as a governess is enough to banish her from polite society, as should have happened long ago."

"*No.*" The word shot from Ward's mouth, hard and implacable. "You may not use Mrs. Snowe's kindness to your orphaned grandchildren to tarnish her standing at Almack's or any other place."

She sniffed. "How do you propose to stop me, Mr. Reeve?"

Ward gave his grandmother a smile that he'd honed inside Britain's most dangerous prison. "When I was fourteen years old, I paid a visit to your daughter. Perhaps Lady Lisette did not share the details . . . in particular why I abruptly returned to my father's residence?"

She flinched. It was a small movement, but he caught it. "No."

He used silence as a weapon again. Then: "I will say nothing to the House of Lords. But if I ever learn that you have spread gossip about my mother's occupation, my siblings' childhood, or Mrs. Snowe's inestimable aid, I will share the details of that visit."

He paused. The duchess tightened her bony hands on her cane, but said nothing.

"Allow me to review the facts," he went on. "My siblings have been raised in France. Since the tragic deaths of their parents, the children have been under the care of a Snowe's governess here at Fawkes House.

If the court comes to the conclusion that they would be better raised by their maternal grandmother, thereby overturning the late Lord Darcy's explicit wishes, so be it."

The drawing room was so silent that the creak of the duchess's knees as she once again rose sounded like pistol shots.

"I shall take my leave."

"May I take that as your agreement?"

"I never lower myself to gossip," she said, all evidence to the contrary.

Ward bowed; like it or not—and *she* certainly did not—the lady was his grandmother.

"I shall next see you in the House of Lords, Mr. Reeve."

He bowed again.

The duchess stopped at the door and looked back at him, her face drawn. For a moment, he thought she was about to relinquish her fight for custody.

"She loved you," Her Grace said instead.

Eugenia? How did she know how Eugenia felt?

"My daughter was not in control of her better self." Torment ran beneath his grandmother's well-bred syllables. "But Lisette loved you. She never forgave me for taking you as a baby and giving you to your father."

He stood very still, surprised by the stab of pain that he felt at her words. He didn't meet his mother until he was fourteen, and she had been alternately charming and violent. "I see," he said at length.

"Believe it or not, I wanted to save your life."

She waited a moment for a response, before she set her chin and walked from the room.

Chapter Thirty-nine

Thursday, June 18, 1801
Fonthill
The country residence of Jem Strange,
  Marquis of Broadham,
  and Harriet Strange, Lady Broadham,
  former Duchess of Berrow

Eugenia occupied herself on the way to her father's estate by sending letters to Susan, dispatching them from market towns she passed through. The first letter told Susan that she was the new owner of Snowe's. The second laid out Susan's objections and countered every one. They had been friends so long that Eugenia had no problem imagining her protests. A third sug-

gested that the new training course for governesses include swimming lessons.

She wasn't busy all the time; tears had a terrible way of smearing ink. At night she lay awake, staring at the rough wooden ceilings of staging inns, hollow-eyed and hollow-hearted.

In the late afternoon on the third day, she finally arrived at Fonthill, only to discover that her father was hosting a number of guests. There was nothing unusual in that; she'd grown up in the middle of a never-ending house party.

Her stepmother, Harriet, had managed, more or less, to rein in her father's love of surrounding himself with interesting people. In the years since they'd wed, she had introduced him to the quiet joys of a more sedate family life.

But a good marriage meant compromise. While Fonthill no longer housed courtesans—or rats, for that matter—it was still frequented by intelligent, eccentric originals who were the marquis's personal friends.

"We have twenty-two to dine," the butler informed her, as he took her pelisse. "Your parents will be tremendously pleased to see you, Mrs. Snowe. They have not yet retired to dress for the evening meal. You will find them in the small salon, if you would like to greet them."

"Thank you," Eugenia said, glancing at herself in a mirror. The woman who looked back at her was tired, but not visibly broken-hearted.

The small salon was light-filled and airy, its doors open to the lawns behind the house. A chessboard in mid-game covered one table, knitting was thrown over a chair, and stacks of books were everywhere.

As she entered, three people turned in her direction: her father, her stepmother, and her godfather, the Duke of Villiers.

"What's the matter?" her father barked, and Eugenia ran straight into his arms, her face crumpling against his shoulder.

"Nothing," she said a moment later, pulling herself together.

She turned from his embrace to Harriet's. Her stepmother met her eyes searchingly and murmured, "We'll talk later, darling."

"Your Grace," Eugenia said, curtsying before Villiers.

"Eugenia," he said, bowing and kissing her hand. His drawl was unaltered by age, although his thick hair was now white, made whiter by contrast with still-black eyebrows. "My dear, you are more exquisite than ever. My duchess will be almost as happy to see you as I am."

"This is a true pleasure," Eugenia said, smiling.

They had been friends ever since she was a precocious young girl with no acquaintances her own age.

Even if Eugenia hadn't loved the duke for himself, she would have adored him for bringing her future stepmother into her life. Years ago, he had brought Harriet on a visit to Fonthill, albeit disguised in male attire.

Her father wrapped an arm around her shoulder and she leaned against him, letting comfort sink into her bones. "How are your children?" she asked the duke.

"Infernal," Villiers replied, his casual tone failing to conceal his pride. "I hope that your appearance signals a decision to rest from your constant labors with that registry of yours?"

"I am hoping the same thing," Harriet put in.

"It is time for a new challenge," Eugenia said, nodding. "I am giving Snowe's to my assistant."

"We are so proud of you for creating the registry," Harriet said. "But it's time to live your life."

"I'll miss it," Eugenia admitted.

Her father's arm tightened. "We have missed you."

"I know how to minimize any sadness you feel about leaving Snowe's," Harriet said. "Stop by the nursery. Our children are squabbling with His Grace's, and even our magnificent Snowe's governess is powerless to quell the storms. Every time I approach the room, I hear screams."

"My youngest has been grumpy ever since the vicar's seduction of Miss Bennifer," the duke said. "It was like a bad play: one moment we had a Snowe's governess, the next she was stolen by a man of God."

"I will be happy to visit the battlefield," Eugenia said. But first she had to change for the evening. No one could remain long in the presence of the Duke of Villiers in a crumpled traveling gown.

She had a burning desire to prove to Mr. Edward Reeve that she was *the* most ladylike woman in all England, and never mind that he was back in Wheatley.

"To the manner born?" She would . . .

The thought trailed off. Ward never attended social events and presumably would not do so until Lizzie's debut, years from now.

Still, she would find a way to show him exactly what he had thrown away.

The moment she entered her bedchamber, Clothilde clapped her hands. "A future duke is in residence!"

"Who is that?" Eugenia asked warily, as her maid began to unbutton her traveling gown. Clothilde couldn't be referring to Villiers's heir—the boy was either away at school or in the nursery.

"Viscount Herries, the eldest son of the Duke of Beaumont."

It took a moment to identify the man in question. "*Evan*? Evan is younger than I am!"

Clothilde shrugged. "He is a grown man. That is the best way, madame. Trust me on this. Men do not age like good wine." She crooked her finger into a C. "Useless to a woman by the time they're forty."

Bathed, draped in silk, and feeling much more herself, Eugenia came downstairs to find the formal drawing room empty but for Villiers, now wearing a magnificent burnt-russet coat with tawny buttons and black trim.

"Where is everyone?" she asked.

"They have traipsed off to the kitchens," His Grace said. "Entirely your fault, I must add."

"Someone made a cake!" Eugenia said, delighted.

"A child of *mine*, baking," Villiers marveled. "Almost inconceivable, and one only hopes not stomach-churning. Shall we stroll together, my dear?"

They processed slowly down the long room, Eugenia's arm tucked under the duke's elbow.

"So, Goddaughter," he said, "who was the lucky man?"

Eugenia let out a startled laugh.

Villiers turned his head; wise, sinful eyes laughed with her. "Would I not notice that my beloved goddaughter has cast off her widow's weeds and become a woman again?"

Eugenia felt herself turning pink. "This is a most improper subject of conversation."

"The only kind that interests me," Villiers remarked.

"Does his name matter? It is finished."

"Names always matter."

Her father and Harriet entered at the far end of the room, accompanied by a group that included children.

Villiers promptly steered her to a sofa. "I trust you will not insult me by asking if I can keep a secret."

"Edward Reeve," Eugenia said with a sigh.

"Ward?" Villiers's eyebrow arched. "He has had a trying year."

"Oh, did you know of the children?"

Silence. Then, "I have not. That young man has been quite busy if he fathered multiple children out of wedlock. Were these children conceived before he betrothed himself to the young lady who is now the Duchess of Pindar?"

"I should have made myself clearer. Lizzie and Otis aren't his." She told him about Lady Lisette's marriage.

"That woman never failed to surprise," the duke said, in a tone of disapproval. "Do I understand that the children appeared on Ward's doorstep, after which he turned to you for a governess?"

She ended up telling him everything.

"Good old Chatty," Villiers said, when she'd finished her story. "What a stroke of luck that he was in the vicarage. It sounds as if the girl is a version of her mother, albeit sane. Do you know that I almost married Lisette?"

Eugenia's eyes widened. "What a terrible mistake that would have been."

"For more than one reason."

"Lady Lisette instead of Eleanor. The mind boggles. I would never have imagined it."

Villiers gave a visible shudder. "Unthinkable. Was it the children that put you off Ward? I can scarcely tolerate my own, so I heartily sympathize if you were overwhelmed by the idea of taking on Lisette's orphans."

"I know how much you love your brood," Eugenia said, slipping her arm back into his. "You cannot fool me."

"I do love them," His Grace said, as if admitting a dark failing. "But they are dirty, they often smell, they grumble, and they do not show proper respect for their elders."

"Villiers blood runs in their veins," Eugenia said, gurgling with laughter. "Surely that explains, if it does not excuse, them."

"Absolutely not," His Grace rejoined. "Do you know what my own heir told me last week?"

That heir, Master Theodore, was eleven and a miniature version of his father, down to the arrogant nose and biting intelligence.

"He said I was too old to wear puce," Villiers said moodily. "When did certain colors become the exclusive province of the young? He's a mere stripling yet dresses as if he were a man of eighty. All in black and white, like a chessboard."

"I trust you immediately ordered a pair of puce gloves for him? And perhaps a coat to match?"

When Villiers smiled, his entire face changed, and Eugenia saw—not for the first time—how fortunate it was for the male half of society that the duke was so much in love with his wife. "My dear Eugenia, you are a genius. I'll have the measurements taken under the pretense of cutting yet another black coat."

"In truth, I would be very happy to mother Lizzie and Otis," Eugenia confessed.

"What on earth did that young fool do to force you to leave him?"

"He didn't want me," she blurted out.

The duke looked down at her sternly. "Let's begin with basic truths, my dear. Unless Ward prefers men—which I doubt—he wants you."

"We had a very enjoyable interlude," she said, striving for a nonchalant tone. "But he has the new responsibility of raising Lizzie and Otis."

She stopped. It was humiliating to confess.

"It's this damn hierarchy, isn't it?" Villiers said, sadness threading through his voice. "Only after taking my children under my roof that did I understand just what it means to be illegitimate. I'll never forget one of my sons telling me in a fit of rage that he would have been better unborn."

"I am so sorry to hear that," Eugenia said.

"He was wrong," Villiers said sharply. "The old ranks are falling by the wayside, and new money is shaping new hierarchies. Look at my eldest: Tobias made a fortune and married Lady Xenobia. Didn't Ward make a fortune on a paper-rolling machine? I recall his father crowing about it."

Eugenia nodded.

"If the man doesn't want to marry a woman of higher rank than he," Villiers said with asperity, "he ought to do it for the sake of those children. The boy has a title."

She took a deep breath. "It's the opposite. Ward is of the opinion that Snowe's Registry has damaged my standing as a lady. He thinks my lost status would be detrimental when it came time for Lizzie to marry."

Villiers was silent a moment and then barked with laughter. "You must be joking."

"I'm not. Granted, he doesn't know my rank—he thinks me a former governess, and told me he had to marry someone 'to the manner born.' But more importantly, he doesn't like the fact I opened a registry. I kept making stupid mistakes," she said wretchedly. "I think the worst was when I unwittingly took Lizzie to a tent-talk."

"A tent-talk?" The duke sounded fascinated. "I haven't sat through one of those rank little gatherings since I was a boy fascinated by hearing the word 'cock' said aloud."

"I didn't listen," Eugenia confessed. "I had no idea what it was until later, when Lizzie asked Ward why it was funny that a bed could fit two men and one woman. You can laugh," she said, responding to his snort, "but Ward was outraged. The talk advertised itself as a lecture on the chemical composition of water, but Lizzie emerged with questions about 'male froth.'"

"I might be a wee bit angry myself," His Grace said. "All the same, it sounds as if Ward has turned into a self-righteous prick."

"No, he hasn't!" Eugenia said, surprising herself with her vehemence. "He's doing his best to be a good guardian. He's utterly determined to provide the children with a conventional life."

"His mother was Lady Lisette," Villiers said, after a moment. "I suppose that's where he got the idea that he should marry someone who conforms in every respect."

"It's truly ironic," Eugenia said shakily. "I was the most conventional woman of my acquaintance until I

opened Snowe's." A tear slid down her cheek and she dashed it away.

"It was just that sort of foolish reasoning that led me to the excruciating folly of nearly marrying Lisette," His Grace said with a sigh.

He drew her to her feet and held out the crook of his arm. "Your father will be worried that I'm giving you evil counsel."

"Have you evil counsel?" Eugenia asked as they began to make their way back across the room.

"Certainly," Villiers said, a devilish glint in his eye.

"Tell me what to do," Eugenia said, wanting to hear that she should go back to Ward and fight for love.

Not that she would listen.

"Take a close look at young Evan—Beaumont's son," Villiers said. "He's over there by the door, looking bored because he doesn't know you've joined the party."

Eugenia sighed. "He's younger than I am. I mean to find a husband who is at the very least my age."

"Oh, not to *marry*," Villiers said gently. "You're not ready for that."

Eugenia gasped. "You *are* wicked, Your Grace!"

"You have had a run of bad luck, my dear, but in truth, a woman's first man after a tragedy such as Andrew's death ought to be an antidote to grief, and from what you have told me, Ward fulfilled his role in that respect. But the second must be for pure pleasure. I suggest Evan. And finally, the third: a new husband. In due course, I shall propose a few candidates for your consideration."

"I shouldn't look for a husband now?"

Villiers had the kind of smile that only a very bad

man could give a woman. "You are a widow; so why not be a merry one?"

"I'm glad that you are happily married," Eugenia said, squeezing his arm. "I would have succumbed to a lure had you thrown me one."

He snorted. "You are entirely too young for me, my dear. A decade between yourself and Evan is nothing, but the gulf between us is insurmountable. Did you know that Evan is an excellent horseman?"

"I did not," Eugenia replied.

"Consider the results of regular and vigorous physical exercise," the duke said, voice grave but eyes dancing. "It develops the body in such attractive and useful ways. Of course, he has brains as well. The lad can't play chess worth a damn, but he knows an absurd amount about medicine."

"I shall take it under advisement." Eugenia leaned closer to kiss his cheek. "You are the best of godfathers."

"I am enormously fond of you, my dear," Villiers said. "We all want you to be happy."

"I shall be," Eugenia promised.

As they neared the group at the end of the room, Villiers said, "I trust that Ward taught you the value of a French letter?"

"All the different colored ribbons," Eugenia said, her smile wobbling before she caught it.

"You are ready for adventure," the duke replied with satisfaction, steering her straight toward Beaumont's heir.

Evan was nothing like Ward.

Ward was big, muscled, and broody, whereas Evan was tall and lanky, with cheerful blue eyes. He stood

to greet them, displaying just the aristocratic, boyish appeal that Andrew had worn so gracefully.

Eugenia extended her hand, and he kissed it.

There was no mistaking the glow of admiration in his eyes. If she wished to be merry, she had the immediate sense that Evan would be happy to help.

Chapter Forty

Fonthill

There was one thought in Ward's mind: he had to bring Eugenia home, before she met someone else.

He needed a carriage. Now.

It was a pity he'd dispatched with his racing curricle, because he could have caught up with Eugenia—who was trundling along in comfort in his large coach. The old traveling coach that had come with the estate would have to do.

Eugenia had said that she loved him. But that look in her eyes when he sent her away, that desolate look . . .

What if someone was consoling her at this moment? Someone who wasn't a bastard, in name and behavior?

His jaw set. She was his. He had hurt her, but he'd do anything to change that. He just had to—

How much could you hurt a woman before she turned her back?

What is unforgivable?

He went to the nursery to bid the children good-bye. Otis calmly accepted his explanation that he was going to fetch Eugenia. "Ruby will be with you and the new governess should arrive in a day or so."

But Lizzie's too-old eyes met his with a sobering doubtfulness. "Are you certain that she'll come back with you?"

He sat down. "No, but I hope so."

Otis had made Jarvis a tunnel with folds of cloth and was trying to lure him through with a piece of bread. "Why did you allow her to leave?"

"I wasn't certain that she'd be the best mother for the two of you."

"That's silly," Otis said, at the same time Lizzie said, startled, "For us?"

"I was wrong."

"She saved my life," Otis said, "that's what mothers do."

"What?"

"When I jumped into the water, she swam to get me and went into the weeds and under water, though she doesn't like putting her head under. It was all Jarvis's fault."

Ward swallowed hard. He had as much as accused Eugenia of allowing Otis to swim in deep water, which was as absurd as everything else he'd said to her.

"Jarvis saved himself," Otis added. "I told you that."

Ward had never asked Otis for details about his illicit swim since he'd been hell-bent on avoiding thoughts of Eugenia. He hadn't wanted to utter a sentence that had her name in it.

"She saved your life," he repeated.

"That doesn't mean she'll come back with you," Lizzie said. "Papa saved your life, Otis, and he—"

She stopped.

Ward sighed. It would take time for all the stories to come out. In their own time, Eugenia had said.

"Give me a hug, you two," he said. "Wish me luck."

Otis leaped up and hugged Ward. "Good luck!" he shouted.

Lizzie came to him more slowly. "If she comes back—will she be our mother?"

Ward nodded. "I hope so."

"Give her this." Lizzie turned jerkily and pulled her bundled veil from under her pillow.

"I won't be back for several days, Lizzie. I don't want to take your veil."

"I am giving it to her, to Mrs. Snowe." Her peaked face was stubborn, her jaw set.

"Are you ready to stop mourning your mother?" He asked it gently, but thought it ought to be said aloud.

"I never wore that for Lady Lisette," she said matter-of-factly.

Otis didn't look up from Jarvis, who had emerged from the tunnel and was triumphantly eating his bread. "She began wearing the veil when Papa died."

Ward grimaced. "I didn't know."

"I didn't tell you," Lizzie said.

She pushed the veil into his hands.

Chapter Forty-one

Monday, June 22, 1801
Fonthill

Susan's answers began to arrive the morning after Eugenia's arrival. The first letters demurred, but the fourth delightedly agreed to take over Snowe's.

"I'm always here if you need me, but I intend to find a new challenge," Eugenia wrote back. She had decided to entice away Monsieur Marcel and become his secret partner in an elegant pâtisserie in Mayfair.

She found she didn't mind the idea of putting Ward to some inconvenience.

On a personal note, Evan was showing an entirely flattering interest. Never mind Villiers's suggestion of an *affaire*, she had the distinct sense that if she gave

Evan the slightest push, he would fall to his knees and beg to make her his future duchess.

What's more, she had got through a whole day without crying. She could add it to the list of courageous things she'd done recently. Learn how to swim, have an *affaire*, not weep for a full day.

Just as her vision blurred, threatening her newly won award for courage, her bedchamber door opened and Harriet entered, a length of shimmering pink silk over her arm. "Look what I have for you, darling." She put it on the bed.

"It's exquisite!" Eugenia exclaimed, blinking away her tears.

"It was to be a surprise for your birthday," her stepmother said, sitting beside her, "but I decided it was a good time for a present."

"How on earth did you have it made without fittings?"

"Clothilde gave my seamstress one of your favorite gowns to copy. She's been sewing madly for the last two days." Harriet held up the gown beside Eugenia's hair. "It's perfect for your coloring."

The gown was cut from a heavy silk so it would curve around the body and flare slightly at the ankles. A gauze overlay was embroidered with vines that curved and curled like the bordering images in medieval Bibles.

Clothilde entered, smiling. "Is it not *délicieuse*, madame?"

"Yes!" If Ward saw her in this, he would realize—Eugenia pushed the thought away. "What are all these small beads?" She peered closer. "Silver? Pure silver?"

Clothilde cackled delightedly. "There are shoes, as well, madame." She held them out.

They were a misty silver silk, with heels and a complex patterns of leaves dotted with silver beads.

"The gown will look very well with the diamond necklace your father gave you when you turned eighteen," Harriet said with satisfaction. "Remember you left it here to be repaired."

"I suspect you have plans for when I should wear this magnificent ensemble?" Eugenia said, tracing the delicate embroidery with her fingers.

"Tonight! I've engaged a small orchestra and invited the neighbors." Harriet twinkled at Eugenia. "Evan will not be able to take his eyes off you."

"I don't—" Eugenia began, but Harriet was already on her feet.

"The footmen will be bringing your bath in a minute, darling. Now I must go ready myself."

"Don't you think diamonds are too grand for an evening at home?" Eugenia asked.

"That necklace was your great-grandmother's; it is not extraordinary except for its sentiment," Harriet said. "I think it will make your father very happy if you wear it."

After bathing, Eugenia stared absently into the mirror while Clothilde fussed with her hair.

What were Lizzie and Otis doing now? It was close to bedtime; perhaps they were in the nursery, playing at draughts and ladders with the new governess. Or Ruby might be overseeing Otis's bath while Jarvis splashed in his own basin.

It was stupid, stupid, stupid, to feel so hollow around the heart, as if she'd lost a family, rather than a mere lover.

She'd only lost an acquaintance, really.

She felt better when she had on the new gown, with diamonds sparkling around her neck and in her hair. There had been life after Andrew, and there would be life after Ward.

Evan was waiting for her at the bottom of the stairs, and the startled wonder in his eyes when he saw her was quite gratifying.

"You are extraordinarily beautiful, Mrs. Snowe," he breathed, bowing as he kissed her hand.

"Please, call me Eugenia," she said, smiling up at him as he escorted her to the drawing room.

"Darling girl," her father said, coming forward as they entered, "I have a present for my shining child." He pulled something from his pocket.

"Oh my goodness," Eugenia breathed, looking down at a pair of shimmering diamond earrings in his palm.

"They match your necklace," he said, pressing a kiss on her forehead.

"Oh, Papa," she murmured, swallowing back tears, because who cried when given diamonds?

Harriet appeared, crowing and laughing, helping her put them on.

"They will glitter when you dance," her stepmother said. She leaned closer and whispered, "Be very careful, darling, or Evan will fall to his knees and offer you a ring to match your earrings."

Ward had planned to make the journey to Fonthill in half the time it would have taken Eugenia, hopefully arriving within a few hours of her.

Instead, his elderly carriage got stuck in the mud three times, its ancient wheels good for nothing but

a dry road. He finally left it at a coaching inn and rented another, which promptly broke a shaft climbing a steep hill.

By his fifth day on the road, Ward was exhausted from lack of sleep; he hardly cursed when the Royal Mail passed them with a rattling of wheels and a loud horn.

He arrived at the Marquis of Broadham's estate aching in every limb. When the front door opened, a lean, shrewd-looking butler glanced at him and said, "Mr. Reeve? I am Branson, the marquis's butler."

"Have I met you before?"

"The Duke of Villiers predicted that you would arrive yesterday." Branson opened the door fully. "The marchioness is giving a ball this evening. Would you care to join them, after refreshing yourself?"

Ward stepped into a marble entry where a chandelier blazed with candles. From his left, through large double doors, drifted the sound of stringed instruments and the light, high sound of a woman's laughter. Not Eugenia's. He would know her laugh anywhere.

It was a waltz, which meant some man was holding Eugenia, a hand at her waist.

"I'd like to see Mrs. Snowe," he said, failing to keep his voice calm.

"I regret you are not dressed for the occasion." The butler's eyes dropped to Ward's travel-worn clothing. "I shall have a bath brought to your room immediately."

Ward's Hessians were caked with dirt; when the carriage had got stuck in a deep rut a few miles ago, he'd put a shoulder to the vehicle alongside his grooms.

He smelled like sweat, if not worse, and his

breeches were splattered with mud thrown up by the carriage wheels.

"Please inform her that I wish to speak to her immediately."

"If you prefer." Branson nodded at a footman. "Roberts will show you to the morning parlor."

"I'll wait here." Urgency was pounding through Ward's body. He crossed his arms and fixed the butler with a gaze that threatened violence.

Branson had the wary air of a man who has encountered any number of madmen. "I shall inform his lordship that you have requested an interview with his daughter."

"I'll tell him myself," Ward said. Before the butler could stop him, he flung open one of the ballroom doors and walked through.

Inside, a few dozen people were dancing.

"It's all right, Branson," a voice said behind his shoulder. "I can take care of our visitor."

The butler withdrew, but Ward didn't glance at the Duke of Villiers. He had eyes only for Eugenia.

She was wearing a gown that made her glimmer from head to foot. Those beautiful curls that had spread across his pillow were piled on her head and held in place with dazzling gems.

Diamonds.

Of course, they were diamonds, as were the jewels at her throat.

Yet the stones faded in comparison to her. The first time he'd met her, he'd thought of a flame: energy and intelligence and beauty in a fiery package no diamond could rival.

"A beautiful woman, isn't she?" the Duke of Villiers said at his side.

One didn't snarl at this particular duke, so Ward bowed. "Good evening, Your Grace."

"Ward," His Grace said with a sigh. "I wish your father was in England. No, your stepmother would be even better."

Ward ignored him, watching the dance with arms crossed over his chest. The moment the music drew to a close, he would stride over to Eugenia and carry her out of the ballroom.

No, that was too primitive.

He felt primitive. A man was dancing with his woman, his future bride, his . . . his everything.

"You are scowling at Viscount Herries, the future Duke of Beaumont," Villiers said, sardonic amusement in his voice. "Dancing, quite possibly, with his future duchess."

His words went down Ward's body like molten lead. He'd be damned if Eugenia married a duke, or a future duke, or any man other than himself. "You are mistaken."

"Well-matched in intelligence—surely you've heard that the young viscount is taking a medical degree, regardless of his rank? Their parents are great friends. Well, you would know that—isn't he your cousin?"

"No," Ward said flatly. "I am distantly related to him through my stepmother."

Viscount Herries was as absurdly handsome as his father, the Duke of Beaumont. His features were perfectly even, as unlike Ward's hard jaw and broken nose as could be. He must be older than he looked, if he was studying medicine.

As Ward watched, the man tightened his grip on her waist and, his eyes fixed on hers, spun Eugenia in

a circle. She threw her head back and laughed. It was obvious to anyone that he was deeply infatuated.

Two young girls standing at the side of the room giggled behind their hands, watching the couple dance.

Damn it, Ward's gut instinct had been right.

The future duke swept her in another circle, Eugenia still laughing, followed by another. One of the girls squealed when she was almost bumped, and Eugenia called a laughing apology over her shoulder.

"None of that matters," Ward growled at Villiers.

"Both of them to the manner born," the duke said dreamily.

Ward registered the sentence and growled. "She *told* you?"

"I'm her godfather," the duke said, his voice sharpening. "Why should she not tell me about an insult she received from a presumptuous halfwit?" Villiers hadn't weakened in middle age: he was a predator still.

Not that Ward would ever—He forced his fists to uncurl.

"As it happens, I am virtually your godfather as well as hers," His Grace continued. "I nearly married your mother, and your father came close to killing me in a duel. Surely that creates a familial bond."

The waltz was slowing at last.

"That bond gives me the liberty to tell you that Eugenia will have in Evan a man who respects and adores her. A man whose mother, the Duchess of Beaumont, is beloved far and wide for her brilliance, her wit, and her decorum."

"That wasn't always the case," Ward said. It was a lame defense; the fact that the Beaumonts lived apart

for many years was trifling compared to his mother's actions.

"The Duchess of Beaumont is no Lady Lisette," Villiers said. "What's more, if Jem—that is to say our host, the Marquis of Broadham—knew that a man had rejected his daughter for being unworthy, he would slay him. Eugenia has wisely kept that detail from him."

"Are you advising me to leave?" Ward didn't bother to look at Villiers. Eugenia was curtsying before her partner, who was kissing her hand.

"Notice the way Evan's leg extends at precisely the correct angle? He's a born duke, that one," Villiers said meditatively. "How *is* your bow? I don't believe I've seen you at many society events."

Ward's hands curled into fists again. He'd had enough.

He strode forward, startling the two girls. Skirted a circle of chairs and headed toward the brightly lit dance floor.

The viscount hadn't let Eugenia's hand go after kissing it. Like a bath of freezing water, Ward realized that the man may be too young for Eugenia to marry. But he certainly wasn't too youthful to be a *friend*—the kind that shares intimacies, as he had so blithely told Eugenia weeks ago.

His boots pounded on the wooden floor, and every person in the room turned to him. Including Eugenia.

She appeared to turn a shade paler but she said nothing. And she didn't drop Evan's hand.

"Edward Reeve?" the Marquis of Broadham came up at his shoulder. Taking in his disheveled appearance, he said, "Has something happened to your parents?"

He shook his head. "I came to see Eugenia."

The marquis's brows drew together at Ward's use of his daughter's first name. From the corner of one eye, Ward saw the marchioness put a hand on her husband's sleeve.

No one spoke.

He could hear Eugenia's breathing as she stared at him. He searched for words as her plump lips tightened into a line. But when at last she spoke, she was impeccably polite, as she had promised in their dreadful last conversation.

"Is there something I can do for you, Mr. Reeve? I trust the children are well?"

"I'm sorry," he said. "I'm so sorry, Eugenia."

Just like that, Eugenia dropped her polite mask—and Evan's hand as well. She folded her arms over her chest as a patch of color rose in her cheeks. "Indeed," she said dangerously. "What precisely are you sorry for?"

Behind him, someone began ushering the guests—including the future duke—from the room. Ward waited until only Eugenia, her father, and her stepmother remained. Except for Villiers, leaning against the wall like a damned bird of prey.

"I am sorry for the things I said to you."

"Are you apologizing for implying that I am not ladylike enough to raise Lizzie and Otis?"

The marquis made a sharp movement. "I am," Ward said. "May we speak in private?"

"No, you may not," her father snarled. "I shall allow you three minutes to explain yourself, Mr. Reeve, and that owing only to my respect for your father."

"Nothing has changed," Eugenia said, eyes fixed on Ward's face. "I am still the person who runs

Snowe's Registry, and who took your sister to a tent-talk, not to mention teaching her to curse."

"I was terribly wrong. You'd be a wonderful mother for the children," he replied, ignoring that litany. He could see she wasn't softening her stance.

"Lizzie sent you this." He pulled a crumpled bundle of black lace from his coat pocket and pressed it into her hands. "Otis thought of sending Jarvis, but I dissuaded him. They need you, Eugenia." He hesitated and then looked her straight in the eye with all the passion and love he felt. "*I* need you."

She looked down at the veil, her eyes stricken. "What made you change your mind?"

"The Duchess of Gilner—"

Eugenia cut him off, her eyes hardening. "She told you."

"Told him what?" the marquis put in.

"Mrs. Snowe, owner of a registry, wasn't good enough to be Ward's wife," Eugenia said. "I didn't have the right pedigree or instincts to introduce his wards to polite society."

The marquis exploded, taking a step forward. "Are you out of your bloody mind?"

"Now that the duchess has told him who I really am, so it's a different story," Eugenia said, her eyes scorching. "*Now* I am good enough to mother the children whom Lisette neglected."

"That's not it," Ward said. "I can't—I can't live without you."

"You could live perfectly well without me," Eugenia said, her voice echoing in the empty room, "until you realized how much my pedigree would help Lizzie and Otis. And with the case against you in the House of Lords."

She hated him.

He had imagined many possibilities he would have to overcome, but not that one. Not hatred.

The words came out of him anyway, forced past the gaping hole in his heart. "I love you, and that has nothing to do with your rank."

"You threw my love back in my face because I wasn't ladylike enough nor docile enough—and that has nothing to do with rank. That is *me*. Whatever you are feeling, it isn't love for *me*."

"That isn't true. I love everything about you, everything that was suddenly gone from my life the minute you walked out of the door," he said, his voice hoarse. "Your brilliance, your joy, your passion for life: *you*."

For a moment he felt hope. He saw her waver. She closed her eyes and he started toward her. Then she looked at him, her resolve firmly back in place. "Whatever your reasons, it doesn't matter. You judged me, found me wanting, and dismissed me like a street urchin begging for a farthing. It's your disdain and dismissal of me that I can't forget," she said. "Please go."

She was a queen from sparkling diamonds to delicate slippers.

"I will still help you with Lizzie's debut when the time comes," she added.

He opened his mouth but she held up her hand. "You are here because you learned of my rank, Ward. Why would I want someone who finds me acceptable only because of my birth? I won't accept that any more than you would accept someone who disdained you for yours."

It wasn't like that. But he—a man who had always

taken his eloquence for granted—couldn't find a way
to explain.

"I gave my heart away too easily," Eugenia continued, "but it will be my own again just as quickly.
Next time, I shall choose someone who knows my
worth—and I do not mean my rank."

Words of explanation, of justification, pounded his
brain. Lizzie and Otis were so young and so damaged. He would sacrifice the world for them, anything to make up for their childhood.

But he had stupidly sacrificed the one thing that
would make them happy.

There was no point in protesting. She was right.
When he'd said he needed someone to the manner
born, he had implied she wasn't good enough.

For him. For Lizzie and Otis.

"You ought to take this back," she said, holding
out the veil as if it meant nothing.

"Please keep it," he said, his voice rasping. "Lizzie
sent it as a gift."

She shook her head. "Children often change their
minds after being separated from beloved objects.
Lizzie will be happy to see it, if only to remind her
of her father."

"You knew she wore it for her father?"

He was confounded. Otis had known Eugenia was
the daughter of a marquis; Eugenia had known that
Lizzie was mourning her father, not her mother.

How had he ever believed he could care for his
siblings, considering all the mistakes he'd already
made?

"Just ask her questions," she said, guessing his
thought because of all the people in the world, she

most often knew what he was thinking. "She will tell you everything."

Ward nodded.

Then he turned and took himself from the ballroom and into the dark.

Chapter Forty-two

$\mathcal{E}$ugenia forced a smile. "This is the sort of drama I remember from growing up."

Three unsmiling people looked back at her. The Duke of Villiers seemed disappointed, her stepmother anxious, her father furious.

"You had an *affaire* with Edward Reeve?" he barked.

Anger went straight up her spine and she flashed, "Considering the house I grew up in, how can you be shocked that I took a lover?"

Her father's stricken eyes, her own seething grief and rage . . . it was too much.

She burst into tears. "I didn't mean that," she sobbed against her stepmother's shoulder. Harriet's arms closed around her, warm and comforting.

"I know," she said in her ear. "We all understand, sweetheart."

"I don't," her father said stubbornly, but he closed his mouth after a glare from his wife.

"We've all played the idiot in our time," Villiers said. "You have to admit, Jem, that you and I have no high ground to stand on."

"I'll go to my chamber," Eugenia said, before her father could turn his anger on his oldest friend. "Please give everyone my apologies for disrupting the evening."

"We will see Eugenia in the morning," Harriet announced, "and she can tell us about her adventures. *If* she chooses to do so, and only as much as she chooses."

Back in her room, she managed to stand still while Clothilde attended to her, removing the diamonds and the silk gown, the shoes, and the rest of it. All the time she felt as if her own breath was searing the inside of her lungs. Why did it hurt to breathe?

When Clothilde left, Eugenia sank onto the edge of her bed. Tears streamed down her face.

Sometimes life didn't give you what you wanted. She knew that better than anyone. Not everyone found true love, or was taken care of, or adored, or pleasured.

Her love affair with Ward was over, truly over.

Over, not because Ward protected Lizzie and Otis—but because *she* had to protect them. She and Ward could never be happy, because he hadn't thought her good enough for him until he'd learned of her family. He didn't love the true Eugenia—the Eugenia who had started the registry, who was planning to open a tearoom, who had ideas about a cookery book.

The last thing the children needed was to find themselves in yet another unhappy home; she sus-

pected that their parents' marriage had been strained, if not worse.

No matter how much love she might lavish on Ward, in the end, he would break her heart. She had bent herself to Andrew's ideas of what she should be, but she had been young. This wasn't a matter of brightly colored gowns: Eugenia couldn't change the fact she had started Snowe's—and in any case she didn't want to.

A piercing sense of loneliness sank into her bones, which was ridiculous. Ward had entered her life only a month or two ago.

No one fell in love that quickly.

Except she had.

First with Andrew, and then with Ward.

There was a gentle knock and her father's voice said, "May I come in, Eugenia?"

"Of course." She stood up and pulled on her robe, then went to the door and let him in.

Her father just opened his arms and she walked into them. For eight years, it had been just the two of them, and though she loved Harriet with all her heart, her father was her mainstay.

After Andrew's funeral, her father had brought her home and stayed with her for weeks, not leaving the house, coaxing her out of bed, making her eat toast, if nothing else. Harriet and her half-siblings came and went, but her father stayed.

"The man is rubbish," he said gruffly.

"Don't you remember that you thought Harriet wasn't a lady?" Eugenia asked.

"Harriet was disguised as a young man and doing a damn good job of it. No duchess I've ever known wore breeches as well as she did."

"No duchess wears breeches," Eugenia pointed out.

"Harriet still does, on occasion," her father said with satisfaction. He tightened his arms and rocked her back and forth. "I suppose I'll see his father at the session for that private act at the end of the month. I mean to say something about the idiot he raised."

"The earl and countess are on a diplomatic mission to Sweden," Eugenia said with an inelegant sniff. "But you do have to go to London and vote against the private act, Papa. The Duchess of Gilner is a harridan who only wants to raise Lizzie and Otis because they're legitimate, whereas she tossed Ward out as a baby."

"I shall." He handed her a handkerchief.

"They'll be shocked to see you, won't they?"

"Who?"

"All those lords . . . You don't attend Lords often, do you?"

"Certainly I do," her father said indignantly. Then he added, with a shrug, "When I haven't anything better to do."

Eugenia stepped back. "I love you, Papa."

He cupped her face in his hands. "You are the most beautiful and brilliant woman of your age in all Britain. If this young ass can't see it, he's not worth a single tear."

"Thank you," she said with a watery smile.

Chapter Forty-three

Monday, June 29, 1801
Beaumont House
The London home of
  the Duke and Duchess of Beaumont
Kensington

*W*ard had always known that his father was powerful, but he hadn't realized how many friends the earl had until he looked around the ballroom of Beaumont House. In the absence of his parents, his uncle by marriage, the Duke of Beaumont, was heading a campaign to ensure that the Duchess of Gilner's private act would be soundly defeated.

There were three dukes in the room—no, four: as

he watched, the Duke of Pindar strolled in, with his wife—Ward's former fiancée—on his arm.

A quartet was playing at the far end, a few couples drifting through a quadrille. The Duke and Duchess of Fletcher were dancing scandalously closely, and if His Grace bent his head a smidgeon, they would be kissing.

One of his father's closest friends, the Duke of Cosway, on the other hand, was arguing with his duchess, but Ward knew them well enough to understand that their arguments were like kisses. A prelude to intimacy.

For a moment a vision of a future with Eugenia drifted through his head. His longing to be dancing and arguing with her twenty years from now was a ferocious burning in his gut.

But the children were the important thing at this moment.

After the court case . . . Eugenia.

The vow beat in his head, the rhythm of the last week. Desire to be with Eugenia gnawed at him, and only iron control had kept him from returning to Fonthill and kidnapping her again.

Once the children were securely his, he would do just that. He could convince her that he loved her and respected her, after he'd become guardian of the children without her help, removing any question of whether he wanted her only for that.

He kept seeing the bleak, betrayed pain in her eyes, and the familiar sense of being gut-shot hit him again.

The thought of her dancing with Beaumont's heir, possibly *sleeping* with him, was a roar of anguish

in his skull. Thinking of the devil—or the devil's father—the Duke of Beaumont appeared at his shoulder. "Mr. Reeve, I would like to introduce you to Lord Bishell, who just came into his title . . ."

Ward bowed as he was introduced to yet another peer who was implicitly being instructed to vote against the private act, or risk Beaumont's wrath—and the Duke of Beaumont was the most powerful man in the House of Lords.

It was becoming clear to Ward that his grandmother was remarkably foolish to imagine that she could garner enough votes to win the case. She knew perfectly well how society functioned and yet she, an embittered old woman, was challenging the most powerful cabal of noblemen that existed in all England.

Ward actually felt a flicker of sympathy for her. She had lived to see her only daughter reviled by all England. From what he understood, Lady Lisette had died without ever again visiting her mother. And now the duchess's bastard grandson would raise the only relatives she had left.

The door opened again. Knowing it was a foolish hope, he turned to see if possibly the Marquis and Marchioness of Broadham—and their daughter, Eugenia—would enter.

The Beaumont butler announced, "Her Grace, the Duchess of Villiers; His Grace, the Duke of Villiers."

Villiers would never pause in the doorway, but he had no need to, because every person in the room turned at the sound of his name. He was famous for his flamboyant dress, but tonight he wore a dark plum coat with no embroidery whatsoever.

"Leo, what on earth has come over you?" their

hostess cried, running over to them. "You are practically funereal."

The duke made a magnificent bow. "It's my hair," he said, straightening. "White hair and black eyebrows. I assure you, Jemma, that putting on some of my favorite coats is like putting finery on a crow."

Her Grace kissed Villiers's duchess on both cheeks. "Sweetheart, how are you? I heard that Theo fell off his horse and broke an arm."

"Taggerty's Traveling Circus came through the village," the Duchess of Villiers said with a wry smile. "Naturally, having seen it once, Theo thought he could stand on his horse's back too."

Ward walked forward. "Your Grace," he said, kissing the Duchess of Villiers's hand. He bowed to her husband. "I am truly grateful for your support."

"You sound like a campaigning sheriff," Villiers observed, raising a thin eyebrow. "Have you some tin mugs to give away?"

"I'm afraid not," Ward said evenly.

"They could be engraved with a pertinent saying. I would suggest 'fools are wise until they speak.'" His tone couldn't have been more acerbic.

"Stop being such a curmudgeon," their hostess said, linking arms with Villiers. "Come. I must show you an attacking combination I have just learned that has no fewer than three sacrifices." With a smile at his wife, she drew Villiers over to a chessboard set out in the corner. Only her ballroom—and perhaps Villiers's—would include a gaming table.

Ward turned to the Duchess of Villiers, an extraordinarily beautiful woman whose hair was still as gold as a guinea even after raising eight children, if one included her husband's six bastards—and one

did, because she and her husband had gathered them all under their roof.

"That's the last I'll see of my husband tonight," she laughed. "Those two talk only of chess if they're within each other's orbit. I'm so sorry not to have seen more of you in the last few years, Ward."

"I lived abroad for some time before I began teaching at Oxford."

"You're being very modest. Your father has endlessly boasted of your paper-rolling fortune."

Ward ignored that. "I apologize if the Duke of Beaumont prevailed upon your husband to attend the House of Lords tomorrow against his wishes."

"Villiers is Eugenia's godfather, so he's feeling grumpy," she replied in her direct manner. "But he will fight for you in court. We have six illegitimate children, Ward. The House of Lords cannot be allowed to delude themselves that we would allow illegitimacy to overthrow a will such as the one written by that poor young lord."

"I am indebted," Ward said.

The duchess smiled at him. "Villiers believes you will make Eugenia happy."

"That is not what he indicated to me."

"He is of the belief that competition can drive a man to recognize his own folly." She tapped his shoulder with her fan. "If you must know the truth, he's peevish because he wagered that you would climb to her window after that scene at Fonthill . . . instead, you returned to Oxford."

"Your husband wagered that I would ruin Eugenia's reputation by surprising her in her bedchamber? That is reprehensible, Your Grace." He shouldn't be so blunt, but he couldn't stop himself.

"Ward," the duchess said with a sigh. "Do remember that we've known you most of your life, won't you? You must call me Eleanor. Of course, Leo thought that. He is so certain of his command of human nature; it does him good to be mistaken from time to time."

"He's not entirely mistaken," Ward allowed. After all, he fully planned to climb to her bedchamber window if need be.

"After I banished Villiers years ago," the duchess said, "my future husband put on a plain black coat—anathema to him to this day, as you can tell by his complaints—and wrote a note under a different name asking me for a drive in Hyde Park. I was in that carriage before I grasped my suitor's identity."

"Are you suggesting that I should pretend to be a different man—legitimate, perhaps? Or a member of the nobility?"

The duchess's eyes softened. "Ward, you *are* a member of the nobility. As are all of our children. What Villiers wanted to prove in his black coat was that the private man, not the most flamboyant rake in London, was in love with me."

"I love Eugenia," Ward said.

"Everyone loves her," the duchess said, with a clear look from her blue eyes. "You will need to move quickly. Evan has told his mother that he plans to make her his wife."

A sound dangerously close to a growl rose from Ward's chest.

"I expect her to attend the hearing tomorrow, sitting in the peeresses' box."

It had never occurred to him that Eugenia might

be there. Not that he knew anything about the House of Lords and their not-so-private private acts.

His former fiancée, Mia, suddenly appeared. With a smile at the duchess, she nudged Ward with her elbow. "Ask me to dance, won't you?"

"It's refreshing to see how friendly the two of you are," the Duchess of Villiers observed. "When I realized that Roberta had once been betrothed to Villiers, I glowered at her every chance I got."

"We are excellent friends." Mia twinkled at the duchess. "I intend to use Ward to make my husband jealous."

A minute later, as they began circling the floor, she asked, "Are you quite well?"

"Not really," Ward replied.

"You have nothing to worry about," she said. "Just look around this ballroom. Why, if someone blew it up with gunpowder the way Guy Fawkes tried to do with Parliament, half the country's peers would be lost."

"You're a novelist to the core, Mia," Ward said, smiling down at her.

He felt a prickling in his shoulders, glanced to the side, and met the glare of Mia's husband. The look in Pindar's eyes actually cheered him up. "I think you're succeeding in making your husband jealous."

"Excellent," Mia said, patently unconcerned. "Now, how are you planning to win back Mrs. Snowe?"

"I shall kidnap her." He had decided to drive the carriage to Fonthill's front door, push past that butler, and carry her out over his shoulder. But if she attended the House tomorrow, he would steal her straight from there.

Mia frowned. "I've written that plot twice, Ward,

and it would *not* be romantic in reality. I always have to finesse the inconvenient fact that my heroine wouldn't have a toothbrush or a clean chemise."

"I brought her maid along last time."

"Last time?" Mia squeaked.

"Vander is on the verge of doing me bodily harm," Ward said, bringing her to a halt in front of her duke, who promptly tucked his wife under an arm and dropped a kiss on her head for good measure.

"Don't be a bear," Mia said, looking up at her husband. "I dragged Ward onto the floor."

"Why?" Vander growled, in a very bearlike fashion.

Ward gave him a sardonic grin. "It seems there's a former-fiancée clause that permits her to organize my love life."

Mia poked Vander around the middle. "Will you please stop glowering at my former fiancé?"

Mia was small, but she obviously wasn't allowing her out-sized husband to intimidate her. Ward considered giving her a congratulatory kiss, but that might push Vander too far.

"I want to make certain that Ward wins the hand of Eugenia Snowe," Mia continued. "I've only met her twice, but I thought her absolutely enchanting."

"Everyone does," Ward said.

Well, with the exception of his grandmother.

"You must make a grand gesture," Mia said earnestly. "Something Mrs. Snowe would never expect. Something that will make it clear that you love her more than you possibly could any other woman, that you treasure her just as she is."

"*I* made one," Vander said. He had both arms around his wife now.

"What did you do?" Ward inquired.

"I wrote a poem."

"You wrote a love poem, because I write novels about love," his wife declared. "It was your way of telling me that you respected my profession."

From Vander's twitch, Ward was pretty sure that His Grace hadn't been considering his wife's novels when he wrote that love poem.

He let a sardonic smile touch the corners of his mouth so that Vander realized that Ward had a hold over him.

The duke narrowed his eyes.

"You must do the same," Mia said, blithely unaware of the silent conversation occurring over her head. "Your grand gesture has to convince Eugenia that you value and respect her as an intelligent woman with remarkable accomplishments."

"What is he supposed to do?" Vander asked. "Hire another governess? From all accounts, he sacked one of her governesses and the other quit. It would be hard to demonstrate respect for Snowe's Registry after that."

"Ward has to make a huge gesture," Mia insisted. "There's India! She'll help." She started waving frantically.

Ward turned as Thorn Dautry's wife, Lady Xenobia India, joined them.

"Hello, Mia darling," India said, dropping a necessarily shallow curtsy, since she was obviously carrying a child. "Mr. Reeve, it's a pleasure to see you. And Vander, you're looking a bit peevish this evening." She went up on her toes to kiss the duke.

"Where's Thorn?" His Grace growled, by way of greeting.

"Here," came a laconic voice. Ward had not seen

Thorn Dautry since he and Vander had helped him rout Mia's uncle, the scoundrel who'd had him thrown in prison.

Now he thought of it, if that old crook hadn't died, he might have had to thank him for stopping his wedding to Mia.

"India," Mia cried, "Ward needs our help. He has to make a grand gesture to convince Eugenia Snowe that he truly loves her."

"Does he truly love her?" India peered at Ward. Whatever she saw in his eyes must have satisfied her, because she turned back to Mia and said, "Flowers?"

Ward shook his head. "Not extravagant enough."

"Excellent!" Mia said, clapping her hands together.

"What?" her husband asked.

"Ward has something in mind. I can tell."

It seemed he was making a grand gesture.

Chapter Forty-four

Tuesday, June 30, 1801
The House of Lords
Palace of Westminster

$\mathscr{W}$ard had barely reached the seat beside his solicitor when a parade of a hundred or so scarlet and ermine clad British peers filed in and took their places along the benches on either side of the Lord Chancellor, who was presiding over the session.

His father had complained that most of those seats remained empty even during the most important bills—but not today. Not in light of the fascinating news that the notorious Lady Lisette had mothered children, *legitimate* children, with the late Lord Darcy. That was news enough, but the fact that Lady

Lisette's mother was sponsoring a private act demanding guardianship of those orphaned children?

The peers crowded on the benches like peas in a cartload of pods.

Ward's grandmother was seated with her solicitors to the right of Ward. She did not spare him a glance.

The case opened with ceremonial blather. A Proclamation of Silence was followed by a turgid list of articles and circumstances and general foolishness, until the private act pled by Her Grace, the Dowager Duchess of Gilner, of the County of Surrey, was called.

Her interminable plea drew to a close with an unambiguous statement: the young Lord Darcy and his sister should not be brought up by a man of illegitimate birth who, while he was to be congratulated for his profitable innovations in machinery (leaving the distinct impression that Ward had been whittling knife sharpeners or the like), had nevertheless been imprisoned in the recent past.

As soon as the word "prison" was uttered, a buzz rose from the benches that sounded like enraged hornets on the move. Neither Ward nor Mia had ever made public the reason he'd deserted her at the altar, disappearing the night before their wedding ceremony.

The duchess's learned counsel concluded with a satisfied waggle of his periwig. "Her Grace feels that there can be no possible comparison between herself and Mr. Reeve when it comes to the ability to properly raise a young peer of the realm, an orphan whose mother has been tragically taken from him."

Lizzie was not mentioned.

Ward's head solicitor bounded to his feet with

an eagerness that corresponded to the acclaim he was receiving by leading this particular case. He launched into an erudite discussion of the fact that Lord Darcy's will assigning guardianship of his children to Ward had been proved in the Court of Chancery.

Fair enough, but everyone in the room knew that was irrelevant. A private act could invalidate Lord Darcy's will, as it had overturned others.

What this case came down to was a show of force on both sides. The Duchess of Gilner had carefully marshalled facts in order to attack Ward's person.

Ward had chosen to marshal people.

One by one, his solicitors called peers to the witness box. Some of them were waiting in the witnesses' benches, but a few made their way from the peers' benches. The Duke of Pindar's explanation of Ward's wrongful incarceration led to a gale of chatter. The Duke of Villiers answered questions in a sardonic drawl, reminding the assembly of his own illegitimate children and daring them to imagine that his offspring would be unsuitable parents.

Few people in all London were foolish enough to go against the Duke of Villiers, especially when he was shoulder-to-shoulder with one of his oldest friends, the Duke of Beaumont.

"In fact," Villiers concluded, "this is a monumental waste of time, and someone needs to state the obvious. I came to know Lady Lisette very well during my wretched, foolish attempt to court her. That was long before she eloped with a young, *very* young gentleman, of course."

The Duchess of Gilner had been staring at her

gloved hands throughout the witnesses' testimony, but she looked up at that.

Ward flinched. In his soft, yet implacable way, Villiers was about to tear his grandmother to shreds. Lady Lisette was no one's dream of a parent—and her failures were about to be laid at the duchess's feet.

Ward didn't want his grandmother ravaged by the duke.

Before he thought the better of it, he stood.

Villiers stopped in mid-sentence. "I cede my speech to the man of the hour." He stepped down from the witness box.

Ward walked over and entered the box.

"This is most unusual," the Lord Chancellor said, his peruke of white curls listing precariously as he watched Villiers return to his seat beside the Duke of Beaumont.

"My solicitors are prepared to call many more witnesses to the bench," Ward said, "but the Duke of Villiers has an excellent point."

"I gather you would like to make a statement," His Lordship said dryly.

Ward turned to the assembly. He hadn't looked at the peeresses' section. He didn't look now either, but he knew Eugenia was there. She may hate him, but she loved Lizzie and Otis.

"I knew Lord Darcy many years ago and he was an extraordinarily kind and guileless young man," he said. "Perhaps those traits made him vulnerable to my mother's courtship, if one might call it that. I have learned from my half-siblings that he grew to be a superlative father."

Rustling from the benches.

"Lord Darcy raised his children to be as gracious and thoughtful as he. For example, though they had little formal schooling, they know Latin and speak French fluently. He was a better father than many of us could hope to be, protecting and caring for his children under extremely disadvantageous situations."

The hum in the room turned to dead silence.

"I am honored by Lord Darcy's trust in me," Ward said quietly. "While I could never have imagined that my school friend at Eton would become my stepfather, I am honored to be part of his family, and I wish to carry out his last wishes to the best of my ability. The Dowager Duchess of Gilner has questioned whether an unmarried man should be allowed to raise children, so I will tell you that I have plans to marry."

Even the rustling of the peeresses' finery and the swish of their fans had stopped.

"I am in love with Mrs. Eugenia Snowe, and I mean to marry her," he said, his eyes ranging over the benches of men before him. "She may refuse me. I will ask her again. If she refuses me yet again, I will raise Lizzie and Otis by myself, because I shall not marry another woman."

His words hung in the air, and finally, finally, Ward allowed himself to look toward the peeresses' benches—only to see Eugenia's back as she left the chamber.

A deep breath seared his lungs. She had rejected him. His muscles clenched and his hands curled into fists. He had to follow her—

He couldn't follow her.

"My half-siblings are mourning their mother and father," he said instead. "Lizzie, who is nine years

old, has chosen to wear a veil, in order to hide her grief from the world."

There was a collective murmur of sympathy from the room.

"I would ask you not to take my siblings from me," he said, keeping his voice even. "Not only was it Lord Darcy's wish, but when she contracted a lung ailment and understood she was dying, our mother, Lady Lisette, instructed that her children be brought to my house."

His grandmother was staring up at him, her brow knit.

"I know that many of you despised my mother—our mother—and I fully understand your reasons. Lady Lisette was a deeply troubled soul. With my knowledge of her character, I was confident that my siblings had been woefully neglected. I am happy to reassure you that, although they had an unusual childhood, they were loved by their mother, as well as by their father. I will give you but one example: young Lord Darcy has a pet rat named Jarvis."

A gasp went up from the peeresses' bench.

"Our mother sewed a tiny velvet cloak fit for the opera for Jarvis, and a satin cloak in case he received an invitation to a ball. Lizzie and Otis were loved by her to the best of her ability. Her wishes should be honored."

His grandmother moved sharply.

He glanced down at her, and back to the chamber at large. "I am blessed in that my father, Lord Gryffyn, and my stepmother, Lady Gryffyn, raised me as one of their own children. If they were not abroad, they would be here at my side. I hope to raise Lizzie and Otis with the same care and respect they gave me."

With that, he made his way back to his bench, looking neither at his grandmother nor his solicitors. He just sat, his gut churning. He was absolutely certain that the vote would go in his favor.

But Eugenia had walked out. She had rejected him. He felt as if a hole had been blown in his chest, but there was nothing to do but sit, bleeding silently.

How had it gone so wrong? How could he have been so stupid? She had said she loved him . . . if only he had taken her in his arms at that moment.

If Eugenia truly loved him, wouldn't she have smiled when he declared himself before the assembled aristocracy?

The Dowager Duchess of Gilner stood. She didn't move toward the witness box or look at Ward. Instead, she told the Lord Chancellor in the firm, fluting voice of the aristocracy, "I withdraw my plea for a private act."

There was a collective gasp. She stared straight ahead, so Ward saw his grandmother in profile. He recognized that nose: he saw it every day in the mirror.

"Very well," his lordship said, and without further ado, he stood up. "This session of the House of Lords is dismissed."

Chapter Forty-five

Eugenia walked from the great chamber and then actually broke into a run down the corridor leading away from the room. The moment Ward had spoken her name, every person in the room turned in her direction.

When Andrew died, she never expressed her grief in public. She wept at home; outside, she kept her head high and her eyes dry. Andrew would have wanted it that way.

But now tears were uncontrollably pouring down her cheeks. She caught sight of an open door and turned into a room, mercifully empty, fell into a chair, and tried to breathe.

Her mind was seared with the image of Ward standing before the rows of peers. He hadn't looked like a gentleman, like one of them.

He'd looked like a king, glancing over velvet-clad lords without a shred of humility. He'd dominated the room from the moment he stood: his face intense, focused . . . commanding. With his words, he had petitioned for guardianship of his siblings, but in truth . . .

He had demanded it. The peers would no more refuse him than refuse the king. The children were his now. Her fear for Lizzie and Otis evaporated the moment Ward began speaking.

She had feasted on the way he looked, her heart yearning, secure in the belief that he was unaware of her presence.

And then—

Then he had stated that he meant to marry her. His eyes had taken on a ferocious intensity as he'd told the House of Lords that she was his, just as Lizzie and Otis were now his wards.

The only sign of tension she spied was when his jaw clenched while speaking of her.

Of the fact she had refused him.

The door opened and Eugenia's head jerked up, her damp handkerchief clutched in her hand.

Ward stood in the doorway.

"What happened?" she managed, coming to her feet.

"The children are mine," he said, striding toward her. Without another word, he tilted her head back and covered her mouth with his. His kiss was the equivalent of his speech before all those lords: it was a statement about her.

He had told a roomful of peers that he loved her, and suddenly Eugenia realized that he had said as much to her countless times.

While kissing her.

While luring her into the lake.

While waking her at night to make love a fourth time, and a fifth at dawn.

She returned his kiss with her entire being. She was his, and he was hers, until death parted them. How could she have forgotten that love was the most important thing of all? She, who had learned far too young that one cruel moment could snatch away love forever?

Ward drew back, still without saying a word, gathered her to him and swept her off her feet. Carrying her the whole way, he strode from the room, down the corridor, and straight to his waiting carriage. She was in the carriage before she could think what to say.

But it seemed no words were needed. His arms closed around her again with hungry urgency and he pulled her onto his lap. They kissed until Eugenia's hair had fallen around her ears and her lips were bee-stung.

When the coach stopped, Ward helped Eugenia to alight on a street lined with large, graceful mansions.

"My London address," Ward said, drawing her up the walk to one of the most imposing of these.

"I didn't know you had a house in London," she exclaimed.

"I bought it before I took the post at Oxford."

The front door opened as they approached, and a liveried butler bowed as they entered. Eugenia caught sight of cream walls and a spotless marble floor, but Ward guided her straight to a closed door at one side.

"Please close your eyes," he said, dropping a kiss on her nose, regardless of the butler.

Eugenia smiled, closing her eyes. Perhaps he brought Lizzie and Otis to London and they planned to surprise her. If so, the children were being uncharacteristically silent, because she could have sworn there was no one else in the room.

Finally Ward brushed a kiss on her lips and whispered, "I meant what I said in the House of Lords. I love you, Eugenia. I love everything about you. *Everything*. Open your eyes, my love."

Eugenia opened them slowly, savoring the way "love" sounded, uttered in that rough, utterly believable fashion.

The room was filled with cakes. Everywhere she looked—on every surface—were spun-sugar confections of every imaginable variety. Two elaborate swans arched higher than her head. An enormous trifle filled an exquisite crystal bowl, which in turn was surrounded by plates of dainty petits-fours. One platter held a cake shaped like a grotto replete with a mermaid, and another held a many-layered confection topped with dancing, gold-dusted cupids.

Unable to speak, Eugenia turned to Ward, knowing her eyes were round with shock.

"I respect everything you do, and everything you are," he said, his voice rough. "I want your *pâtisserie* to be the most famed of its kind not only here in England but in France. I want you to cast Gunter's in the shade. I want *Lizzie* to watch and learn from you. Most importantly, I want you to do what makes you most happy."

Eugenia stared at him as his words sank in. "That's not what you . . . what you said earlier."

"I was wrong. Lizzie and Otis don't need con-

vention or rules; they need you. But I need you most of all."

Eugenia couldn't make herself speak.

"I love you, Eugenia Snowe," Ward said. "I love all of the Eugenias: the prim and proper lady, the brilliant mathematician, the joyous, delicious lover, the owner of a registry, and the future owner of the best tearoom in London."

Eugenia's eyes filled with tears and she opened her arms. Their lips found each other, warm and passionate . . . perfect.

Some time later she turned in his arms and looked with wonder around the room. "Did Marcel help you with these cakes? Where on earth did you find all of them?"

"Vander, Thorn, and I crisscrossed London to find all of them." He hesitated. "It was supposed to be a grand gesture."

"It is truly a grand gesture," Eugenia said, awestruck. She stepped forward to take a closer look at the cake decorated with golden cupids. Each delicacy was more exquisite than the last. And the pedestals were placed at just the right heights to create a perfect display.

"Lady Xenobia India arranged this room," she breathed. "No one else has her eye for arrangement."

"Mia was here as well," Ward said, feeling a bit awkward at the mention of his former fiancée.

"I can't wait to thank them personally," Eugenia cried, not looking in the least disturbed by his mention of Mia. "Oh, look at this one!" She reached toward a small cake with a cluster of spun-sugar feathers on top.

Ward's arm wrapped around her and pulled her against the muscled planes of his body. "Mia is a romance writer," he said. "She said I needed to make a grand gesture."

Eugenia leaned back against him, inexpressibly happy. "I love your grand gesture."

Ward spun her around and their eyes met. "I have something else for you too, from me alone."

"Mmmm," Eugenia murmured. She was surrounded by cakes, and she didn't want even a single bite. She only wanted him.

He gave her a kiss that was measured in the rhythm of their heartbeats. By the time Ward pulled back, Eugenia could scarcely think. "A gesture of my own," he said, his voice husky.

He reached into his pocket and withdrew . . .

A cake.

A small cake, sunk in the middle and cracked on top. It had the surly look that sweet things get when they've been baked too long.

It smelled of chocolate. Burnt chocolate.

"Did Lizzie make this for me?" she guessed, touching the top. Her heart was singing. Those lovely, eccentric, bright children were going to be hers: Lizzie with her too-old, hopeful eyes, and Otis with his inquisitive bravery and deep love for Jarvis.

"Not Lizzie."

"Otis? I'm impressed!"

"Nor Otis."

She looked up. Her mouth fell open.

"I couldn't think of a better way to prove to you that I respect you and adore you—everything about you, Eugenia."

"You baked me a cake," she whispered. It was as

if time stopped around them, as if the world had shrunk to a man and woman and a small, burnt chocolate sponge.

"That's actually the second one," he said. The exasperated tone in his voice startled a laugh from her. "The first one shriveled to the size of a walnut. I left Marcel back at Fawkes House because he won't speak to me any longer, so I had no help."

"I love it," she said, cradling it in her hands. "And I love you." She came up on her toes and kissed him. His big hands circled her waist, steadying her.

Their kiss was open-mouthed and open-hearted, the kind of kiss that lays people bare and vulnerable.

"You are the most witty, beautiful, and warm person I know," Ward said at length, and his words went straight to her heart. "Lizzie gave up her veil for you, and Otis would have given up Jarvis. We love you, Eugenia. All three of us love you so much. Without you, we're a family without a heart."

He shook his head. "I have to warn you: if you say no to marrying me, you will have to say no again tomorrow, and the day after. I will come back with Lizzie and Otis and Jarvis. You'll have to say no to Jarvis."

"Not Jarvis!" Her fingers traced the classically square shape of his jaw.

"Will you marry me, Eugenia? Will you be my bride?"

"Yes," she whispered back, her voice shaking a bit. "Yes, I will."

"Will you promise not to be ladylike?" He was holding her tightly, his face buried in her hair.

"Not all the time," she said, unable to stop smiling.

Epilogue

Eugenia schooled her expression to the polite curiosity that anyone might feel on encountering a pack of two-legged Dalmatians. Or, to look at it a different way, four spotty children ranging in age from three to fourteen.

"I can guess that you've used India ink to create the dappled effect," she said to Otis's best friend, Marmaduke, "but how did you turn your face that sickly white?"

"Cornstarch mixed with rose water," he said. "It's what my nanny uses when she has an afternoon out."

"Mama!" Sally was so plumply adorable that Eugenia couldn't stop herself from bending over and picking her up, despite having already dressed for the evening.

Sally giggled and rubbed their noses together.

Eugenia hitched Sally higher on her hip and turned back to Lizzie, Otis, and Marmaduke. Sally laid her head on Eugenia's shoulder and began sucking her thumb. "Lizzie, I suspect you were the genius behind this."

"We were practicing for the event of an infectious disease," Lizzie replied. "England has been visited by waves of disease for centuries. If we're caught unprepared, we might all succumb."

"I fail to see how drawing spots on everyone's faces will prepare for a wave of the measles."

Otis and Marmaduke, bored of playing at plague, dropped onto the floor and began playing spillikins instead. Sally was blinking, about to fall asleep, her face now mostly clear of cornstarch as it had transferred to Eugenia.

"I had in mind something rare, not the measles," Lizzie said, not at all bored. "Something more like the Black Death. An epidemic—that's what you call it when a great many people die."

Sally gave a little sigh and snuggled closer.

The brilliant intelligence that had made Ward into one of the most successful inventors in England had turned up in a vastly different form in Lizzie.

As if that thought had drawn him, the nursery door opened and her husband walked in. There was a smile in his eyes when he looked at Eugenia . . . a smile that told her just how much he had enjoyed their morning.

Sally had been born seven months after they married, leading Eugenia to decide that French letters—no matter the color of ribbons—were clearly not always effective.

"How wonderful," her husband had told her, his

eyes shining when she told him she was carrying a baby.

"It would have been a disaster if I hadn't married you!" she had retorted.

"I was planning on kidnapping you," her husband had said unrepentantly. "If you hadn't succumbed to all those cakes, I was going to toss them in the carriage so I could feed you on the way to Gretna Green."

Now he strolled over and kissed his daughter's cheek. "Generally, this child looks as clean as a newly shelled egg. Not at the moment, though." He surveyed the speckled crowd. "So who is responsible for all the spots?"

Eugenia sank into a rocking chair, holding Sally's warm body tightly against her. Ward had woken her twice the night before—no, that wasn't fair, because she had turned to him one of those times, waking out of sleep with a desperate hunger for him.

She closed her eyes, allowing the sound of Ward's laughter as Lizzie explained the epidemic that had struck the nursery to settle about her like a warm blanket.

She had two things to tell him, and she was hugging them to her until they sat down to eat together later that night. First, she'd had a letter from Marcel: their venture had just finished its first quarter with an actual profit.

This was wonderful, but the second bit of news was even better. For all her childhood dreams of living in a neatly ordered household, she was now the mistress of a house that rang with laughter and chaos, in which intellectual curiosity and experimentation ranked far above the propriety she had so yearned for.

She wouldn't trade it for a moment—although the baby nestled in her womb would only add to the mayhem.

Lizzie, meanwhile, had moved from lecturing Ward about possible epidemics to telling him about the bird's nest she'd found that morning, when she stopped and put a finger to her lips.

Ward turned to find that that his wife and daughter had fallen asleep. Sally was sucking her thumb just as he used to, her cheek nestled against her mother's shoulder. His heart gave a thump in his ribs that told him, again, how lucky he was.

Eugenia thought he didn't know that she was carrying a baby, but he watched everything about her, driven by a gut-deep need to make certain that his wife was well and happy. Her breasts had grown delightfully larger, and she tired more easily.

She would tell him in her own time, though; he didn't want to ruin her surprise.

"She's having another baby, isn't she?" Lizzie asked.

He looked down in surprise as his sister slipped her hand into his.

"Well, isn't she?"

"I think so. Why do *you* think so?"

"She's sleeping," Lizzie said. "Normally she doesn't stop moving."

"That's true."

"I guessed yesterday, when she didn't want any trifle. Eugenia *never* refuses trifle—except when she was carrying Sally."

Ward ruffled her hair. "You frighten me sometimes, Miss Lizzie."

"Pooh," his sister said. She kicked Otis's leg. "Let's

go see the new puppies in the stable before we have to go to bed."

Marmaduke leapt to his feet, though Otis just gave his sister a mulish look.

"Come on, Marmaduke," Lizzie said, grabbing his hand.

Ward had the feeling that it would be like that for the next fifty years.

He took Sally from her mother's arms and handed her to Ruby before he picked up Eugenia and carried her off to their bedchamber, ignoring her sleepy protests.

She opened her eyes and smiled at him. "We'll name him Felix," she said, before going back to sleep.

"Felix?" Ward snorted. Not if he had any say in the matter.

Then he kissed her, and knew that he would let her have her way, because all that mattered was that his family was safe and together. And that he showed this woman every day that his promise of seven minutes, seven minutes in heaven, would be repeated to the very end of their days.

It would never be enough.

Naughty Children, Pets Rats, and Pornographic Cigar Boxes

Seven Minutes in Heaven is the third in a series of novels which feature heroines with unusual professions for the 1800s. India from *Three Weeks with Lady X* decorates houses; Mia from *Four Nights with the Duke* writes romance novels; and Eugenia runs a registry for governesses.

In the process of learning about governesses, I had a lot of fun reading novels about naughty children. Some of Marmeduke's adventures were inspired by a sequence of 39 books, the *Just William* series, written by Richmal Crompton between 1921 and 1970. Those of you who have read the Nurse Matilda novels will recognize the speckled children in my epilogue.

Lizzie's particular brand of naughtiness—trying to use magic in a vain attempt to control a world that has buffeted her with chaos—comes from an old play by Thomas Middleton called *The Puritan, or the Widow of Watling Street*. And speaking of old plays, Lizzie is

not always right in her quotations, but the plays she quotes are lively and well worth reading.

The remarkably pornographic cigar box that serves as Jarvis's bed is a real box, dated approximately 1803; I posted a photo on my website, www.eloisajames. com, under the Book Extras for *Seven Minutes*. The inspiration for Jarvis is one of my daughter's pet rats named Teddy. You can find a picture of him there as well, nestled on top of his best friend, who happens to be a large dog.

One more inspiration I should add: Gunter's was, by all account, a marvelous establishment. I happily threw myself into exploration of trifles and cakes from the period; the blogger RedHeadedGirl was a big help, sharing recipes from her 1805 edition of *The Art of Cookery* by Hannah Glasse, as well as a recipe for trifle from a 1769 manuscript.

One final note . . . If you've read *A Duke of Her Own*, you may realize that *Seven Minutes* brings one character back from the dead, allowing her to flounce around society once again. We should all be so lucky! But like so many things in fiction, what is so possible on the page is impossible in real life.

A Note from Eloisa

Seven Minutes in Heaven is an extraordinary novel for me, in that both Eugenia and Ward appeared in earlier books as children. A number of links to my other novels follow, each of which connects in one way or another to characters from this book.

In *Desperate Duchesses*, Ward (known as Teddy at that age) is busily running around the house at night, climbing into other people's beds. *Duchess by Night* includes an eccentric, wildly intelligent young girl named Eugenia. The duchess of the title is her future stepmother Harriet, who cross-dresses as a boy to go to a dissolute house party. The Duke of Villiers appears in all six of the Desperate Duchess novels as well as all three of the Numbers series. He duels Ward's father in the first book, *Desperate Duchesses*; his own story, *A Duke of Her Own*, ends with the carriage scene that Eleanor tells Ward about. Finally, *Four Nights with the Duke* is the first novel in which Ward appears as an adult: if you haven't read it, the story of Mia's proposal to the Duke of Pindar, after she is deserted at the altar by Ward (through no fault of his own), is hilariously romantic.

Keep reading for a sneak peek at

WILDE IN LOVE
by Eloisa James

Coming Fall 2017

Hemingford Castle
June 28, 1778

*L*ord Alaric Wilde, son of the Duke of Hemingford, strode down the long, echoing hall of his father's castle. His older brother, the Marquess of North-bridge—or North, as he preferred to be called—walked at his side.

The heir and the spare. The courtier and the explorer. The duke's best beloved and the disgrace.

He and his brother were of equal height, with similar features and cut of jaw. But the resemblances stopped there. Had they consciously tried, they couldn't have been more different.

"No, I did not bed the empress," Alaric stated, stopping at the gilt-encrusted mirror hanging in the castle entry to slap a battered, white, powdered wig on his head. He grimaced at the sight. "Maybe I should change my mind and return to her court. At least I wouldn't have to wear this monstrosity."

"Seriously, there's no truth to the rumor?" North persisted, coming up at Alaric's shoulder. "Blackwell's is selling a detailed etching entitled *England Takes Russia by Storm*. It's set in the imperial bedchamber, and the fellow looks remarkably like you."

Their eyes met in the glass, and North visibly recoiled. "Good God, is that your only wig?" He scowled at the lumpy mound on Alaric's head. "Father won't like to see that at dinner. Hell, I don't like it."

The marquess wore a snowy towering creation that turned him into a cross between a parrot dunked in plaster dust and a fancy chicken. Alaric hadn't seen his brother in four years, and he'd scarcely recognized the man.

"I came straight from the dock, but I sent my valet into London. Quarles should arrive tomorrow, new wig in hand. Not that his acquisition will come close to the elegance of yours."

North adjusted his cuffs. *Pink* silk cuffs. "Obviously not, since this wig is Parisian, enhanced by Sharp's best Cyprus hair powder." Then he grinned. "But I just don't believe it. The famous Lord Wilde didn't bed the empress?"

"All I'll say is the opportunity was there," Alaric said dryly. "She issued a public invitation, in the interests of raising Russian morale."

North gave a shout of laughter. "The burden of improving Russian morale would put some pressure on a man's performance, I'm guessing."

"I couldn't say. I declined the challenge and took the first ship out of Petersburg, which turned out to be damned lucky because here I am, just in time for your betrothal party."

"Fearless in the face of a mountain, yet he flees a lascivious empress," North said. "A sad reflection on England's greatest adventurer since Sir Walter Raleigh."

Just then the family butler, Saxon, walked through the baize door at the rear of the entry and bowed. "Good afternoon, Lord Alaric, Lord Northbridge. The party has assembled in the drawing room." He moved to the drawing room door, ready to usher them in.

"Afternoon, Saxon," Alaric said.

"One minute," North said, adjusting his elaborately tied neck scarf in the glass. "A touch of Casanova in your writing wouldn't go amiss," he said to Alaric. "Enough with the hardship, woe, and duels with two-headed men. On to randy royalty. If I were you, I would have bedded the empress and called it research."

"As soon as you take to the roads and head for Russia, I'll make an introduction. I'm sure you'd love to bed a woman who addresses you as a badger of delight," Alaric retorted.

North let out a crack of laughter. "Badger? Are you sure she didn't mean stallion? Imagine the book sales for a *Stallion of Delight*. Not to mention the etchings."

"Those bloody etchings," Alaric growled. "The duke says that in the years since I left England they've littered the entire country. Actually, I think the word he used was 'defiled.'"

"The way the ladies twitter about you, not to mention collecting various portraits, does not please our father. He thinks your fame is ill-fitting our rank."

Alaric didn't give a damn about rank, though he'd be the first to admit that fame was a double-edged sword.

North had started tweaking the curls that hung over his ears. Bloody hell, Alaric thought, at this rate, they'd be here for an hour. "I'm looking forward to meeting Miss Tallbridge," he prompted.

North had the trick of looking severe no matter his mood, but now his mouth eased. "Just look for the most beautiful, fashionable woman in the room."

Who cared if North had transformed into a peacock in the years Alaric had been away? His older brother had clearly fallen in love. It wasn't an emotion that Alaric would welcome himself, but he recognized it.

He gave North a rough, one-armed hug that risked the perfection of his brother's neck scarf. "I'm happy for you. Now stop making love to yourself in the glass and introduce me to this lovely creature."

Saxon threw open the great doors leading to the drawing room. The room before them glittered with all the things that Alaric most loathed: silks, wigs, diamonds, and insipid faces.

North's gaze went directly to a lady in an overskirt bunched into no fewer than three large puffs.

Other women's arses were adorned with puffs, but Miss Tallbridge's puffs were larger than anyone else's. Alaric could only guess that the puffs equated in some way to fashion.

"That is she," North said in a low voice. He sounded as if he had caught a glimpse of some royal being.

If sheer volume of attire had determined rank, Miss Tallbridge would certainly be fit for a throne. Her petticoat had more bows, her overskirt more ruffles. And she wore an entire basket of fruit on top of her head.

"The Marquess of Northbridge; Lord Alaric Wilde," Saxon bellowed.

There was an audible gasp, as the party registered his presence. Alaric's jaw clenched. He loved writing his books; he hated the fame that had ensued.

With no help for it, he walked into the room.

Miss Wilhelmina Everett Ffynche just happened to be facing the door when the great explorer was announced, which was lucky, because she didn't shame herself by swinging about—as her best friend Lavinia Grey did.

Willa could hardly blame Lavinia: after all, Lord Wilde's image had smoldered from Lavinia's bedchamber wall for the past three years. Faced by the real man, she clapped her hand to her chest and looked as if she might faint.

For her part, Willa didn't feel in the least bit dizzy, but then she had avoided succumbing to the widespread passion for Lord Wilde—which was easy enough if one didn't read his books.

The man who strode into their midst, looking neither left nor right, was wearing sturdy shoes rather than the slippers worn by the other men.

He had no rings, no curls to his wig, and no polish.

Willa snapped open her fan, the better to examine this paragon of masculinity, as Lavinia liked to call him. He certainly wasn't a paragon of fashion.

He looked as if he would have been at home in another time, the Middle Ages perhaps, when men strode about with swords on their hips. Instead he was stuck in a room full of gentlemen whose toes were rendered invisible by the floppy roses attached to their slippers.

"Oh, my," Lavinia breathed, almost too faintly to be heard. "I think I see his scar."

Only then did Willa notice a thin white line snaking down one cheek through skin browned by the sun in a manner that should be objectionable but somehow wasn't.

There were many stories about how Lord Wilde got that scar, and thanks to Lavinia's obsession with the explorer, Willa had heard them all. Her own guess had always been that he fell in the privy and knocked his head against a corner.

She leaned over and whispered in Lavinia's ear, "Personally, I think the imminent demise of his pantaloons is more striking." Lord Wilde's thigh muscles were straining the wool in a manner that was remarkably eye-catching.

Indecorous, but eye-catching.

"Willa!" Lavinia scolded, nudging with her elbow. "That's a remarkably inappropriate comment, even

for you!" But she snapped open her own fan, and her eyes dropped to his pantaloons as if leaded by weights.

"I never before gave much thought to thighs," Willa observed, "except perhaps those frog legs your mother served at her last dinner."

Lavinia scoffed, about to answer, but her eyes grew large. "Willa, he's coming in this direction!"

Sure enough, Lord Wilde and his brother had bowed before their father, kissed their stepmother's hand, and turned, walking directly toward them.

Lavinia actually swayed on her feet, her breath escaping in a gasp.

"He is not coming to *us*," Willa pointed out. "Pull yourself together, Lavinia! The marquess means to introduce his brother to his fiancée, of course."

Their friend Diana Tallbridge had been standing just to Lavinia's right. Her wig was still taller than anyone else's in the room, and the two men were striding toward them like homing pigeons to a roost.

For the first time Willa had some understanding of why etchings of Lord Wilde were plastered to so many bedchamber walls. There was something shocking about the man.

He was so big and—and vital in a kind of primitive way.

Which would be a quite uncomfortable quality to live with, she reminded herself. She herself owned only an etching of Socrates: a thoughtful, intelligent man whose thighs were doubtless as slim as her own.

"Miss Tallbridge, may I introduce you to my

brother?" the Marquess of Northbridge said. "Lord Alaric is recently returned from Russia."

While Diana displayed her remarkable ability to balance half a green grocer's stall on her head while curtsying, Willa discovered that Lord Alaric had sculpted cheekbones, lips that wouldn't bring shame to an Italian courtesan, and green eyes.

Those etchings of him that could be found in every bookstore?

The etchings didn't do him justice.

He bowed to Diana with a finesse that was quite surprising, given the breadth of his chest. His coat was distinctly strained over the shoulders. By rights, a body so defined by muscle should find it hard to bend.

"It is a pleasure to meet you, Miss Tallbridge," Lord Alaric said, kissing Diana's hand. "I am honored to welcome you to our family."

Lavinia made a sound perilously close to a squeak as the marquess turned and introduced her, and then Willa, to Lord Wilde. For her part, Willa had to stop herself from stepping backward. The man was so large that she had the absurd feeling that he might be swallowing up the air around them.

At least that would explain her slight feeling of breathlessness.

In a tribute to their education, Lavinia didn't show by so much as a flicker of an eyelash that she was meeting the man who had been her idol for years.

"Good evening, Lord Northbridge," she said, holding out her hand for a kiss. Then she turned and said calmly, "Lord Alaric, it is a pleasure."

Rather surprisingly, Lord Alaric didn't acquire that slightly glazed look of admiration most men got on meeting Lavinia, but perhaps he was a slow starter.

"I understand that you are just returning from a long trip abroad, Lord Alaric," Willa asked, as Lavinia seemed to be temporarily struck dumb, and the marquess had drawn his fiancée aside. "What do you miss when you're away from England?"

He had been watching his brother and Diana with a slight frown, but her question drew his focus to her.

Lord Wilde's eyes were the darkest green color Willa had ever seen on a man, lined by thick eyelashes. Unfortunately, Willa had a weakness for beautiful eyes.

Beauty was an accident of birth. But eyes? That was different. Beautiful eyes had feeling in them.

Once again she almost sighed, but caught herself. Just barely, but she managed. She squared her shoulders, and to her horror, she caught his lips twitching.

Apparently he expected ladies to sigh, if not fall at his feet.

Cad.

"I miss my family," he said. "After that, in no particular order, mattresses without lice, brandy, welcoming servants, an excellent plate of ham and eggs in the morning. Oh, and the company of ladies, of course."

"It must be an intoxicating experience to be so adored," Willa said, nettled by way he ranked ladies behind a plate of ham. It wasn't a strictly

polite observation, but on the other hand, most of the females in the room were gazing hungrily at him behind his shoulder, as he surely knew.

They clearly put him before ham and eggs.

Lord Wilde's mouth quirked into a wry smile. "Adoration is a bit strong. I think myself lucky that my readers find something to enjoy in my work."

"I beg to differ," Willa said, ignoring Lavinia's horrified frown. "I enjoyed Montaigne's essay on cannibals, but I don't have his image on my bedchamber wall."

"Lord Wilde," Lavinia interjected hastily, "where do you plan to travel to next?"

"I haven't decided." His eyes returned to Willa. "Miss Ffynche, do you have a suggestion?"

"I am not sure where you've been," Willa said. "I must apologize for my ignorance of your books. I think I'm the only person in the kingdom who is so ill-educated on the subject of Lord Wilde's adventures."

His heavy-lidded eyes rose slightly, the tilt of his mouth hitching up a millimeter more. "I assure you that you aren't alone, Miss Ffynche."

"I love your books," Lavinia put in. "I've read every one."

"Thank you," he replied. "Do you have a particular preference for travel literature, Miss Grey?"

Lavinia shook her head. "In fact, I adore novels."

"Do you enjoy novels as well, Miss Ffynche?" Lord Alaric asked.

"No, I'm afraid I'm not attracted to invented stories of any kind," Willa said, not thinking about the implication of her wording, because the man's eyes

were so intent on her face that she truly was beginning to feel slightly dizzy.

"I do not invent the events I describe," Lord Alaric said, his voice even.

"Of course not," she said hastily. Then, unable to resist, "Although, from what Lavinia has told me, wouldn't you agree that your adventures tend to be, shall we say, larger than life?"

"No," Lord Alaric said, seemingly even more amused. "What are you reading at the moment, Miss Ffynche?"

"The fourth book of *Naturalis Historia*." Before he could comment on her admittedly tedious taste in reading material, Willa added, "I shall put it to the side and read one of your accounts. Where would you recommend that I start? With the cannibals?"

Cannibals put an end to his amusement like a dot on the end of a sentence.

"'Cannibals'?" he repeated, his brows drawing together.

"I told you that the cannibals appear only in the play," Lavinia told Willa.

"Play?" The man's body went suddenly still, like a predator lurking in deep grass.

The Marquess of Northbridge cleared his throat, making Willa jump. She hadn't realized that he and Diana had rejoined their group. "*Wilde at Heart* has been playing at the theater in Drury Lane for months," he told his brother.

Lord Wilde's eyes narrowed. "*Wilde at Heart*?"

"I made a special trip to London to see it." The marquess's voice was threaded with laughter. "If you don't mind the advice, Alaric, you should have

skipped breakfast and got to the hinterlands in time to fight off the cannibals and save the missionary's daughter."

It was quite amazing how quickly warm green eyes could turn icily dangerous.

"What in the bloody hell are you talking about, North?"

RAVISHING ROMANCE FROM
NEW YORK TIMES BESTSELLING AUTHOR
ELOISA JAMES

The Ugly Duchess
978-0-06-202173-1

Theodora Saxby is the last woman anyone expects the gorgeous James Ryburn to marry. But after a romantic proposal, even practical Theo finds herself convinced of her soon-to-be duke's passion . . . until she suspects that James desired not her heart, but her dowry.

As You Wish
978-0-06-227696-4

Includes *With This Kiss* and *Seduced by a Pirate*, two stunningly sensual stories in which gentlemen who rule the waves learn that true danger lies not on the high seas, but in the mistakes that can break a heart . . . and ruin a life forever.

Once Upon a Tower
978-0-06-222387-6

Gowan Stoughton, Duke of Kinross, is utterly bewitched by the emerald-eyed beauty, Lady Edith Gilchrist. But after Gowan's scandalous letter propels them to marriage, Edie realizes her husband needs a lesson and locks herself in a tower. Somehow Gowan must find a way to enter the tower and convince his new bride that she belongs in his arms.

Three Weeks With Lady X
978-0-06-222389-0

To marry a lady, the newly rich Thorn Dautry must acquire a gleaming, civilized façade. Lady Xenobia India vows to make Thorn marriageable in just three weeks. But neither Thorn nor India anticipate the forbidden passion that explodes between them.

EJ4 1016

*G*ive in to your Impulses!

**These unforgettable stories only take a second
to buy and give you hours of reading pleasure!**

Go to *www.AvonImpulse.com* and see what we
have to offer.
Available wherever e-books are sold.

AVONIMPULSE

IMP 0811

If she granted him only seven minutes, he wanted every one of them. If he could lure her to his bedchamber, seven minutes would turn into seven days.

O9-AID-270